WITH EXTREI

The blood had dried on his face but the tears still stung and his skin was swollen and red. He looked at the drawn curtains. It was a bungalow. He could make a jump for it, take his chances. There was grass outside. A surge for life made him think about it for longer than he could afford. He felt his bowels begin to loosen. He'd shit himself once already; he wasn't going to do it again.

He drifted further back.

If he hadn't gone for a Chinese maybe they wouldn't have got him. He imagined himself not going for a Chinese. He'd be at home now, in front of the TV. He forged a smile. It was fantasy. They were always going to get him.

They got him in the rain, gutters running with the stuff. Pulled up beside him. Hello, Billy. Then a nothing remark and more chat. Then someone from the brigade wanted to see him. He knew. He could have run. He didn't. There was nowhere to go.

About the Author

Conor Cregan was a journalist and has written two previous novels. He lives in Dublin and is currently writing his next thriller, *House of Fire*, which is set amid the turmoil of Bosnia.

With Extreme Prejudice

Conor Cregan

CORONET BOOKS
Hodder and Stoughton

First published in Great Britain
in 1994 by Hodder and Stoughton
A division of Hodder Headline PLC

10 9 8 7 6 5 4 3 2 1

British Library C.I.P.

A CIP catalogue record for this title is available from the British Library

ISBN 0 340 62305 5

Printed and bound in Great Britain by
Cox & Wyman Ltd, Reading, Berkshire

Hodder and Stoughton
A division of Hodder Headline PLC
338 Euston Road
London NW1 3BH

For Alexander

Thank you to Bernard and Mary Loughlin at the
Tyrone Guthrie Centre, Annaghmakerrig,
where this book was written.

IT WAS THE eight hundred and twenty-first year of the war. Billy Holmes scratched out a final letter to his wife on Peter Rabbit writing paper. The bedroom had a Peter Rabbit theme, even the duvets on the discount-store beds. A man with a gun sat ten feet away from Holmes under one of the bigger wallpaper rabbits. The man had red hair and a pale freckled face and the gun was in his lap. There was a Bart Simpson t-shirt at his feet. The safety catch was off and the gun was pointed at Billy Holmes.

Holmes fought with the tears stinging his eyes. He lost that battle, too.

He looked at his watch. There was half an hour left. They had let him keep his watch. His shoes were gone. First thing they took. And he had no trouser belt. They'd used it on him. They would send everything to his wife. They were meticulous that way. Even made him sign for it. The tears dripped on to his hand and rolled down his hand to the paper and smudged his kids' names. She was pregnant again. Seven months. Lousy timing. His hand began to shake. He could not stop it. Aftershock. He had held himself together right through the interrogation, but now, with the inevitable, there didn't seem any point any more. All life had shrunk to that room, that room and its Peter Rabbit theme and video games and comic books and the crumpled face of Bart Simpson. And it was shrinking more each second.

He had been punched in the face. There were bruises on his temples and below his left cheek. Most of the damage was to the left side of his face. They'd used the good guy-bad guy routine and the bad guy was a right-handed one-time junior boxing champion from Short Strand. He'd split Holmes's lips with the second punch. And two teeth had come loose. They came out later but Billy Holmes could not remember when. They had moved him to the bath.

The bath made him shake more. He'd known they were getting it ready. They left you sitting within earshot. And when they were finished filling it, they let it drip. The drip drove you fucking crazy.

Billy had to hold himself. He dropped the biro on the smudged sentiments.

They didn't want him to admit anything. They said they knew already, that it didn't matter any more. They wanted details: names, dates, contacts, meeting places, information given. Tout, they called him. He knew two of them but they called him tout and the boxer hit him every time they asked a question. And in the bath, they ducked him till he thought his lungs were going to burst. Till he wanted them to burst. He passed out twice, but they wouldn't let him go. They slapped him back to pain. Then the towel. Wet. Around the face. Around the chest. Like a vice. He must have screamed but he could not remember screaming.

The blood had dried on his face but the tears still stung and his skin was swollen and red. He looked at the drawn curtains. It was a bungalow. He could make a jump for it, take his chances. There was grass outside. A surge for life made him think about it for longer than he could afford. He felt his bowels begin to loosen. He'd shit himself once already; he wasn't going to do it again.

He drifted further back.

If he hadn't gone for a Chinese maybe they wouldn't have got him. He imagined himself not going for a Chinese. He'd be at home now, in front of the TV. He forged a smile. It was fantasy. They were always going to get him.

They got him in the rain, gutters running with the stuff. Pulled up beside him. Hello, Billy. Then a nothing remark and more chat. Then someone from brigade wanted to see him. He knew. He could have run. He didn't. There was nowhere to go.

'Finished?'

Holmes looked up at the open door. A full-length poster of George Michael covered the door. A man with similar stubble stood beside it. He was wearing an old American combat jacket with a Vietnam infantry patch on the shoulder and a sharpshooter badge above one of the pockets. He was dark compared to the lad with the gun. Leaner, too. Not a scrap of spare on him. His hair was black with slivers of grey and shorter than it should have been. There was conviction in the eyes, nothing else. It made Holmes shudder as much as the thought of the bath and what was coming.

'I need another sheet,' he said.

Holmes looked for something to hang on to. There was nothing.

'You know where it is,' the man said.

Holmes heard a hint of East Coast America, maybe industrial small town, in the accent. The rest was a mix of Dublin confidence and acquired Ulster staccato. The guy looked like he could kill with the eyes alone.

'You got fifteen minutes,' he said to Billy Holmes.

He nodded at the guard. The guard nodded back and lifted his gun. He licked his finger and wet his lips.

Billy Holmes's world shrank a little more.

Fifteen minutes later John Cusack came back in with two other men, both dressed in European combat jackets, one French, one German. The German jacket still had the Bundesrepublik flag on the shoulder. The man wearing it was bearded and about six-six. The beard hid a scarred chin, the result of a fragmentation grenade on the Lower Falls.

The nut squad, Holmes thought. They had a mechanical method to their movements. Like they were working to a programme. Different from security. Distant. Security got close. Nutters stayed back. Holmes tried to laugh to himself at his joke. The internal security boys had ferret eyes. Tout fever. Suspected everyone. Even themselves, some people said. Holmes couldn't follow the joke any more. The second man had masking tape and a hood.

Cusack told Holmes to get up. The bearded man stood at the door, beside George Michael, .357 Magnum down by his side. It looked small in his hands. Everything looked small. The bloke with the red hair was standing across from him. He had known what to do immediately Cusack had come back into the room. He had his weapon hanging down towards the floor, too. They watched Cusack and the small man in the French combat jacket with the tape and the hood.

Holmes knew the small man with the tape and the hood. The two with the guns he'd seen before but didn't know their names. But Tony McCabe was an old tweed radical who'd wandered into Sinn Fein and the limelight after the hunger strikes, got himself elected as a councillor and then arrested for having an automatic weapon in the back of his car. He'd skipped bail. He wore a baseball cap and he had a frightened face. Maybe a first-timer, Holmes thought. McCabe's hands were shaking. Maybe a loose connection in the machine. Reality had a habit of loosening connections. Theory-heads did gymnastics. McCabe looked like he was going to ask Holmes if there was anything he could do to help. Councillor mode. Like the good guy from internal security when the Short Strand boxer was rearranging Billy Holmes's face.

I don't want to do this, the good guy had said.

Holmes had almost believed him.

Then don't.

Out of my hands.

The smile was a 'fuck you, tout' smile.

Holmes folded the writing paper and stood up.

'Against the wall,' Cusack said.

Holmes looked at each man in turn. Then he looked at Cusack again. He wanted to ask him his name. Stupid things like that. It scrambled his thoughts.

They grabbed him.

Cusack pinioned him and McCabe went to work with the masking tape. He bound Holmes's hands behind his back and covered his eyes and mouth and then wrapped strips around his chest and waist. Holmes knew what he wanted to say now. But it was all happening too quickly. He started to struggle only when the final piece of tape was being wrapped around him. McCabe hooded him then and they grabbed him and marched him out of the room.

There were three others being done that night. The orders were specific. Holmes was to be done and stripped and dumped just over the border at midnight. Then the phone call would go through and they'd get a good slot on the morning news if there were no earthquakes or airline crashes.

It was freezing in the woods above the house. The cold cut into Billy Holmes's last attempts at dignity and he started to cry. His sphincter gave way when they knelt him down and Cusack recited the charges and the verdict of the court martial. It was important to get it all legal. GHQ laid it down in great detail. We're not a bunch of hoodlums, one of them said. The bearded volunteer saw the brown liquid run out of Holmes's trousers and cursed out loud. The wind was coming from the north and there was a low cloud and he almost stepped in Holmes's shit. He cursed again. Cusack told him to shut up.

Holmes collapsed in a heap in his own shit.

'Fuck,' Cusack said.

He told McCabe to pick Holmes up.

This was the problem with touts, Cusack thought. They never ran, but they always had to be held. Nature of the beast. Always needed someone to hold them. Born puppets. Twenty a week and a hole in the head, all for the price of conviction. He looked around.

The red-haired man stood away from them, with his back to them, watching the darkness. He could not understand why. He could not see more than ten feet in front of him.

McCabe and the bearded man held Holmes up on his knees and Cusack took a .32 from his pocket. Not much good for anything else, a .32, but fine for this kind of thing. Close up. Didn't come out. No mess left behind.

He told Holmes he had a minute to make any peace he had to make.

Holmes didn't hear. Because of the wind. And they couldn't hear Holmes crying any more.

When the minute was up, John Cusack put the revolver to the base of Billy Holmes's skull and fired.

1

THE ROAD NARROWED before the trees and the trees were the only cover on that side till the checkpoint. The checkpoint was a macho statement written in corrugated shanty on the green and brown landscape, incongruous, maybe Orwellian if it hadn't been there so long. Behind it, above the village and the low hills latticed with hedgerows, prison-grey cloud spread in a blanket to the horizon, speckled in parts with a rearguard of migrating birds forming up for the flight south. And there was rain.

The rain was soft and in a fine spray and almost horizontal, and it came with the odd sodden leaf carried along on the wind from the east. The wind was cold.

South, over a slow brown river, across a concession road, through a field of uneven grass and grazing cows, beyond an imaginary line that marked the border, the earth punched a low rise into the countryside. There was a wood on the rise, thinning with the fall, some oak and ash and blackthorn, held tight by holly, gorse, and fern. The fallen leaves quilted the muddy ground and the rain ran around the leaves in small rivulets. Water dripped from the trees in large lazy drops.

John Cusack lay on the leafy quilt and adjusted his field glasses. He followed the road from the trees before the checkpoint. They were tall evergreens, maybe fifty feet, heavy with needles on top, thin below. He could see through them to a furrowed field on a hill. The field was fallow and the grass shifted direction in the wind. It was wet and it gave the furrows a kind of wave quality. The field was bordered by a hedgerow that ran across the hill parallel to the crest and joined another hedgerow running from top to bottom. This one had some trees in it, thin trees, like wire sculptures, and they were losing their leaves.

Cusack moved along this hedgerow from the road to a Victorian house. The house was right up against the checkpoint fort. An observation tower stood over it. The tower was a tall corrugated box with an anti-rocket screen around it and green tinted windows on either flank. The south-facing window was removed. Cusack could see one face: young, maybe late teens, his cheeks red, even with the battle paint covering them, and his eyes scared. He had his helmet off. Cusack let the glasses follow the tower to a tree in the garden of the Victorian house and then down the driveway to the road. He focussed in on the road.

A soldier wandered into the scene. He stood against the garden wall and talked into his hand radio. Cusack tried to follow him to the south barrier of the checkpoint. He could see a pill-box, camouflaged and sandbagged and covered in netting, but the grey corrugation at the sides of the road, protection for the soldiers operating the checkpoint, blocked off a clear view and he lost the soldier by the barrel of a General Purpose Machine-Gun. The General Purpose Machine-Gun stuck out of the pill-box and pointed across the road at the shed they used when they wanted to give cars a full search. The shed was shut now. The grey corrugated walls ran on another twenty yards towards the south, bending with the road, into the trees on one side and open fields and hills on the other. Then the road ran for a mile till the border proper. One minute thirty seconds at a constant forty.

Cusack went back to the observation post in the tower at the corner of the checkpoint fort.

The first soldier was still in view. By the barrel of another General Purpose Machine-Gun. It stuck further out of the slit in the observation post than the one in the pill-box on the ground, and Cusack held his glasses on it to see if the second soldier would show himself. He did not. The first soldier put his eyes to the high-intensity optical equipment beside the machine-gun. Cusack smiled and then moved from the observation post across the hill in a sweep and then back to the checkpoint.

It was small. No more than sixteen, maybe less, in the garrison. They were always under strength now. South Armagh patrols used it as a base during the day. Kick-off point for overnighters and long-term observation posts along the border. Flown in from Bessbrook or Crossmaglen. The in-and-outers.

Like the police. The checkpoint fort doubled as a police station three days a week. A few RUC ferried in by chopper for a few hours to fly the law and order flag in the village. For the loyal element. It was about half and half, the village, loyal and disloyal. The checkpoint was up the loyal end.

After dark there would be no soldiers on the road and it would all be controlled from inside the checkpoint fort by a skeleton shift. Just the observation post in the tower and a sandbagged control box sticking out of the checkpoint wall: speak when you're spoken to, no photography please.

But no bollards and spikes either. Something to do with the soil under the road.

Inside the outer wall of green corrugation they had a second smaller wall of breeze block and sandbags that rose to just below head height, and inside that there was an accommodation block for the soldiers dug into the ground and a grey stonewashed house with thin slates on the roof. The house was encased in a wire-mesh cage and sandbagged up to the top windows. And there was wire mesh and razor wire all along the perimeter wall of the checkpoint fort. A small RUC crest on the wall beside the control box told you it was a police station.

Cusack was just high enough to see into the fort. He watched a fat soldier come out of the house and walk across to the control box. His rifle was slung over his back and his helmet was high on his head. There was a shot if you were good enough. The soldier's boots left footprints in the sand. Another man was taking a piss against the inside of the outer wall of the fort, near the observation tower.

The observation tower was planted with electronic equipment. Aerials stood high like a punk haircut. Cusack could see the second soldier there now. His helmet. And there was more optical equipment. Nightvision stuff, thermal imaging units, cameras. A watcher's paradise.

He went back to the road and tried to get a look at the approaches. A car was coming from the south. He followed it. He let his glasses leave it at the barrier in the road with the young soldier doing a licence plate and personality check and follow the road where he could to the village.

From the other side, a dog ran through the checkpoint towards the south. A man in a peaked cap followed on an old bike, jacket collar up, head dipped against the rain. Another soldier on the road let him pass. He nodded. The soldier wiped his face and stood back into the corrugated wall for protection. The rain still got to him. Cusack moved his glasses to the fields flanking the checkpoint. There was a football pitch and an electricity pylon. The pylon was hanging over to one side. There was a tricolour on it. The pitch was a chopper landing pad for supplying the checkpoint and the ground was all cut up. Everything came and went by chopper.

On the other side of the checkpoint, the village went on for a hundred and twenty yards and then tapered out into the south Armagh countryside. There was a crossroads just before the countryside slipped in to the terraced monotony. Both the options, east and west, followed the north-south patterns. East had another permanent checkpoint further on. West was the shorter route. Cusack followed it.

Back at the checkpoint end of the village, there were two derelict houses on one side and a fine red-bricked house on the other. The red-bricked house had a Merc in the driveway. The man who owned it ran a haulage company out of Armagh City and paid a contribution to the cause four times a year for the privilege. His wife was on sedatives and seeing a shrink. Cusack moved the glasses.

One of the derelict houses had a barrier coming out of it. Then there was a row of grey sixties houses, with a break for a shop and a pub. The shop had a petrol pump and the pub had a brown imitation façade. And then a school on the west side of the crossroads. It had good walls, solid. The football pitch belonged to the school. There was a tricolour tied to the top of a lamppost outside the school and Republican graffiti and green, white and yellow markings on the walls. The school bicycle shed was rubble against the wall of a terraced house. A barrackbuster gone off course. Two had been fired. One had hit an old derelict beside the checkpoint. No one was injured; the other hit the bicycle shed and a kid lost his right eye. The kid lived in a house at the end of the row on the east side of the village, across the road from the school. His brother was in the Maze. The houses were built in brick and veneered in painted cement. The paint was monochrome and falling off. They had small windows. Some of the windows near the school and the derelict house with the barrier coming out of it were still boarded up. The barrackbusters again. Launched from a truck in a lane north-east of the village.

The river came from the south and ran north in a curve and then south again to the concession road. The concession road crossed and recrossed the border four times. There was a church on the north side of the stone bridge over the river, before the road junction leading to the concession road. The church was on another hill and there were gravestones beside it all bent at odd angles to their graves and a small line of pine trees running down to the river. The church was on the site of an earlier church and the village got its name, Kill, from the church. *Cill* means church in Irish. It had been anglicised to Kill by the British Army in the 1830s when they were mapping the country. The Victorian house at the checkpoint belonged to the church. They rented it to a retired school mistress who had had a heart attack the last time the checkpoint had been attacked with mortars. She was fat and white and wore tweeds and read Jane Austen. Sometimes the Army put a soldier in her garden. She brought out tea when they did.

There was another church three miles further north. It was Catholic and more modern and there was nothing named after it. It was beside a main road and it had a big car park. Cusack made a mental note of it.

He moved along a couple of hedgerows, up and down hills. The hedgerows were bramble and blackthorn. The brambles still had berries. The blackthorn still had a few sloes. He was moving back towards the checkpoint.

The checkpoint was about five hundred yards from the concession road. The road south ran straight from the checkpoint past the hill where Cusack lay. To his left, a tractor rolled along the tarmacked road from the south to the bridge, and then on past a bungalow with a bed and breakfast sign and a couple of nondescript terraced houses. The houses were shops, and one had an off-licence tacked on to it. The other had a money-changing sign flashing on one of the walls. There was a small wooded lane leading to fields ahead of them and Cusack made a note of that, too.

Cusack swung back to the checkpoint.

The glasses were wet and fogging up. He reached into his pocket for a handkerchief. He wanted to see the patrol. He'd seen it before. Eight of them, moving east to west along the line of the concession road. They'd crossed the border. If they knew it, they didn't care. If they didn't, they weren't asking. They stopped two cars twenty yards south of the border. The cars didn't know where they were either. Cusack knew the routine. ID? Where are you going? Have a nice day. Hearts and minds and SA-80s. Sometimes they told you your name. Sometimes they told you your address. Sometimes they told you where you worked. Sometimes they made you open everything. Sometimes people told them to fuck off home. It worked both ways, the hearts and minds thing. Sometimes. They had young faces, the soldiers. Some of their uniforms didn't fit. And their eyes always ran ahead of them.

A hand tapped him on the shoulder.

Cusack took his eyes from the razor wire around the corrugated wall of the checkpoint fort and a red sign that told you what you could and could not do and rolled on to his side. He looked at the sky and the trees around them, dripping rain, and wiped his eyes.

The man beside him wore a boiler suit similar to Cusack's. He had an old pockmarked face with grey stubble growing to the cheekbones and eyebrows that came down over his eyelids. His shoulders were broad and busting out of the olive suit. One of the seams was about to split.

'Time,' he whispered.

They were over a mile away and they had two farmers using their tractors but everything around them had ears. They'd picked up most of the video and listening gear but you couldn't be sure. Even the people who'd put it there couldn't be sure any more. Every blade of grass, every leaf, every stone, everything, was suspect.

Keep it simple, Cusack said to himself.

The older man looked around him. Then at his watch. There were flecks of dirty rainwater on the face of the watch. Drops of rain running down his face magnified the pockmarks and the grey stubble, and his eyes moved fast in their sockets, left and right, like they belonged to some kind of night feeder looking out for predators.

Cusack raised his hand.

His companion shook his head. His hair was swept back and greasy and the water in it sat like it was glue. He put his hand on Cusack's and showed his watch.

'Come on, Yank,' he said. 'Staters.'

He pointed behind them.

It's okay, Cusack mouthed. He raised his hand again.

The usual Garda and Irish Army patrol was coming from Monaghan Town. Two APCs, a couple of Japanese overlanders and a squad car full of blues. They'd about five roads on which they usually set up their vehicle checkpoints. A kind of predictable alternation. Nothing a simpleton couldn't work out. Otherwise they played safe. Stood and watched and stopped what came and went home.

Cusack trained his glasses on them. Battle camouflage replaced by olive-green duty wear. British kevlar headgear by Israeli surplus. SA-80s by Steyrs. Fear by boredom and overtime. Random death by routine and General Order Number Eight. Number Eight forbade IRA action against the Republic.It was rarely broken.

The Irish soldiers swung their vehicles into position and the gardai took their checkpoint signs out and set them up in the middle of the road. Nothing came. One of the gardai smoked on the sly against the side of his patrol car. Cusack went back to the north. He focussed in on a sign near the checkpoint: 'Blame it on the terrorists'.

He laughed to himself.

I always do, he thought.

'I'm goin', Yank,' the older man said. 'It's my car down there. If they see it, they'll get me. And I don't want to be up before the Special on Monday mornin' facin' two years in Portlaoise. So I'm goin'.'

'Keep your damn voice down.'

Cusack rolled over again, looked him in the eyes and drew his hand across his neck.

The older man wiped his mouth. His lips were pink and the lower one drooped and touched the stubble at the top of his chin.

'Scared, Danny?' Cusack said.

Danny Loughlin did not answer. He lay on his belly beside Cusack and strained his eyes and tried to hold on to his nerves.

'They know me. They know my car,' he said.

'It's hidden. And so what? You're visiting friends. Not breaking any laws. Out for a stroll in your own country. They'll be out of there in an hour. Anyway, they're good cover. And it gives us plenty of time to lie here and get what we want. Unless it's all getting too much for you, Danny.'

'I do my job.'

'Well, then, get me the camcorder,' Cusack said.

'I could do this on my own. I could. My people could get all we need. You want to let people do their jobs, Yank.'

'John.'

Danny Loughlin blinked and wiped water from the end of his nose. He wanted to sneeze but he held it.

'My name is John, Danny. You can call me that. I'd prefer it. Friendly. Informal. Fine?'

Cusack gave him a stare that didn't appreciate argument. Loughlin put up a pretence at disobedience.

'Yes,' he said.

'Good. Get me the camcorder.'

Loughlin slid back on his belly and felt the wet seep through his boiler suit. He reached into some undergrowth for the camcorder bag. The camcorder had a purpose-built zoom lens attached to it. They said you could see into a man's soul with it. Danny Loughlin did not want to think about that. He did not want to think about anything. He wanted to be somewhere else, relaxing, safe, dry. He let his mind run around the area. Landmine over there, pressure pad that way, culvert bomb wherever, hit there, miss there, stiff there. Sometimes he could hear it. Maybe smell it. He did not know if it was the smell or the sight of it that scared him most. He did not care.

He crawled back to Cusack. Cusack took the camcorder and set it up and then ran it across the checkpoint and the village on the other side of the border.

The river had reeds standing along its banks and in places where there were pools there was still green sludge. The reeds shuddered in the wind and the green sludge clung to the still brown water like a beauty treatment. They had a mine on the top of a hill to the right and a bomb in a culvert a mile to the left on the other side of the checkpoint. Maybe the patrol, Cusack thought. They'd tried it a couple of times. Fired a few shots at night, to get them to move towards it. But they always stood their ground and brought in choppers and searchlights now. Maybe a chopper then. Cusack thought about it. A chopper lit itself up. You could draw it in and then hit it with the 50-calibres. They'd hit a few that way. Put holes in one, knocked the tail off a Gazelle. But 50-calibres were heavy and they needed high mounts for anti-aircraft stuff and you couldn't break off a chopper strike so easy with a high mount. Left yourself open to the support choppers.

Cusack ran his eyes along the river. He could see a fox standing in the grass, ears pricked up. He watched it. Then he looked through the viewfinder of the camcorder. A car came through the checkpoint from the north.

'It's too solid. Too well defended,' Loughlin said.

He was on his belly twisting a dead leaf around his finger and peeling the skin off a twig. Little beads of moisture gathered at the blackheads on his nose.

'Not if we surprise them and get inside,' Cusack said.

'Go round it,' he said. 'We're not up to it. There's other targets.'

'Sure we're up to it. You just have to have it up here, Danny.'

Cusack tapped his skull.

'Real prestige, these babies,' he said. 'Remember the last time?'

Cusack hadn't been there the last time. He'd been working for GHQ in America. Buying weapons. Four years ago now. Dessie Hart and what he called his A-team took a Hino truck and drove right into a checkpoint in Fermanagh and blew it up. Then Dessie went and got himself arrested with a .32 and a couple of rounds and two of his lads blew themselves up near Cullaville with their own landmine and a couple more got jailed and another got ambushed by the SAS near Newtownhamilton and the A-team went into cold storage except for random sniper attacks and the odd lunchbox bombing.

Dessie did two years in Portlaoise and went to work with Francie Devine in Tyrone when he came out. Francie and about ten lads from Pomeroy and Coalisland were calling themselves Mid and East Tyrone Brigades then and hitting police stations and off-duty RUC and UDR and really stirring things. Francie and Dessie went back years and Francie Devine was big in Northern Command and Dessie had been a Sinn Fein councillor with a lot of pull in south Armagh and east Fermanagh and Monaghan. It worked like that. Ranks and structures didn't mean as much as personality and loyalty.

Now Dessie had the border again in the Monaghan salient and a couple of good old hands and some new potential. South Armagh, North Monaghan, East Fermanagh, Cusack laughed at the grandeur of the brigades. Six months ago, there'd been three of them doing all of it. Out at night, along the border, over and back, turnips and rabbits and hay and shit, a firefight here and a landmine there, a few off-duty police, a building contractor, some incendiaries, and then back across for a rest and whatever training they could manage.

Training was Cusack's job. Recondo stuff. How to play the SAS game. Harden them up, Dessie said. Even the no-hopers. Cusack felt he could tell a no-hoper on sight. He looked at Danny Loughlin.

'We'll hit what we can hit, Danny.'

'Send a proxy, then.'

'We'd have to follow a proxy all the way in. And then anything could happen. I don't like proxies. Too many variables. Anyway, bad for our image. We can hit this and blow it off the map, Danny. With a bit of thought. You were involved in the last one, weren't you?'

'I was doin' time.'

'Oh, yeah. Well, it'd look good if we did take it. Military-style.'

'Oh, grand, that's grand. What are youse goin' to do? Go up and knock on the door and hand them a bomb with a burnin' fuse?'

'Bit old-fashioned, Danny. That what you used to do, was it? No. But we'll hit this baby with a sledgehammer, and—' Cusack pushed a fist into the palm of the other hand. 'Tells them we're back. Bigger and better. Things got quiet when Dessie was away, Danny. We don't want that to happen again, do we?'

'We did okay with what we had, Yank.'

'Sure you did. Anyway, what are you worrying for, Danny, you're only support fire for this, support, that's all.'

'That's not the point. I don't want my people shagged away on some wild headbangin' shite. And I don't want to go to jail again. You've never been in jail, Yank.'

'You want me to go get my head kicked in Castlereagh just to prove a point?'

'You just don't lecture me on somethin' you don't know nothin' about.'

'I said keep your voice down, Danny,' Cusack said.

Cusack moved the camcorder. He examined the viewfinder. Three soldiers had appeared from the fields in front of the checkpoint's corrugated shields. They were walking in line. One had a radio pack on. The leader crouched into the side of the road by the trees. He rested on his side and pointed his rifle towards Cusack. Cusack picked up the field glasses.

'Patrol,' he said.

He focussed on the two coming up behind the leader. Two more came over the wall from a gap in the corrugation. It led to a hollow and provided cover from the surrounding hills. Two more followed them. They crossed the road in front of the checkpoint and then climbed over a stone wall into the pine trees to his left. He lost them in the trees. He aimed the camcorder where he thought they'd come out. They did. He followed them across the fields. The cloud was beginning to break up in the west and what was left of the sun liquefied on the hills and poured into a small lake Cusack could just see beyond the village. It would be dark in half an hour.

They did not speak in the car on the road to Monaghan Town.

Loughlin swung round behind Ballybay and then took a right on the road to Newbliss to make sure everything around them was all right. His head moved left and right as if he was at a tennis match and Cusack watched his shoulders hunch and his head sink into them and thought Loughlin was maybe turning into a no-hoper. It was not a thought he liked.

It was hard to call Danny Loughlin a no-hoper, and the navy light of early evening and the heavier rain and the headlight contact of the winding and undulating roads kept Cusack's mind away from that and he was glad. Loughlin was an old fighter with a service record that made people who valued such things draw breath. He had been involved since he was a kid and active as a volunteer since he was a teenager. There wasn't a post in the Army he hadn't held and there wasn't a man or a woman who'd been active he didn't know. Fenian to his balls, no compromise, ice for blood, they said. Well, that was the story anyway.

When they got to town, Loughlin relaxed. That was when Cusack got itchy. They stopped at a bookie's and Loughlin picked up the winnings he said he was owed and came out and stood for a bit like he was trying to prove something and then stopped to talk to a man in the street.

Cusack sat in the car twenty yards away, cursing to himself and wondering if the Special Branch were watching. Danny Loughlin had a police record that stretched to the moon and back. Loughlin stood in the rain, with his hands in his pockets, laughing like he was invisible. His head had come out of his shoulders. The other man was tall, like a policeman maybe, and he had a long coat on and a hat that was too big for him and he carried a walking stick and seemed to shake. There was no one else on the street. The town was quiet.

Cusack turned his head and studied the cars around the tourist office. The tourist office was an old colonial market building people had once wanted knocked down. Then they decided that tourist bucks and architectural aesthetics were more important than post-colonial pain and now it was an attraction. There was an art exhibition inside.

No Branch. He could make Branch easier than squaddies in a German bar, he thought. He turned his head again. Danny Loughlin had his hand on the shoulder of the man he was talking to. John Cusack watched them and felt confident. No one knew him.

No one knew him when he ambushed a military police sergeant at traffic lights in Rotterdam. From the footpath. A whole magazine. Then back down a side street and away. They got the MP through his BAOR number plates. Then the BAOR changed the plates and Cusack moved to Germany. No one knew him when he blew up an accommodation block in Hamburg. The excitement was racing in him now. A combination of his frustration with Loughlin and his memories of the German bombing. One dead, fifteen wounded. No one knew him when he shot a building contractor in Newry. Three in the head with a Browning at close range. They could follow this one up with a warning: anyone helping to rebuild this checkpoint will face the consequences.

'Ach, will you go way outta that, Yank,' Loughlin said in the car again. 'It's my patch, everyone knows me.'

'That's the point, Danny.'

They turned round and headed towards Clones.

'Bisto Green,' Loughlin said.

He looked over his shoulder.

'That was, back there. On the blanket years ago, Bisto. Did a hunger strike. Doesn't see so well now. Looks like death warmed up.'

Cusack could not find a reply. He had a respect for hunger strikers that went beyond reverence. It was the sheer will involved. He almost worshipped it. Cusack had a special place for will.

'Hundred and fifty quid,' Loughlin said. 'Fancy a few pints?'

'No can do, Danny. Can't be seen with you. Shouldn't be in this car with you any more. If Dessie knew I was taking you to your nag earnings, he'd throw a fit. Drop me off, Danny, get that video taken care of and then get to bed. I'm going to. I'm bushed. Why Bisto?'

'What?'

'That guy.'

'He was always sayin' "aah". Anythin' you said, Bisto said "aah". Still does. Never says much more than "aah". Good man, Bisto. Stiffed eight Brits in his time, Bisto. And look at him. Tappin' me outside a bookie's. That was what he wanted. Knows where to find me, Bisto. Where to tap me. So I give him a few quid. That okay? He deserves better. Than that. Much better. For what he's done.'

Cusack could not reply. They turned off the road and drove past a travellers' camp. There was a young girl sitting in the doorway of one of the caravans. She had long hair and a stick. A dog moved its head in and out of the road lights. The dog was tied to a rusting car. The girl threw the stick past the dog and the dog ran at the stick. It could not get to it. The leash was too short. Cusack thought it was tragic and comic.

They drove on through what looked like the heavy setting of a washing machine, and the navy evening darkness turned into black night darkness and vision sank to the level of the stone walls and the grass banks and the lower ends of the hedgerows and the broken tarmacked road. Danny Loughlin lit a pipe and pushed his tobacco into the pipe with his thumb, and the tobacco left a black stain on his thumb, and Cusack pulled the car into a road that was not a road except that it was marked on the map as a thin red capillary. It had a centreline of grass and potholes full of dirty water and it wound through trees to a farmhouse. The farmhouse was whitewashed and squat and it had a corrugated barn to the left and a ring of trees around it. The car headlights caught the heavy drops of rain against the whitewash and the whitewash was cracking and revealing the stones behind it. Water ran from a drainpipe on to the path in front of the door. There were flower pots in front of the door, clay flower pots, and the flowers were dead and the water ran around the pots and into the grass. John Cusack looked at Danny Loughlin before he got out of the car. He wanted to say something but he could not think of anything to say. The rain ran down his neck into his back and he felt a strange exhilaration.

2

OVER THIRTY MILES and ten hours away, at another farmhouse, the rain had stopped and the dawn cold bit hard into flesh and sinew and bone and light began to infiltrate from the east.

Tim McLennan could make out some of the detail of the house. There was a hole in the roof on the right and two of the windows had planks of wood nailed across them. The front door had flaking paint and a crack running along the bottom of it. And there were bats. They got in and out through the hole in the roof and he could see them now coming in from the vanishing darkness. A few birds started to sing. Two on one side, one on the other.

He tried to ignore the cold but the cold would not go away and he knew that he did not want it to go away because it was the only thing keeping him awake. He had had four hours' sleep in the three days they had been there. Three days rigid, watching this house, lying there, covered by netting, eating compo rations, soaked by the rain, shivering, pissing and shitting in plastic bags. He nudged the trooper beside him. The man jolted and raised his head. He had the kind of stubbled weatherbeaten face McLennan had learned to take for granted. The mouth was thin and there were scars and divots on the skin and a boyish excitement in the tired eyes.

'I was asleep, Staff,' he said.

McLennan pointed to his watch. They had agreed. When the sun rose they would abandon the observation post and call in the chopper to pick them up. Across the garden, about twenty yards, the other two men in the OP were set up. McLennan stretched his head to see if they had fallen asleep. He caught the face of his corporal, smiling. A smashed nose spread itself into the man's cheeks. His hair was what the Foreign Legion call *boule à zéro*. He had a Legion tattoo on his right forearm. The corporal put two fingers up to him and then made a sleeping signal with his hands. McLennan shook his head. He slipped back into deeper cover.

The tip had been solid gold, Intelligence said. Top-rate source. They'd said that before. They always said it. And four out of five OPs ended in pneumonia or diarrhoea and nothing else. McLennan reckoned he'd spent the night in most of the farmyards and gardens of derelict houses in every county in Northern Ireland. This one was between Cookstown and Pomeroy and it was wetter and colder than he could ever remember. To his left he could see the silhouettes of mountains, appearing slowly out of the darkness. The cold came from the right. From the east wind and Lough Neagh.

He tried to move without moving, possible if you were a contortionist, something to relieve the nearly unbearable pain of the dawn cold. He reckoned the cold had eaten away most of his legs and was getting ready to chew at his balls. He moved his muscles and the wet ganged up with the cold and made him stop. He needed to piss.

The chopper had dropped them off with a regular patrol. Then they'd had to hack their way through brambles and blackthorn to get here. By the time they got into position, they were torn up by the hedges and shredded by barbed wire. Better than being blown up. Better to hack your way through and rip your skin off than follow a nice neat tail and step on a pressure pad or trip a wire. The first time he had gone out on patrol, a lad had hit a pressure pad. That was so many years ago now, he thought it might have been someone else he was thinking about. Way before he went special. The poor bastard stepped through an open gate. It all looked fine. There were fresh cowprints in the mud. He stepped through smiling with his left hand up and his weapon out. Then the earth shook and the man came back with no face and no weapon and no left hand.

He tried to count the years back but he could not. Join the UDR and save Northern Ireland from the Fenians. Everyone in the area joined. The schoolmaster was the major and the newsagent was the sergeant. They got him in his shop. Two in the head. Motorcyclist and passenger. McLennan looked at his watch and checked his weapon.

The solid-gold tip-off said there was a stash in the house. Right there, in front of them. Neglected to be specific. What kind and how much. Gold tips had a habit of being debased by the time they reached OP teams. Interests protecting themselves. By the time the stuff made it from a Tasking and Coordination Group through Int and Sy Group to them it might be down to a nod and wink. He wished he could see through walls.

They could have gone in to take a look. Maybe jarked the weapons. Maybe left a present. Or maybe got one themselves. It might have been a set-up. It might still be a set-up. They'd done that. Rang the hotline with the best information and all the directions. Given it to some chinless wonder from Intelligence. Sucker-kill by proxy. It had worked a couple of times. The new lads fell for it back in the early days. Some people who should have known better fell for it later on. But bites made people shy. People were older and wiser now. The movements were more subtle. No one moved without checking a dozen times. No one breathed without checking the air. The safety catch on his G3 was on.

He slipped the safety catch on his weapon off, adjusted the fire selector and put his hand on the grip. Compact-look, seven point six two stop. You needed that against these lads. Nine-mil was too soft. Okay for the stakeouts in plain clothes on Belfast side streets but bloody useless against active-service players in the countryside. Body armour and assault rifles. Five point five six assault rifle stop, minimum. He had a sidearm, too, an SIG-Sauer, and two grenades on the back of his belt. The grenades were only for emergencies. In case the whole brigade turned up. He checked that line of thought. It wouldn't happen. Francie Devine's boys were too smart for that. Three police stations and thirteen kills in twenty-five months. East Tyrone or Mid Tyrone Brigade, they weren't particular. Devine moved like he was a shadow at high noon. And the local Taigs were Chinese monkeys.

They had four of Francie's lads under twenty-four hour watch and the bastards still managed to make hits. Fuckers, McLennan thought. They laugh at us. Have to catch them red-handed before we can do anything. Only way to deal with them was like this. In their own coin. And pray Francie turned up. Snuff Francie and East Tyrone and Mid Tyrone go with him. Like Dessie Hart across the border, out of Monaghan. Back in business, Desmond Charles Hart was. Another wild boy. Pit bull. Checkpoint Charlie, they called him in the pubs after the Fermanagh job. Smooth, that. Well organised. Well executed. Twenty to thirty players, maybe more. Real professional. Way above their usual standard: the off-duty cops blown to bits in front of their kids or the UDR men caught on their doorsteps, pissing into their y-fronts. He was angry now and he tried to stop his anger getting stronger. He could not afford to let it. Fuck it, he thought. Just fuck it. They were getting smarter and stronger and he was still fighting with one hand shoved up his arse.

McLennan rubbed his eyes and watched the rest of the day appear.

They knew each other, much more than he liked to admit. Like lovers engaged in some exotic mating ritual. He knew all the main IRA players, and maybe the main players knew him. TAC HQ had their lists and the IRA had their lists. There were lists everywhere. Every bloody tom knew the main players in his area and the players knew the toms, even the ones who didn't wear uniform, even the four-man special teams who chose their own weapons and came in just to hit. No yellow card on OP/React.

If it was a set-up, maybe the IRA boys were freezing their balls off just the same. Not likely. Booby trap was the most likely. Pressure pad beneath the window. Tripwires everywhere. Timer set off by outside pressure pad. The possibilities for violent death were endless. It didn't help to think about it. McLennan felt his stubble. He imagined what he looked like. The urge to piss got worse. Pissing was the worst problem. Shit usually stayed solid unless you contracted a chill. Then the whole hide got washed out and the opposition could smell you a mile off. But if you kept your bowels firm you could manage a shit if you had to. It wasn't easy and it left an uncomfortable feeling but you could manage it. Pissing was murder. There was no use pretending. The bag saw about a fifth of what came out. The rest went over you and your partner and when it came to his turn he could get you back. Made for strange relationships.

There was a curtain hanging loose in one of the windows. When they'd first set up, McLennan's OP mate had elbowed him and said he saw something move in the window. So they watched the curtain. They watched it for eighteen hours, mouths dry, face muscles frozen, fingers on triggers. All eyes on that curtain. A break in the cloud in the middle of the first afternoon ended the curtain stakeout. A spider was weaving a web between the curtain and the window.

'Car. Staff – car.'

McLennan froze. The pain of the dawn cold left him. A rush of adrenalin nearly forced his eyes out of their sockets. For a few seconds the freezing turned to a giddy shaking and McLennan fought to steady his weapon. He took a whiff of the urinous oily air and pinched his hands. His partner brought the Armalite at his side to a firing position. McLennan hoped to

Christ the others had their ears pricked. There was a radio link but you couldn't be sure. Not in this war. The other side had everything. Sent their new volunteers to college to gen up on chemistry and electronics. Coming into the movement now with PhDs. McLennan cursed. The car was about thirty yards off and slowing.

Trade.

The car stopped at the gate. The gate was shut. McLennan willed them to open it. Open it and bring the car in. If they did that, they had them cold. They could hit the tyres. No way out. And that was the aim. Give them no way out. No quarter given, no quarter asked for.

One man came to the gate and opened it. The gathering light showed his combat jacket. He was big, well over six feet. McLennan could almost feel his heart somersaulting.

Contact.

The man walked to the door of the house and looked around him. He walked along the front of the house twice and then stopped at the door again. Then he went round the back. He passed within two yards of McLennan. McLennan saw the weapon in his hand. Browning, maybe. Maybe a Beretta. Hard to tell. The hand was gloved and the man's face was bearded.

He went round the house one more time, very slowly.

Shit, McLennan thought. Maybe he was going in the back. They'd no cover at the back. The door was planked shut. All the windows were planked shut. He listened. No sound. Come on, come on.

McLennan kept willing the moves.

Bring the car in. Come round the front, friend.

The bearded man checking the house came round to the front door and waved the car forward.

McLennan nearly stood up and cheered.

The car came forward, slowly, inching over the gravel driveway, crunching the stones one by one. It stopped right at the door. McLennan waited. Everything would be on his signal. His call. OP/React. They knew that in the other hide. They would wait.

Two more men got out of the car. McLennan was writing the story already. The one HQ in Lisburn would release. It was falling into place. He waited. The two who got out of the car were thinner and shorter than the bearded fellow at the door. One looked like he was a kid. He had thin hands and they were shoved into the pockets of his anorak. Stupid, son, McLennan thought. He watched every move. No way they were going to get near anything they had. No way they were going to fire a round in anger.

'Mornin', boys!'

McLennan's G3 was already firing when the last word came out. The trooper beside him was up on one knee emptying his magazine into the bearded man at the front door. McLennan thought it looked like the fellow was being nailed to the door. He tried to get his pistol into a firing position but the high-velocity Armalite rounds had broken his spine and ruptured his heart and lungs before he could get his finger to the trigger. He headbutted the rotten door and fell through the splintering wood, dropping his weapon on to the concrete doorstep.

The second hide sent the man on the far side of the car into a comic frenzy against the side of the vehicle. Seven point six two-millimetre Heckler and Koch and 5.56-millimetre Armalite kisses smothered him. His head smashed against the windscreen of the car and rounds hit his body from three sides. Some of McLennan's had passed through his target and the car and into the man on the other side. McLennan's target screamed as the rounds struck him. McLennan watched the body jerk and dance and the man put his arms and hands up as if he expected to deflect the bullets. One struck his throat, another hit his elbow and a piece flew off his elbow and spattered the car. McLennan could see stains on the car window but the light was not yet good enough to make them out for what they were. Then the car exploded.

The flames went up and then out and knocked McLennan and his companion off their feet. On the other side of the car his corporal was screaming in an English Midlands accent but McLennan could not make out the words. McLennan fell back into a bush and dropped his weapon. He landed on one of the grenades he had attached to the back of his belt. The grenade dug into his back and McLennan thought it had gone through. He groaned and groped around in the pre-dawn and burning-car light for his weapon.

'Tim, Tim, he's moving, Tim.'

The trooper was grabbing his rifle and switching magazines. He had a spare one taped to the one in use. It unbalanced the weapon a bit but it was quicker for reloading during a firefight and a little imbalance didn't make much difference at a few feet.

'Get him, Vinny, get him,' McLennan said.

He had his weapon again.

The IRA man nearest them was on his feet and scrambling over the garden wall to the road. The soldiers in the other hide fired at him. They missed. Vinny Richards fired and a round struck home and pitched the victim into a ditch at the far side of the road.

'Hit, Staff, hit!'

'Go! Go!'

McLennan was up now, shouting orders.

'Corporal Evans, secure the scene, secure the scene and radio for QRF back-up.'

'Staff!'

McLennan rubbed his back as he moved towards the man in the ditch. He was lying on his back with his head in the water. The water was over his ears and up to his eyes. He was burnt and full of holes. McLennan counted twelve. Skin from his face had melted and shrivelled and hung to one side in a small ball. His legs were spread. One of them twitched. McLennan knelt down. He felt for a pulse. It was there.

'I'm alive.'

McLennan looked into his eyes. They were moving. He could see breathing too. Erratic. The chest was straining.

'I'm alive, I'm alive, get a doctor, get a fuckin' doctor.'

McLennan examined his face.

'Now let's see who we have here,' he said.

He pulled a piece of paper from his inside pocket and examined it with a pencil torch. The face was fifth down. Thirty. Involved since he was sixteen. One jail term. Possession. Seven kills down to him.

'Malachi Hart. Well, well, well,' McLennan said. 'Your mug doesn't do you justice, son. Well, it wouldn't, would it? Not now.'

'Get me a fuckin' doctor . . .'

'You're dyin', Mal,' McLennan said. 'Nothin' anyone but me can do for you now. Not Francie. Not even Dessie. And I'll just let you bleed if you don't cooperate. You'll be gone in a minute, Mal.'

'Fucker. If I live, I'll fuckin' . . .'

'You'll what, Mal? You're not goin' to live, Mal, you're goin' to bleed to death. Now where's Francie Devine these days?'

He touched Hart's body with his rifle.

'I tell you what, Mal, tell me where Francie Devine is, then I might help you.'

'Suck your prick, Brit.'

'Then shut your fuckin' Fenian mouth and die, Mal.'

'Bastard . . .'

'Francie! Where's he hidin' out?'

'Fuck you, fuck you . . . get me a fuckin' doctor. Y'Orange bastard.'

McLennan shook his head and stood up and tapped Hart's running shoes with his boot. The running shoes were torn. A piece of sock stuck out of the side of one of the shoes.

'Maybe you just might live, Mal,' McLennan said. 'Maybe you just might, mightn't you? And then you'd get better and do your whack and get out and be back to your bad old ways and before I know it you'd be takin' a pot at me or blowin' some poor widow or child or some poor fucker to kingdom come, Mal. No way, Mal. No way. You should have stayed with Dessie in the Free State, Mal. Where's Francie?'

'Fuck you – Christ, I'm freezin'.'

He coughed blood. It dribbled down his chin. His chin was pointed. The blood dribbled down his chin and ran into the water.

McLennan put another magazine into his weapon. He cocked the weapon and took aim.

'Cunt. You better back off, bastard,' Mal Hart said. 'Do it well, fucker.'

McLennan backed off a few feet and took aim at Hart's heart.

'Oh, Jesus . . . I'll see you . . . I'll—'

A three-round burst hit the area around his heart.

'Area secured, Tim.'

McLennan turned. Chris Evans stood holding his rifle over his shoulder. He was cut on the forehead and the cheeks and there was a burn mark above the cut on his forehead. The dawn had arrived.

'Bloody car, Tim,' Evans said. 'Someone hit the tank. Ted's caught a bit more than me. Face and body are badly burned. I've radioed for a medic. Vinny's giving him some morphine and basic. The other two are out of it. Stiff. I think we'll let the local toms go into the house and see what this lot had in store.'

He looked at the dead body in the ditch.

'You stood back?'

'Yeah.'

'Good. Three nil, the regiment.'
He raised his fist.
A chopper was coming in from the east with the rest of the light.

3

ON A HILLSIDE in south Armagh that morning, in a customised hide, the 'Song for Liberty' from Verdi's *Nabucco* flowed through a thirty-five-year-old woman's brain as she lined up the PSO-1 sight of a Soviet SVD sniper rifle on a British paratrooper's chest. The rangefinder scale in the lower left of the sight is graduated to the height of an average man. She placed the horizontal line on the scale at the foot of her target and followed the curved line to the head and calculated the range. The 7.62 round in the chamber was armour-piercing. Muzzle velocity 2,720 feet per second. The target was walking.

The target was about the same age as the sniper. He had a small scar on his cheek and a moustache. There were five paratroopers visible. But the timid morning sun on cloud silver had picked him out. She could see the light-rays bounce off his red beret and winged badge and the back of his tight blond haircut. This was the maiden patrol for the new battalion in south Armagh. They'd come in by chopper the day before. Maggie O'Neill had watched it all and now she wondered if any of them really expected anything to happen. Then she stopped wondering and let the music take over.

The trigger was at the point.

The target raised his hand and made a signal and two paratroopers behind him ran on ahead and took up positions in a ditch. The target examined the road ahead with the sight of his SA-80. Maggie O'Neill relaxed her body and waited for the music to guide the shot.

He folded the moment the round struck. Dropped like some imaginary strings had been cut. She saw his mouth open, then there was no more time to watch. Direction-finders would be on to her in a few seconds. The watchtower on the high ground to the east. She pulled the earphones of her Walkman off, slung the rifle over her back and scrambled down the ladder to the barn floor. The barn smelled of shit and urine and it had a mist of dust and hay floating around in tunnels of light from the gaps in the corrugated walls. She was counting seconds.

On the broken south Armagh tarmac the target, a sergeant from Gloucester, was already dead. Deep red blood ran from the exit wound at the back of his body, split into little streams by the broken tarmac, and snaked towards the grass and the bubbling ditchwater at the side of the road. One of his soldiers held the sergeant's head in his arms and spoke a prayer, trying to keep his compo rations from spilling out on to the broken tarmac. Two others fired off rounds towards the south, shouting curses. A corporal yelled at them to hold their fire until they had identified a target. The radio operator was screaming into his mouthpiece:

'Man down, man down . . .'

A black and white cow watched them through a hedge.

Maggie was already across the border when she saw the Lynx sweep low over the fields around Crossmaglen. Her new hide was a simple camouflaged net over a ditch between some trees. She lay on her back, holding her rifle, and watched the chopper sweep across the border. It hovered about fifty yards to the right of her. She could see the waist gunner swing his GPMG in an arc. There was a second somewhere. She could not see it but she knew it was there. The Lynx made two sweeps at treetop height and then headed north again.

Couldn't risk it, she thought. Even with cover. But the mouths'd be saying back in Monaghan they should have had a 50-calibre ready for the chopper. Mouths always said things like that. Jumped out of their skins if you asked them to take a weapon but were full of tactical bullshit over a pint.

The lower half of her was wet with ditchwater and she could feel the sweat begin to cool on her upper body. Her mouth was dry. She wanted to take her balaclava helmet off. The itching was getting so she couldn't stand it. She continued to count. She never carried a watch. She preferred her own method. From the time she began to the time she finished she never stopped counting.

Another ditch ran through high nettles to a culvert and the culvert allowed her to run along a hedgerow out of sight of the north and the choppers – there were two of them now – racing up and down the supposed line of the border. She was still counting.

The engine of the Ford Sierra was already running when she got to the farmyard. The cloud was breaking up in the gathering wind and the low morning sun was bouncing in Morse flashes off the whitewashed walls of the farm buildings and a sheepdog was playing with a ball near some chickens.

Maggie had dumped the rifle in a hole between the culvert and the farm. She stuffed her balaclava and the surgical gloves she wore into the pocket of the olive boiler suit she had on and ran her fingers through her short hair. Then she pulled down a duffle coat hanging over a piece of machinery and put it on. She got into the car. The seat sank under her. There were furry dice hanging from the rear-view mirror. There was hay on the floor of the car and a couple of dirty newspaper pages. The driver drove out on to the main road south.

There was no talk in the car. If the driver knew who she was he did not say. You kept to what you were supposed to know. He was a driver. That was all he did. He picked people up and he dropped them off. And for that he got expenses. It supplemented the social welfare and the farm income and allowed him to feel he was doing his bit without making him do anything he couldn't handle. That was the way they ran it. You did what you could. It accommodated all points of the commitment spectrum. He believed. But not enough. They knew how to make use of that.

He didn't even bother looking at Maggie O'Neill. She shoved her earphones back into her ears and listened to some eighteenth-century choral music.

He dropped her at a house on the road to Carrickmacross. She could dump her boiler suit, gloves and balaclava there, burn them and take a shower.

The owner had more commitment than the driver. He allowed an upstairs room to be used for meetings and he and a brother owned a sheep farm in Connemara with a sixty-foot bunker under an outhouse, packed with bags of fertiliser, electronic timers, a score of Romanian AKMs and thirty thousand rounds of ammunition. He'd been interned in the fifties for a couple of years, had gone to the States then, come back, renewed old contacts and become active again after Bloody Sunday. His wife had left him for it. She'd stormed into their bedroom one night and laid it down in front of him. A bomb had gone off on a shopping street. Two women had been blown to pieces. They'd had to shovel the pieces into plastic bags. It had been on the news. Give it up or me up, Harry, she said. Harry McCusker never saw his wife again.

He was pouring water on a box of herbs when Maggie came in. There were two men sitting at a bend in the road, on a grass bank, playing chess, drinking bottles of Heineken. One was young, about twenty, with a tweed jacket and a disordered face, like he'd been half rearranged and forgotten. He was too thin for his clothes and there was a hump in his spine. The other was older, square and balding under the tweed cap he was wearing. His nose was wide, spread across his face, and he drank whiskey with his Heineken. He kept the whiskey in a silver flask. The two of them were road workers and they were there for a reason and knew better than to ask too much about anything. The younger one had a walkie-talkie in his pocket. The older man made a comment about Maggie, something innocuous, meant as a boast. He looked over at McCusker and raised an eyebrow. McCusker, who looked like a schoolteacher, shot back at him with a look that cut him in two. He went red and downed his Heineken and whiskey and told his young friend to finish his and get back to work. The job was done; whatever was supposed to happen had happened. Danny Loughlin would be in touch.

'You're wanted again,' McCusker said to Maggie.

She had showered and he was burning her gloves in a fire. Maggie was combing her hair in a mirror. Going through a dinner menu in her head. She was still counting.

'Already. When?'

'You'll get a message.'

He watched her small body move in front of the mirror. The jeans he had given her hugged her bottom and made him want to reach out and touch her. Her hair was combed back and wet and she had some freckles on her face and cold blue eyes that smiled even when they were serious.

'Anythin' on the news?'

'Bare details.'

'Score?'

'One nil, here. But they got three lads this mornin' over at Pomeroy. I don't know the details. They've given no names.'

'Shite,' she said.

She took a deep breath and exhaled, slowly. McCusker thought she looked even smaller when she was exhaling. She wasn't that small. Maybe three or four inches over five feet. In high heels she could give him a run. He let his mind imagine her in high heels. Then he told himself to lay off, concentrate on business. He could get a woman later. McCusker needed a woman every time he was involved in something. Even at a distance. It was that or jerk off. He preferred to have someone with him. Helped him with his fear. Some day they'd come. He was convinced of it and it didn't matter if it was true any more. It was his dread. Maybe a four-man team in untraceable cars. It kept him awake, shitting himself sometimes, gun under the pillow. They got your name one way or another. Then you went into the computer with a rating. And if they thought you were worth it they sent a team across to get you. You never knew until the bullets were in your skull. Then it was too late. He was never specific about who they were. They were just they. Over there. On the other side.

He looked at Maggie's face in the mirror. It was a young face but the eyes looked like they'd seen more than they should have and they had a distance in them, like they were trying to protect something. And she talked as if she was always drawing on some hidden reserve deep inside her.

'Want a drink?' he asked.

'Not on,' she said. 'Did you get all that shoppin' I asked for?'

'Downstairs. Real little housewife, aren't we?'

'Not your concern.'

'No.'

A second driver took her to a small village between Monaghan Town, Castleblaney and Clones. A place where people watched and said nothing. It had a wide main street in a kind of market-town layout except there was no market and very little town left except those with families and those too old or too young to go. Most of those left were on the dole. There were two shops and three bars. One of the bars was a shop and one of the shops was a sub-post office. The bars had faces that looked inbred and the faces had a timidity that verged on embarrassment. The main street was broken up with potholes and if you stopped there people talked about nothing but the potholes – and maybe the weather. A man had been elected to the local council on the pothole issue. No one had ever been elected on the weather issue.

The private bus from Dublin was pulling up at a petrol pump outside a shop when the Ford car dropped Maggie and her shopping off. A few eyes followed her. No one said anything. She worked shifts in Dundalk. Everyone knew that. Because she told them. It was better to tell them and have them feel they knew than have them talk. And men gave her lifts all the time. Most men in the area wanted to give her lifts. Most men in the area wanted her. Sometimes when they'd had a few and they knew there was no one who would say it to her, they said they'd like a bit of her. They didn't care about her husband or what he thought.

Brian O'Neill was a bit of a joke. She did not want to admit it. Loyalty to him. What it said about her. She looked over at the road leading to Monaghan Town and the site. The site was empty except for an old shopping trolley and a tractor wheel. His site. For his hotel. He had the plans, he'd get the permission, he said. There were plenty of lads around who'd like to see a hotel built. Who'd put the money up. There was always an inane grin on his face when he was talking about the hotel. The kind of grin you see on gamblers throwing their last dice or turning their last card over. Cliff-edge sense. Except Maggie had a feeling her husband was way beyond that now.

There wasn't going to be a hotel. The banks would take the site and the house and anything else they could, and even if they didn't get the site, no one in their right mind would build a hotel there. Who for? She asked him that. Her Brian. She called him her Brian and the villagers called him her Brian, as if he was a child. She asked him that when he spread the plans on the table and told her what he was going to build as soon as the money arrived. The money was coming from a different place every week. There was a fountain on the plans, right in the forecourt. Kitsch on kitsch. Sentimental bad taste. His style all over. He spread the plans out after dinner every night.

It did not seem to matter that he was out of work, that the banks sent letters every week, that he was up to his neck in court summonses. He was going to build his hotel, right there, right at the edge of the village, right on his site, build it and run it and everything would be fine again.

Things had been fine when she'd met him. Fast-car fine. She was down from Belfast, working in Blaney. Brian O'Neill always drove a Merc and people said he was a millionaire. The family had a quarry in Tyrone and a boat business on Lough Erne and the Shannon. There were other businesses but she never got too deep into the whole thing. All she knew was the businesses vanished one by one and each time a business vanished a new set of letters would arrive and Brian would toss them in the dustbin. He still drove a Merc except the models were older and third- and fourth-hand. But he always had plans. She'd liked the plans when there was still a possibility they might be real. When he could make you believe in him. The never better language of futility in the face of cold reality. They'd had a kid quick and then another just as quick and Maggie cursed herself for being swept along by whatever it was this Brian, her Brian, had.

She walked through the drizzle to the end of the road. There was a stone wall around the site and a broken For Sale sign at the far end. She had not seen that before. She did not know if it was old or new. She did not care. She stood and looked at the field. It would not be a big hotel. You just couldn't on that site. Brian said it would be a huge hotel. And when he was in one of the boozers he bought drinks with the housekeeping and said it was going to be a massive hotel and he was going to give jobs to everyone in it. They cheered and took his drink and then said he was a thick cunt behind his back.

Maggie put her shopping bags on the wall and placed her hands on the wet stones. The Dublin bus was moving on. It left a student behind. The student was tall and he had a male-model face and romantic hair. She might fancy him, she thought. If only. She did not continue with the if onlys. She was relaxing for the first time since the job. She could feel her body releasing itself. An old woman walked along the opposite side of the road. She had a headscarf on and her body moved in an overweight motion. Her legs were big and bent. Maggie said something she did not mean and the woman answered with something she did not mean. Maggie picked up her bags and headed home.

The radio news gave pencil-line details. Her job followed the Pomeroy ambush. No names in either. Statements, condemnations, expectations. She sat down and looked out of the window at the street. Two cars passed slowly. Maggie started to shiver. She felt her body and her body was sore and she could not stop it shivering. She saw a woman with big breasts trying to run across the road outside. She tried to laugh. The woman's breasts almost tipped her over. Maggie made coffee and drank it with both hands around the cup. Upsurge in violence, expected retaliation, revenge, answers, all the stars of the Northern Ireland soap bounced out of the radio in predictable order. Voices and statements ran into one another and she could not be bothered to figure out who was saying what. She went into the living room and picked up a photograph of her husband and herself on their wedding day. She did not remember where the photograph was taken and she did not really want the man in it. She sat down and let the shivering take over.

'Let me go,' she said.

Then she opened her jeans and put her fingers between her legs and rubbed.

She was still counting.

Counting had always been part of it. Count Brits, Maggie. Just sit there and count them. On a wall in Andytown. In school uniform. Holding a tennis racket or something like that, watching them and counting them. She could fancy them, too, that was okay. Smile at them, Maggie. Make them think you're their friend. But count. Fifteen of them broke the door down and tore their house apart.

The fucking cunting sniper ran this way, you bastards.

One of them was in the middle of the road, dead duck from the duck squad, in the middle of the road, bleeding from the head into the gutter, glass eyes. She remembered the glass eyes. Death was always glass after that. Fragile. Broken.

Another fragment came at her. A gun battle at the corner of Whiterock Road and the Falls, her pulling Patricia Murphy to the hot paving stones, Patricia's screaming, summer heat, soldiers running and screaming and kicking in doors. No casualties.

They broke the door in during *The Likely Lads*. Up the stairs, pulled her brother, Pat, down the stairs, kicked him, hit him with rifles, cursed, fucking bastard, fuckers, bastards, back and forth, she counted till she lost count, and her mother was on the kitchen floor, crying and screaming, on her hunkers with this para standing over her, asking her to stop, Daddy standing with his fingers spread against the wallpaper, paras tearing up the carpet and the floorboards, watching *The Likely Lads* when they could.

You Cahills are up to your fucking necks in it, marked. Dead, my son, dead. Pat was dragged out and thrown in the Saracen with three other lads from the street. Maggie counted them.

She boiled an egg and made toast. She cut the toast into soldiers. She dipped the soldiers into the boiled egg and put them into her mouth. The plans for Brian's hotel lay in the corner of the kitchen. Beside the Trivial Pursuit and other games.

Sell the bloody site, Brian, sell it and clear our debts and we can hang on to the house. For the kids, Brian.

Brian always shook his head. No way. I'm buildin' this hotel. I'm seein' someone today and there could be good news. If we can get the money and the backin', the plannin' permission is a certainty. That's how it works. If we can provide one bloody job around here, they'll build the damn thing for us. This is our future, love. The kids', too. I'm not throwin' it away. I've had setbacks, but I'm stronger for it. Do you not see?

Maggie was too busy counting. Duck-squad times. Corner to house one, corner to house two. Ten lads lined up against a wall on the Springfield Road, arms out, up on toes, fingers spread, a hiding to the one that moves, checking, cursing, pushing. She ran along the line, ducking under the lads to see if Pat was there. She knew all of them but they said nothing. The duck-squad leader called her darling and held her schoolbag while she looked. She pulled her skirt up above her knees. The platforms made her look taller. Pat wasn't there. He was in a house in Lenadoon, making a bomb.

You should have been there, Pat, she thought.

Brian never saw an angry soldier, never heard a gun, never felt a bomb. Nothing. It was like she was an alien describing another planet when she tried to tell him. He did not want to know. Most of them did not want to know. Some of them admitted it. The rest paid lip service and made good speeches when they had too much to drink, but they did not want to know. She hated them for it. For placing it all on her shoulders. You expected help. Any they got was Band Aid stuff. It was always a running retreat. Maybe if they'd put their money where their mouths were, the lip-service rebels, it would all be over by now, she thought. But they couldn't, could they? They were scared and revolted. Revolutions got done by a very few, that was always the way. By a very few and then legitimised by the rest later when the revisionism came along and you found out that all those people you thought despised you were actually helping you. But that was people. The mob. Public opinion, the pollsters called it. One and the same. Second-guessers. Fence-sitters. Waiting for a result. Sure things.

Her mother went on Valium and never came off it. Her father died of a something she was not sure of. She didn't go to Belfast any more. That was part of her play. She was out of it. Long time gone. Not so much as a parking ticket. Only banks and building societies trying to get her house and a husband trying to build a hotel. She laughed. She had ceased to look for logic in life. The business she worked for in Dundalk was an IRA front. For money. Clean as far as the Branch knew. Nice factory on the industrial estate. IDA grants even. Then a fundraising unit comes in one day armed to the teeth and leans on the boss for a contribution. The stupid pricks were lucky not to lose their kneecaps. The army council went apeshit. One of the girls in the office called the gardai and three carloads of Branchmen arrived and lifted two of the fundraisers. The Branch were all sympathetic when they came to interview the boss. Told him to put in a panic button, direct to them, to press it if the subversives ever called again. He was sweating. Had to have a cuppa. Maggie didn't know whether to laugh or cry. The lads who got picked up got time. No one in the Army shed a tear. The boss put in a panic button. Orders.

She found herself picking targets through the window. And counting. A lover spoke to her on a distant thought. Shankill tones. She sat and watched a talk-show on Sky. They had a satellite dish. They had everything and they owned nothing. She flicked back and forth to Sky News but they kept showing the same reports. Police tape and a reporter with no details. Names being withheld till next of kin are told. Senior sources were quoted. British and Republican. So long as they were senior. She did not recognise the piece of south Armagh where her target had died. She did not use die. She used another word. She knew she meant died but she did not use that word. He was gone. Tagged and bagged and ready to go home. There was nothing there now but soldiers and tape and two RUC men with Rugers who looked like they wanted to be somewhere else.

Who the hell were they? The Pomeroy dead. She wanted to know. They were people she knew. They had to be. She could make a call. One call and find out. But she did not want to find out. She just wanted to know. For no reason. She would not feel sorry. She was beyond feeling sorry. She never felt sorrow or sadness any more when they lost volunteers. She felt anger, she felt hatred, but nothing else, and even the anger and hatred were reheated stuff, from way back. You had to protect yourself. Keep going. That was the bottom line and you did what you had to do to keep going.

That led her back to Brian and his hotel and she wanted to pick up the plans and tear them up and scatter the pieces over the site.

Then Maggie O'Neill closed her eyes.

4

THE LYNX FLEW at treetop level, lower where possible. The engine's metallic whine drilled into Tim McLennan's ears. He sat hunched in the back, one leg bent, one flat, hugging his equipment. Vinny Richards sat beside him. Evans at the other end. The fourth man in the team, Taylor, was in hospital in Belfast. They'd stayed with him for an hour in Armagh, watched him shake, second-degree burns right up the body, the stink of burning human flesh, the giddy talk of fear and pain, young toms staring, trying to ignore it, feeling their guts tighten just thinking about it. There but for something, McLennan thought.

He watched the patchwork quilt of green and brown and grey, fields and mountains, rivers and lakes, drift by, beneath and around him. There was a great emptiness about the place. It had an underused feeling. Like people were busy with other business. Like it was waiting for something to happen. And Lough Neagh was a huge tear in the distance.

His land, he thought.

He could see roads he had travelled and towns he had visited and houses in the towns where friends lived or had lived and farms outside the towns where this or that friend of this or that friend of a friend or relative lived. It was all interconnected, a grid of support, all the links established over generations, all the protections. You needed protection. Because he could see the places where he wasn't welcome, too. Where all he could expect was a bullet. They wound their way in and out of the good stuff like a cancer, he thought, those places, sometimes only a house away. And breeding faster. Bloody-minded. The bloody-mindedness of the perennial loser. Creeping cancer.

From treetop height it had a board-game quality. The pieces were there. Taig, Prod. Move the occupants of that farm to that town. Let them set off a 200-pound car bomb. Then move that platoon of soldiers to that field and let them ambush a few gunmen. He felt he could reach out of the chopper, past the waist gunner on his GPMG, reach down and pick up the pieces and move them about. Checkmate.

The Lynx followed the M1 and the Lagan and left the H-Blocks of the Maze Prison on the right and swung a wide hemicircle before heading north along the line of Lough Neagh to Aldergrove. The RAF base had an isolated emptiness about it, and a certain depression pervaded it, a direct contrast to the international airport beside it. A C-130 sat on the tarmac of the RAF base and a British Airways shuttle was taking off from the international airport. The Lynx came in low to make its landing. A Puma passed them on the way out. Other helicopters sat on the ground, blades hanging lazy, loading, unloading, uniforms and guns, guns and uniforms.

McLennan watched a platoon of skinhead paras with their cam-cream faces and their scared eyes tool up and squash themselves into a flight of Pumas. They played with the safety catches on their rifles. On, off, on, off. One man slapped another on the shoulder. His mate did not look at him. He concentrated on the outside.

McLennan slid off the Lynx and threw his equipment over his shoulder and slung his weapon from his neck. More outgoing toms passed him as he walked across the tarmac. At a distance. There was an understood distance. One of the paras was an officer, young, maybe early twenties, first-tour face, getting-to-know-the-men body language.

The officer stopped talking to his sergeant and followed the SAS trio till he realised he was going to look stupid. The contact-groupie look, McLennan thought. A kind of frustrated jealousy. Ordinary green just didn't get into contacts much any more. PIRA didn't wait around. So the toms just went through the figure-eleven motions and hoped to Christ they left with the same amount of live bodies they arrived with.

The paras around the officer talked about their dead sergeant in south Armagh. They had nervous lips that talked big and dried out in seconds. Two of them wet their lips with their tongues. The officer said something bland and then turned back to McLennan.

Tim McLennan might have saluted him except he did not feel like it and he knew he did not have to with a first-tour sub. Para or not. Para pansies, he thought. A mixture of past envy and present contempt. They came and went, toms, in and out, tour after tour, round and round.

The officer made a move to salute and then stopped and answered a query about Crossmaglen from a young tom with a backpack that looked like it was about to split. The para sergeant yelled at someone ahead of him.

Tim McLennan was busy preparing his evidence.

There'd be no problem. But it was important to get the story clear. They were challenged, two of them had guns, we opened fire to protect ourselves. They had given the bearded bloke's automatic to Mal Hart. Squared better with the RUC when they came. The third man's gun never got fired. It was in his pocket with his hands. So they fired it for him. He would have wanted it that way, they said, laughing. And it made it all look clean. The rest was for Army Information and Press Relations to handle. No one was going to spend too much time crying for three terrorists caught red-handed at an arms dump. Five AKMs, probably from the Libyan shipment, a few hundred rounds of ammunition, three revolvers and a sawn-off shotgun. The press relations people would make a nice story out of it. A few of the local liberals would whinge about shoot-to-kill. The Shinners would get all sanctimonious. Cry murder. Like their lads were out for a stroll. But that was part of the war, too. Contacts didn't just begin and end in the field. They were just the bang. Waves of sanctimony could do more damage than an assault-rifle bullet or an explosion if they were directed the right way. Each side did it. It worked itself out. And McLennan could live with it.

It was the others he couldn't stand. The civil liberties people who complained that they should have wounded the opposition, taken them prisoner. Nice and neat. He shook his head. He knew only one way to shoot. Anyone who shot to wound never shot again. What the hell else did they think people shot for? You went out to kill. That was it. War: big boys' games and big boys' rules. The other side knew it, they understood it. And if the shoe was on the other foot, the regiment could expect no different.

He was left facing an argument he did not want to have. With the reconciliation people. They looked on the whole thing as some unfortunate misunderstanding that could be sorted out by some kind of quiet chat around a fire. No fucking way. No fucking reconciliation with that. They wanted to take it all away from him. Everything he was. This Irish Republican Army, and all its fellow travellers: its constitutional nationalists and Free State jelly republicans. Couldn't do it themselves but took the benefits the

Provos gave them. He was British, the turf he tramped night after night, the roads he walked, the fields he slept in, pissed in, shit in, they were Ulster, his Ulster, and his Ulster was British. He hated the middle-grounders worse than the Provos. The Provos were honest, you knew where they were coming from. They made no bones about it. They wanted the country united and the Brits out. Fair enough. Except he was a Brit and he wasn't leaving till they carted him out in a box, and even then he'd do his best to get back. But the in-between boys, the 'let's recognise both traditions' lads, they were the worst. They took it away from you, smiling at you. Both traditions. He laughed. Everything was a compromise with them. They believed in nothing. Just prices and deals. How could you recognise both traditions? They were mutually exclusive. A child could see it. If it wanted to.

'You can't suddenly tell an Englishman he's German.'

'Sorry, Staff?'

McLennan looked at Evans as if the man had asked him to jump from a great height without a parachute. The corporal was stirring a cup of tea. He had a slice of bread balanced on the cup. The burns and tears on his face looked designed. He had a kid's face. It had all the features of adulthood but it was a kid's face. Something missing. They all had it, the ones from over the water, no matter how long they'd been at it. They just didn't know what it was all about. To them it was just another job. Another contact. They never got into the politics of it. Just went where they were sent and shot who they were told to shoot. Fine, up to a point.

McLennan poured milk from a half-pint carton into his tea.

'Nothing,' he said.

He was tired now. They were supposed to get showered, eat, sleep and then report. The routine. Everything was routined. McLennan couldn't think past the cup of tea. He was too tired to sleep. And too high. Contradictions like that were a way of life on OP/Reacts. It would subside. The high feeling. Contact fever. Slowly. It would slip away and mundanity come back. Then he could sleep. He could feel the mess slipping between his legs. He could smell himself.

'You think he'll be okay? – Ted, Staff?' Vinny Richards asked.

It was Yorkshire sounds mixed in with East End pronunciations. It did not mean anything. It was unwind conversation. Small-talk.

McLennan nodded. Richards bit into a biscuit.

McLennan walked over to a table and pulled out one of the chairs and sat down. All the wet of his combats seeped into his body and he shivered. He placed his sodden boots on another chair and folded a piece of bread and ate it. Mud from his boots slid off the leather and dripped on to the floor.

'Tim!'

'Boss,' Evans said. He stood up and came to attention as much as he could. Richards didn't even get that far.

'At ease, lads. As you were.'

McLennan hadn't bothered to get up. He could see the captain in a mirror on the other side of the room. The mirror had a girlie calendar beside it. McLennan was eyeing up Miss September. She wasn't his type but the way this tour had gone and the way he was feeling, he didn't care. He'd lost count of the amount of ambushes and stakeouts they'd set up this tour, and this had been the first contact. First blood to the troop. First blood should have meant something. He had not had a successful contact in two tours. But he felt disappointed, almost cheated. Because, for him, it was just a piece of PR. To show they were on top of things. To show Francie Devine and his boys they didn't have a free run. Except the Provos had scooped them again in south Armagh, and maybe if there was a need and a chance and the guts in Downing Street, they'd be sent out again for another show of strength. It still wouldn't mean anything. No one would make the real decision and let them loose. Afraid of the mess. Instead they used the Army as a lid and called what was underneath acceptable levels. He shook his head. No one noticed. Eyes were on the captain.

'Three kills, Tim. Congratulations, boys.'

The captain was a couple of years younger than McLennan and from a better-off background, and greying at the temples. He had a solid paratrooper body even though he'd spent most of his early career in an infantry regiment. His eyes had something romantic in them that McLennan could never quite pin down. And he always stood on his toes like he was desperate to get stuck in. They had that on him. He'd never go out on an OP. Officers didn't any more. Gave you pips and clipped your wings. McLennan wondered what he would do when his pips arrived. He did not want to give it up. He could not. But his commission was wet to dry ink away. He dropped the commission. He was too tired to get into that wrestle. Anyway, it brought him to his wife and he did not want to think about his wife.

A commission would mean out of the field and probably far away. There was a temptation but it was only that. He had made up his mind that morning, well before that probably, probably when Eric Johnson was crippled, even before that maybe, maybe as far back as Robbie Wilson losing his eyes, but, officially, that morning, that he wanted to stay. This was his war and he wanted to stay and fight it to the end.

He laughed to himself and his stomach expanding was the only outward sign that he was laughing. Maybe they'd keep him here, and in the field. Make an exception. He was a local lad and a local lad had an edge they weren't going to let go of. Anyway, the pips, if they came, would be a sop to effort more than anything else and McLennan knew he wasn't going any higher. NCO in officer's clothing, someone had said in the mess. McLennan was going to hit him but when he thought about it, he decided it was the truth. He half laughed to himself again. There were two chances of him getting what he wanted. His wife was back in his head. Decisions piling up like shit, he thought.

'Yeah,' he said to the captain. 'One of ours was wounded. Taylor. He's bein' treated in Belfast at the minute.'

'Yes, I heard. Bad luck, Taylor. And the paras have taken a casualty over XMG way this morning. Sniper. Dead. Still . . .'

Bob Stone held himself and tried to decide what to say next. He wanted to ask about the contact but he had to play it cool. He'd never been in one in Northern Ireland. He'd done other stuff but never here. And that annoyed him. Made him feel less than he should in front of his men. He stood with his hands behind his back and worked some saliva into his mouth.

'Right,' he said. 'Good. The press will be screaming over this one. It's terrific, though. I was beginning to think we'd go through this whole tour without a contact. Wait till it gets around the squadron. Drinks on me, tonight, I think.'

It was just a bloody game to him, McLennan thought. In a league. He wasn't much different from Evans really. If you asked them about the place, they couldn't tell you much about it. If you asked them if they felt they were in Britain, they'd look at you and think for a while and smile and say yes. But it was just orders with them. Caretakers for people who couldn't make up their minds how to get shot of the place. Fighting an ad campaign. Nothing more. People who winced at the sound of an Ulster Protestant accent. They got embarrassed on the Twelfth. They got embarrassed when you started getting into religion. For God and Ulster. McLennan had it tattooed to his right arm. He was a teenager when he'd had it done. They were all having it done.

If we have to go into a united Ireland, if you force us in, we'll be wiped out in a couple of generations. Those that got left behind when the border was drawn, look at them. Down to three per cent and droppin'. We'd go the same way.

McLennan was letting a basic mistrust of Northern Ireland politics rise to the surface. A result of overexposure. More dangerous than UV rays. Duplicitous machinations that would put a Byzantine court to shame. Fudges, half-measures, contradictions, lies, a suffocating mixture of inertia and intent. He let his mind freewheel.

The English would drop him and all he stood for if it suited them, he was sure of it. He could be British and still mistrust the English, there was no contradiction there for him. British could betray British that way. For two decades they'd said they were staying and everything they did told him they were going. And history was on his side. They'd done it everywhere they'd ever been. He tried not to think of it like that but he could not stop himself.

And then we'll be on our own, he thought. Pieds Noirs. Backs to the sea. They all say we won't fight. I will. You want to take all I am, all I'm ever going to be, you better do it over my corpse.

He grinned at the captain. The captain moved from one foot to another and put his hand on McLennan's shoulder.

'Proud, lads,' he said.

His voice had that clipped confidence that Sandhurst seemed to dish out with the rations. McLennan raised his cup. A worm slid out from between his bootlaces.

'Success,' he said. 'Success, shit, piss, and worms.'

The captain laughed. Evans and Richards laughed with the captain. McLennan watched the worm crawl along his boot.

'We'll talk when you're ready, Tim. Good show, lads.'

'Sure.'

He raised his fist and dimpled his cheeks. These bastards were so sure of what they were, McLennan thought. And when a tour was up, they'd slip back to England, slip out of uniform, slip into a woman and forget any of this really existed. It was like some giant training ground to them, and if they didn't feel like it they need never see it again as long as they lived.

He came from here. The place was in his blood. The towns and farms he had seen on the flight back to base came into his head. Hills he had walked in and mountains he had climbed, trails and lakes and rivers, where the good fishing was, where the worst bigots were. He had asked himself a few times, in moments of imposed reflection, usually up to his face in rain and mud, if he was a bigot. Seriously. There had to be some in him, he concluded, in that kind of divide, and he let it go at that. Tolerance was a luxury he could not afford. Let me see them be tolerant when they know a lad three miles away has walked into a bar and machine-gunned four of your friends. And you can't get the bastard because there isn't enough evidence. But you can see him every day. Walking down the street, going into a shop, buying fags and booze, putting money on a horse. And he knows you can't touch him.

McLennan was back in the great swamp of policy again and he didn't want to get bogged down in it now. Not after a contact. What he wanted now was Carol. Carol and all the comfort she brought. He thought about her and a time they had been together and then about his wife and a time they might have been together and then he stopped thinking.

'How long do you need, Tim?'

'Boss?'

Stone was sitting on the edge of his desk, lighting a cigarette. His hands had scars running up the fingers. They were too regular to have been accidental. When people asked him he just shrugged it off and said he'd been careless. He was perfect SAS, Stone, just the right mixture of competence and insanity. McLennan tried to apply the description to himself and could not figure out which was the stronger in him. Stone used football analogies. I don't play any more, he'd say, smiling, just coach from the sideline. He had all the body movements of a football manager and most of the jargon, too. His hair was combed back to cover a bald patch beginning to show on his crown. He wore a coloured scarf around his neck.

'For this business?'

'Few days, sir. Back by Monday.'

'Okay. Fine. You deserve something after this morning. Home, then!'

'This is my home, sir.'

'Yes. I'm sorry. My mistake. You know what I mean. Anyway, I'll give it to you, Tim. All sorted out by next week, you think?'

'Yeah. I wouldn't ask if I didn't think it was necessary.'

'No. I'm sorry for prying, Tim. Another mistake. I'm nosy but I have to be. Maybe I need a leave.'

He hadn't made a mistake. He knew what was under McLennan's nails. Stone knew how many lumps of dandruff he had in his hair.

'So, it's going to be sorted out, then?'

'Yes, sir.'

'You can call me Bob when we're alone, Tim. The commission will come through, Staff. I'm sure of it.'

'Sorry, boss, tired. I don't know. I wish – a few months and the whole thing will be sorted out for good.'

'No regrets?'

'No.'

'I'm sorry, but I have to ask. It has a bearing. You sure you won't have one of these?'

He showed McLennan the cigarette packet.

'Tryin' to give them up.'

'Good. You all right? I mean, the contact. You don't want to see the MO or a shrink or anything?'

'Would you get away, Bob. Give me the men and let me loose. I'd have the whole fuckin' lot of them in a week. Every bloody one.'

'Yes, well, we can't, Tim, can we? Orders.'

'Mustn't offend the sensibilities of the Home Counties. Cricket, all that. Must be seen to play fair. We don't play fair now, what's wrong with admittin' it and goin' all out? I guarantee it'd be forgotten in a year.'

'Not by the other side. And not by the rest of the world.'

'Scare the shit out of the South.'

'Maybe. But you're closer to all this than me.'

'Your country too, Bob.'

'Oh, yes, yes, of course. But the problem is more delicate, Tim. Has to be handled with care. Fifty, a hundred years ago, we could do what you say. Not now. Now we have to catch them with their fingers on triggers. You can take them out then. You have that.'

'Thrill. That way we beat them fair and square.'

'We'll get there. Her Majesty's Government is not going to let a shower of fascist bootboys tell it how it should operate. Her Majesty neither. And you will hold her commission soon, Tim. Just like me. As long as that's the case, we'll defend her realm to the last drop of our blood.'

'That's nice to hear. But – may I speak frankly, boss?'

Stone indicated the question was unnecessary.

'I think you're talkin' bull, Bob,' McLennan said. 'They've been around for over a century – we've been chasin' them for twenty years – and they're here until they get what they want or we wipe them out. It's down to that. Otherwise I'd better learn the "Soldier's Song". I mean, come on, Bob, what kind of country allows a rebellion to carry on inside its borders for this long and continues to let the rebels walk free? When is a terrorist not a terrorist? When he's a fuckin' Fenian.'

'Okay, Tim, okay, enough of the political lectures. We've gone through all this before. I'm well aware of PIRA's capabilities. I've read all the reports and summaries. I still say we'll lick them. Anyway, methods are a policy matter. If you want to get into policy I suggest you go and get yourself elected. Otherwise, relax. You're tired and emotional, Tim. You may say things here you'll regret later. Let's agree that we're on the same side.'

'Are we?'

Stone got up and walked around behind McLennan. A classic trick of superiors. Come at you from behind. And you can't twist without seeming insubordinate and feeling childish.

'Of course we are. And if you think differently, Staff Sergeant McLennan, I suggest you consider your position within this regiment. Come on, Tim, we are on the same side. And you had a successful contact this morning. That makes up for the para we lost in south Armagh. And Malachi Hart, too. Dessie's little brother. Just the kind of thing we want. That'll hurt the bastards. So what's the problem?'

'My problem is sometimes I understand the men I killed this mornin' more than I understand what I belong to. I mean that if this was goin' on in – where is it you come from, Bob? – Surrey – if this was goin' on in Surrey, every Provo that ever lived would be behind bars for a million years or dead. They wouldn't be allowed to twitch without riskin' a bullet. You'd have them all on treason charges and the Tower would be workin' overtime. We had a state with one third of the people out to wreck it from the beginnin'. One third of them. And we were expected to treat them with kid gloves. Did we try to undermine the Free State by claimin' jurisdiction over it? No. Did we ask the Protestants down there to start shootin' policemen and plantin' bombs? No. All we wanted was to be left alone. To be allowed to be what we wanted to be. British. And then because we get tough and the television cameras happen to be over, what do you lot do? You take our parliament away. You humiliate us before the world. You make us look like a bunch of crazy fascists. Then you sign a lump of our sovereignty over to Dublin. My father fought fascism. For your people. For his people. Dublin never did.'

Stone sat down in his chair and stubbed his cigarette out in an ashtray beside a photograph of his wife.

'You're tired, Tim. You won't admit it but you are. It's been a long tour, maybe too long, and you're tired. I'm going to have the MO have a look at you.'

'I don't need that, sir.'

'I'm ordering it. And then you head off. And for Christ's sake, cheer up. Try and spend some time with that kid of yours.'

'I want to bring him here.'

'Yes, of course. I know how difficult this must be for you, Tim. If I can help, you know? Look, we'll talk again next week, when you're sorted out. Okay? Try and use the time to relax, Tim. I know it'll be difficult. Okay? Remember, your first loyalties are to your monarch, her government – in its functional sense, of course – and your regiment. You go wherever we send you. Desert or bog, it's all the same. Don't ever forget that, Tim. Now, come on, this tour has taken it out of all of us.'

He was going to say more. About how Ulster could get to you. But he decided not to.

'Can I ask you somethin', Bob?'

'What?'

'Do you believe this is your country?'

'Of course, Tim. This is part of the United Kingdom.'

'Yeah, yeah, Bob, but do you believe it's as British as – as Finchley?'

Stone stood up.

'Staff Sergeant McLennan,' he said. 'This is the United Kingdom and I have sworn to defend its integrity with my life. I will to the best of my ability. And so will you. And that is as much as we get to ask.'

McLennan stood up and came to attention.

'Sir!'

'Good. Now bugger off, Tim, there's a good chap, and don't let me see you till next week.'

McLennan turned on one heel.

'And Tim . . .'

McLennan stopped at the door.

'We will defeat them, Tim. Look. I don't want to go too deep here, but we're following a major line that could lead to something big in the next few weeks. TCG South's even bedding down with Security Service. That'll give you an idea of what I mean. I'm meeting the L/O this afternoon. Can't say more. But stay loose, Staff. Use this weekend to unwind. I know that's a tall order, but try. Come back fit and ready to get stuck in again.'

'Yes, sir.'

McLennan didn't go to the MO. He said he would but he did not go. He could not face it.

Outside on the airfield, familiar rain touched Tim McLennan's face. He reached into his pocket and pulled out a packet of cigarettes and took one out and put it in his mouth. He looked up at the pale grey sky and watched the water run from the tops of the buildings, down drainpipes to gutters. McLennan threw the cigarette away.

He thought about casualties. When Robbie Wilson lost his eyes; when Eric Johnson had his legs blown off in a booby trap.

Stone would never feel what he felt. Not unless the Provos stepped things up in England. And even then there would never be the same intimacy of experience.

He tried to think about Robbie Wilson's eyes but Robbie was too close and it was too painful. So he moved on to Eric Johnson. Eric was a little more distant – he'd moved to Scotland – and McLennan had been able to do something about it.

Eric Johnson had been a policeman and a basketball star. A local hero. Good and tall. They'd had to adapt the squad car he was in. He came out after breakfast and checked the underside of his car. Except he was too tall to do a thorough job. They must have known that. They had it well hidden. And camouflaged. So Eric got into his car and the mercury in the tilt switch tilted and Eric Johnson's basketball career ended with his police career. He lost his legs almost at the groin and lost his wife after that.

You could lose your wife other ways. By not being there. Then it was down to the question, who lost whom? McLennan didn't dwell on that. He preferred to concentrate on things he could deal with. Like Eric Johnson. They'd been to school together. They were at each other's weddings. Back to wives, and McLennan had a feeling he wanted to discuss something but would not admit it to himself. The rain increased and the wind twisted it and swung it into his eyes and he wiped them in case it would look like he was crying.

Ach, don't mind, Timmy, Eric had said when he came out of hospital. I could be dead.

There's worse things, McLennan said to himself.

Eric's wiry hair was scalped back, for the stitching they'd had to put there. He coughed a lot.

I could have caught it in the stomach, he said. Another inch this way, another centimetre that way. They went through all the permutations.

Then they drank whiskey and laughed.

'I got the bastard who did that,' McLennan said to himself.

'Talking to yourself, Tim?'

He was in the armoury, drawing a personal weapon. Evans was stripping an Armalite. He had the buttstock in his hand. The whole place reeked of gun oil.

McLennan looked at Evans and raised his eyebrows.

'You were rabbiting.'

'Was I? Gettin' to be a habit.'

'Dangerous.'

Standard personal protection weapons were Brownings but McLennan preferred a Walther P5. He drew some spare ammunition clips with the weapon. He smiled when he thought about the shock on the face of the lad who'd done Eric Johnson. Thought he was safe, hiding in Donegal. Peter somebody. Or the Gaelic version of it. Working in a warehouse. Night-watchman. McLennan got hold of the file and then got hold of an untraceable Chinese Type 67 pistol. Silenced. Easy to get when you know where to look. Nice touch that. The Provos thought it was the Sticks. The Sticks denied they existed any more and said it was an internal Provo execution. Army black caught hold of this and put it about that Peter had been a talker. Sowed a nice bit of doubt. That was good. Weedy lad, he was, this Peter whoever. Lost look about him. Wore a denim outfit. The jacket was too small. McLennan remembered the jacket most of all. One between the eyes, two to the heart and then one into the mouth. One of the wonder-boy Protestant defender associations claimed the credit in the end. Revelled in it. Issued five statements. They'd thought about joining one when they were kids, Eric and Tim. The U something or other. The corner boys who liked to play muscle and make a little illegal on the side. Beat their wives when they had to prove something to the other lads. And if they were really brave they might go and machine-gun a bar or a chip shop. They never joined. Eric got into the police and Tim got accepted by the UDR.

That evening, Tim McLennan pulled his car out of the RAF base and on to a closed road for the international airport. A Land Rover pulled into the base with a helmeted soldier sticking out of the roof. The rain had stopped.

5

PEOPLE WHO THOUGHT Dessie Hart was a vicious murderer said he was a ruthless psychopath, a hardened terrorist, addicted to violence, at it so long he couldn't stop himself even if he wanted to: people who thought he was a freedom fighter said he was a dedicated soldier, brave, intelligent, ruthless, yes, but only where necessary and in a good cause, a man who had given everything to the fight to free his country. There was no common ground in these views, except the word ruthless, and according to your taste and your needs that is a good or a bad quality.

Since his release from prison, Hart had been trying to re-establish his border unit at the level of efficiency and expertise it had had before he'd been arrested. It had been a slow process – not only were people gone but a lot of knowhow was, too. And morale was static. Settled into a routine. He'd had to break that without breaking the people he had left. And recruit new blood. But new blood was another problem. The gap between the experienced and the inexperienced volunteers was galactic. You could give a man gun lectures and firing training but combat was an acquired taste.

Border units like Hart's were organised on a quasi-commando basis. They were larger than the usual IRA cells, usually between ten and twelve active volunteers with another twenty or thirty company auxiliaries and assorted hangers-on, under people like Danny Loughlin, who did back-up work.

Their structure was somewhere between flexible and soluble depending on who was in charge, and their activity was limited only by the degree of ambition of their leaders and the zeal of their volunteers.

Hart's unit moved in and out of activity in small groups, depending on who was available, what kind of medium-term strategy they were following, and what the British were doing. They normally worked in teams of four or less. Usually less. Everyone carried what they needed. Anything else was picked up on the way. Each volunteer carried a rifle and ammunition and a .357 Magnum and a knife. They wore a whole wardrobe of military gear, scrounged, bought, stolen, from wherever it could be got. They had balaclavas and surgical gloves to prevent forensic tests linking them to evidence and when they came in from the field they burnt everything that might be used as evidence. Patrols usually followed a set route along the border, setting up ambushes, setting mines and booby traps, pot-shooting, always on the move.

Sometimes they would wait for days for a British patrol to turn up, in the hope that the patrol might walk where they had a booby trap set or a landmine planted in a culvert. Sometimes they set a lure or opened up with rifles to manoeuvre a patrol into a bomb.

Over the months, Hart and Cusack had stepped up the operational activity of the unit: a few single killings, a couple of mines, a mortar job with the engineers, cooperation jobs with Francie Devine's unit in Tyrone and north Armagh – nothing huge but enough to get the notice of people in Lisburn whose business it was to note such things. Now Dessie Hart wanted a spectacular, something to complement Francie Devine's campaign against the police stations in Tyrone and Armagh and raise the level of the IRA campaign along the border way above the flea-bite strategy it had sunk to when he was away. And although he did not want it to, the death of his only brother had added an extra edge to this desire.

In a small room, up a narrow staircase, over a shop, on a street off the Diamond in Monaghan Town, Hart poured water into a glass. The water had a slice of lemon and herbal leaves in it. It left a sandy residue on the inside of the jug and the bottom of the glass. Behind him, a dozen wooden chairs were stacked in fours and a card table lay against the wall. Hart sat at a desk. The desk had a leather top and the jug left an imprint in the leather. The leather was green.

Hart had been a Sinn Fein councillor for the area for five years and he still did work for the Party when he had time. People who went to him when he was a councillor still came to him because he was good at sorting out problems. There was a Sinn Fein office on another street off the Diamond but he did not use it for Army business. He kept his Sinn Fein business and his Army business separate. He did his Sinn Fein business in public and once or twice took cups of tea out to the Garda Special Branch detectives who followed him when they got the chance. In the eighteen months he had been out of jail they had put a special effort into keeping an eye on him. It was a problem. Not one he couldn't deal with. But a problem all the same.

When he had to, he lost them, and when he was on Army business he had to lose them. Sometimes it took hours but Army business got the time. Army business took precedence over Sinn Fein business. To Dessie Hart, Sinn Fein business was Army business except it wasn't illegal. He could have said it wasn't as dangerous but Loyalist hit-teams had changed all that and even south of the border wasn't safe any more if they got to know your routine. So Hart didn't have a routine.

He drank from the glass of water and shoved a set of black and white ten-by-eights across to John Cusack.

'They've done a dummy,' he said. 'It checks out. Straight in, straight out. Everythin's ready.'

'What about these guys who've been lifted?'

'That's it, isn't it? If we let it go, then the operation goes up the spout. They haven't come for the bomb. They haven't made a move on anyone else. We've had dickers all over the area. No Brits around. The lads won't talk. They're good lads. It's just bad timin'. A seven-day thing. They know the drill. Command say we should go ahead anyway. Otherwise the campaign gets holed unnecessarily. And you're perfect, John. No previous. No one knows you. And you're qualified in explosives. So you get elected. You could slip in and out and no one would even know you'd been there. Boom. The pressure gets released if this one doesn't go down. Be a shame. To leave a gap. Plannin' this for weeks and those dozy fuckers had to go and get themselves lifted.'

'Yeah, what the hell,' Cusack said. 'I just hope there's not an army of Sass waiting for me. And me holding the fuse. I don't want to end up like—'

He was going to say he didn't want to end up like Mal but he held himself.

'There's boys there already. They've checked it out. They'll follow you. Anythin' like a blade of grass out of place and you get warned off. I'd use those lads only there's none of them have ever done this kind of thing. No real experience. It's gettin' to be a problem. Attrition. This needs an experienced lad, this one.'

'And the checkpoint?'

'Still on assumin' we haven't got a major tout in Tyrone. Mal and Bik has Francie lookin' under the floorboards.'

He choked on his Adam's apple. Cusack wanted to say something but held back and let Hart speak.

'I'm meetin' Francie after the funeral, okay? I'll be able to go over it with you then. But the plan as it is stands, I think. We'll go over all that again. When we see who we have. I want to have a look at all our video stuff at the same time. To see if there's a need for any change. If not, the Fermanagh blueprint stays. Why change it?'

He swallowed again and Cusack wanted to reach out and touch him. It was a hard moment and Cusack was angry because he could not deal with it.

Last time out, Hart had assembled volunteers from all over – Fermanagh, Monaghan, Armagh – and hit a checkpoint near Newtownbutler. Months of planning and watching, timing and dry runs. The checkpoint was at a t-junction and they came at it right after dark, late afternoon, twenty volunteers, twelve in the assault group, eight covering, blocking the roads. They used fertiliser bags to block the roads and armour-plated a Hino to attack the checkpoint. He went over the plan in his head, by letters. Everyone had a letter and the whole thing went down by letters. A drove the Hino into the checkpoint. B stood up in the back and opened up on the soldier on road duty. C and D opened up on the furthest pillbox with a GPMG and an AK. E used a flamethrower on the nearest pillbox. F and G threw grenades and poured more AK and a second GPMG into the watchtower.

Then A reversed the Hino through the steel gates and H, I, J and K hit anything that moved inside with AKs and grenades.

Finally, L followed them in with a Japanese van packed with five hundred pounds of explosives.

It was all over in under five minutes. Two soldiers lay dead and three wounded and the checkpoint was wrecked.

The assault group fought a running retreat to the border in the back of the Hino, under cover fire from the secondary units. Two weeks later, Dessie Hart was arrested with a revolver and ammunition and jailed for two years in Portlaoise and the Hart offensive splintered into single killings, lethargy and takeover stunts in Cullaville.

'I'd like to have been there for that one, Dessie,' Cusack said.

'This'll be better. We'll do the lot of them. Really injure them. Show them they can't even hide in their biscuit tins any more.'

Hart was balding from the front and there was a scar on the right side of his head and the scar was white in a kind of tanned scalp, and when Hart got excited the scar stretched and looked like it might tear. He had two fingers missing on the left hand and he left that hand flat on the desk when he was talking. Cusack went to the window and pulled the laced curtains back and watched the street.

'Dessie,' he said, 'about Danny. We might have a problem with him.'

He imagined the 1974 bombing in those streets, among those people, and thought he had felt something then even though he had not and could not even remember where he was or what he had been doing when it happened. No warning, bits of car tearing through shoppers. He swore to himself and looked at the black and white photograph of the north Armagh market town they were going to bomb.

'What do you mean?'

'He's dead against this. The checkpoint.'

'Danny'll be fine. Been away from it too long. Rusty. Needs a little encouragement. That's all. Anyway, I need him on the fifty-cal. He's all I can get for that. We're stretched. Francie can only supply four now out of his own lot. I've scraped around and come up with some possibles. I'll let you know. So you see, John, we're not runnin' over with experienced volunteers at the minute. I was hopin' to get some extra help from Newry but with this lift, everyone's divin' for cover. And I need units on back-up. We're tight for people. Francie's gettin' the guts of two back-up units from Strabane. But that's not ready yet. So Danny's in.'

'I guess.'

'His lads have done a good job up to now. You leave Danny to me, John. Politics, John. I'm good at that. Sure I used to be a councillor, I should be. You stick to the military stuff. That's why you're here. Together, we'll do fine.'

'Your looks and my brains.'

'If you like.'

'I could use tomorrow to make a close recon of the checkpoint.'

The checkpoint had become an obsession for Cusack. Like it stood for something more than a single target in a campaign, like it was a kind of cornerstone and if they destroyed it something bigger would topple. He could not explain his feelings and he did not like to look on them as obsession, but it was an obsession.

'No,' Hart said. 'Straight back, John. I don't want to put any strain on operations and I don't want to lose you to somethin' stupid. I don't have too many people without records, John. You're valuable. You should be back in Germany, you know. You're perfect for the Continent. Or England.'

'I've done the overseas thing. I want to be here. The war zone. I'm useful. You said it yourself, Dessie. GHQ agrees.'

'It's okay by me. I'm not complainin''. GHQ might, eventually. Danny'll brief you on the bomb job and support. Okay?'

'Danny?'

'Come on, John. So he's cautious. Maybe we need that. He's been around a hell of a long time.'

'There was too much caution round here when you were away, Dessie.'

'Well, there isn't now. Maybe Mal and Bik Hennigan could have done with some.'

'Yeah. I'm sorry, Dessie, I'm sorry. How are you son, anyway? How's your dad taking it?'

'He's seen it before. I can't let it get to me, John. Cloud my judgment. Mal knew what he was about. He took the risks.'

'Do you think it was a tout?'

'I don't know, John. Maybe they just got unlucky. Francie's paranoid. Says he has three bastards he wants to nut straight away. Tony McCabe's boys are goin' to comb. They'll probably be askin' questions here. I hate that. Upsets the troops. Tony's become a real pain in the neck since they gave him security. Struttin' around like the Grand Inquisitor. He's never been on a job, you know? Except that tout thing with you. And he fuckin' threw up then, didn't he?'

Cusack looked at the ceiling.

'And Francie's talking tout?' he said.

'Francie's spittin' fire. He lost the head, I'm told. Jesus, I hope he's all right. He's a fuckin' temper, Francie. Him and Mal were close. He was like another brother. You know? Ah, Jesus, John, I can't believe Mal's dead. Wee Mal.'

Hart began to cry. It happened quickly and Cusack thought it was just something in his eye and looked away but when he looked again he saw that it was not and Hart was wiping the tears from his cheeks. He pulled a handkerchief out and wiped his face and blew his nose. The whites of his eyes had expanded and the brown and grey pupils had hardened and he was winning back control.

'Don't tell anyone, John,' he said.

Cusack shook his head.

'Course not, Dessie.'

They looked at each other for a while as if each of them was trying to figure out what the other was thinking. And Cusack thought of a bully he had known at school who sold insurance now. He touched the collar of his leather jacket and pinched the Yin and Yang badge and felt the fear he had felt when he had been bullied by the guy who sold insurance and he became angry again. The anger was against the bully first, because he was easy to be angry with, but it spread and Cusack felt it spread and soon it was getting out of control and he had to fight hard to control it. Dessie Hart folded a piece of paper and then tore it into strips and placed the strips into a neat pile. There was a knock on the door before either of them could do anything.

Hart indicated to Cusack to get behind the door. Cusack did it. He pulled a .357 Magnum from the small of his back and looked across at Hart and nodded.

'Who's there?' Hart asked.

'Dessie.'

Hart paused before he replied. There was a routine with the shopkeeper and this was not part of it. He looked over at Cusack.

'Who's that?'

'It's Maggie, Dessie.'

Hart's face relaxed.

'Maggie!'

He was already out of his seat. He pulled the door open and Cusack stuffed his gun into the small of his back and came out from behind the door and tried to look like he had not been standing there ready to blow her brains out.

'Come in, come in,' Hart said.

He looked over at Cusack and called him over with his hand.

Cusack's eyes went from the door to Hart and back to the door and Maggie O'Neill. Then he stayed with her. He tried to get them back to Hart but he could not. He could feel his heartbeat quicken and the palms of his hands sweat. Hart stepped back and then rubbed his eyes to get rid of any hint that he might have been crying. He almost started laughing with embarrassment.

'Maggie!' he said again.

'I got a message,' she said.

Hart went over to her and put out his hands. He took her hands in his and shook them.

'Yeah, yeah,' he said. 'Success! Well done! Listen, I've double-booked, I think. Today's upside down.'

'I heard. Mal. Oh, Dessie, I'm so sorry.'

Hart nodded. Cusack had backed off to the window again. Looking out of place. Maggie nodded to him briefly and then turned back to Hart. They were still holding hands. Cusack folded his arms and then unfolded them and put his hands in his pockets and leaned back against the wall. He tried to stop his pulse rate going up but he could not. Everything he had been thinking about, everything that had seemed important, left him, and he could only watch the small woman holding Dessie Hart's hands. Hart looked at him.

'Will you give me an hour, love,' Hart said. 'Usual place. Okay?'

She nodded her head.

'Fine.'

She glanced at Cusack and he smiled and she thought about smiling because he had a nice smile and good teeth but she knew she was in on something she should not have been in on so she did not smile. But she did look at him for longer than she had to and Cusack knew he was going red and tried to hold the look but he could not do it. Maggie pulled her hands away from Hart's and looked at Cusack again and took him in.

There was a silence and then she left.

'Good woman,' Hart said.

'Yeah,' Cusack said.

'Good-lookin'. Eh, John?'

Cusack did not answer. He had turned his back so Hart would not see he was going red. And he wanted to watch her on the street. To draw the curtain and watch her walk and see her move. He did not, though.

Hart was already back at his desk going over something and Cusack had to abort what was developing inside him and watch the image fade. It did not completely fade and if he had not had things to do and a job to concentrate on he might have been able to bring it back in full, but that did not happen and he had to drop it in favour of what was being planned.

When they had finished, Cusack went down to the shop and let himself think of Maggie. It was not much but after a couple of minutes browsing over the newspapers and thinking he was better able to do what he had to do. The shop was small and it sold cigarettes and sweets with the papers. It had a tiled floor and when the shopkeeper, who was one of Danny Loughlin's men, came to tell Cusack it was fine to leave, Cusack heard him walking with a limp on the tiles. He bought a bar of chocolate and an evening paper.

Outside, it was cold, and Cusack pulled the collar of his leather jacket over his neck and read his paper.

Dessie Hart watched him from the curtains. Hart had begun to cry again. This time he did not try to regain control of himself and the crying released him from where he was caught and when he was finished he felt like a great weight had been lifted from him. But it did not help him with the sadness he felt over his brother's death.

When he met Maggie O'Neill again it was almost dark, and they walked down a narrow country road near the Cavan border that might have been a lane only people called it a road. Hart carried an umbrella and it kept the rain off them and added another layer of cover. She was waiting for him by a metal gate. Standing against it with her anorak hood up and her hands in her pockets. The anorak was blue and the end of daylight made the blue in the anorak look like shadow in the trees and hedgerows of the narrow road. Maggie wore glasses.

When Hart walked up to her she put out her hands and took his and when they had held hands she put her arms around him and held him.

'I'm so sorry about Mal, Dessie,' she said again, like it had somehow been her fault.

Hart nodded and slapped his hands together. He had a very angular nose and it made his face come out at you with an intensity that fell between commitment and concern. Maggie did not know which. His skin was rougher and some raindrops were caught in the rough skin.

'Past, Maggie,' he said. 'Past. Has to be. Okay?'

She nodded.

'You did a good job this mornin'. Bloody good job, girl.'

She was going to say something about the girl bit but she decided to allow Dessie his slip into unreconstructed chauvinism. It was something she was used to in the Army. You had to be really good to get anything like respect. Otherwise it was orders and people asking you to wash the dishes.

'Thanks,' she said. 'Jesus, I thought I'd walked in on a raid there before.'

'Yeah, sorry about that muck-up,' he said. 'I'm up to here with things. We're really gettin' goin', love. I just wish we'd enough people for everythin' I wanna do. It's always the way. That's why you're so valuable. He's a good man, John. Been doin' a lot of work for us. You'll be meetin' him again. It's what I want to talk to you about. He was a Marine. He's helpin' whip the lads into shape. Anyway, I know we shouldn't be seein' each other so soon after this mornin' but I need you to give me back-up on a job we've got planned. It'll be soon. Next few weeks.'

She turned to him. Rain touched the loose stones around her. A dog barked. Two trees to her right were tipped over and they looked like inebriate giants. Water ran by her feet.

'What kind of job?'

'Big one. Very big one. Like I said, I need everyone I can get.'

'I thought we agreed I'd work to my agenda, Dessie. Keep me away from other operations. Single jobs. Danny's boys providin' the cover work. It's been workin' well up to now. Nice attrition rate. What's the job?'

'A checkpoint.'

'Another one. Checkpoint Charlie strikes again.'

'Enough of that,' he said. 'You did well the last time.'

She had been B. She'd shot the first soldier. She could still see his face. She could see all their faces but his was younger and the cam cream did not hide it or turn it into something from a children's television series. He was real and his face was young and he couldn't even get his rifle up. Half a magazine. He fell spreadeagled. Like he was pretending.

'I don't want you for the assault,' Hart said. 'Just cover. Last-line cover. You'll be this side of the border. Nothin' unless you have to. Then just a single to keep them occupied. We have a Barret Light Fifty.'

He laughed.

'Icin' on the cake,' he said.

'I've not used a fifty.'

'Yeah. You'll have to practise. In the dark. Over a mile. Only you can do that.'

'You flatter me, Dessie. You're the real politician. Move over, Gerry, here comes Dessie.'

'No chance. Francie Devine's cooperatin'.'

'Jesus, Dessie, things move when you're around. Christ, I was the Army down here till you got out. Me and a few lunchboxes.'

'Will you do it? I could order you but I want you to volunteer. Anyway, there's a couple of new lads around and it's good to have some more old hands. You know what I mean?'

'You make me sound ancient. When would you need me? For how long?'

'I'll be in touch. You'll need to practise somewhere safe. Danny'll arrange that. On your own. I'm gonna take a few of the lads on a refresher course with John and Danny. Get them moulded. You don't need to be there. But I want you to know what's goin' on. Any problems?'

'No. But I'll have to give Brian a cover.'

'Does he need one?'

'Somethin'. And the kids.'

'Just leave the bastard.'

'I can't, Dessie.'

'No. Well, your mother. Somethin' like that. Say your mother called. I'll have someone talk to Brian if he gets nosy. You can ring nights, for your kids. I'll let you home when I can. Are you with me? I want this to work, Maggie. For Mal now. You liked Mal, didn't you? All the birds did. He was good-lookin', Mal. We always said that at home. I want this to work for Mal.'

She smiled.

'For Mal,' she said. 'Will you be at the funeral?'

'I want to be. Danny says no. They'd lift me as soon as I showed my face. Or shoot me. Life or death. It's an easy choice.'

'I know how you feel, Dessie. I know.'

'Thanks.'

He kissed her on the cheek and kept walking. She walked back to where a Ford Escort was waiting for her.

She was cooking dinner when her husband came in. Their kids, a boy and a girl, were setting the table. Brian O'Neill was copper-haired and tall and he had a moustache. The moustache was thick and it hung down around his mouth and lengthened his face. His face was tired, the skin was pale and drawn and broken and right under his eyes it was dark and swollen. He was fat and he wore his belt the way fat men do when they will not admit they are fat, squeezing the flesh over the belt and leaving it hanging loose instead of tucked away. He used to be thin but that was a long time ago. When he had money. When he had a new Merc.

Maggie watched him go through the motions of coming home. He came up behind her, put his arms around her waist, kissed her on the neck and buried his head in hers and smelled the smell of her hair. His smell was aftershave and boredom. Maggie could name the aftershave. The boredom was a general smell. She felt his prick harden. He touched her cheek with his face.

'Hi,' she said.

She put her hand up and rubbed his face. He put his finger in the red sauce she was stirring. It was hot and it burned his finger. He did not say anything. He did not taste the sauce. He wiped it off his finger with a piece of kitchen towel. Then he let his other hand wander to her groin. She held it there until she thought maybe one of the kids might see. Then she pulled it away and made a face at her husband, affection mixed with irritation.

'I'll wash my hands,' he said. 'Have they washed their hands?'

'I'm sure they have.'

'Have you washed your hands, kids?'

They looked at their mother. She looked at her husband.

'Get up and wash your hands,' he said.

'We have,' his son said.

Eoin O'Neill was thirteen and acned and as tall as his father. His father went over to him. Eoin blushed and showed his acne more. He looked more awkward than usual.

'Let me see.'

Brian O'Neill grabbed his son's hands.

Every bloody evening, Maggie thought; he does it every bloody evening.

She stopped herself and drew on a residual warmth and familial bonding. Eoin wore his hair like a sheepdog. Shaved up to the ears and then thick and hanging over his eyes. He had a girlfriend. Maggie'd seen her. They held hands and sat on a wall.

Affection turned to anger.

A boy had touched her daughter, Maeve. She was tall the way girls of fifteen often are. And big. She'd let him touch her. Maggie'd flipped, run around the house, screaming. She found them on the couch one afternoon, after a job. Home early. Watched through the open door. Her daughter and whoever the hell he was half dressed, his bottom moving at her, her schoolgirl legs and their schoolgirl socks wrapped around him, her head back and her eyes closed, like she knew what she was doing, like she was enjoying it. He had his mouth on one of her breasts. Her hands were down between his legs.

We didn't go all the way, honest, Mam, we didn't. I didn't let him, honest, please don't tell Daddy, please, please. I love him.

Maggie hit her. Right across the face. The mark was there for hours. It was an out-of-control slap, nothing more. Desperation.

The news had given the dead para a name. Stephen. He had a wife and a two-year-old. They showed a picture. He was smiling. He had a nice smile. She did not recognise the picture. The uniform, it was the uniform, always the uniform. He was a victim of the uniform. It killed him. Everything it stood for killed him.

She was hitting back. For all the mess of being born a working-class Taig in Belfast. Every shot said fuck you to them. Fuck you and your fucking army and your fucking police and your fucking system. She felt herself shake. Like she was committing a crime by wanting revenge. It was that simple sometimes, she thought. Screw the politics, screw the aims and screw the polemics. Just to hit back. To feel them suffer like we suffered. With their toffy accents and their pinstripe bullshit. We're as good as you. You can't take us out. She found herself getting high on this when Brian was making love to her.

Maggie was somewhere else and trying to fake pleasure.

Her body stiffened and she dug her nails into the sheets and thought of Stephen from Gloucester and then Malachi Hart. She had known Mal Hart longer than Dessie. And better. Dessie was quiet, pensive, shy, maybe distant. Monastic. Mal was a lad. Always coming on. Stud to the Provo groupies. Made a try for her. She said no. She regretted it. She could feel more anger now. That was good. Fuckers. And they got Bik Hennigan as well. She'd done a couple of jobs with Bik. Bomb under an RUC man's car. Ambush near Keady. Culvert south of Coalisland. The culvert killed a civilian. A woman, a mother. It was hard to listen to her family and hear the tears and the condemnation.

Bik was a family man.

She didn't know the third guy but he had a name she knew and she figured he was from a family near Coalisland that had a son in the Kesh and a daughter working for Sinn Fein in Donegal. The daughter had a thing for Tony McCabe. But Tony was gay. Kept it quiet, though. Real close-hand player, Tony. Ambitious and close. Did the Sinn Fein bit when he had to. Good for the press, the quotable quote. Wrote short stories, had a book published. Tony had plans.

Brian O'Neill came without penetrating, on Maggie's leg, in a single motion, with a single stretched cry from deep within him, and she held his head to her breasts and kissed it.

'I'm sorry,' she said. 'I'm tense.'

He did not answer. He had gone way beyond discussing her frigidity or his impotence.

Maggie found herself counting again.

6

TWO DAYS LATER, early November blew cold breath on late October outside Newry and John Cusack touched his car brake with one foot and pressed the clutch with the other and came down a gear.

The policeman was bent in the driver's window of the car in front. There was one soldier covering him from a crouched position at the side of the road. Cusack looked around for the others. The drizzle had stopped and the sun was throwing rainbows between the broken clouds and on the watery film of the road surface. The wind had picked up. It was gusting from the south-east and the soldier crouching at the side of the road kept his head turned to the north. Long grass touched his camouflaged face and some loose blades clung to the camouflage and then blew away. A hundred yards down the road there was an identical set-up for the stuff coming north. All very low-key. Low-intensity, the best analysts in the best universities and polytechnics called it. Cusack kept his eyes focussed on the RUC officer.

The policeman had pulled his head from the car ahead and was laughing. The long hair of the driver stuck itself out of the window just enough for the wind from the south-east to toss it about in strands. The back window of his car was covered in mud and Cusack couldn't see any more of him. The policeman cast an eye at Cusack and then back at the driver of the Mazda with the dirty back window and Cusack had a sudden feeling of possibility.

He shot a glance in his rear-view. Five, maybe six vehicles behind him, stretched out round a bend. He sifted through the landscape for other soldiers. He spotted three, one of them could have been two – the colours on the hill kept changing. Cusack rubbed his chin. He moved his hand around his face in a single movement to feel for sweat. There was a small drop on the side of his nose. He licked his finger and wiped the side of his nose and dropped his right hand between the seat and the door.

The policeman waved the car ahead on and signalled Cusack to move forward. And all the self-preservatory anxiety John Cusack had inside him told him to push hard on the accelerator and go. The instinct was sharp and definite, like pain. He put his foot to the pedal and stared the RUC officer right in the eyes. The officer was stooped. His flak jacket was too tight. He had a rip in one of his uniform sleeves. The sleeve flapped in the breeze. It showed his watch. Cusack looked back at his face. He had broken lines on his face. His eyes were watering from the wind and his nose was running. Cusack's eyes went down his torso one more time, down the flak jacket, to the Ruger revolver at his hip. He had a wedding ring.

Cusack let the handbrake down. Very slowly, very cool. A kind of sensory disengagement. He glanced at his watch without letting the policeman see he was doing it. The phone call would already have gone through: you have fifteen minutes to clear the street.

Fifteen minutes of panic and chaos and people running the wrong way and RUC men screaming warnings no one could understand. They'd clear it in twelve minutes. Just enough time, maybe a few casualties, some collateral, some legitimate, a couple of police maybe, left too long. Then the main street of a north Armagh market town would have the features torn off it. He took a second look at his watch. He was behind time. This was dangerous.

He'd taken the main road to allay suspicion. The car had been left for him. Drive the bomb in. Leave the van. Walk off nicely nicely. Buy a paper. Go round the corner. Get in the car. Read the paper for a couple of minutes. Check. Move off. Dickers kept an eye and gave him the okay. Then back across the border. Don't take side roads. Take main roads. Go with the daytime traffic. You couldn't predict a mobile vehicle checkpoint. Stay cool.

There was no reason they should be on to him, but if they were they'd get him at the permanent checkpoint after Newry. With the spikes and the automatic bollards. The bollards could send a car into orbit. He calculated the risks.

They'd be shouting in the streets of the market town. He could see it. He'd watched one once. Stood with the bystanders and watched a 500-pounder rip concrete and stone and glass into fury. Showered with pieces of market town. Nearly knocked off his feet by the blast. They got an RUC officer then. Cusack looked in his rear-view.

More cars behind him. And an Ulsterbus. Too crowded. His mind conquered his anxiety and he eased forward the few yards to the policeman.

'Good mornin', sir,' the RUC officer said.

Cusack liked to think he could place them by their accent. It gave him an extra feeling of being on top. Things like that mattered to him. He replied in kind to the officer and smiled.

'Nice day it's turning into,' he said.

'American, sir?' the officer said.

Cusack nodded. He was overdoing the American thing, part of his cover for the bomb run, but he hated his accent when he heard it in the raw. It always sounded like an alarm bell. It was going, it had been going for years, and he had to try to sound really convincingly American now, but in a country where accents changed by the street, it would never quite go. And that was a weakness in the long run. Anything that singled you out was a weakness. And somewhere someone was trying to identify weaknesses and all the time calculating.

The policeman leaned his hands on Cusack's car.

'We're just checkin' vehicles, sir, routine. Could you show me some identification.'

Cusack reached into his inside pocket and pulled out an American passport. It was fake. If he radioed it in, they'd tag it as fake. Not immediately. But it would unravel and the young married policeman would remember his face and Lisburn would put a name to the face and a life to the name and any edge he'd had up to now would be gone. Cusack dropped his hand between the seat and the door again. The .357 was under the seat on that side.

'Business or pleasure, sir?'

The policeman was flicking through the pages of the passport.

'Sorry?' Cusack said.

'You in Northern Ireland for business or pleasure?'

He was examining Cusack's corduroy jacket and French cotton trousers. There was a briefcase on the passenger seat and a raincoat lying across the back window.

'Some of both, I guess,' Cusack said.

He glanced at his briefcase.

'Might be investing. Have to examine the options. You know – with the Troubles going on.'

The policeman closed the passport and looked around him.

'Where?' he asked.

Cusack looked at him. There were two tears running from his left eye. He wiped them and moved his head to show he was waiting for an answer.

'Where's the factory goin' to be?'

Cusack felt his heart miss a beat. He lifted his hand from between his legs and placed it on the steering wheel.

'Belfast, I think. Though we've been offered a site in Derry – eh, Londonderry.'

'Aye. It's all right, sir, you can call it Derry if you like. I'm from there.'

Cusack throttled up the accent and increased the volume, stretching every syllable he could manage without breaking his vocal cords.

'Okay. Listen, can I turn off for Monaghan Town around here? I've got a meet there with some people in a coupla hours.'

'Competition?'

'Maybe.'

'Everybody needs them.'

'What's that?'

'Jobs.'

'Yeah. I guess.'

'You'll see a roundabout down the road, sir – take the right exit. Before Newry.'

A soldier behind him radioed through the car registration. The policeman turned his head to him. The soldier moved his rifle towards Cusack's car, keeping it pointed down.

The policeman turned away from the car and stepped back. He still had the passport in his hand. He walked to the front of the car and then to the back. At the back, he stood and took his own note of the licence plate. The soldier was still waiting. It was a hire car. From Dublin. Someone else had hired it in the name of Cusack's passport. They could have stolen one. But the computer was getting too good. Escape runs needed clean vehicles. Cusack let his hand drop again. Kneejerk. He stopped himself. Not here. If they wanted him, they'd hit him further down the road. Not here in the middle of this lot. This was the size-up. The soldier was speaking through his radio again. Cusack watched the policeman in his rear-view mirror. His mouth was drying. He sucked hard for saliva. Dry mouth was a dead giveaway. He lifted his hand from between the seat and the door. The soldier nodded. The RUC officer started walking back to him.

'That's fine, sir,' he said.

Cusack looked at his boots. They were dirty, and the lobes of his ears were red. The soldier's boots were shining and he had no earlobes. The policeman rubbed his running nose with his fingers and handed Cusack back his passport. Cusack lifted his hand from the steering wheel and gave a kind of a wave. It allowed the breath he had been storing up to ease out between his teeth.

When he'd passed the northbound checkpoint and an armoured Land Rover with the confidential telephone number on it, Cusack turned on his car radio and left the main road at the roundabout before Newry. He swung west and then south-west away from the wind. It was against the plan and Dessie Hart would hit the roof if he knew but Cusack figured he was through now and that feeling gave him a surge of confidence that almost made his heart burst. They'd be concentrating on mobile VCPs once the bomb went off. Putting on a show for the public. To demonstrate they were doing something. They wouldn't be expecting to pick up a bomber at a border crossing. He felt a certain invincibility and it was a good feeling. If anything happened, he could play the lost American. And maybe there was more. Maybe he wanted to press it. See how far it could go.

The roads were empty except for vans and tractors. Friendly country to the left, enemy country to the right. He moved further left and had a feeling of being right. Like a booster. Fortress south Armagh. The whole place was alive with electronics and observation posts and low-level chopper patrols from Crossmaglen and Forkhill and foot patrols that jumped out of the hedgerows at you. This was what it was about for Cusack. A kind of live advertising poster for his argument. The soldiers were the outsiders. They couldn't even use the roads without risking a landmine up the arse. These were marcher lands. He knew the place well now, he knew every town and village and what had happened where and when.

What he was doing now was another risk. But it was worth it, he felt. To get a first-hand close-up. It was a chance to feel the target. They might get him there. It'd be ironic, he thought. If they were on to him and they lifted him at the Kill permanent checkpoint.

He opened the car window and took in the small-farm smell. The bad land of the hills turned from black and brown to a kind of dark green further down. Trees huddled together in clumps, to protect the fields and themselves from the wind and rain.

He saw the village when he came round a bend through a heap of cow shit and a pool of stagnant water. A kid in wellingtons stood at the side of the road with a stick in his hand. Cusack splashed him with the shit and water and raised his hands and shrugged his shoulders. The kid raised his fingers and started running after the car, screaming. His face was flecked with cow shit and his jumper was dripping water. Cusack didn't stop.

The businessman cover was an old play. Got them in their prejudices. Provos just didn't wear business suits. He'd once spent three days in Belfast, posing as the same American businessman. It was a GHQ fundraising thing. IDB lunches, executive drinks, tours of potential factory sites. They hit him with a sales pitch he hadn't seen since he'd sold real estate in California. He brought up all the old investment fears. They countered with a charm offensive that gave a whole new meaning to the word normal. They kept telling him New York was a far more dangerous place. He told them he wasn't keen on investing in New York either. They took him for more lunches. The company he said he represented did exist. GHQ had set it up three years earlier to help clean money. It was a good front. They got a whack of cash from the IDB and promises of more if they opened another factory. They never opened anything. They had a shell in south Belfast and a heap of going-tos and maybes and a piece of ground in Newry but nothing ever happened and there were no jobs. It worked well for laundering.

He laughed to himself. He was disobeying Dessie Hart's orders.

What could Dessie do? Blow his kneecaps out? You had carte blanche in the field. Whatever you could do. They wrote the script later.

Cusack had only done one kneecapping. First thing he'd ever done. He figured it was a kind of test. To see if he was genuine. It was a mixed-grill job from Strabane. They took him over to Donegal to do it, then dumped him back in Strabane. He was a skinny guy with a habit. Got high one night and screwed up a weapons dump. All the stuff was ruined when they found it. Rifles, ammunition. He'd done it before. With a Lee Enfield number four they had for sniping. It had to be kept at a constant temperature. Otherwise the wood warped and the whole aim was off. They always warped eventually.

The thing was to slow the process down, get the best from the weapon.

So they dragged this kid into a car and took him to a sports hall in Donegal and knocked him about and put a 9mm bullet through each ankle, each knee, each hand and each elbow. Cusack helped hold him down. They put a sock in his mouth and an Armalite to the back of his head. He passed out after the second bullet. His muscles rippled and jerked when they were holding him down, like he was having a fit. He tried to be brave the whole way to Donegal, talking. Head covered on the floor of the car. Tried to talk about sport and women. Cusack found bits of bone on the sports hall floor when they were scrubbing it down. Little pieces. Like from broken pottery. He threw them in a toilet.

'Hey, mister, you drowned me!'

Cusack was stopped beside the shop in the middle of the village. Beside the petrol pump. It was a small shop and it sold basics. He was crouching by his car, looking at the checkpoint. He'd stuck a penknife into the tyre. The car was sinking down on that side. There was a news flash about the bomb on the radio. Five injured. The main street of the market town was devastated. Then the usual: condemnations, calls for internment, seal the border. Loyalist threats to step up their attacks on Catholics. He felt good. It was a combination of elation and right.

He listened to the air escaping from the tyre.

The boy in the wellingtons was running along the road, holding his stick in the air. A foot patrol ran from the front gate of the checkpoint fort, along the main street on both sides, past Cusack, north to the crossroads, soldiers crouching and covering each other, then running, boots stamping along the road to the crossroads. Cusack froze while they passed.

The boy stood in front of Cusack. Dirty water ran down his legs and the shit spots were drying on his face. But none of that registered with Cusack. All he could see was the eye. It was like someone had melted the lid-skins together. He wanted to prise them apart, show the eye.

'You did this, ye bastard,' the boy said.

The soldiers were at the crossroads, point man heading west. Paras. One had red headgear. A middle-aged man came out of the shop in a pullover with a hole in the belly and his hands in his pockets. He had a red face and hair coming from his chest below the collar of his shirt.

'Grand day,' he said.

It did not mean anything.

His eyes followed the soldiers. Two cars came through the checkpoint from the south. Then a truck. Then a tractor. He watched each of them. A driver waved. He waved back. Then he shoved his hands back in his pockets. Another car came through the checkpoint.

'You drowned me, mister,' the kid repeated. 'He drowned me.'

He looked at the man who had come out of the shop.

Cusack was trying to watch the checkpoint and the soldiers at the same time. He sharpened his American accent some more.

'Sorry, kid.'

'You fuckin' drowned me. He drowned me.'

The tail end of the patrol took up positions at the crossroads. The NCO in charge took the radio handset from his radio man and spoke into it.

'I've a busted tyre. And I need cigarettes,' Cusack said to the man beside him. 'You got cigarettes in there?'

He kept looking at the boy's eyes.

'What you starin' at? You starin' at my eye?' the boy said.

'Go along, Paddy,' the man from the shop said.

The foot patrol was disappearing up the road heading west. Escape route number one, Cusack thought. You could come in on that road but it was unapproved and they'd be more suspicious of anything coming from that direction. East ran you right into a bigger permanent checkpoint. Approach from the south and out by the west.

The NCO held back with his radio man. Cusack walked around to the boot of his car and pulled out the spare. The boy followed him and kept talking. Cusack was watching the NCO.

The soldier watched for a few seconds. Then he said something to his radio operator and walked over to Cusack.

'Run along,' the shopkeeper said to the boy. 'Your mam will be lookin' for you.'

The boy made a face. His eye made the face ugly.

'Need a hand, mate?' the NCO said to Cusack.

He was fat, with a scar on one cheek and a pointed nose. He had nicotine stains on his fingers and Cusack thought he could smell the cigarettes from his mouth.

'No, it's okay. Busted tyre. I'll just change it.'

'Fine. But you'll have to move it back. We don't let people park this near the checkpoint. Security. Right, Mr Ryan?'

The shopkeeper did not reply.

Cusack looked confused. 'I'm a stranger here.'

'Who isn't, mate. You're not supposed to park here. Rules, you see.'

'What about the gas pump and the shop?'

'Pump's out of action, isn't it, Mr Ryan? Park back there if you want to shop. You can get petrol after the checkpoint. There's a place on the concession road.'

'A cop directed me this way. I'm going to Monaghan Town. Am I on the right road?'

'Yeah. There's better roads. There's been a car bomb north of here. Someone just drove it in and walked away. Don't listen to police officers. They don't know much. Thick as bricks. You'll be okay. But get that fixed. If you hang around too long, I'll get it in the ear from my C/O. Got identification?'

Cusack walked over to his car and pulled out the passport. The radio operator radioed the licence plate of the car in. The NCO didn't pay too much attention to the passport.

'Where you from?' he asked.

'States.'

'Yeah, but where?'

'New York.'

'I was there once.'

He smiled and the cam cream he wore on his face almost fell apart. Cusack smiled back and the soldier handed him his passport.

The boy was staring at the soldiers. He looked at John Cusack and then back at the soldiers.

'Bastards! Youse are bastards!' he shouted. 'Fuckin' bastards!' He pointed at his eye. 'See this, hey youse, see this, youse did this. Youse like blowin' children's eyes out. See them, mister, they fuckin' did this to me. That right, Mr Ryan, that right?'

'Paddy,' Ryan said. 'Paddy, get home and stop that cursin'. You think your mother will like that?'

The radio operator had his back to the checkpoint and was pointing his rifle at Cusack and Ryan and the boy. The boy raised his fingers. The soldier responded in kind and laughed. The NCO gave Cusack his passport back and the two soldiers moved off. The boy went to run after him but Ryan caught him by the shirt collar.

'I said get home, Paddy. I thought you had a patch for that eye. You shouldn't be out without it.'

'Our Rose says I look like a pirate with it. I don't want to look like a pirate.'

He looked at Cusack.

'Moshe Dyan,' Cusack said.

'Who's he?'

'Israeli general. Won a war.'

'I'll be him, then. I'll be – what is it?'

'Moshe Dyan.'

Paddy turned and walked back to the crossroads, whistling.

'You're a Yank,' Ryan said. 'I'll give you a hand. Don't mind him.'

'The eye. What happened?'

'The boys threw a mortar at the checkpoint. It missed. He knows what happened. But it's in the family. You know. It's always in the family. Blood. Now let's get this wheel changed. Let the brake off and we'll push you back. Jaysus, you were lucky you were goin' slow. Could have had a nasty accident, son. Could have killed yourself.'

Cusack turned his head and watched the soldiers move down the road west.

'I've a meeting in a hour. Looks like I'll be late. Nice countryside you got here. I like it.'

Cusack was hoping to Christ the American accent would hold up talking to Ryan.

'It's nice enough. Except for that.'

He nodded at the checkpoint.

'Yeah, I noticed. Still, terrorism and all. You know?'

'I'll help you fix your wheel.'

Cusack had attacked his first patrol near another permanent checkpoint. Dessie Hart and another lad with him, over a year ago now. Scots regiment. Eight of them. Right before dawn. Cusack did the shooting and Dessie Hart and the other lad triggered the mine. The explosion almost took Cusack's head off. It left him with a headache. It killed one soldier and wounded two more. The rest of the patrol were running around like headless chickens, shouting and cursing. The wounded soldiers screamed a combination of fear and insanity. Cusack felt the explosion under his feet before he got the blast in the face. It broke windows around them. Then they opened up with small arms. The firefight went on for five minutes. Till the choppers and the searchlights arrived.

'He was in the school when it hit,' Ryan said. 'Young Paddy there. Could have killed him. Mad. They put that thing there and we're like sandbags for it. They could put it further on only they're scared the boys will stick half a ton of explosives under them. So we get the shite when it flies.'

Cusack's mind was back on a hillside, watching his first ambush. They could hear the screaming over the chopper noise. One of the wounded was calling for his mother. You could hear the words clearly. It was a still night except for the choppers. Two more choppers came in and landed in a field back from the border and back-up patrols jumped out. An officer with an English accent was barking orders, splitting his men into sections, demanding cover, shouting through his radio handset for more information from the patrol under attack. They couldn't even find each other for fifteen minutes. Cusack wanted to shout at them, tell them where their wounded were. He could see everything with his nightsight: soldiers darting from hedgerow to hedgerow, searching, cursing, shouting; and the screaming got worse.

One of the wounded was lying at the edge of the crater. He was buried except for his head, and his leg was lying on the other side of the crater. One of his friends had crawled over to him and was trying to get some morphine into him and get the mud off him. The firefight had kept them from getting to the wounded. About a hundred yards away, Cusack saw the other man. He was holding his stomach in. It was seeping out through his fingers. One of his mates stuck a bayonet through the skin flaps to hold it together. The voices spoke panic.

Medic, medic, where's the fucking medic . . . ?

Move on down . . . move, move, move. Get the bastards. Get them.

Cover, fucking cover . . . give me cover . . .

The voices were deep Scots ghetto, a combination of fear and aggression. Desperation scratched into their faces and overlaid with cam cream. Hart and the other two pulled away but Cusack stayed to watch.

'Right, hand us the spare,' Ryan said.

Cusack had stopped fixing his wheel. He pulled his head up and looked at Ryan and then did what he was told.

The shop was musty and there was an overwhelming smell of chocolate. Delicious and revolting at the same time. Cusack picked a couple of bars of chocolate and three packets of cigarettes and a newspaper. He wanted to buy the shopkeeper something but the man would not accept anything.

'You'd do it for me if I was in your country,' he said.

Cusack wanted to say he was. But he did not. He nodded.

Fucking country, fucking bloody country, an officer had said at that first ambush.

Cusack had had a clear shot. The officer stood tall in the field, holding a radio handset, walking behind his radio operator, talking. He was maybe forty, maybe a major. He looked like he had a ramrod inserted in his back. Cusack could see everything about him. In the grey-green of the nightsight. It was a clear shot. To the head. Except they had the choppers and the choppers could spray GPMG from their waists and GPMG could tear him apart. The smart move was to sit tight on the south side and watch. Dessie'd wanted to take a video for propaganda. They'd decided not to. Another smart move. This was the kind of war the folks with the cash didn't need to know about.

The Scots lads dragged the wounded soldier with no leg by the shoulder straps. Along the ground. Cusack could see one of his fingers hanging loose. Three soldiers covered the retreat to the chopper with their rifles and a chopper hovered overhead and threw its searchlight in a wide sweep. Cusack was in trees. The searchlight touched a lake and a river and threw a pattern into the night sky. The officer kept asking for details and the dead man's name. No one could give it to him. They weren't sure who was dead.

The dead man was brought back in a bag, in pieces. The explosion had blown him apart. His head and shoulders were lying in another field, the rest of him was spread out around the crater in shreds. He was about nineteen. He had baby eyes and a chain around his neck. His mates called him Sandy. Sandy's remains spilled out after they had packed them into the body-bag and ran down the stretcher legs on to the floor of the chopper. One of the wounded men had Sandy's insides on his arm. His own right arm had been severed and it lay on its own in the chopper beside the second soldier's severed leg. He was sitting up, morphined and out of it. His face was a bloodied mess of shrapnel wounds, holes held together with metal and blood. Blood from his wound ran through the grooves of the seat and washed back and forth with the movement of the chopper. There were pieces of stone and gravel and leaves in the blood.

Cusack told himself not to feel anything. It was hard not to. Right there, staring into this chopper, listening. He countered it by telling himself they'd shoot him on the spot if they found out where he was. Anyway, it was their fault for being there. That was the bottom line. They had only to go or even say they were going. He was going to say no one had asked them to come. He did not. But they had come and they were responsible for what happened to themselves. They could end it tomorrow. Until then, war was war.

In his car again, he thought of the kid's eye.

He drove through the checkpoint. A soldier told him to have a nice day. A couple of helicopters hovered overhead, a mile apart. Soldiers took up positions along the concession road. Cusack drove south.

7

TIM McLENNAN ALMOST didn't go to meet his wife. When he heard his mother had been injured by a van bomb, the only thing that made him go on was his mother's insistence that she was fine and her pleading with him that he should at least meet his wife, at least talk to her. And his own desire to see his son.

In their suburban garden near Hereford, his son's football seemed to hang in the air for a moment, like it was deciding, before it struck the kitchen window.

It hit dead centre and the window and the reflection of the garden in it dinged and distorted. Anne McLennan did not move from what she was doing. She let her eyes rise and saw her son with his hand over his mouth. She winked. His father lay on the ground with his hands in the air. He sat up and shrugged his shoulders at his wife. She made no reply.

Marty McLennan was eight. He had a small port-wine stain on his face. His eyes were his father's, his smile was his mother's, his hair was chestnut from somewhere way back in both their families. This was the fifth time he had seen his father in the last two years. Anne McLennan hadn't seen her husband in six months. She hadn't slept with him for a year. It hurt. She watched the water run from the tap over the lettuce, stroking her fingers over the leaves, small pieces of dirt caught in the veins coming loose in the water, and the water was silver in the sunlight. Her son was at the window, mouthing.

'Sorry, Mum.'

The sound made it through the window. She winked at him again. Water hit the bottom of her sink and rebounded into her eye. She blinked and the blink looked like a wink to her husband and he winked at her and then picked his son up and put him on his shoulders. Anne McLennan raised her arm to her eye and rubbed it and held back her tears. Tim ran round the garden with Marty on his shoulders. She stopped what she was doing and sat down and pulled out a filtered cigarette and a metal lighter and put the cigarette between her lips and lit it and drew. Her lips were dry and she wet them with her tongue while she smoked. She felt her body shake and she could not stop it.

'I scored, Mum, I scored!'

Marty trailed his triumph by a few milliseconds. His mouth was wide and the muscles in his face were all contracted so that it looked like all the skin was being pulled from behind his head. It made him look like an elf and his smile was dotted by two of the biggest eyes she had ever seen. She held out her arms.

'Give Mummy a hug, Marty,' she said.

He ran to her arms. She hugged him close to her. His skin was wet. His hair was stuck to his forehead. His hands were dirty. The nails had grit under them. One nail was cracked. He kissed her cheek and she felt his warmth and the sweat of his body on her cheek.

'Love you, Marty,' she said.

'Yeah, Mum.'

Tim McLennan watched from the kitchen. His wife saw him. His son did not. The pupils in his wife's eyes narrowed. He could not see into her any more. The narrow pupils covered the retreat of her eyes and sealed her off. He looked at her body. It was a good body. It was a body she knew how to use. Images of her using it flashed in his brain. He cut them off. Her skin was pale and she had thin shadows under her eyes. The eyes retreated a little more from Tim McLennan.

'Go and play in the garden, Marty,' he said. 'Mum and me want to talk. I'll be out in a bit.'

His son turned in his mother's arms. His eyes were wide and welcoming and McLennan wanted to take his son and hug him and not let go.

'A wee while,' he said to Marty.

Marty looked at his mother. She nodded. He looked back at his father. He nodded. Then Marty nodded. Anne McLennan sniffed and reached for a handkerchief in her pocket. She turned her head from her son and her husband. Tim McLennan watched her hand move across her breast and her breast touch the wool of her polo-neck and made a gesture with his head and his eyes to his son.

'Go on,' he whispered.

When Marty had gone, Tim McLennan pulled up a chair and turned it round and sat leaning his arms on the back of the chair and his chin on his arms.

'He's happy,' he said.

Anne McLennan was replacing the handkerchief in her pocket. She stubbed a half-smoked cigarette into an ashtray on the arm of her chair. Then she glanced across at a painting on the far wall above the television. She tightened the muscles in her face and pushed her lips into each other. Any colour in her lips disappeared and for a moment it looked like she had no mouth. She sniffled. She wished she had not. She wished she could just face him off. Without feeling like she was a dam about to burst.

She reached for another cigarette.

'We have to talk,' Tim said.

She nodded. Her hand shook, lighting the cigarette.

Tim slid his hand across his head. The hairs were tightly crewcut, brown except for one or two copper and a few grey. His hand was conditioned and covered in small brown hairs. Below it, his face had a permanent half-tan and a uniform shave. The skin sat well on the bones. There was very little overhang.

'My solicitor says—'

'Your solicitor?'

'My solicitor. He says we can do it without too much—'

'Hassle?'

'That's not what I was goin' to say. I want this to be as painless as possible.'

'You're not putting down a dog, Tim. You're not neutralising one of your terrorists. You're breaking up a home. So please don't couch it in officialese. I don't want this. There's a funny thing, isn't it? I must be a right laugh. Sitting here, telling you I don't want you to leave. Make you feel good, does it? God, I feel so small.'

'Please, Anne, please. I'll look after everythin'. You won't have to do a thing. Anythin' you want, you can have. I've told Jimmy that. He's my solicitor. I've told him I want you and Marty taken care of.'

'I'll explain that to Marty. I hope she's worth it, Tim, this police bitch. I hope – I hope she – just tell me, just tell me, is she a terrific . . . ?'

She held herself back because she could not say the word she wanted to say and she hated herself for not being able to say it. Inside, a vacuum had sucked everything there ever had been between them out and she was empty of thoughts and memories and filling up with hate. She wondered if he realised how much she hated him for what he was doing. If maybe he did think he was behaving like some kind of gentleman. There was a line, from somewhere. She spoke it without knowing.

'Tread softly for you tread on my dreams.'

He bowed his head.

'Anne, I'm sorry,' he said. 'But we have to sort these things out. For your sake. For Marty's sake. We have to. I want to give you everythin'. I won't even try for custody. Just let me see him when I can. Just let me do that.'

'You know you have a beautiful voice, Tim. Lovely lilt. You could be telling me you were going to kill me. It would sound the same. I wonder does it sound the same to you. Do you understand?'

'I think so. I didn't – it's not somethin' you can foresee.'

'No. Though you might tell yourself a little lechery can go a long way. I suppose that was how it began, Tim. A look. Bored with me. Couldn't remember me. Away so long you were probably asking yourself who that strange woman in your house was. I never fancied anyone else. That hurts. That bloody hurts. I wish to Christ I had. Just something.'

'We were driftin'. I was away. This business. It's not good for families.'

'What, creeping around ditches in Ireland? No, I don't suppose shooting people keeps you adjusted for the average suburban estate. She let you do it on razor wire? Get dressed up in combats and cut each other with knives before orgasm? You're a bastard, Tim.'

She could not hold herself any longer. Tears came out singly at first, along her nose to the edges of her mouth and then her eyes overflowed and she put what was left of her second cigarette into the ashtray and her head in her hands. It was uncontrollable and Tim made no attempt to stop it. He just sat there, watching and listening and wanting to leave.

'You're a bastard,' she said.

It was mixed up in tears and crying and Tim could see the tears running over her hands and on to her jeans.

'A bastard.'

'We have more in common,' he said.

She looked up at him. Her eyes were wide and red and full of tears and her mouth was wet and tearstains streaked her face like warpaint. She reached for her handkerchief.

'More in common? Uniforms, you mean? You like uniforms, Tim? I could have worn a uniform if that's all you wanted.'

'That's not what I mean. I mean we understand one another. Carol's there. She knows.'

'Knows what? And you're saying we don't have anything in common any more? I know every inch of you, Tim McLennan. We have a son together. Out there. Or had you forgotten? A son. Marty. We made him. You and me. Now unless—'

She stopped herself, looked around the room and then said it.

'Is she pregnant?'

'Of course not.'

'Oh! Only people like me get pregnant. That's our role. Nice little wives, waiting. This Carol, has she ever waited? What the hell do you mean, nothing in common. I've shared your life for ten years, Tim. I know every muscle, every bone, where you hurt, where you like to be touched, how, when. Does she? We speak the same language, we're from the same country, what more can we have in common?'

'I don't think you'd understand, Anne. Even I'm not sure.'

'But you'll break up our family.'

'It's broken already, Anne. We haven't been man and wife for over a year. And don't put it all down to me. Every time I asked you to come over with me, come visit Mum, come live for a bit while I'm on tour, what do I get? No, you don't want Marty growin' up there, in that environment, with those people. Well, they're my people, that's my environment. I grew up there. It's not some colonial backwater. Like you said, it's supposed to be your country. You bloody English.'

'Bloody English, bloody English. I'm not the one buggering off on his family. I'm not the one screwing some police tart blind in the back of a Land Rover. Like that, does she? Feel of the military. Like some Sass, darling? What was it, some kind of get-off thing with you, Tim? She pop every time she saw you? Big SAS man. Walk-on-water brigade.

You believe all that rubbish, Tim? Come down to earth, for God's sake.'

'I'm fightin' a war.'

'A war! That's a laugh. We lose more on the roads every year.'

A catalogue of images appeared to him in no order, images and faces and smells and noises. And the television. The television was a big player. The television and aftermaths. The television was an expert in aftermaths. You never saw the befores, very rarely you saw the durings, but you always saw the aftermaths. Like designed sets or gallery installations: urban mutilation, rural ambush, and variations on the themes. The variations were endless. The combinations infinite. He heard his mother's pleas again and remembered the stock picture on the hotel television. Always a lone soldier, he thought. Always a lone RUC man. It was an art form: control-box post-atrocity realism. And the police tape was the frame.

'Tell that to my daddy,' he said. 'Tell it to my mother. She was a minute away from that bomb. A minute more and my mother would be in pieces all over the high street. As it is, I should be there with her. So should you. They dug a piece of metal the size of a nail out of her leg. She's on a walking stick and more Valium. Do you know what I'm talkin' about? I should be with her, Anne. She's my family. She's Marty's family. He should be with her. And if you'd any feelin's you'd be with her, too. They set off another one today. That's three. Jesus, when I think of it. I nearly want to puke. Not a war! What the hell do you think it is?'

'I don't know. I don't know. I don't bloody know and I don't bloody care. No, no, that's not what I meant. I don't know. I don't want that for Marty, Tim, I don't. Your poor mother. You know this'll kill her.'

'Don't you use that. My mother's been through more than you can imagine. She'll understand.'

'I'm sorry, Tim, I'm sorry. Is she okay? I mean, is she—?'

'Yeah, she's okay. Bit of shock there. It wasn't that bad. She'll get by. It went through flesh. They let her go quickly. That's a good sign. Valerie Wilson's over with her now. Robbie and her are keepin' an eye. But there's four others who aren't out of hospital. And I probably know them. Do you understand? Christ, it just keeps comin'. Look, you could try ringin' her, Anne. And let Marty talk to his granny.'

'Yeah. Jesus, I don't know, Tim, I just wish to Christ – oh, I don't know, I want my family. I just want my family.'

'Your family. Your family. What about my family? What about when I want you to be with me? You forget that too soon. You think I liked bein' alone. Night after night. Either up to my neck in mud or slotted into a barracks regime. You think I never wanted you there with me. Just one touch, just one touch, I used to think. Then I could keep goin'.'

'Keep going, keep going. Where? For what?'

'That's just it, Anne, that's just it.'

'Please don't talk like that. You have no right. Do you have a pet name for her? No, don't answer that. I don't think I could stand it. I'm taking Marty to Kent at the weekend. Mummy and Daddy are going to have all of us down. You're invited.'

'Please, Anne.'

'Pathetic, aren't I? There you are, bonking this – this Carol – rotten and I feel all the guilt. There's no justice, is there? I'm still in love with you, Tim. I hate you. I hate you so much I think I could kill you now but I'm so in love with you I'd take my clothes off now if you asked. And I hate myself more for that.'

'Anne.'

'Don't patronise me. You're getting what you want. I'm being walked on. My dreams. I won't ever forgive you. I won't. And I'll teach Marty not to. I'll make him hate the very sound of your name. I promise you. I want something. I want to feel I have something for this. I know you're not supposed to but I want my pound of flesh. Hell hath no fury, eh? Pathetic.'

He was going to tell her she would get through it, that it would pass, but he could not get the words out. He stood up and came over to her and crouched down and put his hands on hers.

'It's over, Anne. I can't go on. I don't love you any more.'

'No. I won't hear that. I won't. I will not. I will not. Bastard.'

She shoved his hands away. He stood up and stepped back from her. He glanced around the room. He could not remember buying anything for that room. Except a lamp in the corner. It had a black stand and it moved. It was ugly and both of them had known it was ugly when they bought it but neither of them wanted to tell the other. They didn't want to hurt each other.

'Do you love her?'

Tim shook his head.

'I could.'

'Could?'

'She understands things.'

'Where do you do it?'

'Anne.'

She couldn't help it. She tried. To be mature. Whatever mature was. Stiff-upper-lip stuff. Best of British. But she could not help asking. Every detail. She had to know every detail. Where, how long, when, what, which, why? Most of all she wanted a why she could live with. And she knew she would never get one. Her neurons were giving her images, filling in the gaps, and she was starting to cry again.

'I want to see you hurt, Tim. And if I can, I will hurt you. I want to see you in the pain I'm in. I want to see you humiliated like this. Because you've destroyed me. And don't come on with some kind of philosophical get-out phrase: you still have your writing, Anne, you have Marty, you have another children's book out next month. And a short story in *Woman's whatever*. I'm destroyed, Tim. And there's nothing will ever put it back together. And people who say different don't know what they're talking about. You're a bastard, Tim. God, I want to hurt you. I want to scratch your – your – your fucking eyes out.'

'I'm sorry. I want Carol.'

'How did I ever get mixed up with you? You and your bloody soldiering and your bloody soldier's ways. Is this honourable? What do the regiment think? Conduct unbecoming. They should break you. I'll go to them. Tell them what a bastard you are. Jesus knows you put me through enough to get this commission. Officer and gentleman. I don't think so. Is it more important than her? It was so important for you. The Queen's commission. Through the ranks. Yes, sir, no sir, three bags full, sir. You're no gentleman, Tim McLennan. Hypocrite. Bloody hypocrite. It means nothing to you. All the garbage you spout. All the high morals and codes. All bull. You're out for yourself. You don't give a shit for anyone else. And when another little tart in a tight uniform comes along and gives you the eye, will you dump this Carol and mount her? It's just some macho thing with you, isn't it? What I can't understand is why you took those vows with me. You remember, in your precious church. Whatever it was. That man with the Ian Paisley accent. Scared the shit out of me, he did. Scared, on my wedding day. I thought I was in some kind of comedy. Thou shalt not, thou shalt not.'

'That's it, mock my church. You think I'm some kind of redneck? All high and mighty. Daddy in the right clubs, went to the right schools. Very embarrassin' bringin' home a redneck. I am not a redneck.'

'And what would your God think of this?'

'He will understand. I have faith, Anne. You'll never understand that. Carol—'

'Don't you fucking mention that bitch's name to me. Don't. I won't hear. For Christ's sake, Tim. For Christ's sake. Look at what you're doing. Look. Think of Marty. What'll it do to Marty? Please.'

'Maybe you'd better get a solicitor, Anne. Make it easier on yourself. I'm goin' out to play with Marty. You decide what you want, how you want to play this. I'll go along with whatever you want. I just want to see Marty when I'm over. Maybe take him for a couple of holidays. When I've leave.'

'With this Carol? Over there?'

'Maybe.'

She was biting her upper lip. Her pupils had relaxed and light from the kitchen was bringing out a kind of purple and brown mix in her eyes. The whites were bloodshot and red and her face was stained with tears. She wore no make-up. She did not need to. She had a young face and it could stand alone except for the eye shadows. She stood up and walked over to her husband.

'I love you,' she said.

'I'm doin' what I have to do.'

'You always did.'

She turned away.

'There was a river. And I was watching it from a bridge. There was a bit of it I wanted. I had it all mapped out. The water was clear and the sun lay on it and rolled in it and then sank into it. You could see small trout in it. They were brown. And they moved quick in the water. So I went down to the bank and lay down and put my hands out and tried to get that piece of river. But it was gone.'

She swung round and hit him across the face.

'Bastard.'

He touched his face. There was a small tear on his cheekbone. No blood. But he could feel the skin flap. He licked his finger and then touched the tear in the skin with his wet finger. It stung. Nothing he noticed. She had backed off. Her hands were shaking. Her mouth was open. Her pupils were pinpricks again. She undid the band at the back of her hair and shook it free and then pulled the ponytail back into shape and replaced the band around it. Her hands had stopped shaking.

'If I told you I killed a man last week would you try to understand me?' Tim McLennan asked his wife.

He did not know why. There was no answer he was looking for. He should not have said anything. Against the rules. He had never broken them like that before. And for nothing. There was nothing else she could say. He wanted to kick himself. He was looking for sympathy. It was one more thing he could have done without.

'If you told me you killed two hundred I wouldn't understand you, Tim. Maybe I have never really understood you. Maybe you've been playing me. Making the right noises. It's hard to see the same man now. I'm at a wake and there's no corpse. There'll be a funeral and no grave. There is other damage, Tim. High-velocity rifles aren't the only deadly weapons around. Look at me. Reduced to this. I used to think I had it so together. Friends came to me for advice. If my friends could see me now.'

She made an attempt at a line of the song but stopped.

'I'll play a while with Marty,' Tim said.

'Play soldiers, Tim.' She laughed. 'You can be the good guys. Make sure when you're killing your son you do it cleanly. Single mark. For his sake.'

She took out her handkerchief and blew her nose. Then she took another cigarette out and lit it and smoked it. Tim moved his hands in a kind of vain defensive gesture. He had been expecting her to say sorry or something. Come up and touch his cheek. Something. But she was smoking. Standing there with her arms folded, smoking. And he could think of nothing to do.

'I'll go out, then.'

'Yeah. I'm going to wash my face. I'll ring your mother. Barbara's pregnant. She told me to tell you. So there. And Uncle Maxie's in hospital for his prostate. Auntie Molly's on to Mummy all the time. Poor Mummy. We all lean on her. She likes you.'

In the garden, Tim McLennan played with his son again. There was a lawnmower in the distance and some of its sounds made Tim stop and think. The rain came as the light faded and Marty ran past his father and kicked the ball at the garden wall where Tim had planted a creeping bush one time. The ball hit the bush and leaves ready to fall fell and Marty cheered and felt the rain touch his face.

Upstairs, his mother watched and hated.

8

THE WOOD TURNED black at the edges and the yellow flame split in two and touched tongues. The wood caught fire and the touching tongues became one again and climbed to the top of the stove. Danny Loughlin threw another piece of wood in and watched it catch. He took a pair of black metal tongs and picked a piece of coal from the enamel basin beside the stove and placed the piece of coal on the burning wood. It hissed and crackled and small jets of steam and oily tears came from it. Loughlin thought he saw a face in the fire. But the flames moved and the face was gone.

'I think he's fuckin' mad, John, but he won't bloody listen. He'll put the whole set-up here knee-deep in shite. All of us. For no reason.'

John Cusack sat in an armchair across the room. He wore jeans and a black sweatshirt and his hair was wet. The jeans were not his and the sweatshirt was too big.

'It's his brother, Danny, his only brother. I don't think we can stop him. I won't try.'

'You won't? And what if he's lifted?'

They were in Cavan, a farmhouse between Shercock and Cootehill. Isolated, tree-covered. The house was mid-nineteenth century and it looked like it had not been touched since then. It was grey and solid and behind it was a yard of concrete and low huddled brick and angled slate, running with slurry. There were cattle in the fields around and a solid gob of mist smothered the landscape.

The farmhouse was one of about a dozen isolated places, in what they called unoccupied Ulster, which they had unfettered access to. Safe houses, billets, call houses, they had different names. In a couple, they paid for the privilege, in the rest, the owners did it because they wanted to.

When they wanted to use a place they made a phone call and sent the back-up people in. The active-service volunteers followed when the all-clear was sounded.

'Talk to Dessie yourself, Danny,' Cusack said.

Loughlin did not turn to him. He could see a reflection of his pockmarked face in the flames and the grey stubble that rose to his cheeks and the eyebrows that came down over his brown eyes. The eyes looked like stagnant pools when he stayed too long in front of a mirror.

'He won't listen to me,' he said. 'He'd listen to you. What does he want to do, read out some kind of Fenian-dead speech?'

'He wants to see his brother buried.'

'Mal was a wild lad. Never looked. Too fuckin' gung-ho. Like some others I know.'

'What's that supposed to mean?'

'Nothin'.'

Cusack leaned forward. He put his hand to his hair and felt the wet hairs and squeezed some of them. Water dribbled down the side of his face. It tickled his skin. His skin was shaved and he could not feel any of the stubble that had been there before.

'Jesus, Danny, you're not back on that again. This operation goes, Danny. What the hell do you think we're running here? Some kind of damn fairground game? This is an army and an army fights wars and wars are risky. Ask that lot over there about it. Who dares wins. You try and minimise the risks, but you take the consequences. We all know that. Look at Mal. He got unlucky. But he would have been the first to say he accepted it. It happens. Okay?'

He picked up a glass cup and drank some coffee. Then he took a packet of cigarettes from his pocket and a disposable lighter from the table beside him and lit the cigarette. He drew on it three times and then blew the smoke out.

'I'm just bein' practical,' Loughlin said.

'And that's fine when it's needed.'

'It's needed now. It's practicality – not bravado – wins wars.'

'Maybe if you were real practical you wouldn't be fighting this war,

Danny. I mean, people are not exactly lining up, asking us to fight, are they? I mean, maybe we could make it real easy for ourselves by just dumping arms and going home. But we don't, do we?'

Loughlin was fighting to keep his argument going but he knew it was already lost. They had tested a 50-calibre machine-gun that morning and the sound of the firing and the feel of the weapon had made him wet himself. He did not tell anyone. And when they were finished and kicking a soccer ball around, he went in hard and the thing turned into a maul in the mud and he had to change his clothes like the rest of them.

'Yeah, well, you've still gotta be practical,' he said. 'And we're gettin' too ambitious. Too complex. Too many workin' parts.'

He shook his head.

'We're well able,' Cusack said. 'If we're not, then we might as well pack up and go. Look, we have to go for this one. Because it's there, Danny. And because we're here. That's it. Look at Francie Devine's boys. They've hit three cop stations already in two years. Three of them wiped out. And look what Command's done the last couple of days. Things are moving, you know? Not bad for a bunch of mindless terrorists.'

'Yeah, bet you're pleased with yourself there.'

'With the team, Danny.'

'The bombs are fine. Exactly what I want. Minimum risk to volunteers, maximum damage to the enemy. Good payback. That and the flea bites are fine. It's this Rambo stuff I don't like. A couple of police with Rugers is not the same as a bunch of soldiers in a checkpoint. If one thing goes wrong . . .' He drew his hand across his neck and made a choking noise. 'And this A-team rubbish. You and Dessie – you've been listenin' to Francie too much. Francie think's he's invincible. Even after what happened to Mal. Oh, no, no touts in his set-up, had to have been a civilian. He just wants someone to stiff. He nearly went for Tony McCabe yesterday, you know that? Got him by the throat.'

'You know everything, don't you, Danny?'

'I have to.'

Loughlin poked at the coals with a poker and closed the door of the stove. He pulled himself up from his knees with the movement of a hydraulic machine. His corduroy trousers were suspended by a pair of old clip-on braces. He wore a collarless shirt and a grey scarf. He put his hand in his pocket and took out a packet of pipe tobacco and went over to the wooden table by the window and picked up the pipe lying on it and went back to the stove.

'Think about what we did with those bombs yesterday and the day before,' he said. 'Good solid operations. Everyone got out fine. And we leave a few of their towns lookin' for plastic surgery. We hit them and they don't hit us. They can take bigger hits than we can. This isn't even, John.'

He took a penknife from his pocket and scraped burnt residue from his pipe and flicked it into the stove. Then he tapped the pipe on the side of the stove and emptied what was left into the flames.

'Anyway, who says they aren't on to youse. All this pimpernel shite, John, you ferryin' bombs and Dessie fuckin' off to funerals. You're gettin' like Francie, youse are, takin' too many risks. They're not stupid over there. You shouldn't have done that drivin'. I said that to Dessie. There was no need. I could have found someone. If Dessie'd fuckin' let me.'

'Newry screwed up. Dessie needed someone. I had a cover, so we went with it. I'm here now. We did it. You said it yourself.'

'You could be leadin' us all into a lot of trouble, son. I've said this before and I'll say it again. You stick out like a page three girl's tit, Yank. Look at you. Everythin' about you says you're different. And different in this war is dead.'

He shoved some tobacco into his pipe and lit it.

'I've done okay up to now. The other day went fine. Even managed to do a bit of recon. Waltzed right through them. Stopped for a chat with the bastards.' Cusack laughed.

'So you say. You can overdo the Marine rubbish, you know. I seen too many hard lads in Miltown to put much faith in it. Give me people who are clever, lads who know how to hit without risk. I prefer that. You boys are too high. Too fuckin' high.'

'You just don't want to do this, do you, Danny?'

'You know my feelins. I don't make a secret of them.'

'So we just keep to the same old stuff? A bomb here, a bullet there. So we can feel we're doing our bit. Hope they'll get tired and go away.'

'Long war, Yank. That's what'll win it for us. We'll outlast them. We're here long-term and they're not. So long as they're here, we'll fight. It only takes one of us with a gun and that's the fight.'

'And we're here for ever? That's stupid. How long is the long war?'

'As it takes. It's been goin' on for centuries.'

'So we just go on flea-biting? Come on, Danny, you think the Brits really give a shit if we kill a cop here or a workman there? Even a Glaswegian knacker in para dress? They mind when we look strong and hurt their pockets. It's economics and propaganda we're fighting here. Raising profile. Sucking cash. This war will be decided in the headlines and the balance sheets. Make them hurt in their pockets and make them look bad. Their entire strategy is based on containment. Acceptable levels. And they have a whole colonial population to waste. We can't let them contain us.'

Loughlin sat down in a wooden chair beside the table and opened a newspaper. Cusack's bomb was on the front page. Big picture of the scene. He counted the number of times the word terror was used. An old woman suffering from shock had taken a piece of shrapnel from the van in her leg. It had a picture of her being lifted into an ambulance.

'If it's all getting too much, you can always stand down, Danny,' Cusack said. 'No one would hold it against you. You've done more than enough. You know that.'

'Don't patronise me, son. Sure, stand down. Do the tours, appear at rallies, listen to Sinn Fein total strategists debate the shape of the new republic. Is it true you got Martin Burke out of the Royal Vic on the end of a pile of tied-up sheets?'

'GHQ work, Danny, can't talk about it. He's a good lad, Martin. Gentleman.'

'He's a fuckin' psychopath. I seen Martin pump a whole magazine into a tout for the fun of it. Get a grip, John. We have our bad ones. Everyone has. And Martin Burke's one of them. He was really in with Mal Hart. Wanted to stiff that DUP boy crowin' about Mal on the television, Marty did.

'Martin'll be along on this one, Danny. He's a good volunteer. Remember that.'

Loughlin had his head bent, scanning the newspaper.

'We can take it, Danny, it just needs planning and discipline. Council want this kind of operation done. Command want it done. Francie wants it done. Dessie wants it done. And we will do it, do you hear me? We will do what's necessary. And if it means banging a few heads together, then I'll do that. Take it up with Dessie if you don't like it.'

'You're in real thick with Dessie, aren't you, Yank? He likes all that Marine shite, far too much. We've been doin' okay, you know. You want the list of successes we've had? And I don't mean stickin' two pounds of Semtex in a shoppin' mall and blowin' some civilians into a thousand pieces. This is the real thing down here. This is our land and we call the shots. Those bastards over there they shit themselves every time they come out of their holes. United Kingdom! They can't even walk along their own roads without us sendin' them into orbit. And we were at it long before you came, Yank.'

'I told you, Danny. I'm as Irish as you are. I was born here. I went to school here. Okay, I spent some time in the States, but tell me a Mick who hasn't. Come on, Danny, we've put some good operations together here over the last year. That upsetting for you, is it?'

'What are you sayin'?'

'Think we don't know about your little sidelines? War has its profits, Danny.' He touched the side of his head.

'You fuckin' . . .'

Loughlin came at him. Cusack stood up and shifted to the left and caught Loughlin with a kick to the top of the calf. The older man went down on his knee and Cusack rabbit-punched him. Loughlin pitched forward on to a couch. Cusack came down on top of him and grabbed his hair and dug his knee into his back. He pulled his head back until the neck was at snapping point. Loughlin could hardly breathe.

'You're forgiven, Danny. But cut it out from now on. It's not good for our image. And if you ever come at me again, Danny, I'll break your fucking neck. Clear?'

Loughlin fought. Cusack pulled harder. Loughlin gave in.

'Clear.'

He let Loughlin go. Loughlin slumped on the couch and tried to get his breath back. There was a knock on the door. Cusack did Loughlin's clothes up and slapped a little colour into his cheeks and shoved him into a sitting position. Loughlin's colour drifted back to pale. The door opened.

Betty Loughlin was a small woman with very white hair and a face that had fallen half an inch since she had been a local beauty queen. She had a gentle down on her skin that could only be seen in sunlight and she wore a kaftan and glasses. She looked at her husband and then Cusack.

'I've got some, John,' she said. 'New clothes. They're in your room. Okay?'

'Thanks, Betty.'

Her husband did not speak to her.

She took in the situation, made a choice in her mind, covered it in mental gymnastics and fatuous arguments she did not believe, turned and left.

Betty Loughlin followed her husband because she loved him. She was not in the IRA and she had never wanted to join but she cooked when she was asked and washed clothes and made phone calls and shopped because of Danny and because she wanted to.

Later, when Cusack was in a bedroom, dressing, Betty Loughlin stood at the door. She knocked on the wall to let him know she was there. He looked up from where he was tying his shoelaces and smiled. She had very elegant fingers. Cusack watched them spread out over the wall beside the door.

'Maybe you should leave Danny out, John,' she said. 'Maybe he's reached the point, you know. I've seen it. He was on the Brookeborough raid. Did you know that? Great friend of Fergal O'Hanlon's. That was a terrible thing they did to Fergal and Sean South.'

'It was a hell of a mess. That whole campaign was a hell of a mess. Good men dying for nothing.

'Oh yeah, tell me about it.'

'We need him, Betty. When this one's done, we'll see. I've told him no one would mind if he stood down.'

'I'll bet he took that well.'

Cusack smiled.

'He's a proud man, Betty.'

'Far too proud. He believes, you know. I don't want you to think he doesn't believe. He's been through too much not to. But—'

'He's losing it.'

She didn't say anything.

'It happens,' Cusack said. 'People like Danny, they've been at it too long.'

'You include me in that?'

'You're stronger. Much stronger. The Brits don't know what they're up against, do they?'

'I don't believe any more, John,' she said. 'I'm not sure I ever did. I do it for him. I'd do it for you. But I don't believe. I'd like to. And sometimes when I've had a few or I've read a book or they're really layin' into us on the television, I get a sneakin' belief. But it never lasts. I'll do it for you and

Danny and for the dead lads and the prisoners. I'll do it for them, but don't ask me to do it for a cause.'

She folded her arms.

'That's the way it is.'

He smiled. It was a patronising smile.

Betty felt there was more to it than that, but something inside her told her not to pursue it.

'Anyway, the troops are gatherin'. Dessie's here,' she said. She laughed. 'I'm makin' lunch. I make a good camp follower, John. If it wasn't this camp, it'd be another.'

'You can follow my camp, Betty, wherever it goes.'

'That a promise? You're a good man, John. Don't get too good. Sometimes too good is worse than bad. Do you understand?'

He did not.

She led him down the stairs through the hall and the living room to the kitchen. The kitchen was clouded in steam from a boiling pot. There was a smell of cheese and a loaf of bread lay in slices on the table. A smaller woman was at the sink. She did not look at Cusack. She knew not to. Her husband was out farming and keeping watch. There were other watchers, too. Betty pulled an anorak from the back of a chair and gave it to Cusack.

Outside, the mist was sitting on the roofs and there was a drizzle. The rain sent ripples through the slurry puddles to grooved concrete. Cusack pulled the hood of the anorak up and walked across the farmyard to a stone outhouse.

The outhouse had hay and two animals in it and steam rising from the floor and a rustic smell that hit the kitchen cooking right in the nose and knocked it out. There was a trapdoor at one end, under one of the animals. It led to a tunnel that ran for sixty feet to a small shed in the corner of a field at the top of a hill. They had never had to use it. Loughlin had had it built as an escape route for planning meetings, and there was a bunker off it for storing weapons and practice firing. There was nothing stored there now. Stuff was shifted all the time. The Quartermaster's Department lived in a permanent state of nomadic paranoia. The Quartermaster General was a second cousin of Danny Loughlin's on his mother's side but they didn't get on. Danny still thought he deserved something for his time on the Army Council years ago.

The outhouse in the yard was fine for planning meetings when the gardai and the Irish Army weren't on a sweep. The bunker did for the other times. There were others in other houses, and you'd have to search hard to find them.

Cusack stood before a group of six, sitting on milk crates. Danny Loughlin sat with a board on his knee, a notepad on the board and a pen behind his ear, smoking his pipe. He drummed his fingers on the board. His hands were hairy and the veins bulged under the sagging skin. The veins were purple and they looked like they might burst. There was a jug of water on the ground and some glasses around it.

On Danny's right were two young men who might have been brothers. They were distant relatives and the fat fellow nearest Loughlin was the better volunteer. The other was fine, but not as good. The fat fellow was called Tate for some unexplained reason and the thin one, who had a hair-lip and shaving nicks all over his face, was called Ger. Tate was a second-generation volunteer. His dad, Paddy Byrne, had been a well-known Belfast republican. Ger's brother had been shot dead by Loyalists in a random shooting. He had a job as a carpenter on both sides of the border when he wasn't active. He was a Kelly from Armagh and the Kellys from Armagh and the Byrnes from Belfast were related by marriage. Tate was wanted. Ger wasn't. Cusack smiled at the two of them and moved to Dessie Hart.

Dessie Hart's mouth was thin and sad and his eyes were hanging on the edge of their sockets. He'd let his body sink and it looked weaker.

Cusack put his hand on Hart's shoulder when he got behind his chair.

'How's Des?' he said. 'I think Mal'd be proud of us.'

'I think so, John.'

Hart put a hand on John Cusack's. It was a moment of genuine affection.

'There'll be a few early winter sales in Armagh and Tyrone, I think,' Cusack said.

'Maybe we should go and see if we can get a bargain.'

Everyone laughed.

Cusack was already moving to the babyfaced teenager sitting beside Dessie. He had a familiar face except that Cusack couldn't pin it down and he was already looking at the woman opposite.

'This is Bruddy, John,' Loughlin said. 'He's teamin' up with us. Right?'

'How're you doin'?'

Bruddy extended his hand.

Cusack had already skipped past Bruddy and straight to Maggie

O'Neill. A surge of feeling made him hesitate.

'And this is Maggie.'

'We've met,' Cusack said.

'Maggie Oakley,' Dessie Hart said.

They all laughed again.

Maggie O'Neill bowed her head and looked to Betty Loughlin for support. But Betty was already leaving. She knew when to come and when to go, when to speak and when to shut up. There was food to get.

Cusack shook Maggie's hand and looked straight at her. She turned her eyes down.

'I've heard of you, Maggie,' he said. 'I'm pleased to meet you – formally.'

He nodded his head as if he was agreeing with himself and did not let go of Maggie's hand. She shoved her hand in further to hold the grip. He felt it squeeze against his and if he had let up she might have hurt him.

'And I've heard of you, Yank,' she said.

Then she looked at Dessie and Danny.

'So we've all heard of each other. Let's hope no one else has.'

No one responded. Cusack ran his eyes over her and felt himself move. Maggie looked at her watch and thought about her kids and then looked back at Cusack for a moment.

Cusack shot a glance at Tate Byrne. Tate looked at Loughlin for support. And Ger looked at Tate.

'I heard your name in 'Blaney last night,' Cusack said. 'You've been putting it about, Tate. You know the orders about that. Especially in your position. You'll have the Branch all over you. I don't care what you do with your fucking dick so long as you do it in private.' He slapped his hands together. 'What I do care about is when you go screwing wives around here and then husbands get jealous and you draw attention to yourself. And when you draw attention to yourself you draw attention to us and that isn't on.'

'Yeah, Tate, you're gonna have to give it a rest,' Dessie Hart said. He looked at Loughlin. 'I don't know where he gets the energy. Honest, I don't.'

The men all laughed. Maggie did not.

'I thought we were here for a meetin',' she said. 'I've got other business. I don't want to piss around, Dessie.'

'Sure, Maggie, you're right. Tate, lay off the women. Sit down, John.'

Hart's posture redefined itself and he looked like a leader now. His receding hair gave him the edge on everyone except Danny Loughlin. It was complemented by a pointed nose and a direct way of speaking. When Dessie Hart spoke to you you stayed spoken to.

'We have a war to fight,' he said. 'We took three fatalities last week and gave one back. They're not good odds. But we'll come back. That was good, John. And yesterday. They're callin' it our revenge for Pomeroy. Let them think that. We've a few bigger surprises planned.'

'Maybe too big,' Loughlin said.

'You got a problem, Danny?' Hart said.

Loughlin shrugged. Then he shook his head.

Cusack got up and backed away from the group. He leaned against the plain concrete wall and scratched his tight haircut.

'Look, I know Danny's not totally convinced but here's how it is. We hit ones and twos, that's fine. Keeps things ticking. But ten, fifteen or more. That's when we get the headlines. And not just here and in London. That's when we get the American networks. Cable news. It's like if we stick a bomb in Belfast. We get a few seconds down a running order after Princess Di and right before the animal story. We stick one in London, we get the headline. Put a big enough one in London and we get headline after headline. Knock out a strong point and we go from pain in the ass terrorists to real threat. We get days for the same effort. We gotta use what we have to maximum effect. Be efficient. It takes the same planning to kill two as twenty. It takes the same planning to explode a thousand pounds as a hundred pounds. We have to think scientifically. Use our technology.'

He moved towards Tate. Tate nodded. Maggie looked at Dessie Hart. Hart was writing in a notebook.

'There's no one disagrees with that,' Maggie said.

Loughlin turned his head away.

'Only way to go,' Hart said. 'John's right. It's a kind of target inflation we're runnin' up against. Each time we hit a target, the value of that target goes down. It's like printin' five-pound notes. The more you print the less they're worth. Single targets are fine but they just don't have the same value any more. So we have to up the ante. That's the way of it. We can't just stay static. Otherwise we're losin'. We've gotta push. I'm fine with the long war, Danny. I just don't want it longer than it has to be.'

'But that's our strength, Dessie,' Loughlin said. 'Commitment.'

'Aye, Danny, but you've gotta add a bit of tactical and strategic sense. Otherwise you're just beatin' your head off a brick wall. And all you end up with is a sore head. You've gotta see the armed struggle for what it is: one part of a total campaign. A very important part, but a part all the same.'

'Is that Sinn Fein speakin'?' Loughlin said.

'That's Council speakin', Danny. That's strategy speakin'.'

'Sure,' Cusack said. 'And it's all with us. We set the pace in this war. They can only react.'

'I hope they know that,' Danny Loughlin said. He laughed.

'They will, Danny,' Cusack said. 'Because that's the way things are going to go here.' He looked at everyone, individually. 'Okay?' he said.

There was a gap in the talk. People looked at each other. Cusack looked at Maggie.

'Right,' Dessie Hart said, 'to business. The permanent checkpoint at Kill.' He rubbed his eyes. 'This job is now our focus till we see it through to a conclusion. And I want to be completely ready when we go. No loose ends. Now we're gettin' new volunteers in. I think Ger has someone who looks good – yeah, Ger?'

Ger nodded.

'Okay,' Hart said. 'And we have support from Tyrone and I've got a couple of other lads in the pipeline. But I think we'll have to push our deadline back, John. This business in Tyrone at the minute needs time. And we need more trainin'.'

Cusack was going to argue but Hart continued speaking.

'Just a delay, John, not a cancellation. I'll leave the organisation of trainin' to you. Okay?'

Danny Loughlin grinned at John Cusack.

'For how long do we delay?' Cusack asked.

'Until we're ready, John. Until we're absolutely ready. There's more work to be done. And that's what we'll concentrate on. Danny has a place organised, don't you, Danny?'

'Nice and secluded,' he said.

'I guess that's it, then,' Cusack said.

'Come on, John,' Hart said. 'I said delay, not cancel. Soon as we get the all-clear, it's business as usual. Maggie, you'll train separately. I don't want everyone together. And Tyrone are lookin' after their end of things.'

Cusack sat down, deflated, beside Bruddy, and tried to figure out where the hell he'd seen him before. The puzzle mixed with his feelings on frustration and he concentrated on Maggie.

Betty Loughlin came through the door with sandwiches. She had a black cat at her feet and the cat jumped up on the table and walked around, stopping in front of each one of them. Maggie stroked its back.

'He's lookin' for somethin', Maggie. He's a cute little so-and-so, isn't he?'

Cusack looked at Bruddy again. Then at Maggie. He felt his heartbeat increase again. He threw his eyes back to Bruddy but they kept going back to Maggie and each time they did, she looked at him for a few seconds and then down at the floor.

'I'll bring beer in an hour,' Betty said. 'That okay?'

'Right, love,' Loughlin said.

She left. Her cat followed.

Loughlin saw Cusack shooting a glance at Maggie. Maggie half smiled. He had direct self-assurance, Cusack, the kind you picked up in the States, something you didn't get in Ireland, and it made him stand out. She thought about that and then about her kids and finally about her husband. Then she stopped. Cusack had picked up a sandwich. He was chewing and listening to Dessie Hart and Ger Kelly talking about a weapon and looking at Maggie when he could.

'By the way,' Danny Loughlin said. 'Bruddy's Billy Holmes's brother, John.'

9

McLENNAN CAME BACK from England with nothing settled. The same morning a Catholic taxi driver was wounded in the head by Protestant gunmen in Belfast and a soldier lost his leg in a booby trap in Tyrone. Tim McLennan drove to his mother's.

On the main street of his home town, his footsteps crushed broken glass and the powdered dust of bomb damage rose in mushroom clouds from the floors of the dismembered and disembowelled shops and McLennan smelled the smell of burnt rubber and charred wood and scorched metal. And the gutters ran with water. Two cars on the other side of the street sat paintless and tyreless and glassless, silvery black and yellow, like they had been stripped and left naked. There was a car seat down the street and one of its springs lay beside it. The spring was rusted.

At the centre of the explosion, there was a crater in the road and the buildings had collapsed. There was an exposed fireplace on one of the new gable walls, with a candlestick and what looked like the base of clock still sitting on it. The candle was broken and tilted to one side. There was a crater in the road and water ran into the crater. A lump of chassis was embedded in the new gable wall with the fireplace. It all looked like some modern art statement. He stopped and spun around on his heels and followed the explosion out both ways. The street channelled the explosion right down itself, like some ignorant halfwit collaborator. Scorched walls, torn façades, drainpipes at grotesque angles in twisted-limb pose, slates picked off roofs and tossed around like autumn leaves.

There was a butcher back in business across the street a hundred yards up, where the damage was less. No windows, men on the roof, glass splinters mixed in with the sawdust on the floor. McLennan walked across the street. There were small pieces of everything on the street. Coins and half a wine bottle with wine still in it and two postcards with greetings from the town across them. They were wet and burnt at the edges. There was a glove and a packet of cigarettes and the tape from a cassette tape, piled neatly in a heap, and a polystyrene fast-food cup. He stopped outside the butcher's shop. He stood at the window.

'Bit of a shambles, Harry,' he said.

A heavy man with a girder frame and single-span-bridge shoulders cast an eye through his gouged-out window. He had a high hairline and a single eyebrow and his whole face came to a focus at the dimple on his chin. For a second he paused and maybe he wanted to say something hard and hurting. McLennan saw the pause. He waited.

'Tim! Tim McLennan. How's about you, Tim? Would you look at you?'

He came over to the window and wiped his hands in his uniform and then shoved one of his hands at McLennan.

'How are you, Harry? Bit of a mess here.'

'Too right, Tim. One more like this and I'm gettin' out. That's for sure.'

They looked at the street together. Harry Patterson shivered in the cold of the morning and the wind. They had been in the UDR together once. Then the newsagent around the corner, who'd been their sergeant, was shot dead and Harry Patterson resigned. Never the fighting type, he said. Meat was all he knew. And with the supermarkets and the car bombers it was enough of a war just trying to keep the family business going. Some people held it against him when he left the UDR. McLennan went through a period of not talking to him. Nothing designed. They just didn't meet much any more. McLennan didn't do much to avoid Patterson then but he didn't do much to meet him either. That was all over now. And McLennan could not remember when it had come to an end and why. Maybe it had run its course or maybe McLennan just liked to feel he had friends in his home town.

'How much was it?'

'A thousand. Fifteen hundred, maybe. They say fifteen hundred and they ought to know. Bastards. I heard your mother was nearby. Is she okay? I meant to get our Vicky to call round. But this . . .'

'It's all right, Harry. I understand. She's fine. Bit shocked. You know? And after Dad – and, well, you know yourself.'

'I do, Tim, I do. Well, how are you? I'd offer you somethin' only the electricity's out. They tell me the buildin's unsafe, too, but I can't afford to lose the business. You know? I've a lad doin' it for me on the QT. Just to get movin'. You still in the forces, Tim? I heard you were in Germany or somewhere like that? That true?'

'A bit. I'm home for a bit now.'

'Jesus, we could do with a few more troops. I don't know. Maybe they want it more than we do.'

A woman had come into the shop. She was young and she should have had a pretty face but her face was hard and McLennan thought there was some of that powdered bomb-damage dust on her skin. He was going to answer Patterson but Patterson had turned to the woman and her face with its hardness and the dust of the bomb halted McLennan mid-thought.

'Business, Tim,' Patterson said.

Two more people came into the shop. A man asked Patterson if he was open. He smiled and made a joke.

'Listen, I'll see you, Harry. I'm gonna take a look around.'

'You do that, Tim. Tell your friends what you seen.'

There was an unwritten rule that you never said out loud a man was in the forces. McLennan nodded and stepped back from the window and saw that half Patterson's name was gone from the shop sign. Patterson was weighing meat.

McLennan stood in the middle of a circle of bricks, beside a broken tree. The tree had fallen forward on to the street and touched the road with the tips of two branches. There were other shops in business, on the fringes, behind wooden façades and masking tape and swollen polythene. In death there is life, McLennan thought. It was a nothing thought. Just something to console himself.

Carol couldn't see him. Traffic branch were snowed under. Something to do with parking tickets. She had time off in a couple of days. She could see him then. McLennan wanted to smash the call-box phone. It gave him an insight into phone-box vandalism. All the worst kind of helplessness happened in phone boxes and you were always short of enough change to get what you wanted to say said. He walked down the centre of the street and noticed a girl sweeping glass in a clothes shop. She had a tight skirt and a ladder in her stockings and McLennan let his eyes wander over her body. Two dogs went for each other in a side street and a ghetto blaster threw Van Morrison around on the wind.

The music brought him to a contact he did not want to revisit. They had a radio and it got turned on in the firefight. Years ago. He could not put a date on it. Firefights and contacts ran into one another or seemed to be reruns or repeats of earlier contacts. He did not want to be alone.

He looked back at Harry Patterson's and wished they had more in common and he could stay and talk. You lost it in fragments and each fragment did not mean much in itself. What the hell could she have to do with parking tickets that could be so important?

Tonight, Tim, I can see you tonight, can you see me tonight?

I've got to stay with Mum, Carol. She needs me tonight.

Not to worry. See you later.

It was slipping away. She could not see the urgency. His town and two more had been disembowelled and she was messing with fucking parking tickets. He thought back to Anne.

The whole trip to England had been a waste of time. Except for seeing Marty. If Anne could just see this, he thought, just smell it and feel it, she would understand, see what he was saying was right. They were under attack and they had their hands tied and all they could do was watch and wait for the next one. And when every town in every county in the province was in this mess, would they untie their hands then, allow them to hit back in kind? He shook his head.

His mother had a neighbour in and they were drinking tea from china cups with chocolate biscuits and slices of fruit cake laid out on plates in parade-ground fashion. Neither of the women ate. His mother's wound was smaller than he expected. She was on more sedatives and she had stopped shaking. Her skin was still transparent and he felt he could see right through to her heart and the cracks in her heart were longer and wider. She was not a handsome woman: her neck was too long; her mouth frowned even when she was smiling; her breasts were falling, stretched and falling; and her eyes were a cold grey, like she had closed down except for what she could run without too much thought. It was not true. She still had reason to live. To keep going. Her son, her grandson. McLennan pushed thoughts of his son away because they were too painful and he could not stand such pain then. Not watching his mother try to smile at him with that frowning mouth.

'You're sleepin', Mum?' he said.

She hadn't slept more than four hours a night since her husband's death.

It was down to two now. But McLennan felt he should ask, just so she could say yes, and they could agree she was fine, that the trauma was over. Her blue rinse was vanishing and he wanted to tell her to take it all out and leave her hair the way it was meant to be.

'Have you eaten, Timmy? Have a piece of cake. I can cook somethin'. Let me cook somethin'.'

There was a degree of happiness, even in her frown. They had not come to the subject of Anne and Marty yet. It took the neighbour to bring that up. She was small and round and she wore too much lipstick. And when she mentioned Anne and Marty, there was a silence and then eyes from his mother and some embarrassed quips from McLennan and a shift to the mess the bomb had left in the centre of town.

'I have to go to Belfast this afternoon, Mum,' Tim McLennan said. 'You'll be okay? I'll be back for dinner, okay? I'll see you then.'

He hated himself for doing that. Lying to her. But he just could not stay with her, there, knowing what would come up. Not then.

The contact with the music was three lads with a holdall. RPG and a couple of assault rifles and balaclavas and latex gloves. And the radio. Two teams of four. GPMG on a hill above them. One of them just sat down when they shot him, sank down on the grass and bowed his head. One of the rounds took the side of his head off. Part of his ear lay on the ground beside him.

'You'll keep her company, Mrs Musk?'

'I will, Tim, I will.'

She made faces and the words appeared on her lips without any sound and McLennan thought it was ridiculous. As ridiculous as her name and the strange smell she always carried around with her. Her son was in the UDR. He was in the UVF, too, but she didn't know that.

'How long are you here for?' Mrs Musk asked.

'Ach, I can come and go, Mrs Musk. When I've the time. You know. I might call round and see Robbie Wilson, Mum.'

'How is Robbie?' Mrs Musk asked. 'Our Ian would like to see youse. I'll give you where he's at, Tim.'

'Okay, Mrs Musk. Robbie's doin' okay. You know Robbie. Always looks on the bright side of life.'

He whistled some of the song. Neither of the women understood.

'Leave Ian's address on the table for me,' he said.

'I will. Youse were great pals, weren't you?'

McLennan smiled and nodded. He had never been great friends with Ian Musk but there was something more than friendship at stake here and the fact that Musk had been with them in the UDR and was still in it gave him a status that went beyond friendship. McLennan smiled at his mother and hoped she would not smile back.

'See you later,' he said.

In Belfast, he walked around. Nowhere walking. Killing time. Trying to make decisions. He walked through the taxi rank at the top of Castle Street. Groups of women with bulging shopping bags and heavy coats pushed themselves and each other into the taxis. Provos, he thought. Provo taxis. Up and down the Falls. Fenian public transport. He wondered if he stood long enough would they make him. Did he look like a squaddie? He turned and faced Divis Street and the Lower Falls. There was an Army checkpoint in the middle of the road where the two streets met. The APC had a confidential telephone number and the soldiers had visors on their helmets. He looked from the checkpoint to the observation post at the top of Divis flats and from there to the mountains and then back to the checkpoint and the taxis. They were like ants, he thought. And where they were going was another country.

He walked on up Castle Street and turned right into Queen Street.

Another contact. Sometimes, he felt, he could map the whole province out in contacts. One there, two there, three there, isolated bites. They'd come along in a car and one of them had stood up through the sun roof and let off an RPG at the gates. The return fire missed the attackers and their car and killed a passer-by, looking in his glove compartment. Keystone, he thought. They brought you in and briefed you and told you to hit. And the information was always selective. Always someone protecting a source, or sheltering a policy. The layers were endless. There was a time when the regiment had a free rein, when it was there and not there, when they were pushing. But the whole thing had shifted, the rules had changed somewhere and they were cosmetic now. A media event.

The Ulster Says No sign was loose on City Hall. He never liked City Hall. It smacked of imperialism and he was not an imperialist. Its features were anachronistic, like the costumes of some badly researched period drama. What the hell was Ulster saying no to? There were so many options. He stood and watched and wished Carol was with him.

When the divorce was through he'd marry her. Marry her and maybe try and get Marty. Move them into a house near his mother. Give her a family. That'd make her happy. Carol could leave the RUC. They'd work something out. More kids. He wanted more kids. Brothers and sisters for Marty.

An RUC Land Rover swung into Donegal Square and round the back of City Hall. Two more followed it. They had a Dalek feel about them. He put his hand in under his jacket and felt the Walther and put his other hand in his pocket and touched the spare clips.

It began to rain when he was on Great Victoria Street. And the rain was thin. He walked against it and felt it on his eyes, sharp and cold, and it made him shut his eyelids till he could see no more than the path at his feet. The clouds went from grey to dark grey and black and the blackest cloud swung in from the Cave Hill direction. And the rain got heavier. He stopped and sheltered in a doorway.

Where are you going, McLennan? he thought. What are you doing with yourself, boy?

He had no answer. He should have reported back to base by now. AWOL, he thought. It had a liberating effect. But it was not true. He'd phoned Stone. Another day, Bob. Family troubles to sort out. Well, there was a truth in that. Stone was his usual overunderstanding commanding-officer self.

McLennan stared across at the Europa and wished he had a room and Carol and thought about a time they had been together. They were lying together. In some bed. Her head was on his chest. They were not speaking. It was a perfect moment, he thought. Perfect understanding. He phoned her again.

'I can't speak now, Tim. We're really pushed, love. Go to the flat. Make coffee. Watch a video.'

'I need you.'

'I know you do. God, I wish I could. I really do, love. Offer's still open for this evening. Think of it? Lots of—' She interrupted herself and whispered. 'Look, I can't talk, Tim, they're a nosy lot here. You know, I'll ring you when I can.'

'I'm fallin' in love with you,' he said.

She did not answer.

'Did you hear me?'

'Yes. We'll talk about it. I'll ring.'

'Are you?'

'What?'

'Fallin' in love with me?'

'I want you, love. I do. Now I must go. I really must. Traffic's falling apart without me.'

A car backfired outside the BBC at the junction of Bedford Street and Ormeau Avenue. People ducked. One woman screamed. McLennan did not move. He had coffee in a coffee shop on Botanic Avenue. There was a vehicle checkpoint out on the street. Two RUC and four soldiers. One of the soldiers faced south from a vegetable shop, beside the carrots and cauliflowers, rain running down his helmet, dripping from the rim in large drops, down his neck, and he hunched his shoulders with the feel of the rain on his skin. McLennan watched him try to shelter under the shop canopy but he could not see what he wanted to see from there, so he opted for the rain and tried to avoid the stream of water running from the canopy above him. McLennan laughed to himself.

You could be knee-deep in it in south Armagh, he thought. The thought did not go the way he had expected. He should have been glad he was there, in that coffee shop, out of the rain, drinking coffee, time on his hands, alive, clean, warm, safe, in Belfast, his old home, the Lord in his mercy, I'll tell me ma; but then he thought of OPs and contacts and shit and fear and he felt like he was dead. It was not a bad feeling, it was not much of a feeling at all, and that was the problem. The rain eased off and he left the coffee shop and walked through the vanishing daylight to the Botanic Gardens.

It was a different city this end. It had a different colour, a different finish, a different feel. There were no hard edges. Nothing that told you there was a war. No peace line, no slogans, no murals. People looked like they enjoyed themselves.

Maybe money was all that was different. Money insulated. Best defence in the world, money.

He sat near the palm house and watched a shuttle heading for London. The noise outlasted the vision of the plane and he leaned back in his seat and watched students from Queen's drift by. How many of them gave a shite? He tried to tell from the faces. And when there were no students he shifted to mothers with children, and when he could not figure out how many gave a shite from their faces he tried to tell religions. It wasn't so easy down here, out of his territory, where the money did the dressing. Good camouflage, money. Prods and Taigs, Taigs and Prods, they all looked the same. A lot of new Catholics had moved into south Belfast. Upwardly mobile Fenians with degrees, ambition, attitude and wine cellars. He felt left out. They were getting degrees and living like there was nothing wrong and he was up to his eyes in mud and risking his life. He let himself feel superior. Like he knew something they didn't. He needed it then. Watching them. With their don't-care walks and their don't-care expressions. They didn't seem to care at all. It might as well have been a million miles away. And he could not tell religions.

The ball rolled to his feet and the baby boy tripped his way to the ball. McLennan picked the ball up and handed it to the boy. The kid's hands were too small and he could not hold it.

'He likes to kick it. Remember when we used to kick balls?'

McLennan swung his head. A bearded man, about six foot and built like a blockhouse, was standing by the railings across the path. He had his hands on the railings and his head was turning around on its axis, like he was checking for something.

'Don't you know me, Tim?'

McLennan knew the face but he could not pin it down. He thought about going for his Walther but did not. If it had been a hit, he'd have been dead by now. He cursed himself for letting someone get that close.

'Lenny, Tim, Lenny Beggs. Remember?'

McLennan tried to rearrange the last vision he had of Lenny Beggs and match it with the man looking at him. The jet-black hair was new, the big nose was the same, the dark-rimmed NHS glasses he couldn't remember. Beggs wore cotton trousers and an anorak over a tweed jacket. Two of his teeth were yellow on the left side of his mouth and he had a scar running from his chin to his cheek. The scar was the result of a knife fight in Belfast in the mid-seventies. McLennan remembered that. And he had hands the size of fishpans.

McLennan remembered more. He'd been a good centre half in their soccer days. Hard man, Lenny Beggs. Hard Man Beggs, they called him. Sounded great on the Shankill when they were kids and they needed a really hard man to put the boot in for them. But that was then. That was when he'd had an interest in soccer and they'd lived on the Shankill. Lenny still lived around the Shankill and they called him other things now. He had different interests. Things that made a walk with a kid and a ball in this park something more than routine.

'Lenny Beggs! Christ Almighty, you haven't changed much,' McLennan said.

He was still thinking about going for his gun.

Beggs made an attempt at a smile.

'You have. You're bigger than the little snot I remember. Been doin' weights, Tim?'

McLennan did not rise to the bait. He moved his eyes around the park.

'Just put on a bit, Lenny,' he said.

'So you've met my wee boy, Tim McLennan. What do you think? Chip off the old block?'

'I hope not.'

'You don't mean that.'

McLennan was going through all he knew about Lenny Beggs. Sifting through files and rumours and evidence and chit-chat. Been busy, Lenny, he thought, very busy. There were two conflicting emotions in him: one was a complete suspicion of Lenny Beggs and the other was a swelling in his heart that he could not control – childhood memories, empathies, something shared, and it was in danger of wiping away what he knew about Beggs.

'I heard you were away again,' McLennan said.

It wasn't anything more than bait. Beggs knew it.

'Oh, no, Tim. Not me. Law-abidin', that's me. Loyal son. You're thinkin' about years ago. That was at Her Majesty's pleasure. At her pleasure. Always glad to give Her Majesty pleasure. I was a wild lad then.'

McLennan was going to ask what was new. He did not.

Beggs had been involved with a Shankill Road vigilante group in the early seventies, when he was a teenager. They caught a barman from the Falls one night and gave him the thousand-cuts treatment. People who heard it said he was begging to be killed when they'd finished with him. Beggs was convicted and given a pleasure sentence and then ten years later he was fingered for another killing on the word of a supergrass. But the case fell apart. By that time, Lenny had moved up the ranks of the loyal organisation he belonged to, running drinking clubs and squeezing cuts from taxi drivers and building workers. There was talk of drugs but no one ever proved anything. Lenny had learned the value of distance. And he hadn't lost some of his more instinctive functions. There were other things he hadn't lost either.

'You were indeed, Lenny,' McLennan said. He kept shaking his head. 'What are you doin' down this end of town? Way off your usual beat. I heard you never moved from there.'

'Gossip, Tim, like everythin' about me. Careless talk. And you know what that costs. It used to be your beat, Tim. Don't get many visits from you now, son.'

McLennan was still twisting his eyes to see if Lenny Beggs had anyone with him. There were three guys in the park now who looked like they should have been arrested on suspicion of something. Maybe they were Lenny's people, maybe they weren't. McLennan leaned back and felt the Walther and watched the three of them move.

'No,' McLennan said. 'Always meant to. I've been too busy, I suppose.'

'So I believe.'

Beggs moved over to his son and picked him up and the kid laughed. Then he put his hand out. There was a tattoo on the wrist.

'Long time no see, Tim.'

McLennan did not take the hand. He watched the three watchers. One of them had a paper. The light made features difficult but he could see a moustache and a pair of white socks. Beggs held his hand, almost testing McLennan. McLennan still did not take the hand. Instead, he stood up and touched the kid's head and rubbed it.

'Nice lad, Lenny. Now what's all this about? I'm armed, Lenny. And I'll have you and whoever's with you dropped before you can blink if you don't answer me now.'

Beggs looked around him and shrugged his shoulders.

'Oh, come on, Tim, come on,' he said. He spread his arms in a defensive gesture. 'I don't know what you mean, Staff Sergeant – or is it Mr McLennan yet? I heard rumours, Tim, that you might be in for a promotion.'

'I could have you just for sayin' that, Lenny. I told you, I'm armed.'

'Hey, I believe you, I believe you. But I'm not. I'm just out walkin' my wee lad. A man's still allowed to do that, Tim, in this here province of ours. Might be a time, though, when he isn't.'

McLennan looked at each of the watchers in turn. He gestured with his head to Beggs.

'Yeah,' Beggs said. 'Not very good, are they? I'm trainin' them in. Sign of the times, Tim. It's not all that safe for a man in my position to come to a public park. There's evil men in our society, Tim. Anyway, I'm glad to see you're okay. How long's it been?'

'I never counted, Lenny. Maybe twenty years.'

'Is it that long? Where'd all the time go?'

'I know where some of yours went, Lenny.'

'You always were smart, Tim. Quick with your mouth. I used to like that about you. Good fun. You and that mate of yours. What was his name?'

McLennan figured Beggs knew. But he answered anyway.

'Robbie. Robbie Wilson.'

'Yeah, Robbie. Good soccer player, Robbie. Too bad, too bad.'

'What is?'

'Oh, nothin'.'

Beggs laughed and put his son down. He pushed the ball along the path. The kid chased the ball and McLennan thought of his own son and must have given it away by his face because Beggs asked him if he had a family. McLennan knew by the tone Beggs already knew but he answered that question as well. The small-talk went on, minute after minute, McLennan watching the watchers, but it got smaller.

Then McLennan walked over to the railings and leaned against them. He watched Beggs try to watch his son and turn to talk at the same time. Beggs called the kid over and the kid refused to come.

'Mutiny,' McLennan said.

'Ulster backbone,' Beggs said. 'Knows how to say no.'

He folded his arms and tried to figure out when he'd last seen Lenny Beggs. It was on television. A strike. And there was Lenny – combat jacket, scarf around his mouth, black sunglasses. It was ridiculous him trying to disguise himself. Lenny Beggs stood out like a whore at a church tea party. But there he was, standing at a barricade of cars and buses and barrels, holding a stick in his hand, mouthing on about betrayal and sell-out, and threatening. He did not have a beard then. But he did have a slight speech impediment, a stammer when the sentences got too big. And during the pauses, he threw his head back like he was getting ready to butt someone. The interviewer stood back. He had no speech impediment now, Lenny Beggs.

Beggs lifted his son up and then grabbed the ball and stuffed it in one of the pockets of his anorak.

'Yeah, I like to get out with the family when I can. Walk around. You should come down to visit us some day, Tim. There's people down the Shankill would like to see you again. Been hearin' things. Good things. Bit of a star, Tim.'

'I don't know what you're talkin' about.'

'No. No, I don't suppose you do.' He smacked his hands together. 'Well, I better go. The wife'll kick up hell if I don't get him back for his tea on time. Orders. Nice seein' you, Tim. I'll see you again, maybe. Maybe we could meet – for a drink, like. Talk over old times.'

'I don't think so, Lenny.'

Lenny looked around and smiled.

'Well, chew on it,' he said. 'Enjoy your walk. Love to the wife.'

He winked. McLennan had an inclination to pull his gun out and drop Beggs there and then. But he did not. And afterwards he would ask himself why he did not respond.

He watched Beggs walk off with his son in his arms. The three watchers vanished with him. McLennan felt for his gun again. It could have been a coincidence. He looked up at the deepening sky to see a pig. Then he swung around in a circle. Bad day, Tim, he thought. Just a bad day in a bad week. He tried to ignore what had happened, then he tried to figure out what it had all been about. Neither worked. He was left with a picture of Lenny Beggs, almost unreal now, like he'd stepped out of a time warp and then stepped back into it. McLennan felt a chill. It might have been the dropping temperature. He took a taxi to where his car was parked and he drove out of Belfast along the Shankill without stopping.

10

OVER A HUNDRED and thirty miles away on the other side of the border, Danny Loughlin watched a stag step out of the treeline of a conifer forest. It was brown. The trees were green. The day was dying bright. Fragile. There was a wind from the west. Showers every half-hour. Hail once. The crosswires of the telescopic sight fixed on the animal's right eye. The animal moved. Loughlin twisted his body to follow. The stag looked round and took three more steps and looked round again. The wind blew patterns in his coat. Loughlin could see scars in the hair. He was an old stag. He had an old stag's eyes. Loughlin held his sight on the eye. The eye had a residue of scum in the corner and the pupil was wide. Alert. The stag pulled its head around and looked at Loughlin. Loughlin fired.

'Shit, Danny!' John Cusack said.

The bullets hit the stag's head first. One through the eye. Whisper shot. Silent. Armalite and noise suppressor. The rest of the magazine followed. Twenty-nine 5.56mm rounds: five more to the head, and the animal's knees were already folding; ten to the body in three groups, and the animal's legs had gone completely; the remainder into the jerking flesh while it lay on the ground. Small pieces of flesh and bone were scattered around the stag as it was hit and blood came from its mouth.

'Great!' Loughlin said. 'Bloody great.'

He looked at Cusack beside him. Cusack shook his head.

'That's thirty rounds wasted, Danny. Thirty rounds. You better eat that sucker. Lead and all.'

'You bet I will. That skin is mine. Did you see that? Some shot – eh, Dessie? I can still put them where they count.'

'Deer don't shoot back,' Cusack said. 'But then that suits you, Danny, doesn't it?'

Loughlin frowned and looked to Dessie Hart.

'I hope your aim with the fifty is as good,' Hart said.

'You could always get someone else. Someone better.'

'You're it, Danny. I don't have anyone trained on the fifty I can spare. Cover fire, Danny, that's all.'

'Yeah, I know. I said I would and I will.'

Hart blew air out his nose and furrows appeared on his brow, one by one almost.

'Come on, let's get back to the job. I never trust these places,' Hart said. 'We've got a lot to get through. And I want to do it quick and get out.'

'Sure, Dessie.'

Loughlin saw a pattern in the freckles on Hart's head where the hairline had receded. There was a scar in the freckles. Dessie'd been hit in the head years ago in a firefight near Keady. They all thought he was dead when they got him over the border. He got pains in the head now and again. And he had trouble with his left hand in very cold weather, but he was still going. They couldn't kill Dessie Hart, Loughlin thought.

Hart saw that look on Loughlin's face. He turned away.

'Show me the man who can get that kind of on-target with one of these beauties on full automatic,' Loughlin said. 'I was one of the first to use one of these lovelies. When you two were still watchin' *Blue Peter* I was out. Dundalk was El Paso and the Armalite had a meanin' all of its own. Bet you don't think much of it, John?'

'It's a good weapon, Danny. Light. It's had its problems. The AKs are better for what we're doing.'

He picked up a Rumanian AKM from the holdall at his feet.

'Boil it, freeze it, kick it, dump it, and it'll still come good when you need it. Best in the world for a guerrilla army. Don't need much training to use an AK, Danny. Sentimentality's fine but we gotta be practical, like you keep saying. Old hands like you can go with the Armalite if you like, and the G3s and FNs, but the new lads should get one of these till they prove themselves. We have enough of these. We don't have enough of the other gear.' Cusack stopped himself. 'Anyway, that's not the damn point here, is it?' he said.

They walked along a mud track to the forest. The forest ran up a slope for about five hundred yards. All around them there were forests running along the hillsides. It was good protection. A river ran down one of the slopes, through a gap in the trees, and small streams fed the river from every side. The ground was bog and brown topped with heather and long grass. Most of it was wet.

Hart knelt down beside the stag and touched it with his hand. He could feel the warmth of the animal draining away. Blood ran down the brown coat to the mud and the grass. Hart touched the blood. He raised his finger and stood up and went over to Danny Loughlin.

'First blood, Danny,' he said. 'Good luck. I hope it carries.'

Loughlin smiled.

Hart drew his finger across Loughlin's cheek. Loughlin touched his cheek.

'Maybe this thing will work,' he said. 'Venison and lead for dinner.'

He crouched down beside the stag and ran his hand across its body. Then he tried to lift it.

'Come on, lads, give us a hand,' he said.

'You killed it,' Cusack said. 'It's your load.'

'Yeah, but I did it for us.'

'I didn't ask you to, Danny. Neither of us did. We don't need this. Dump it or carry it yourself. But it's your load.'

'Dessie?' Loughlin asked.

'It's up to you, Danny. We've business to take care of,' Hart said.

He looked at Cusack and smiled. Loughlin scowled. He tried to get the animal into position so that he could throw it over his shoulders. He could see Hart and Cusack had something between them, something shared, something he had lost, or maybe never had, and it made him angry. He said something about queers to himself. They could go fuck each other. He'd do it himself.

'I put the first shot in the eye,' Loughlin said.

'You did that, Danny,' Cusack said. 'Clean kill. That's what it's about. You think you could do it at night at maximum distance?'

Loughlin's face went into the boggy mud and he swallowed some of the bog water and spat it out and pulled the dead stag over his shoulders and tried to lift himself up from the knees. He did not get up. The animal was too heavy and he was unbalanced. He fell back into the mud. Cusack and Hart laughed. They turned and walked back down the track.

'Drag it, Danny,' Cusack said. 'On all fours, if you have to. They used to make us do things like that in the Corps. Gunnies with the sense of humour of the Marquis de Sade. Okay, maggots, you're going to suffer. Prepare yourselves to suffer. I'm telling you, Dessie, you guys don't know what real suffering is. You hear that, Danny?'

Loughlin was dragging the stag by the hind legs.

Their camp was a canvas bivouac over the remains of a stone cottage on the edge of a treeline. There were smaller trees to the left and right, young saplings taking root. No one knew who had lived there or how the cottage happened to be so far away from anything. There was nothing resembling a road leading to it. They had hiked overland from a drop-off point about three miles away. There were some tracks and firebreaks for the forests but the mud had made them impassible even in four-wheel drives. They hiked with backpacks and weapons. They took it in turns to carry the 50-calibre machine-gun and its mount. It was beside the wall now, covered in a tarpaulin.

Tate and Bruddy were at the bivouac, preparing food. Ger Kelly and a Dundalk volunteer named Eddie Barnes, who sniffed like he was a cocaine addict, stood guard on two high points with walkie-talkies. Eddie had an Armalite he didn't really know how to use and Ger had an FNC. The FNC had a folding butt. They each had field glasses and nightvision goggles. Danny Loughlin had dickers around the area, at a distance, but Ger and Eddie were there in case trouble came from anywhere else. Anyway, Cusack and Hart wanted the whole exercise to be military, let people get the feel for being in the field.

There was no real need for the guards to be armed. IRA General Order Number Eight kept engagements with Irish Army personnel and gardai to a minimum. Number Eight was more a recognition of practicalities than any moral considerations. Bank robberies in the south had often ended in gun battles with the gardai. And when the IRA had kidnapped a newspaper executive in Dublin they'd ended the operation in a gun battle with gardai and Irish soldiers. Two gardai were killed. A certain amount of revenge was taken when another attempted kidnap ended in the ambush and capture of the IRA unit by gardai.

Bruddy Holmes stood up when John Cusack reached the bivouac. Cusack nodded to him and then sat down on a rucksack and started to strip the AKM he had been using. They had been firing weapons all day, practising positions and tactics. The area was one of three they used for training. The other two were in Sligo and Donegal. People around who could hear the shots were people who would keep what they'd heard to themselves. But there weren't many people around. It was poor country.

'What we got to eat?' Cusack asked.

He did not look Bruddy Holmes directly in the eyes. He could not. It made him judge and he did not want to judge. He wanted to give him the benefit. But Billy Holmes followed his brother like a shadow and an organisation that put so much weight on blood ties couldn't ignore bad blood any more than it could good.

'Bangers, soup, eggs, burgers, sir,' Holmes said.

Cusack threw his eyes to heaven and then over to Tate.

'Would you ever cut the sir shit out, Bruddy. None of that here. We're all in this together. Aren't we?'

He reached out and dipped his finger in a pan full of sausages and put it to his tongue. The grease was bubbling. The fat spat out over the side of the pan. Tate had cut up buns and onions. He had them beside each other on an enamel plate. They could have brought nothing, scavenged from what was around them – deer, rabbits, hares, anything else they found – but Hart wasn't doctrinaire about lifestyle and he knew the limitations of the people around him. Cusack couldn't argue. They'd done the in-country thing, when necessary, days spent trying to suck nutrition from a squirrel or a rat, nights waiting for a patrol to come along. Then move on to the next site and repeat, back and forth, till the mud and the rain flowed with their blood and they were so close to pneumonia they could hear their insides crying out for a rest.

There was a pot of soup beside the sausages. The soup was thick. It had flecks of burnt wood in it. The pot Tate had cooked it in was black and there were lumps of soup stuck to the side of it.

'I just thought – I don't want people to think what happened to Billy affects me,' Bruddy said.

Cusack gave him a pep-talk. It was mechanical.

'You're your own man, Bruddy, I hope,' Cusack said. 'You do what has to be done, you'll do fine. Okay?'

'Yeah.'

'And group your shots, Bruddy. Ones, twos and threes. Anything else is for getting out of trouble or just a fucking waste of good ammunition. You know the kind of organisation goes into getting ammunition? I'm telling you, Bruddy, think about it. And keep your body down. Give them the smallest target.'

Bruddy nodded. Any kind of acceptance made him excited. 'He wasn't such a bad lad,' he said.

Cusack did not answer.

Bruddy turned a few sausages. The fat rose and spat in all directions. Cusack had stripped his rifle. Spots of rain were coming down on the bivouac.

'Jesus, I'm starvin'.'

Hart was rubbing his hands together. He had the hood of his combat jacket over his head. He shoved in beside Cusack.

'He wasn't such a bad lad, was he?'

Hart looked at Holmes and shook his head.

'Who?'

'Billy.'

'Leave it, Bruddy,' Tate said. 'Leave it be. There's no sense bringin' it up. It's done. And it was done right. Right, John?'

'Yeah.'

Cusack looked at his watch and then stuck his head out of the bivouac. A drop of water touched his lips.

'Bad weather for this time of year. Good for some. Gives us more dark. That's good. Bad weather and dark. Hurry up with the grub, Tate. Bruddy, go see what's up with Danny. Dessie, where'd he go?'

'He's still draggin' that bloody stag, John. It'll take him all night, I'd say.'

'Not fuckin' likely!'

They all stood up out of the bivouac. Loughlin was coming. He had the stag's head over his shoulder and a knife in his hand. His shoulder and that side of his combat jacket were drenched in blood. Deep red, almost black blood. His hands had blood on them, too.

'There's nothin' left of it. You mad bastard,' Hart said.

He had a gap between his teeth and when he raised his voice there was a whistle. Loughlin stood before them and threw the stag's head down at Cusack's feet. Pieces of skin and sinew and hide were trailing from the head.

'Where's the rest of it?'

'I dumped it. We could have had venison if you bastards had helped me.'

'And what if someone finds it?'

'No one will. I stuffed it in a boghole. You know, you've seen them used. Hide anythin' in a boghole. There's a Brit about twenty miles that way . . .'

'Hey,' Cusack said.

Loughlin had put his foot in the stag's mouth.

'No discussing operations, Danny.'

'Right, I forgot.'

He pulled a small flask from his hip pocket and unscrewed the cap and swigged it. Then he offered it to Cusack. Cusack shook his head. His eyes tightened and his skin became pale and Loughlin could see the vein at his temple pulsating.

'No,' Cusack said.

'I forgot that as well. You don't on duty. Well, I do. My father told me never to trust a man who doesn't know when to take a drink, know that?'

He offered the flask around. Tate took some. Hart refused. Holmes pulled up his hood and went back to his sausages. Cusack checked the mechanism of his AKM and then put the safety catch on and placed it in the holdall.

Hart pulled a sheet of paper from inside his combat jacket and unfolded it. Three drops of rain touched the paper. He reached over and grabbed some chopped onions and put the pieces in his mouth and chewed. He felt the sting of the onion rise through his nose. The paper had a rough diagram on it. The checkpoint in the centre. He had arrows coming at the checkpoint, double-lined arrows filled in the middle, and there were letters. He moved his finger across the diagram.

'Anyone got anythin' they want to say about the plan?' he asked. 'Danny? And I mean the plan, Danny, not the operation.'

Loughlin went to speak and then checked himself. He pulled his pipe from his pocket. There was blood on it. He rubbed the blood off with rainwater from the grass.

'If we catch them cold, then we're in and out before they know what's hit them,' Cusack said. 'And we have a textbook operation.'

'Danny,' Hart said, 'once the bomb goes off and you're out of there and back across the border to your second position, keep firin' till you get the word we're clear. Okay?'

'Sure, Dessie. Who'll be my driver?'

'I'll let you know. We might have to switch jobs, so everyone gets to know everyone else's job. You just concentrate on what you have to do, Danny. And non-stop into that tower, Danny. No let-up. We'll be dependin' on you. We're gettin' the explosive and armour-piercin' rounds the day after tomorrow. I don't care if you don't score hits. Just keep the bastards in that tower scared shitless. Right?'

Loughlin nodded. His throat moved out and in.

'And if there's any kind of trouble with the Hino, we'll dump her and move back this way over these hills and under your cover to the back-up transport here and here. Right?'

'See some mile records bein' set, then,' Tate said.

'This is serious, Tate,' Hart said. 'I want everyone aware. Any chance you get, go over the maps you've been given.'

He repeated himself. Like he wasn't sure himself and had to hear it again.

'Anyway, all of youse all know your positions for now.'

They nodded. Hart moved his hand around the diagram.

'These two pill-boxes. There shouldn't be anyone in them . . .'

'Shouldn't?' Loughlin said.

'Won't, Danny,' Cusack said.

'Tate, this control box. I was thinkin'. We'll hit it with an RPG and a flamethrower – one of the Tyrone lads is checked out on a flamethrower – but I want you to spray it with GPMG as well. Then you can back Ger and Danny against that tower. And when we smash the gate, you and Ger just spray whatever's sprayable with GPMG. You know? Everythin'. Okay?'

Tate went serious and nodded.

'Prisoners?'

'No. Tyrone tried taking a couple of prisoners last time out and they got a volunteer with half his arm torn off for their trouble. No prisoners. If we do this quick enough the bastards won't have time to get out of bed. We'll hit the accommodation block with an RPG and the flamethrower to keep them occupied but the bomb'll do the real damage. Right, we're inside, Danny's keepin' the OP tower pinned down, we're pourin' fire from our side at it and anythin' else. Then the Hino pulls out and the Hiace with the bomb drives in under our cover. John!'

Cusack took over.

'The bomb's placed and the fuse set for one-twenty. That means everyone back in the Hino pronto. No delays. So get fit. You could lose a few pounds, Tate. Anyone gets left behind we're gonna be picking him off the walls. We have to be on the escape road when the bomb goes off. It's our main cover. Border time west from this crossroads, two minutes fifty seconds. We'll have at least two ASUs covering this route and two more for diversions on this road east.'

Holmes put his hand up as if he was in a school classroom. Cusack sighed.

'Yeah, Bruddy.'

'Why don't we just go back down the road we came on, it's shorter.'

'Two reasons. One, that's the first route they'll follow up. And two, the Hino'd have to turn one-eighty out of the checkpoint. Too difficult. No. Keep the movements simple. Straightforward.'

Holmes nodded. Cusack looked at Loughlin. Loughlin had lit his pipe. Smoke trailed off around his eyes.

'And the bomb?' Tate asked.

'Five to seven hundred, I'd say. Engineers are still calculating. These walls should do a lot of the work for us. Increase the impact. But it's the key to this operation. Getting the bomb right inside. Right here. Like you did in Fermanagh, Dessie.'

Cusack turned to Loughlin. 'I know Danny thinks a proxy would do the trick.' He looked at Danny Loughlin with a respect that made Loughlin uneasy. 'Besides the obvious disadvantages of a proxy, like the fact that the fuckers are shitting themselves and don't always do what they're told, there's security problems. It's a weak link in the chain. And anyway, the best we could hope for would be outside on the road. We'd have to use more explosives, there'd be less damage to the objective, more collateral damage. We thought about getting one in here, this house next door. But they watch everything there from this tower. It'd be impossible. Anyway, we want to show them we're a serious threat, not a bunch of hoods. Put the wind up them. They build these things to make a point and we can blow them up to make a point. War. Dangerous, I know, but they all are, and if we play it right, it'll go fine. Okay?'

'What about if we just rolled a truck at them,' Danny Loughlin said. 'Back it with fire from this position. The way Francie Devine did at Aughnacloy. Remember that? You were banged up, Dessie.'

'It didn't work, Danny,' Hart said. 'The incline isn't good enough for a runaway. Anyway, runaways do just that. They go all over the damn place. Maybe in someone's front door. Not smart.'

Loughlin felt humiliated and his face showed it.

'We've put a lot of preparation into this,' Hart said. 'We've run dickers in and out and back and forth through that checkpoint. And remember, there'll be a skeleton crew here. The rest of them kippin'. Danny's boys will be checkin' for patrols right up to the off. If anythin' looks wrong, we scrub. If it goes accordin' to plan, we'll wipe this fuckin' thing off the map.'

'Five hundred pounds plus is big, isn't it?' Bruddy Holmes said. 'It's a small place, Dessie.'

'You have a problem, Bruddy?' Cusack said.

Holmes looked around him and thought.

'No,' he said.

'This end of the village will probably sustain a fifty-plus percentage. Maybe even civilian fatalities. But I think we can live with it. The checkpoint end is Brit. There'll be no tears for them and when our people see what we do to that checkpoint, they'll be cheering us. Might even get us a few more volunteers. A lot of the houses will be fucked up but the NIO can pay for that. Kids will love us if we fuck up their school again. Last time, they were dancing. What we've planned is safer than a runaway and a proxy. But we can only take as much care as the success of the operation allows. If it comes to it, civilians take their chances. We're not going into the village passing out leaflets.'

'We're goin' in heavy,' Dessie Hart said. 'Heavy as needs. Give them somethin' to think about.'

'Seems like it's all worked out,' Danny Loughlin said. 'Sure what could possibly go wrong.'

'With you along, Danny, nothin',' Hart said. 'The flamethrower'll add a psychological edge to things. Fear factor. Flamethrower really scares people shitless. And in combination with the RPGs and the GPMGs, it'll give us a punch that'll knock them out. So, straight in, straight out, like this, lads. Surprise is our main weapon. We'll catch them unawares and we'll wipe that fuckin' thing out. Then we drive straight out, turn left and leg it, as they say. Danny?'

Loughlin's mouth was moving, like he wanted to say something.

'You know something, Danny?' Cusack said.

Loughlin slapped his leg.

'The Hino'll get through that gate?'

'It will,' Hart said. 'Reinforced. It's been worked out. Mathematically. Anyway, you don't have to do anythin' more than work the fifty, Danny. Just work the fifty and fall back and cover us. Simple.'

Loughlin played with his pipe and nodded.

'Unless you're sayin' you won't do it,' Hart said then.

It caught everyone off guard. Loughlin's face lost colour.

'If you don't want to do it, okay. But I think you should tell me now. Do you understand? I need you on this one, Danny. I need heavy fire to cover us. We'll have cover behind you, Danny. Second-line cover. So think about it, and tell me now if you don't want to do it. There's nothin' stoppin' you standin' down. There's nothin' stoppin' you goin' home and sleepin'.'

Loughlin looked at the others. Then at Hart. Colour returned to his face.

'I said I'd come and I'm good for my word. You know, this reminds me of the Custom House in twenty-one. Remember that?'

He got no reaction.

'But if it's on, then I go,' he said.

'Glad to hear it, Danny.'

'Anyone else got anythin' to say?'

No one said anything. They looked at Loughlin with a look he did not need.

Loughlin broke a twig. He let his face twitch and tried to stop it. He could not.

When they had eaten, Bruddy Holmes and Tate Byrne relieved Ger Kelly and Eddie Barnes and Hart went through things with them. Cusack sat outside the bivouac on a fallen stone. He let his gaze drift over the stone walls and the grass and moss growing on them. He was confident. They could do this. They could take this target. They had the will and when it came down to it will was what counted. Pull the trigger and drop the enemy. It was a simple calculation and the purity excited him. This was it, what he'd come for. Operations like this. Compensated for having to pump some stunned reservist in front of his wife and kids.

He had killed one in Portadown. The bloke drove a delivery van. They followed the van and walked up behind him when he was opening his front door. Four to the back of the head. He hung on to the key. Don McLean was playing on a radio in the house and there were kids playing on a swing two houses up. The reservist lasted a couple of days in hospital. His wife opened the door and her husband kind of stood there, hanging on to the key in the door, and then fell into her arms. Cusack was backing off down the driveway. She watched him and said nothing and a kid came round the side of the house and asked him who he was. He didn't like that. He did it but he didn't like it. But this was war and you had to do things you didn't like.

'What if we do blow that fuckin' village apart, Dessie?' Danny Loughlin said. He said it quietly, while Hart was stripping a rifle. 'And there's some of them our people?'

Hart shrugged his shoulders.

'If they didn't build their forts beside civilians then civilians wouldn't be in danger. Like John says, this is war, Danny. We try to minimise casualties. We do our best. If the locals stay inside and hit the floor they'll be okay. Maybe they won't have any roofs on their houses, but they'll be okay. Best we can do. The firin'll give them plenty of time to take cover. Everyone'll get a chance. Except the target people. Anyway, these five houses are all Orange. So who gives a fuck there? We'll keep the collateral damage down. Good plannin', Danny, it's the key here.'

Loughlin dipped his head. He had been hoping for more from Hart.

'Ach, maybe what happened to Mal and Bik's gettin' to me,' he said.

'And you think it doesn't get to me?' Hart said.

Loughlin turned away.

'I'll go give the lads a cuppa,' he said.

'I could do with a woman,' Eddie Barnes said.

He threw his hair back and kissed the air with his lips. His lips were too big for his mouth and they spilled out when he moved them. His hair was shaved up to the level of his ears and then thick and falling to one side. He wore jeans and a pair of climbing boots. The climbing boots had a gash in one of them. He'd torn it crawling over a rock with Hart and Cusack, trying to outflank Danny Loughlin and Kelly. It was a tag game Cusack had invented, one on one, two on two, three on three. The aim was always the same. A kill.

'You need your fuckin' balls taken off,' Dessie Hart said.

Barnes made a face because he was new to the group and he was unsure of where he stood. He'd been in a cell based around Dundalk, doing bombing jobs into south-east Armagh and south Down. Then the unit leader went and got himself arrested for leaning on a Chinese restaurant in

Dundalk and was banged up in Portlaoise for a couple of years. The unit went into a slump. Two members ended up being kneecapped when they went into the insurance fraud business for themselves. It wasn't so much that they went into the business as that they didn't bother telling Northern Command or GHQ. The unit was stood down and there were attempts under way to get things moving again. They'd put a couple of bombs on the Dublin-Belfast railway line and rolled a bomb down the track at the checkpoint between Dundalk and Newry. One soldier was killed. Eddie'd already drifted west into the Monaghan-Armagh axis where Dessie Hart held sway. He even moved house and got engaged to a girl in Castleblaney.

'Is that Maguire lassie not good enough for you?'

'She's my regular. But a lad needs more. Ask Tate. Tate fucks anythin' that spreads. Tate's a fuckin' stallion. I'm learnin' from him.'

'That Maggie's a bit of all right,' Ger Kelly said. 'Could throw a lot over her. I heard she was a wild one. I have family in Belfast. They knew her there. Bruddy knows her. But he won't say.'

'Bit of respect,' Cusack said. 'Show a bit of respect.'

Ger looked at Eddie and they smiled and then looked at Hart and the three of them laughed.

'Bit of gra there, John?' Hart said. 'Do I detect a bit of gra?'

Cusack pulled his .357 from a shoulder holster. He unloaded it and then reloaded it and spun the chamber and replaced it in the holster.

'I just think volunteers should give each other respect.'

'She's a nice woman, Maggie. Married, though. Kids. Husband's an eejit. I know his family. All stuck up, them O'Neills. They had money and they flashed it about. Brian was always sayin' how he was going to this and that and all he did was lose it all. He wanted me to burn down a dance hall he had. Offered me money. Me. Money.'

'What did you do?'

'I said no.' Hart smiled. 'Wasn't enough. Wouldn't have even paid for the petrol. But Maggie's a good woman. Remember that, Eddie. She's a good volunteer, Maggie. Keep it in mind.'

'Yeah, sure, Dessie.'

John Cusack put Maggie O'Neill from his mind. Her body stayed longer than it should have. He got rid of her face but her body stayed. The last time he'd had anyone was a year before, maybe more, he could not tell exactly, in Dublin. A pick-up and a drive in a taxi to her flat on the north side. She was a radiographer and she was hot as hell and the evening was hot as hell and they sweat buckets up against her door and on her floor and on her stairs and on a table and then in her bed. It was lust on his part and vacuous and she went on about out-of-bodyness and spiritual experiences. Then she left him lying in bed and went out on a call.

'Weapons check in ten minutes,' he said.

11

ROBBIE WILSON'S FOOT slipped on a small granite stone and he lost his balance and had to grab Tim McLennan's arm. His fingers dug into the oilskin and if you looked you could see small indentations from his nails in it. He had delicate fingers, almost feminine, with no hair and a skin that looked too young for his age. His nails were even and extended only a couple of millimetres out over the ends of the delicate fingers. There were scars on the fingers and on the rest of his hands.

'Nearly went there, Timmy,' he said.

'Nearly, Robbie. Just hang on there. You hang on.'

It was the second day Tim McLennan had not reported back.

Wilson linked tighter. He could feel the damp breeze on his chin and the right side of his face. He had no feeling on the left side of his face. He imagined the day: grey tarp, westerly coming round from a south flank, long grass balancing remains of rain in a gentle dance, water running around the stones at the edges of the track they were on, pulling tiny grains of mud and stone with it to the lake. There was fencing both sides of them, and blackthorn in spaced clumps, still holding a few sloes, bottom-of-the-tray sloes, past their sell-by date. In the fields, and if he listened hard over the wind he could hear them, sheep destroyed the dance of the grass. There was a tall rhododendron around. Planted. He could not remember where exactly. He reached up and pulled his cloth cap further down over his forehead. His forehead was sensitive to temperature.

They walked down the track and Robbie listened to the sound of their boots on the granite stones and he knew when they were at the boathouse.

The boathouse was a small brick building with a red roof and the leftovers of a bird's nest wedged between the roof and a wall. The roof was corrugated. There was a slip running from the boathouse to the water. The door was padlocked. It was a metal door and it had been scratched with graffiti and was rusting at the hinges. The padlock was rusting, too. The rust on the padlock was deeper than the rust on the door. The graffiti were indecipherable.

'Tell me what it's like, Timmy. Tell me,' Robbie Wilson said. 'And leave nothin' out.'

'It's the lake, Robbie. You know. It's there. It's always been there. There's a few birds left over there. I don't know what. Maybe swans. Wait for a better look. There's tall trees on the far bank and runnin' up the hill. The fields on the right are empty.'

'What colour?'

'Green. They're always green.'

'Look again. Harder.'

McLennan looked at the fields sloping into the grey tarp. There was a silver there he had not noticed before and it came and went with the breeze. He told Robbie Wilson.

'I knew it. I knew it. See, I knew it,' Robbie Wilson said. 'Go on.'

'The water's dark.'

'Come on, Timmy, you can do better than that. Superman Rambo, you can do better than that. Everythin'. All the movements, all the ripples. I can hear it and I can imagine it, just confirm it to me. Just that.'

'It's ripplin' over there, where the birds are, near the reeds. I can't tell you what the birds are yet. A couple of them are dark. They're smaller than swans and they don't look like ducks. Maybe they're lost. Flyin' south and lost. It happens. There's a lighter shade of dark to your left and small waves in the middle. It'll be bumpy. You still want to go out?'

'Yes. And the trees around?'

'Losin' leaves, those that can. The spruce are their usual selves. For ever.'

'Any sign of fish? Any ripples? Shouldn't be this time of year.'

'No. It's boggy to the right, further down this bank. There's high grass and the water is in among the trees. Plenty of moss. Mud's knee-deep over there, I'd say.'

'That'll be the rain, Timmy. Terrible amount of rain we had this last month. More than usual. Not so cold, though. I can tell with my head. No hair but a good temperature gauge when it's naked. Let's go.'

The water was well up the slip, almost at the door of the boathouse. Robbie Wilson stood and took the air in through his nostrils while Tim McLennan got the small boat and the oars and pushed the boat into the water. The boat was fibreglass. There was a metal walkway leading from the boathouse to a pontoon anchored to the bottom of the lake. The lake was too dark to see the bottom except at the edges and at the edges the water lapped in a kind of whiplash motion, threatening, holding and then coming in small foamy tongues before receding. Tim told Robbie about that when they were in the boat.

McLennan had the rods and tackle in two bags hanging from one shoulder. When Robbie was settled, he gave him the bags and put the oars in the rowlocks and began rowing. The oars cut into the dark water at a sharp angle and it changed colour when they had passed through. Tim didn't tell Robbie this. He was too busy getting his rhythm and thinking his own thoughts. He thought in snapshots: a girl on the London shuttle with a scared-of-flying mouth, an RUC patrol on the Shankill, his mother's garden sinking into winter sleep. Robbie Wilson didn't ask Tim McLennan about any of that. He just imagined.

When he was rowing, McLennan stared into the bottom of the fibreglass boat, trying to isolate individual strands of fibreglass. There was a pool of dirty water at Robbie Wilson's end of the boat and he followed the dirt as it rolled with the boat. He did not look at Robbie Wilson. He could not. He could look directly at him for short periods, glances, when he was talking to him or guiding him, but he could not just sit there and stare. Not at those eyes. They weren't ugly. The plastic people had done their best to make them up. There were small scars all around the eyes but they might have been crows'-feet. And the lids came right down so that all you could see of the inside was a streak of white. But Tim still could not bear to look too long. Robbie Wilson knew that. They could say things like that to each other. Tim said Robbie should wear glasses. He bought him a pair. Robbie refused to wear them. He said he wanted people to know. To see and to know and to ask. And when they asked, he told them, he told them everything, in exact detail, almost scientific, time after time. A witness, he said.

A car bomb. Three hundred and fifty pounds. He knew everything about it. How it was made, what kind of car it had been packed in, who'd driven it, where they'd placed it, how long a warning they'd given, all the nuts and bolts. They'd stuck a few of them around the bomb for good measure. He'd studied every detail of the bombing. One in thousands. They got a farmer to drive the car. The car was stolen. The farmer's wife and kids were held hostage. The car was a Ford. The wife was a piano teacher. One of the kids had asthma. There were three men holding them in the house. Two others followed the farmer to make sure. The timer was an acid-condom device, the bomb was mostly fertiliser. It was packed into a drum. One of them got twenty years for it. He was in France now. Had renounced his earlier ways. The proportion of terrorists re-offending was very low. Only the hard men kept going back for more. But they were all that was needed. Darwinian selection. Maybe the NIO should have encouraged more of the wets to rejoin. The warning had been ridiculous. A combination of fear, incompetence and sheer don't-care. He'd been in buying a tracksuit. Had just paid for it and was walking out of the shop. Stopped to look at a pair of soccer boots. Good at soccer, Robbie Wilson. Got a Linfield trial.

He could remember the bang, he thought. He could not be sure. Everything slowed. In that instant, life went into slow motion. And five people died.

Two died with the bang. One woman beside the car and an RUC officer, yelling at everyone to get away. He could see the RUC officer's face. It was young. His skin was cherry and his eyes were blue and wide open. Robbie Wilson remembered the eyes. The woman was blown to bits. They found her head fifty yards away, her right arm in among some tailor's dummies, some of her entrails hanging from a broken gutter. Her head was crushed. She had worn glasses.

The RUC constable was killed by the shock-wave first. Massive internal injuries. One piece of the Ford went through his chest and came out through his right hip. His hat was blown down the street and was still lying on the footpath three days later. Robbie could not remember where he had heard that. Most of the blast was channelled towards the RUC constable. Robbie was at the other end of the street. At first, he thought he was only knocked off his feet. He tried to get up and he could not. There was silence and then screaming and then he passed out. But he could tell the doctors what happened after that. Without being told. They told him he was imagining it. He'd passed out. He was already blind. A shop window took his sight away. An optician's. He always laughed at that. Lacerated him. Pieces of his clothing and flesh were found at the back of the sports shop stuck to the wall. His abdomen was split open and the only thing holding his guts in was his shirt. He had burns all over his body. They'd put a petrol can in with the bomb, for added effect. Economic target. Their logic was inescapable. First blast the street, then watch it burn. Eight shops caught fire. They didn't get it out till the next day.

Three people died at his end of the street. A man and his four-year-old, crossing the street, and a delivery man sitting in his van reading the *Mirror*. The kid was disembowelled by a piece of Ford Escort the size of a penny. It went right through him and took some of his spine to the end of the street. His father was shredded by shrapnel. His limbs were all taken off. He lived for a few hours. He had one hundred per cent burns on one side of his body. He had heard the warning and was trying to shield his son. The delivery man was found in his upturned van. It had been burnt out. He was burnt to death inside it. They could have got to him except no one heard his screams and the van looked such a mess no one thought anyone could be alive in it. And it was a matter of saving the saveable then.

Anger. Robbie Wilson summed the whole thing up with that word when a newsman had come to interview him. He would not say anything else. The bomb was anger, the deaths were anger, the mutilations were anger, the reactions were anger. He could not think of any more to say. Now he walked around and people saw.

They were fishing, back to back. Rods out over the side of the boat, lines disappearing into the rolling darkness of the lake. Cast and reel. Through rolling surface to still waters running deep. The lake was cold and the cold from the lake got into the damp air and made it hard and sharp. Tim could feel it in his toes and it brought him back to OPs and contacts and in the stillness of the lake he could see action. Robbie Wilson could not see anything.

'There's mute swans over there,' Tim said. 'And they're mallards in the bullrushes.'

'How white are the swans?'

'Pretty white. Very beautiful. I hope we catch a pike.'

'We should. It's a good time for pike. There were leaves on the ground at the bank. I felt them. They were wet. Tell me if you see anythin', Timmy.'

'I will.'

It was like that and the wind rocked the boat and they did not speak until Tim saw the otter. He did not look at Robbie and Robbie did not need Tim to look at him. It was understood. They were friends and friends did not have to explain. Just like friends did not make judgments. And Robbie did not say anything to Tim about leaving his wife even though he thought it was wrong. McLennan thought about that when he was fishing for the pike, thought about that and the bomb that had torn Robbie Wilson's sight away from him and other bombs and shootings and other friends with no arms and legs and some dead and he was glad his friend had said nothing about Anne.

'There he is, there he is, he's just above the water,' Tim said when he saw the otter. 'Nice coat. He's going. He's gone.'

Robbie Wilson had turned in the direction of the otter and followed it through Tim's words.

'Do you remember Mark Green and the otter, Timmy?' Robbie asked.

'I do. Do you hear from him?'

'He sends some letters. Not many. He's settled over there now. Best Protestant Jew in Ulster. Do you remember the Twelfth when he stuck the Pope's picture on the lodge banner? Do you remember that?'

'I do.'

This was for Robbie. It was understood. Things he could describe. And Tim should only answer with a couple of words.

'He was a great boy, Markie. Good at rugger. Could have had an inter-pro cap if he hadn't upped and gone to Canada. I thought he was stupid. I bet there's a bit of him still wants to be back in Northern Ireland. Do you?'

'I do. I do.'

'Watch that otter. He'll be after our fish. Markie nearly died of a heart attack when the bloody thing took his. Could have had an Irish cap, Markie.'

Robbie stopped there. That was an area of disagreement. Tim hated the idea of Northern Irishmen playing rugby in green Irish jerseys in Dublin. Not when we're fighting a proxy war against them, he said. Robbie said it was a good way to promote understanding. Tim said there was nothing to understand. They were out to get Northern Ireland. It was in their constitution. The Provos were just the thin edge of a southern wedge. He could see no difference, he said, except the Provos had an honesty of purpose the other lot didn't. And for some reason he could admire that. They never got further than that. Robbie always wanted to talk dialogue but he knew it was pointless with Tim. Tim was Tim and their friendship was more important than some academic notion of cross-border dialogue.

'Do you remember him with Helen Wright? You would.'

'I do, Robbie. Where is she?'

'Portadown, I think. I heard she married a health-food salesman. Nicky Frankel says she saw her a couple of weeks back. Nicky's up the spout again. God, Terry Frankel never gets off her. They must be at it mornin', noon and night. She was a good ride, though.'

'Who?'

'Nicky.'

'How do you know?'

'I do. I just do. I can see it now. Oh, it was beautiful. There she was, lyin' there, you know the way, lyin' there, naked, spread in front of me like good margarine. Cryin' out for it. I can see it now. Summer's day, good beer, good rock and roll, sun on your back and Nicky screwin' like a rabbit. Always liked to go until the fellow's sacks were drained, Nicky. That's what she said. You could hear us in Newtownards. She was a noisy cow, Nicky. Oh, I know what I'm talkin' about. Was it like that for you?'

'How do you mean?'

'With Helen.'

'Nah, Robbie, nah.'

'I didn't think so. I can tell. I have a whole new sense focus. Happens when you lose your eyes. Everythin' else is heightened. I can hear pulses sometimes, isn't that funny? One door closes, another opens. That's how I look at it. I could have been killed, couldn't I? I could be like Eric. Jesus. I'm lucky if you see it that way. It's all a matter of how you see it. And one of the bastards has given up the ghost because of what happened. That has to be good.'

'There's others.'

'It's a slow process.'

Tim McLennan did not answer. He felt a tug on his line. He tested it. The tug got stronger.

'What's happenin'?' Robbie asked.

'I think I've a bite, Robbie.'

'Shite. Terrific! Pull the bastard in.'

'Easy. Easy. Let him come. He'll come. There's a time. There's always a time.'

It was a pike and he was big. He was struggling on the end of the line and the rod bent in the struggle. Tim reeled him in methodically, pulling on the rod and reeling in the line, slowly, giving and taking, holding his breath. And he held his breath till the fish was in the boat. It was about two and a half feet long and it was an oily green on top and then patches of oily green and lighter green going on yellow and then lighter green going on yellow fading to a silver sheen underneath. And it thrashed about on the fibreglass, sliding towards the dirty water at the back of the boat.

'Is it good, is it good?' Robbie Wilson asked.

'It's good, Robbie, it's good,' Tim said.

He grabbed the pike by the head and pulled the hook from its mouth. The pike's teeth touched his skin and the fish made an attempt at his finger and McLennan pulled some small forceps from a bag under his feet and wedged the mouth open. He could see a fish louse emerging from one of the gills.

When the hook was free, he took a white priest-stick from the bag between his feet and hit the fish on the head and it shook for a bit and then stopped moving.

They caught two more. And Robbie Wilson caught a second and let it go because it was too small. McLennan wanted to kill it. It was fifteen inches, maybe more. But Robbie said no.

On the bank Tim McLennan put a thin branch through the pikes' gills and balanced the branch on his shoulder. The branch was dead and they walked on dead leaves. Robbie Wilson kept asking Tim to tell him what it was like.

'I know what it was like, I know,' he said, 'but I want to see if I was right. I have to know, Timmy. I could picture it, you know.'

Tim was still trying to figure out what had happened between Helen Wright and himself. He might have lost his virginity with her but he could not remember. There were others and it might have been one of them. Helen was the one everyone wanted. She wore a green uniform and had a shorter skirt than anyone else. She had good legs. It was probably her. They lived around from the McLennans, the Wrights. The father was a driver or something in the bus company. He had a heart attack. She had a couple of brothers. One was a policeman. Everyone seemed to have a policeman in their family. Policemen got paid well. Young policemen drove good cars and pulled women at dances. The downside was wondering who was waiting outside the gate for them. But between the job and the gate there was a good life if you wanted it.

'We're takin' a gang of kids to Scotland next month, Timmy,' Robbie Wilson said. 'Did I tell you that? Cross-community thing. There's a centre. They can meet and talk. I think it'll be good for them. You know?'

He was hanging on to Tim McLennan's arm again. Helen Wright was still on McLennan's mind. She had this long brown hair and it blew nice in the wind.

'Jesus, we went on one of those years ago, do you remember that? Shankill meets the Falls for three days. I don't know.'

'I don't remember that, Timmy, are you sure?'

'Yeah. You were there. You and Bony Craig got into trouble for writin' something about the Taigs on the wall and then there was a punch-up. Over The Sash.'

'I don't remember. Sometimes my old memory lets me down.'

'It was a long time ago. We were kids. Fifteen or so.'

'I wish I could remember.'

Tim slapped him on the back.

'I hope it goes well for you, Robbie. I hope.'

'I know you do, Timmy. And it will. We'll bone these and eat them with the kids if you want. Would you like that or is your mother expectin' you? Valerie would like to see you, talk to you. The kids, too. But we could go round to your mother's if that's what you want.'

'I'd like a pint.'

'We can do that, too. Good day, eh?'

'Good day, Robbie.'

Tim gutted the fish by the car and threw the guts in a ditch. Then he wrapped the fish in newspaper and placed them in a plastic shopping bag. Robbie sat in the passenger seat of the car and smoked a cigarette. They both knew they weren't going to Robbie's house or Tim's mother because Tim's mother would only talk about Anne and Marty and Tim did not want to talk about Anne and Marty and Valerie would try not to talk about Anne and Marty because Robbie had told her not to and Tim hated Valerie trying not to talk about Anne and Marty worse than his mother's talking about them.

'How's your mum, Tim?' Robbie asked.

'Physically, she's fine. Few stitches. The news made more of it than it was. She didn't like bein' on the television. Said they showed her thighs when she was bein' put into the ambulance. Prudish, my mum. But up here—' He put his finger to his temple. '—never over Daddy. Never. She's on everythin'. Bit dazed. Doesn't sleep. I'm gonna stay over there when I can. For her. You know, with all this mess and what not. Well, you know, Robbie. You and Val have been good. Thanks.'

'Oh, nothin', Timmy. What are friends for? Good woman, your mum. Good woman.'

'Aye. I think I'm AWOL, you know.'

'Jesus, Timmy. You serious?'

'I think. I rang and left a message. Told a pack of lies. Can't go back yet. Need this. Jesus, I do. I'm a bit tired, myself, Robbie. Ah, sure they won't touch me. I'm too valuable. You know? Ach, I don't know, Robbie. This past year's been – you don't mind me goin' on?'

'No, Timmy. You go on there. I know what you're goin' through. And you were always there for me, son.'

'Christ, when I saw the town, Robbie, and then Mum. The bastards, Robbie. They're fuckin' wreckin' the province and we're powerless. I'm just a tool of a glorified public relations firm. I do stunts for them when they need it. Does it not get to you?'

'Sure it does, Timmy. Sure it does. I carry it with me every day. Sometimes I get so angry I think I could kill. Sometimes. Then I calm down. You know John Hume's always quotin' Gandhi. You know, an eye for an eye just leaves everyone blind.'

McLennan was leaning against the car with his head back on the roof. His eyes were closed.

12

THE CLOUD HAD cleared and the stars were out in their hundreds. Cusack followed them to the horizon. The horizon was a cluster of trees on a hill. The trees were swaying. The temperature had dropped and the wind chill made it worse. It was past one. He slid over the rock and crawled a few feet on his knees and elbows. Three yards ahead of him he could see the silhouette of a human body and the barrel of a rifle. He took his knife from its inverted sheath on his right shoulder. The knife was short and dark. It had two sharp sides. And it was perfectly balanced. Under the ribs or the back of the skull. And twist. Always twist. They taught you that. The Corps. When they taught you to kill. The enemy. The enemy? Whoever they said. You stood up and said, Sir, yes, Sir, and never thought. They didn't teach you to think. They didn't pay you to think. They taught you to kill. They paid you to kill. The enemy. Cusack tried to count the stars.

In Central America, he had killed the enemy. In the Philippines. Other places. Jungle places. A teenager with a million-dollar budget. Want to know what it's like to spend a million dollars in a couple of minutes? Join the Corps. Do what they tell you. Ask no questions. Sir, yes, Sir.

There was a pueblo. A few shanty houses. Rural corrugation. A pig squealing. The smell of open drains and garbage heaps in the summer heat. And the sweat. That was what was different about Ireland. He never sweated except when he was scared and that was a good sweat. It complemented the cold. The cold had a purity about it. Even when it hurt. But the pueblos only had the sweat. They had sweat and claustrophobia and they had death. All kinds. Set up your killing ground and wait for the first movement. Then let loose with the technology of the First World on the undernourishment of the Third. The first one dead would always be an early-morning piss. Maybe a screwing couple if they had to get away. But screwing couples mostly died in their beds. And when it was over you left what had to be left and the right people put out the right statements and no one bothered doing too much about it because pueblo campesinos didn't rate much of a quote on Wall Street.

Cusack placed his rifle down and moved.

One village became another and ambush became air strike. Couldn't order a drink in some states but he could call in a multi-million-dollar air strike. And when he couldn't do it, he trained others to do it. He told them to kill the enemy the way he'd been told.

He had Bruddy Holmes down on the ground and the knife to his throat. Holmes's eyes had a terror in them Cusack recognised. He was looking into Holmes's eyes for the first time. He couldn't help it. There were other eyes there, and Cusack held the stare for longer than he needed. Then he shoved it all away and put his finger to his lips. Then he pulled the knife away.

'Tie him,' he whispered.

Tate Byrne came behind him. He had plasticuffs and a black hood. He tied Holmes's hands and feet and hooded him. Cusack sat in Holmes's position. Hart had put out two flanking watches: Ger and Eddie. But they were too far apart in the dark. You could drive a regiment through that gap and neither of them would see it. Cusack cursed. Make them pay, he said to himself. Make them pay and make them learn. That was the brief. Trim the fat, Dessie said. No pain, no gain. Prepare for pain. Make 'em or break 'em. I'm going to break you, boys.

He signalled to Tate. Tate moved on towards the second watch, Ger Kelly. Cusack followed him through the nightsight on his rifle. Grey-green. Ghost feeling. Tate crept up close and waited.

'Ready?' Cusack said through his walkie-talkie.

'Ready,' came back on the radio.

'Right – go.'

Tate moved on Ger and caught him cold and Cusack rushed him from behind.

Ger didn't know what hit him till the AKM barrel was in his mouth.

'Freeze, Ger,' Cusack whispered.

Ger's sculpted head melted into the darkness and he dropped his weapon to the ground. The rifle fell on its butt. Cusack reached down and picked it up and grabbed Ger's radio from him. Tate bound Ger the way he'd bound Bruddy Holmes. Cusack moved on ahead. Three left. Static. Static position without defences. He grinned. No pain, no gain. Prepare for pain, lads. Tate dragged Ger over to Bruddy Holmes and took up the position Cusack had told him to.

Eddie Barnes was out on his own when he should have been with Danny Loughlin. Hart had told them to move wide of Holmes and Ger Kelly. He was going to use them as bait and then swing round them when Cusack and Tate made their move. But the whole plan was better than the sum of the parts. Cusack cursed again. This kind of basic shit should be inside, natural, he thought. He threw himself at Eddie and knocked him into a tree stump and rolled him over and twisted his arm.

'Fucking watch yourself, Eddie,' he said.

He hit him in the plexus to wind him and cuffed him and hooded him. Then he tied his feet.

'Stay there and shut the fuck up, Eddie. Shut the fuck up and think about staying alive. Because if you go on like that out there you're dead. And if you're dead then like as not someone else gets dead.'

Cusack crawled behind a rock and watched the bivouac with his nightsight. There was a string of smoke rising from behind the wall. Cusack cursed one more time and crawled forward between two rocks. The ground was soft and wet and the wet and mud seeped into his clothes and the cold night wind bit at him where it could. Tate was making his way around the flank.

'Position,' he said on the walkie-talkie.

Cusack answered.

Behind the bivouac wall, Danny Loughlin was smoking and swigging from a flask. Cusack watched the smoke and then looked left and right of the bivouac. Dessie. Where was Dessie? He went through the permutations. Dessie and Danny, Danny as bait, Dessie as flanker, Danny pissing around, Dessie on his own. Cusack had to decide. He could swing into the trees and come round behind the bivouac, over the wall. He tried to control his heart. It was up a gear and the beats were like a bass drum at a rock concert. He could feel warmth now. He was sweating. Fear sweat. Excitement sweat. Where every move meant something. Everything on an edge. You live more in three minutes than most lifetimes. Addictive. He felt his head swell and the confidence wanted to explode. He had them.

Dessie Hart was about twenty yards behind Danny, and moving away.

Bad moves, boys, bad moves pay bad, Cusack thought. He told Tate about Hart. Tate followed Dessie Hart. Cusack moved.

He played it like every tree had a tripwire, every step might be a pressure pad. Jungle fever. Every leaf, every stick, everything is the enemy. You against it all. They had the numbers, it should have been easy for them. Only Danny was soft. Soft and getting softer. Stopping for a smoke and a swig. Maybe the cold was at him, probably more. Probably lied to Dessie. Said he was moving. Left Dessie exposed. Cusack could see him now. His rifle was against the wall outside the bivouac.

Danny Loughlin replaced the hip flask in his pocket and stubbed out his cigarette. Not as good as a pipe, he thought, but it would do.

'Freeze, Danny.'

Cusack was on the wall above him. Loughlin went to go for his weapon. Cusack kicked it away. Tate radioed that he had Hart. Cusack stepped down. His AKM was two inches from Loughlin's head. Tate frog-marched Dessie Hart with a Heckler and Koch G3 touching his nose and Dessie screaming curses at him, telling him the exercise was over, they'd won, let him up. Tate and Cusack laughed.

The moon was low and covered by a patch of left-over cloud except for a crescent.

'Okay, okay, you've got us, John, you've got us. We give up,' Hart said. 'Exercise complete. Drinks on us.'

Loughlin reached into his pocket for his flask. Cusack jumped at him and kicked the flask from Loughlin's hand.

'Tie him,' he said to Tate.

'John, let us go,' Hart said. 'That's an order.'

Cusack walked over and put his foot into Hart's back.

'Shut up, Dessie. You're prisoners. You think the Sass would let you go if they got you? No fucking way. You lads are dead. Down, Dessie.'

Tate Byrne looked at him to confirm the order.

'Tie him, Tate. And hood him.'

'Come on, John, it's done, you've won,' Loughlin said. 'Up the Marines.'

'Shut up, Danny. Tie him and hood him, Tate.'

Tate hesitated again.

'What about the others?'

'Do it.'

Loughlin went to get up. Tate didn't move. Cusack put his boot into Loughlin's chest.

'I'll put one between your eyes, Danny,' Cusack said. 'Face down. Both of you. And don't fucking move.'

He fired. One shot. Into the ground beside Loughlin.

'Jesus, John.'

'Fuck.'

'John, come on, John,' Hart said. 'Let me up.'

'Shut the fuck up, Dessie, or I'll do you, friend. Tie him, Tate.'

Tate did as he was told. And he put plasticuffs around Hart's legs so Hart couldn't move. Then he and Cusack went out into the night and frog-marched Eddie Barnes, Ger Kelly and Bruddy Holmes back to the bivouac. They all protested. They got no answers. Tate kept looking at Cusack, waiting for him to call a halt. Cusack did not. They threw the three prisoners flat on their faces beside Loughlin and Hart and plasticuffed their legs. The rain started to turn into sleet and the sleet hit the bivouac tarp like silenced bullets. Cusack stood away from Tate and smiled at him.

'Victory,' he said.

He raised a fist and Tate grinned a fat hair-lip grin and raised his fist.

Then Cusack raised his rifle and pointed it at Tate.

'Drop it,' he said.

Tate didn't react. There was reaction in his eyes. Cusack could see a thousand decisions being made. Reaction contemplated. The sleet showed itself in the clouded moonlight. All around, the stars crept in and out of straggling cloud. Tate put his weapon down. The movements were deliberate. First to his waist, then to his knees, then the ground.

'Jesus, John,' Loughlin protested. 'Cut the shite.'

'I said shut up, Danny.'

'Come on, John,' Dessie Hart said. 'Enough, I'm freezin'. Come on.'

Cusack lashed out with his boot and caught Hart on the back of the head.

'Shut up!'

Tate had his hands out wide. Cusack indicated he should put them on his head.

'Come on, come on, I haven't got all fucking night. Down.'

He came at Tate and pushed him into the mud. Tate's mouth swallowed mud and sleet and he cursed Cusack. Cusack knelt on his back and tied his arms with the plasticuffs. Then he tied his feet and hooded him.

'What the hell's goin' on?' Bruddy Holmes asked.

He'd been trying to obey Cusack's order to shut up but he was afraid now.

'What's happenin'?' Eddie Barnes said.

'I don't know,' Tate said. 'Maybe Mr John here—'

The words didn't get out. Cusack kicked him between the legs.

'Shut up. Right. Now all of you listen. You're all prisoners. Dead meat if I say so.'

He clicked a small handheld radio.

'Romeo Foxtrot, Romeo Foxtrot, this is Alpha one, over. Targets secured. Send the QRF bird. Send the QRF bird.'

'Jesus, John!' Loughlin shouted. 'You a fuckin'—'

'Shut the fuck up. You're maggots, you hear? You're fucking maggots and you maggots are going to wish you'd never been born. In five minutes, you bastards are going to wish you'd played our little game a bit better. Isn't much of a game now, is it, Danny?'

'Jesus Christ, he's a fuckin' tout,' Hart said. 'You're a fuckin' tout. You bastardin' cunt. Fuckin' fucker.'

'Jesus, Cusack, you fuckin' tout bastard. I'll fuckin' have you. I swear, you bastard. I swear.'

'Sweat, Danny.'

'What's happenin'? What's happenin'?' Bruddy demanded.

'The fucker's a tout,' Eddie Barnes said, 'the fucker's set us up. They're comin' to pick us up. Jesus, do you not see?'

'You cunt,' Loughlin said. 'I always knew you were a fuckin' cunt. I fuckin' told GHQ we didn't want you. Bastard. Fucker. I'll hang your fuckin' balls over my shoulder.'

'I'm going to take special pleasure in seeing you bruise, Danny,' Cusack said. 'We've a lot to ask you. Nice holding cell waiting. Then some of the big boys from the Hereford Gun Club want to spend a few hours in your company. Nothing official, mind. This one's unofficial. So we can keep you for as long as we like. No yellow cards where you're going, son. Now the rest of you can make it easy for yourselves by learning that talking is just a word away. We'll get what we want from you any which way, it's just a matter of time and how much agony you can endure. I seen boys go for days. Hands smashed. Nails pulled out. Electric stuff to the balls. Some guys get so used to that they get off on it, eventually. Come all over the cell every time the thing is switched on. Most scream. You should hear them scream. You like to scream, Danny, you fucking shit? You're going to get all the chance you want.'

'Fuck you,' Ger Kelly yelled. 'Fuck you, John Cusack.'

'I said shut up.'

Cusack cocked his rifle and put it to each of their heads.

'We could just finish it here. Maybe that'd be better. We could get what we wanted from you maggots in half an hour. Then we waste you. It's our choice. I can make it happen easy or hard. Which is it to be?'

The bound and hooded men struggled in the mud. Bruddy Holmes wet himself. He could feel the warm liquid against the cold of his skin and it stayed warm for a few seconds and the feeling was good because it was warm. But when it went cold it was worse than before.

'Shit, Bruddy, you're fuckin' pissin' yourself. Jesus, he's fuckin' pissin' himself.'

Cusack laughed.

'That's it, that's what we want. Ten minutes. The chopper'll be here. You ready for this, Bruddy? You able to stand up to what we're going to do to you. No Geneva Convention, boy. We'll work on you till you beg to die. You're a maggot, son, like all these fucking maggots. Murdering sons of bitches. You think any decent human being could belong to a gang of murderers like you bastards. You see Danny Loughlin over there? You see him, son? Danny Loughlin. Soldier of Ireland. Man of the people. Well, we've got Danny up for twenty at least. And then there's talk of him stopping a bus full of Prod workers about fifteen years ago. Night like this. Whoever did it – and we think Danny might have been there – whoever did it put heavy-duty firepower into those boys. That right, Danny?'

'I don't know what you're talkin' about. I hope they fuckin' get you, son. I hope they use a knife on you, slowly. Peel you, you bastard.'

'Some of our lads are with your wife now, Danny. With her, with Betty. Imagine that.'

'Bastard!' Loughlin yelled.

'Don't worry, Danny, nothing unless she wants it. But then again—'

'You fucker. I'll fuckin'—'

He tried to move but he could not even get his head up. Cusack slapped him over the back of the head and then shoved his head down in the mud.

'You're dead, Danny. We'll stick you on a roadside with a tout sticker on you. They'll say you were a tout. We'll stick all of you with tout stickers. Then the boys will spend the next ten years wondering who was a tout and who wasn't.'

He moved over to Holmes.

'Your brother was a tout, Bruddy. You hear that? A tout. Your brother, Billy. These lads put one into his head. Left him lying in south Armagh with nothing but a plastic bag for company. How the fuck did you end up in an organisation that could do that to your brother? Tell me that.'

'And who was the trig—?'

Cusack smashed his fist into Danny Loughlin and Loughlin felt like all the air he had ever had inside him had been pushed out with that punch.

'Come on, Bruddy,' Cusack said. 'Your big brother. I bet he was a hero to you. Jump into bed with him when you were scared nights? Like now. Wish he was here now so you could jump into bed with him. Fuck it, Bruddy, these bastards killed your brother. And you're with them.'

'He was – he was – I don't know. He was toutin'. They found he was toutin'. And touts—'

'What happens to touts?'

'They get dead,' Dessie Hart said.

'Shut up, Dessie, or I'll whack you. I'm talking to Bruddy here. Little brother of the tout, Billy Holmes.'

'Leave him alone.'

'I said shut up, Dessie.'

Cusack was kneeling at Holmes's head. He talked right into his ear.

'Are you willing to die?'

He could smell Holmes. Not just the piss. There was a smell and he had smelled it before. In Central America. He could not remember the country or the town. They had all looked the same. Maybe it wasn't in a town. There was a room. It was hot. He was sweating. There were mosquitoes. The suspect was in a chair, bound. Two men in civilian clothes were taking turns hitting him. They took ten-minute shifts. His face was changing colour, very slowly, and the angles of the bones were shifting so that the face was not the face of the man who had been dragged in. There were no questions. He could not remember questions. The men just beat the suspect in turn. There was a radio off in the distance and rock music. One of the men doing the beating had a Yankees baseball hat. The other drank Coke between shifts. And they put their hands in warm water after hitting the suspect. Eventually, their hands changed colour and lost shape, too. The suspect died without saying a word. Blood trickled from his ear.

'I said are you willing to die, Bruddy Holmes?'

'Leave him, you bastard,' Ger said.

'Solidarity. That's good.'

'Come on, John, this isn't real, come on,' Tate Byrne said. 'Enough.'

'Not real, not fucking real. I'll show you real. You want me to prove it's real. One of you dies now. One of you. You select the bastard. I'll give you one minute.'

He stood on Tate Byrne's back and shoved his boot into the spine.

'I'll snap it, Tate.'

He clicked the radio again.

'Romeo Foxtrot, Romeo Foxtrot, on my signal, on my signal, over . . .'

Cusack pulled the silenced Armalite from the holdall in the bivouac. He cocked the weapon and put it to each of their heads.

'Silenced,' he said. 'Won't make a sound. Thirty seconds.'

He took aim and fired. The round hit home beside Dessie Hart's head. Hart jerked.

'Fuck, that's—'

'Shut up, shut up, that was a warning, Dessie. You see, I'm fucking serious. Now decide. Ten seconds. Who's going to die? Eddie?'

'You can't expect us to—'

'To what?'

'Please, John,' Ger said. 'Please don't do this.'

'It's you then, Ger.'

'No,' Holmes said.

'All of us,' Dessie Hart said. 'Kill the lot of us, you bastard. How long have you been with them?'

'All of you? Suits me. Fine with you, Danny?'

'I'll see you in fuckin' hell, Cusack.'

'How long, John? How fuckin' long?'

'They sent me to get you lot. You can take that as a compliment. Now say your prayers if you believe. You can have another minute.'

'No, please, don't.'

'Do it.'

'Bastard.'

'Cunt.'

'Where's this fuckin' chopper? I don't think the . . . you fuckin' bastard, Cusack.'

Cusack began to laugh. He started slowly and then could not hold it in any more so he let it echo around the hillside in the sleet and the wind and then Hart laughed and when Hart laughed Byrne laughed and Tate laughed and they all knew what was happening.

13

THE BOOT HAD caught him in the ribs. One of them broke. McLennan felt like he'd been stabbed. He yelled and rolled over and flattened out in the mud. The mud went into his mouth. He could taste it. It tasted like rocks and it ran on to his tongue and down his throat. The mud was swallowing him. He lay there in the mud and felt any left-over warmth being sucked out of him. The pain in his side evened out. McLennan drifted.

Then a hand grabbed him. He felt the fingers tear skin from the back of his neck. He was wrenched from the mud.

Come on, Paddy, get a fucking move on. Fucking Mick cunt, get the fucking lead out or I'll RTU you here and now. Fucking move, you miserable piece of Irish shit.

The NCO lifted McLennan on to his feet. The rib stabbed him again and he spat and snotted mud. He tried to wipe his eyes. He could see the NCO and pieces of landscape, parts of the puzzle. He had a rifle hanging around his neck and a pack on his back. The pack squeezed the rib and made McLennan think his insides were being pulled out through his ribs. He was fighting for breath.

I think my rib's broken, Corporal, he said.

You think I give a fuck, Mick, you think I give a fuck if every bone in your body is broken. Get the fuck up that hill. You hear me? You die when I tell you to die. Do you hear me?

Yes, Corporal.

One foot in front of the other.

McLennan could see the small line of camouflage moving among the rocks further up. He could hear shouting behind him. He did not look back.

He was moving. One foot in front of the other. Pain tearing into his side. He held his side with his hand, pressing it in like he could press the pain away. He could not. He moved.

Where the fuck did we get shit like you, Mick? Where the fuck? Jesus, what's that shower of fucking wanking pansies you come from?

McLennan did not answer. He wanted to turn his weapon in the direction of the corporal and kill him. Put a whole magazine into him. But his hands were occupied keeping the pain in his side to consciousness levels. Maybe more than one rib was broken.

Answer me. Answer me when I talk to you.

UDR, Corporal.

What the fuck kind of regiment is that? What kind of bent camelwankers come out of that shit?

McLennan knew he was not supposed to answer that.

I'll tell you, I'll tell you, stupid fucking Micks like you, you cunt, you big prick Mick, cunts like you who fuck their mothers and their sisters and their sheep before they wank. Do you hear me? Answer, cunt!

Yes, Corporal.

You want to get into this regiment. You want us to let you sit with us. Jesus, if I had my way, it'd be paras only. And none of you fairies. I've seen fairies like you crawling in the dirt, begging, do you hear? Begging, and that's the way I get my rocks off. I'm going to break you, Mick, do you hear me? Break you. I always do.

Up and the rain came down and the rain came with sleet and the rain brought mist and it made it so McLennan could not see more than two feet ahead. His side was burning but he kept going. His face was cut, he could feel blood coming from it, he did not know where it had been cut, but blood and mud were dripping on to his hand in a kind of ugly mix, like some artist was preparing to redraw him. And beside him, the voice of the inferno. Abandon all hope or whatever. And McLennan hated him. He had hated before but he did not think he would ever hate like this again. There was no hate imaginable that would ever compare with his hate for this tormentor. Beige beret, rakish angle, tattoos, lean, white, tight and mean, all the airborne bull in one body.

Fucking move, fucking move, I want you to die, do you hear? I want you to die. Will you die?

McLennan tried to turn his head but he could not, not without so much pain it made him want to pass out.

Answer me, prick. Will you die?

A slap caught McLennan across the face. He felt like his face had been dinged and was out of shape.

Yes, Corporal.

Good! Move! Move! This is the regiment, do you know that? Nothing like us in the whole universe. Do you believe that?

Yes, Corporal.

Queen's killers. That's us. Queen's killers. We take out the outtakers. You've seen the movie, you've read the book, you've bought the t-shirt and the souvenir mug, now experience the reality.

He shoved his hand into McLennan's backpack and pushed him. Then he leaned in close to McLennan's ear.

You hate me, don't you, Mick? You hate me, and that's good. Want to do me? Want to do me? You haven't the balls. Playing soldiers at weekends. That how you began? UDR. Wankers. What are they . . . ?

McLennan opened his eyes. He could see the outline of his hand, dull, unformed, and the curtains and a gap in the curtains and the light from the street. His heart was pounding. His mouth was dry like ash. He could feel sweat at the back of his knees and between his legs. He shot his eye around the room. There was a chair and a table and an open wardrobe and a dressing gown hanging from the door. He touched his side. Then he reached over to the dresser beside his bed and pulled his watch down. Midnight. He sat up. Midnight had a feel all of its own. A whole life began at midnight. A different world. He'd worked as a night manager in a supermarket once, for six months. Wars liked midnight. He'd spent so many midnights lying waiting that at times all there ever seemed to be was one endless midnight. There was always a feeling of stillness, of waiting. Midnight was a waiting time.

In the kitchen, he made tea. He had the Walther in the pocket of his dressing gown. He'd had it under the covers with him in bed. Safety catch off. Dangerous maybe but better dangerous and alive than safe and dead. They didn't wait for people to take safety catches off.

He heard footsteps. He did not move. He was sitting in the kitchen, in a corner, lights off, away from the windows. Too easy to spray a window. An inspector had been done through his window, making coffee. McLennan waited. His body was stiff, tense. He thought about

Carol. It helped him relax. He could have done with her now. His thoughts got more erotic. He needed her. Thc way she did it. He liked that. Took tension away. She had the randiness of a mistress. And he liked that. He sipped his tea.

'Tim?'

It was a whisper. The head at the door had white hair. It was a good head. Old face. There was a warmth there. There were lines and age but the warmth was more visible.

'It's okay, Mum, couldn't sleep. Havin' tea.'

'I thought I heard you come in. I went to bed early. Did you have somethin' to eat?'

'I did, Mum. Robbie and me. We had a grand feed. We caught three pike too. There's a pike in the fridge for you.'

'That's good. And you're fine?'

'Fine. It's a good time of the day for a cup of tea.'

'I'll leave you, then.'

'I'll see you in the mornin', Mum.'

'Okay, Tim. Thanks for stayin' over, Tim. It's nice to have you here, son.'

'It's good to be here, Mum. You okay?'

She nodded.

'I'll be fine, Tim.'

He had wandered to the Killing House. Target, decision, hold fire or kill. Move. Next situation. Ready. Target. Decision. Terrorist. Double tap into the torso. Right. On. Up. Target. Terrorist. Fire. Dead. Fucking cunt, McLennan, you've killed a civilian. He sank against a wall and reloaded. Fractions, he thought. Fractions of a second. People didn't understand. You were shitting yourself and you had fractions to give and take life. Always put your man down, no matter what it takes. No shooting except to kill. A wounded man shoots back. A dead man stays dead.

He did not sleep the rest of the night. He had learned to rest without sleeping, he told himself. There was more to it, maybe to do with dreams and what they told him about his fears. Not the fears of life and death, fears he could control, fears he could use, these were other fears, hidden, kept down, only breaking through when he was weak, fears of place and time and belonging, fears he could not control, fears he did not want to face, and his excuse was good enough to get him through the night and back to base that morning when he might not have gone. He sat all night, watching the darkness, holding the Walther, waiting, and when he faced Stone in the daylight, he had exhausted most of his fears and sunk back into simpler unquestioning function.

Stone stubbed a filtered cigarette into a steel ashtray and lit another. He was leaning on his desk. The lines in his face were anxious, defined and deep and anxious, and when he spoke to McLennan he stretched forward like he was trying to get closer. McLennan sat back in his chair with his right foot up on his left knee.

'Look, I really must know if you're not A1, Tim. I can't have my senior NCO under par.'

McLennan nodded.

'So, are you going to tell me?'

McLennan shrugged his shoulders and pulled a stick of gum from the packet in his hand and undid the paper and the foil and bent the gum and shoved it into his mouth.

'For Christ's sake, Tim, I give you time off, a day's extension, when I'm stretched as it is, and you calmly leave a message – a damn message with some typist – saying you're taking another day off. I mean, what the hell do you think we're doing here? This is the British Army, Tim, not some New Age hippy collective. I ought to have sent the redcaps after you, Staff. Well?'

'My mother,' McLennan said. 'She needed me with her. You weren't here, Sir. She was this close – Sir – this bloody close. Took a piece of shrapnel.' He showed with his fingers. 'I'm sorry, Sir, it won't happen again. I – this divorce and all, I've had a lot on my plate the past few days.'

Stone pulled back and drew on his cigarette. His face had relaxed. His body language was conciliatory. He leaned back and turned his head to the wall behind him and looked at the maps.

'You can talk to me, Tim,' he said. 'You know that. How do you think it would have looked for this commission if it had gone into your record that I'd had to send the redcaps after you?'

'I said I'm sorry, Sir.'

'Look, all I'm saying is talk to me, Staff. Come on, Tim, we've known each other a long time. I know you think I'm a chinless public-school wonder sometimes, a real Rupert. You think I like it? It can be a damn difficult thing to live down. Especially in a regiment like this. My father was in this regiment with Mayne and Sterling. Do you know that?'

'You've said.'

'So, things are expected.'

He stood up and turned completely to the maps.

'Look – what I'm trying to say, Tim, is we all get stressed out now and then. The thing is to watch it and get to it before it gets us. Bit like what we're doing here. We watch them and wait for them and get them before they get us.'

'Sir.'

Stone turned.

'Bob, Tim. Bob. We're alone. I'm your C/O, Tim. Problems, you come and talk to me. Okay?'

'Bob.'

'So what's the situation?'

'Under control, Bob.'

'I know it's an awful thing, Tim, I know. My brother went through it. Damn near killed him. You see, I do understand. And I'm sorry about your mother. She's okay, though?'

'Ach, I don't know. They have her on drugs. I was thinkin' I might spend free nights, time like that, at the house. I'd be contactable.'

Stone thought for a moment.

'Okay,' he said, 'sure, why not? I think we can facilitate that, Staff. Within limits, of course. Security considerations and your duties here take priority, Tim. But I can be flexible. Okay?'

'Thanks, boss. She's – well, this divorce and – well, she never got over my father's death.'

'No. Listen, I won't pretend I know what that did to you. But it all serves as a reminder of what we're up to here. And I've got to ensure that we're up to scratch, right up to scratch, Tim. You never saw the MO.'

'No, Sir.'

'How about an hour this afternoon?'

'Is this an order?'

'If you like.'

McLennan rubbed his nose and smiled at his superior. Stone tapped his fingers on the map nearest to his hand. It was a border-area map, with red stickers on it. There was a larger-scale version of the place he was tapping his fingers on to the left of that map. McLennan tried to focus on the larger-scale map. Stone stood looking at McLennan and then folded his arms and smiled.

'Okay, okay,' he said. 'Lecture and bollocking over. How about we get down to business? Oh, there's a commendation for you here somewhere, from way up high, all the best kind of stuff in it, and a signature that ensures commissions.' He searched through the papers on his desk. 'It's here somewhere. By the way, you over that perfidious Albion trip you were on the other day?'

'Sir?'

'You know, the prophecy that says HMG and Co. are going to serve you and yours up to a united Ireland, garnished, with a side order of chips?'

The you and yours section of Stone's question stuck in McLennan's mind. He filed it.

'I was tired. Post-contact bitch syndrome.'

'Where'd you dig that up? Satellite television? I told you you should have seen the MO. It's here somewhere. Damn. I'll find it. Anyway, let's get down to earning that fabulous salary HMG pay us for dealing with the armed rebellion within our borders. Okay?'

McLennan noted the 'within our borders', too, and wondered what Stone was thinking. Stone returned to the maps on the wall.

'Right,' he said. 'To business. Now what I'm saying here is for you and me only, Tim. This permanent checkpoint – here – yeah, here, at, eh – yes, ironic, really – at Kill. See?' He laughed. 'Come here and take a look, Staff.'

McLennan got out of his seat and walked over to the map wall. Stone had his finger at a border crossing between Armagh and Monaghan. He was trying to get a cigarette out of its packet with the other hand. The cigarette broke in his hand and he cursed.

'Well, we believe they're going to hit it – PIRA.'

McLennan looked closer.

'I think I mentioned it to you the other day. Well, it's looking better than average that there's going to be a considerable terrorist attack on this checkpoint, twelve to fifteen, maybe, in the attack group, a dozen or more terrorists backing them up. And others. I mean, big, Tim. And what's more, led by Dessie Hart and Francie Devine.'

McLennan gave away his feelings.

'Yes, I thought that might get the blood circulating,' Stone said. 'Now

TCG South, Security Service, Int and Sy Group, including our good selves, and E4A are all in on this one, Tim, and, as I say, it's not one hundred per cent, but all the indications are that Hart and Devine are going for a spectacular and, from what we can make out, going for it here.'

He slammed his hand into the map and then lit a cigarette.

'Do we have an inside source?'

'I can't say. Security Service are dancing around with grins as big as water-melon segments on their faces. They virtually begged to get involved. RUC Special Branch are talking it down at meetings. But they're always doing that. There's bad feeling there over assets. My guess is it's hot. Hotter still since you hit Mal Hart and crew. Brother Dessie's distraught, they say. And Francie Devine's hopping mad over it. Our watchers say there's more than the usual movements going on in Tyrone. It could be just Francie sending people around looking for informers, but it's probably more. Tony McCabe and two of his chief security heavies have been seen in Coalisland. One of them's that boxer fellow from Short Strand. Twice since the incident. What do you think?'

'I'm thinkin' why did TCG South let us take out those three last week if they had this up their sleeves? I don't think the Tyrone lads are gonna be too keen to go out again after what we did to them.'

'Yes. Well, let's say that was a calculated risk.'

'Jesus. Great minds?'

'It could work to our advantage.'

'I see. You have to have eyes in the back of your head to see advantages here.'

'Revenge, Tim. A very basic instinct. We took out three of Francie Devine's heavies. And one of them turns out to be Dessie Hart's little brother. What would you do if you had a major hit planned and that happened?'

'Call it off till I found out if there was a tout in the Tyrone outfit. But then I bet you're a step ahead of me, Bob.'

'I don't like that word, tout. But then I must bow to your right to a little localese.'

'Gone native, you mean, Bob.'

'Don't be too smart, Staff. Anyway, they might just find their—' Stone held his breath for a few seconds and looked at McLennan. '—their tout,' he said.

'I bet they will.'

'Ours not to reason why, Tim.'

'Ours but to do and die.'

'Quite. Anyway, it's Dessie Hart's play, this one. Hart's unit are the main force. Tyrone are coming for the ride. Making up the numbers, so to speak. And this is Dessie Hart's comeback show. You know, Checkpoint Charlie and all that rubbish. So with brother Mal pushing up the daisies, I'd say Dessie-boy wants a real spectacular under his belt. What do you say, Staff?'

'I'd say you know a lot more about this than you're sayin' – Sir.'

'Did you know that the shortest distance between two points is actually a curve, Tim?'

'When?' McLennan said.

'What?'

'When's this gonna happen?'

'That we don't know – yet. It's ongoing. And that's where you come in, Tim. We want to get more information on Dessie Hart's gang. Now the Garda have them under watch when they can, but Garda watch can be – how shall we say? – uneven. They vanished last week and then Hart was seen giving out tea and biscuits at a Sinn Fein do. And now he's out of sight again. Commitment isn't absolute in the security services that side of the frontier, is it? And I doubt the boys in blue over there will be all that keen to deliver Dessie and his lads into the welcoming crossfire of a regimental Type A ambush. Very bad for their image. So the ball's in our court, really. Look here.'

Stone opened a file on his desk and laid sheets of paper with photographs stapled to them out on the desk. The first photograph was an old one of Dessie Hart. The attached paper had a summary of Hart's career and a couple of lines rating his danger level and the necessary approach. Dessie Hart rated the same handling as anthrax, according to the report. McLennan wasn't impressed.

'Information from that side of the frontier's always patchy at the best of times but we do know Hart's players have been together for a team meeting at least once in the last couple of weeks. These two – eh, Kelly, Gerard Kelly—' Stone put the usual English stress on the second syllable of Ger Kelly's Christian name and McLennan took two more computerised personality summaries and held them in each hand. '—yeah, and that chap,

Byrne, Tate Byrne, they're old cronies of Dessie Hart. Took part in that job Dessie carried out near Newtownbutler in Fermanagh—' Again Stone used the wrong stresses when he was pronouncing the words and McLennan wanted to tell him just to point out what it was he wanted to show. Stone went on. '—a few years ago. Before friend Hart went inside for another spell. Now that was textbook stuff. I mean, our boys were caught with their trousers down. They hit us with a metaphorical sledgehammer. Wham! You have to give it to Hart. If he wasn't a terrorist, he'd probably be one of us. Definite officer material there. The thing is, we'd really like to have a fuller picture, so to speak. Be nice to get some ears on what's going on over there, see who's with Dessie now, how they're going to play it. More exact information.'

'That mean there's no one inside?'

'It means we want more information. Now, from what we know, Hart's just itching to go. Devine's gang have been taking most of the glory and Hart has been helping out and rebuilding his own team. But Dessie's anxious to get back to scoring form. Hit top of the league, so to speak.'

'So we want a listener?'

'Exactly. Look.' Stone pointed to the biggest map. 'These farms. Here and – here. See? Known safe houses. They're perfect for a team getting ready to hit that checkpoint. Isolated, covered, difficult to snap, even from the air. Now we have photographs of this area, taken from OPs, choppers, et cetera, even some taken from a Vulcan and a couple of satellite jobs. They're okay but we've never got anything of any substance. The odd blurred face. And anyway, photographic intelligence has the shelf-life of fresh fish. I digress. Now this one here. See? It's about four or five miles back from the target – depending on whose maps you buy – behind Castleblaney. Now – as far as we can gather – Dessie's made this place his base for the moment. As I say, information's sketchy on this place. Too far away. Hard to get at. Not everyone's there at the moment. And people come and go. It's a kind of transit camp. A bit iffy for a listener, I think. But here, this other farm – see here, it's back about two miles from the border and nicely tucked away, forests and hills all round – if we could get an ear in there and Dessie moved his troops there for the attack – well, it'd make the job that much easier, wouldn't it?'

'We'd have to be sure he was goin' to use it.'

'Of course we would. It's the one we're interested in, Staff.'

'So you must be sure our friends are goin' to use it,' McLennan said.

Stone smiled. 'Straightforward job, Tim,' he said.

'So you're sure.'

Stone shook his head.

'Doesn't concern you, Staff. But I'll say this, it does seem a good jump-off point for Hart's group. And what's to lose? Straight in, straight out. Overnight job, I'd say.'

'Nothin' to lose, if it goes well,' McLennan said. 'You want me to take a team south?'

'Seems logical. We can have a listening post set up here, photography from a satellite. Won't be great. Just what goes in and out. But having an ear there. Now that'd be something. What do you think?'

'What's the endgame here, Sir?' McLennan asked.

'Minimum force, of course, Staff. And wipe out the whole bloody lot. Off the map, so to speak. I thought we'd agreed on that. Get maybe a dozen of them. Quite a feather.'

He went back to one of the maps on the wall and drew a line with a pencil from Cookstown to Monaghan. 'Knock out this whole axis.'

'What if they just use a proxy bomb? You know, strap some bastard to the seat of his car. Then we're left with a mangled checkpoint, dead bodies everywhere and egg on our faces? I mean there's no evidence they're goin' to try another Fermanagh, is there?'

'Security Service is sure it's a full-scale assault. Hart and Devine, Tim, that's their way. Wild bunch. Look, I can't say more. But we are watching them, Tim, all the time, you know that. I'm stretched enough as it is. I won't order you to go south. If anything did go wrong and you were compromised, you'd be in enough excrement to bury your chances of a commission for a while. That's how it is, Staff. But then it's a straightforward job. In and out. No reason you shouldn't do it in a night. I think we should give it a go. Security Service are with us. Boss says okay. Haven't discussed it with the RUC. Best not to, I think.'

'No. What if they sweep? Could blow the whole operation.'

'We've thought about that. HQ thinks it's an acceptable risk. They won't be expecting it. And as long as you don't leave a calling card, there should be no problem. Yes?'

'So simple.'

'I can't authorise weapons but if you feel you should have defence, there's a store available. Unattributable stuff. Silencers and barrel changes. Plausible deniability, as they say. Could be Loyalists.'

'I am a Loyalist.'

'Yes, but I mean the wrong kind. Anyway, as I said, it'd be a straight-in-straight-out job, Tim, no bother. Look here. I've been examining this. There's the border. You could cross here, make your way through this forest land and round from the back, here. The people who own it are a seventy-year-old farmer and his darling wife. They're paid. They'll be asleep.'

'Sure?'

'Absolutely. Security Service have had a look at the place.'

'So why don't they do this?'

'Policy, Staff. Policy. HMG and HQNI aren't altogether keen on Security Service people doing black-bag jobs in Eire. Not since the agreement. Creates a bit of a fuss if things go wrong. They can run agents all right, but this kind of job is best left to us. Frankly, we're a darn sight better at it than those bastards.'

'Right. Sure, why don't we just go across and get them all and say it was the UFF or the UVF?'

'Of course, Tim. Just tool up and go. And take out anyone else who happens to turn up. Come on, Staff, it's not bad, this. It's slow but we're getting there.'

'As you say, slow. I just hope a proxy doesn't turn up one fine evenin'. Might be a shock for some poor sod. Ach, I don't know, Bob. Kind of source that can give information like this, if it's good, would have to be well placed. Must be Dessie himself.'

'Ignore sources, Tim. It's Security Service's ball and they're extremely jealous of their sources. This job's in our hands now. We have the information we need and we're acting. We simply follow orders. GOC says go. All hands to battle stations. We'll need help from Hereford for the interdiction when it's time. And we have the cooperation of the local paras. Poor sods, as you say, sitting there, waiting, doing as they're told.'

'They know?'

'The checkpoint commander does. He's a new lad, trying to impress, I'm told. Don't you just love it? This hasn't just cropped up, Tim. We've been watching them for months now, months. Security Service, E4A, Int and Sy Group, all of us. It all says the Security Service material is on the right track. They've sent fifteen scouts through that checkpoint in the last three months. That should say something. And we've spotted at least eight people watching it from Eire. Infra-red has its uses. But we have to get the plumbing in order. I feel this one, Tim, I feel it. And if this comes off, well, you were the one who said you wanted to be let loose on the bastards. Here's your chance.'

'I've never been to the Free State.'

'Never?'

'No.'

'Funny. I've been on holiday a couple of times. Lovely place. Kids adore it. My wife's family have connections in Cork. We take a house. Never?'

McLennan shook his head and took the gum from his mouth.

'I'm not sure I like the idea of goin' over there.'

'You don't have to like it. Just put an ear on them, Tim. We'll run a recce in a couple of days. Okay? And you can ship down to a safe house at the end of the week.'

'Big turnout at Mal Hart's funeral yesterday,' Tim McLennan said.

14

A GREY-BROWN CAT slipped through the railings of the gate and watched Maggie O'Neill with yellow eyes. She could hear the noise when she got to the front door. From there it sounded like a fight. For a few seconds she stood in the porch, head close to the door, breath condensing on the black paintwork. The cat moved under a bush and watched a bird that had come to rest on the wall. The bird looked at the cat. Maggie opened the door and slid in and closed it.

The noise was upstairs and now it was not a fight any more and Maggie stopped thinking about how she would get to the .357 Magnum in the hot-press. She hung her bag over the post at the end of the staircase. Two schoolbags lay side by side at her feet. One of them had a heart on it, the other a Rolling Stones logo and 'Elvis Lives' running across it diagonally in capitals. The noise got louder and deeper and Maggie climbed the stairs.

There was no mystery any more. It was just a matter of getting there unheard. It was not hard. Soft footsteps, timed to the noises she could hear. She avoided parts of the stairs and landing where she knew the boards creaked. She stopped at the hot-press and looked at it. The noises had words now, and the words were struggling.

Maggie moved forward to the open door of her bedroom. She stood at the door and stared at the mirror on the sliding doors of her wardrobe and the two figures on her bed in the mirror. Then she froze.

The boy's bottom had a pimple on it and her daughter's nails gripped it and then moved up his back and Maggie could see her fingers digging into his spine and his bottom moving and her daughter's legs wrapping around him and unwrapping and spreading and she could hear the noises and the words they were speaking over and between and under the noises. But she could not see their faces. And for a moment, she could pretend it was not her daughter and this was not her house and that was not her bed and she could feel something for these two lovers, watch them love each other, urge each other, tell each other they loved each other, watch them make love and listen to the sound and smell, the smell of love, and see the touch of love and want them to love, like it would bring her back to somewhere she had once known, somewhere she did not think she would ever go again.

The climax brought her out of her trance.

Her daughter's face appeared from behind her lover's head, appeared and then threw itself back, and she shoved her pelvis up at the boy and lost control and cried out when he cried out and rocked with him, wrapping her legs around him, pulling at him like she was following some teenage guide to lovemaking, going through motions with the aid of a Sunday tabloid, everything at the right time, all the sounds, all the right words, all the right feelings, and then the script was gone and she and her boy cried out in a kind of shocked pleasure and both rose together and then fell to the bed.

Maggie grabbed the boy by the hair and wrenched his head back and pulled him off the bed. He hit his head on the floor and rolled over and then Maggie slapped her daughter across the face and her daughter put her hands up to defend herself and screamed.

'Mam, Mam, no, Mam, please, please, no.'

'You little tart.'

'No, Mam, please, please.'

Her boyfriend was picking himself up and trying to decide whether to do something to save the girl he had promised to love for ever a couple of seconds earlier or just to grab what he could of his clothes and leg it. Maggie had her daughter by the hair and was screaming curses and pulling the girl over the bed on her belly, her daughter screaming back and crying and trying to hold back her mother's blows.

'Please, Mrs O'Neill, please,' the boy shouted.

He was trying to get his underpants on. Maggie threw her hand back and caught him across the face and he almost lifted into the air and cracked his head on the wall.

'You little shites, little shites, oh, my God, wait'll your daddy hears about this.'

Maggie had lost all control now. There was no sense in trying to reason.

Whatever had to be exorcised was on its way out and there was no stopping it. The boy picked himself up and grabbed what he could save of his clothes and ran. Maggie dropped her daughter on the floor and chased him down the stairs. He was trying to get his pants on and Maggie kicked him on the stairs and he fell forward and saved himself from going through the window at the end of the stairs by hanging on to the post at the end of the banister.

'Get out, get out of my house,' Maggie O'Neill shouted, 'get out and don't you ever go near my daughter again, you little pervert. I'll fuckin' break every fuckin' bone in your fuckin' body, you rapist, you little shite.'

He grabbed his schoolbag and Maggie caught him with another blow to the head and knocked him against the hall door. She was crying now and when his head rebounded from the hall door she hit him again and then opened the door and hit him again and shoved him through the door and kicked him when he was through and shoved what remained of his clothes out after him.

'Get out, get out!' she yelled.

Two women across the street stood and watched, too embarrassed to move. A car stopped and then started and stalled. Maggie yelled at the driver and he tried to get his machine going again and stalled twice. The boy had reached the gate and was trying to get through it with Maggie slapping him around the head and four of the neighbours watching. The cat and the bird continued to stare at each other.

The boy got through the gate, tearing his shirt, and when he was through he thought it was over. But Maggie was not finished. She ran back into the house and got a brush and came after him with the brush and chased him through the street out of the village through an audience of paralysed onlookers who did not know whether to laugh or run away themselves. The boy kept running for half a mile after Maggie had stopped.

'Oh, they'll all love it round here. Look at that O'Neill girlie, wee tart, isn't she? Puttin' it about with everythin'. Like a wee bitch on heat.'

Maeve O'Neill sat across the room from her mother in a dressing gown, crying.

'Mam, oh, Mam. I love him, I love him.'

'Love? Love? You're fifteen, you don't know what love is. Wait till your daddy gets home. He'll beat you into tomorrow. He'll kill your man. Little shite. Who is he?'

'His name's Sean. He's from Clones. Oh, Mam . . .'

'I don't know, I just don't. Here! In my home! In my bed! Jesus, girl! Jesus!'

She slapped her hands together.

'Did youse use anythin'?'

Maeve shook her head.

'Are you on the pill even?'

Maeve shook her head again.

'Oh, Jesus. Well you better pray you're not up the spout, wee girl. I promise you your father'll kill you, he will. And we can't afford another mouth to feed. Did you think about that when you and him – when youse were – Jesus, my daughter – when youse were screwin' in my bed. Jesus, I could fuckin' kill you. I could fuckin' kill you. You little bitch.'

'I love him.'

'Don't talk to me about love. Don't ever say that word again. You think we haven't enough problems? What possessed you, girl? You promised me. You promised me after last time. Never again.'

'I know, Mam, I know. But I love him.'

'You loved the last one – that Paddy.'

'It just happened. It just happened. Didn't that ever happen to you?'

'That's not the point. You're fifteen, for Christ's sake. What age is he? I'll have him done for underage sex. Where the hell did you learn all that, girl? Where? Have I not told you? Have I not? And I don't suppose you ever heard of AIDS?'

'It was our first time. His, too.'

'Oh, you know that, do you? He told you, I suppose. You're the only girl for me, Maeve. I've been savin' myself. Jesus. I can't believe this. We have all the trouble we can handle here and now this. You've your exams to think about, girl. Did you even consider that? If you're in the club. Babies don't look after themselves. And I've to work, or hadn't you noticed?'

'Sorry, Mam, I'm sorry. I won't do it again, I promise.'

'Fuckin' right, you won't. No more out. Nowhere. I swear I'll kill you myself if I ever even hear you've been near that little bastard or anyone else. Jesus!'

'Don't tell Daddy, Mam, please, please don't tell him. Please!'

'I don't know what I'm gonna do with you, Maeve. I just don't. Do you see what you did was wrong? Do you?'

'Yes, but . . .'

'But what? It was wrong. You're a wee girl, for God's sake. A wee girl.'

'But I love him.'

'Oh, don't talk to me about love. Do you know how many lads I thought I was in love with till I married your Daddy?'

'I don't know, Mammy.'

'Dozens of them. And they all loved me. Look, love, I'm not sayin' love isn't great when it happens but wait till you're sure, till you're old enough, love. Wait. I know it sounds cruel but it's for your good. You see, you're young and you're changin', Maeve. You have all these feelins and you don't know where they're comin' from. I know. But it's not so simple out there. Things are harder. And the world doesn't forgive the way I do. I do it for you, love. I do everythin' for you. I want you to have a good life. I want you to meet someone nice and marry him and have babies and a good life. I want you to feel proud of yourself. Feel you've achieved somethin'. But you have to listen to me, love. Listen to what I tell you.'

'But I love him.'

'Enough of that. I don't want any more of that. You don't love him. You think you do. You're in love with love. It happens. I want to take you to the doctor tomorrow, okay? Come here. Come here to your Mammy.'

Her daughter stood up and walked over to her mother and bent over and then knelt down and put her head in her mother's lap.

'It's okay, it's okay, I'm with you, love, always with you,' Maggie said.

'Do you love Daddy, Mam?'

'Yes. But there's all kinds of love and maybe your Daddy and me love each other in a different way to the way we did before.'

'Did you ever really love anyone else?'

Maggie leaned her back in the chair and watched a tree move outside. She ran her hand through her daughter's hair and felt her daughter's tears.

'Oh, yeah, lots of times. There was this one lad. When I was about your age, I think. I was mad about him. He was lovely. But I only knew him a couple of days and I never saw him again. It was a youth-trip thing at home. He was a Prod. So, you see, I know what you're feelin'. Ach, sure then there were others.'

'Did y'ever do anythin' with them?'

'No. We didn't.'

'Would you have liked to?'

'I told you, it's best to wait.'

'Did you wait?'

'Yeah.'

'That's nice.'

Maggie left her daughter for a moment for an argument over a repossessed car.

'I love you, Mam,' Maeve said.

'I know, love,' Maggie said. 'I know.'

'Things'll get better, won't they, Mam?'

'They will, love. They will.'

Outside, a car door slammed. It was loud enough to be heard in the house and Maggie jumped up and went to the window. Brian O'Neill saw her looking through the curtains and smiled. She gave him a smile back and then looked through the gate at the car. It was another Merc. Brand new. The licence plate said it. But you could tell from the way it sparkled in the cold late-afternoon pre-sundown light, raindrops glistening and shivering in the cold wind and the cold dying light and Brian O'Neill standing in the street, almost asking people to ask him about his new car. Maggie O'Neill turned to her daughter.

'Jesus, I don't believe it,' she muttered to herself. 'A new fuckin' car. Jesus Christ!'

She clenched her fists.

'Mam?' Maeve said.

'Go get cleaned up, Maevie. Please. Please. And tidy upstairs, for God's sake. What time's Eoin finished football practice?'

Maeve looked over her mother's shoulder at the curtained window.

'Seven, I think. Daddy's got a new car.'

'Yeah, he has. Go on. We'll keep all this to ourselves, won't we? Girls.'

'Thanks, Mam,' Maeve said.

She kissed her mother and ran upstairs.

The front door opened and closed. Maggie did not look up at her husband. He stood in the doorway of the living room, holding a briefcase in one hand and a bunch of flowers in the other. Maggie folded her arms and tried not to cry.

'What's that?'

She pointed outside.

'The new car, love,' he said.

'The new car! Yesterday, they came and took our old one because we couldn't meet the payments and today you're here with a brand spankin' new one. Oh, great, just great. Just like that. It must be me, Brian, because you're obviously sane, Brian, you obviously know what's goin' on. I'm just the one that lives in the world where they take things away when you can't pay. You've found some way of reversin' that. Bravo, Brian. Shite!'

'You like it? Come and have a look.'

'I don't think you heard me, Brian.'

He grinned. 'Sure I did.'

He handed her the flowers. She put them on the floor.

'Peace offerin',' he said. 'For yesterday. I'm sorry. I got carried away. I shouldn't have lost my temper. Please say you'll forgive me, Maggie. Please!'

'Oh, yeah, why not, Brian. This upside-down world of yours. Sure, hit me again and I'll love you for it.'

He put his briefcase down and came over to her and went down on one knee.

'Princess, princess. Remember when I used to call you my princess? Remember?'

He flopped back on to the carpet, crossed his legs and leaned towards her.

'Get into the best dress you have, love, I'm takin' you out. We're celebratin'. Oh, are we celebratin'! You betya. Brian O'Neill is back. Do you bastards out there hear that? Brian O'Neill is back. Fuck the lot of youse. Oh, Maggie, Maggie, you're beautiful, beautiful. Get dressed up and let me wine you and dine you and then bed you for hours. Hours. I love you. I have an investor. A lovely bloody investor.'

She stood up and walked past him. Then she turned.

'What are you talkin' about, Brian?'

'For that. For that site youse all laugh at. For my hotel, my dear. My bloody hotel. Man from Dublin. Property developer. Heard about it from some people I know there – see, I get around – likes the idea, wants to meet. We're goin' to be rich again, Maggie, rich. You watch.'

She shook her head.

'You have to be kiddin'. Someone as crazy as you are rings up and says he wants to jump from the same great height and you go out and buy a new car when we couldn't afford the payments on one six years older and light-years cheaper. Jesus Christ, is my whole family gone fuckin' mad? Or is it just me? Am I missin' somethin'? Have I been wastin' my life? Yeah, yeah, it must be me. I must be missin' it. You see, I was always told that you shouldn't spend what you didn't have. I was wrong, wasn't I? I should have followed the Brian O'Neill way. Always spend what you don't have. Always put your faith in pipedreams. In fact, the bigger the fuckin' fantasy, the better. My God, Brian.'

'No, no, it's true. I checked him out. The company's fine. They've invested in things likes this before. Over in Donegal, down in Cavan, all along the Antrim and Down coast. Leisure, Maggie. The future. They see potential.'

He pulled himself up from the floor and took his coat off and laid it on the couch beside her. Then he went to hold her but she stood back. He came at her again and she shoved him away.

'Don't, no, don't, Brian. You're seriously tellin' me there's a chance someone will put money into your scheme to build that hotel out there? I suppose this bastard wants to buy the Brooklyn Bridge, too. Why not sell him the keys to heaven while you're at it.'

'It's a good site. And we can buy up more land around it. Make it special. You offer people somethin' special and they'll come, no matter where it is or how much you ask. That's business. You never did understand business, Maggie. Never.'

'No, no, I didn't, I suppose. No, no, leave me be, Brian, please. Just leave me be. I want to go out. I want to go out on my own. Get the kids their tea. Take them out in your new car. Oh, God, let me out of here. Just let me out. Go tell your daughter your good news, I'm sure it'll make up for the bedtime stories she missed.'

She pushed by him and grabbed her coat from where it hung over the banisters, pulled a scarf from one pocket and walked out. She slammed the door shut.

She was sitting on the wall, staring at her husband's site, when he came. It was dark. A car passed her and its headlights caressed her for a moment and then moved on. Brian O'Neill walked slowly with his hands in his pockets. Light from a chipper on the main street stretched out on the black road surface. Maggie tucked her knees up into her chest and put her chin on her knees. It was not so cold now. The wind had died. There was a gentle breeze that tickled. Maggie could hear it in the trees to her right. A kind of whisper. A shadow moved on the surface of the grass in the field in front of her.

'I knew I'd find you here,' he said.

He put his hand on her shoulder. She did not respond. He pulled a package from his coat pocket and handed it to her.

'I made you a sandwich,' he said. 'I have tea ready. I'm gonna go and pick up Eoin. Okay?'

Maggie nodded.

She took the package and opened the greaseproof paper and took the sandwich out. It was cheese and tomato and the cheese was a processed slice. Maggie took a bite and crushed the paper in her hand and handed it back to her husband.

'I have to go away for a bit, Brian,' she said.

Another car passed.

'Oh!' he said. 'How long?'

'Just a bit.'

He put both hands on her shoulders and leaned his head on hers. She reached back and touched his head and then put her hand on his.

'You won't ever leave me, princess, will you?' he said.

'No, I won't leave you.'

When she said it she didn't know if she meant it but she said it anyway because it seemed the right thing to say and she hoped it was true.

'I do all this for you,' he said, 'and the kids. Look – use your imagination, love. Imagine a palace here. Imagine it. Ach, sure we'll be millionaires in a year. You believe me, don't you?'

He hugged her.

'Of course I believe you, love. Why shouldn't I? Tell the kids I've gone to see Mam. I'll ring when I can.'

She kissed his hand.

'I caught Maeve with a boy this afternoon,' she said. 'In our bed.' She laughed. 'At least someone's gettin' use out of it.'

'Maeve?' he said.

'Yeah. Our wee Maeve, Brian. Screwin'. Our daughter with some Clones shite called Sean. I caught them. I nearly killed your man. I just lost the head. Poor Maeve, she thinks she's in love. Don't say anythin'. I said I wouldn't tell you. She thinks the world of you, Brian. It'd kill her if she thought you knew. Please don't say anythin'.'

'No. Jesus Christ. I'd have killed the little bastard. She's only fifteen. Christ. Who is he?'

'I don't know. But don't press it, Brian. Please. For me. I feel a bit of a hypocrite lecturin' her. Poor wee Maeve. She wants to be in love.'

'It's gonna get better,' he said. 'I mean it. We'll build and things'll be better. You've been great, Maggie. I mean, I couldn't have survived without you, love – what age is this Sean fellow?'

'I don't know. Around Maeve's, I think.'

'She's not pregnant?'

'I don't know that either. I don't know everythin', Brian. I can't do everythin'.'

'Yeah. My God, Maevie. I'll beat the shite out of him if I get my hands on him.'

'I said no, Brian.'

'Right. Would you like to stay in my hotel?'

'I'd love to,' she said.

The following night she was on a beach in Donegal, lining up the laser-guide nightsight on a Barrett Light Fifty rifle on a side of beef. The distance was one mile and the round hit the target in the top right quarter. She adjusted her sight and waited for the wind to die down and let the music from her Walkman melt into her mind and when it was right she fired again.

15

IN THE DINING room of a three-star hotel south of Belfast, Carol Russell reached across the table for two and touched Tim McLennan's hand.

'You're not with me, love, are you?'

He cut a piece of filet mignon and dipped it in the mayonnaise on the side of his plate and pushed some lettuce and tomato from his side salad on to his fork and lifted the fork to his mouth.

'I'm a bit away, I suppose. You know? Mum was screamin' last night.'

He put the food in his mouth.

'How long are you going to stay there nights?' Carol asked.

McLennan chewed his food and took a sip of wine from the glass beside him and swallowed the food and the wine together.

'As long as she needs me.'

'Mummy's boy.'

'That's not fair, Carol.'

'Yeah, I'm sorry. I thought I'd have you tonight. I haven't had you for a couple of weeks now, Tim. I miss you. I want to have you. I need you, love.'

'There's a lot happenin'.'

'I could come over. Keep you both company. We could make love in your bed.'

'No, Carol!'

'Just kidding, Tim. Just kidding. Mae still doesn't approve, I take it.'

'I don't discuss it much.'

Carol finished off her wine and McLennan took the bottle from the bucket and poured some more into each glass. The bucket was on his side and the water running down it had spread out on the white tablecloth to the sugar bowl. The ice in the bucket had melted to discs and the label was coming loose on the bottle. Carol touched his hand again.

'You look tired,' she said. 'Are you looking after yourself, Tim?'

She smiled.

McLennan squinted and moved his lips like he was about to say something.

'Poor Tim,' she said. 'The weight of the world. I could give you a rub. Come back for an hour and I'll get the oils out and give you a rub.'

'I wouldn't leave.'

'Would that be bad?'

'I promised. I'll get a free night, I will. I'll make one. We can get a room somewhere. Not back at your place. Somewhere we can order food and drink. You know? Special.'

'Always the romantic. Are you making an indecent suggestion to a police officer?'

'If you like.'

'I do.'

He nodded and ate some more of his steak and pushed a congealed heap of sautéd potato around his plate and finished off his glass of wine.

'We'll have to get a taxi if you keep knocking back wine like this, Tim. Or I'll have to arrest you.'

'I'm fine.'

'No, you're not.'

'I miss him. I miss Marty. It was only over there I realised it. He should be here.'

'Well, bring him over. You're his father. You bring him over.'

'You think?'

'Yeah. You do what you want, Tim McLennan. You follow your instincts.'

She smiled and McLennan put his knife and fork together.

They did not have dessert and they did not have coffee. McLennan paid the bill and they walked around the hotel grounds for a couple of hours and when they had finished McLennan drove her home and wished he had not promised to stay with his mother. His mother was asleep when he got home and that lifted his spirits and he poured himself a whiskey before he made coffee.

It was late and he was drinking coffee when the doorbell rang.

McLennan put the cup down and went to the door and then stopped before he got there. He had assumed it was Carol. He bollocked himself for the assumption. Then he took the Walther P5 from his jacket pocket and moved over to the living-room window. You could see the front door from the living-room window. There was a spyhole in the door but if there was someone there intent on doing him harm and they sensed a presence at the door and they were out for a kill they could pour rounds through it. He'd thought about getting an armour-plated door. But he wasn't there very often and the windows would have to be proofed, too. And, anyway, if people wanted to get you then they'd find a way. Bombs did the same as bullets, less discreet but just as effective. You couldn't beat a desire for life and a personal weapon. He was as good as ten of them, he felt. Then it didn't matter any more.

Lenny Beggs was shuffling his feet on the doorstep. He looked foolish shuffling his feet, like a little boy dying for a piss. McLennan came to the door and watched Beggs through the peephole. His whole body was wide-angled, like he was being spread with a knife. His mouth was open. There was frozen breath coming from it in clouds. He was smacking his hands together. Then squeezing his nose. Mucus stuck to his hands. He had a wide nose. It was wider in the wide angle of the peephole lense. And big dark eyes that bled into the night. His eyes were drifting. Sharp black eyebrows that would put you on your guard any other time in any other light looked grotesque on the spreading face over the drifting eyes.

Jesus Christ, McLennan thought. Mr Fuckin' Inconspicuous. The original prick in tight jeans.

He opened the door. A small breath of the night touched his face. It was zeroish. No rain. Not much wind. Some stars. The stars looked like you could pick them. Beggs made an attempt at a smile.

'Tim,' he said.

'Lenny.'

The snot had dried on Beggs' fingers. He was rolling it into balls. He stopped shuffling. He made to come in but McLennan looked at him and he did not.

'Hows about you?'

'What the fuck are you doin' here? You followin' me, Lenny Beggs? The other day in Belfast, now this. I hope you've a good explanation, son, or I'm gonna be annoyed. You're beginnin' to imitate a rash, Lenny. And I have an irritatin' feelin' on the back of my neck.'

'Aye, well, look, it's bloody freezin', Tim, can I come in?'

'Why? It's one in the bloody mornin'. And I don't like bein' followed, Lenny, not by you, not by anyone. Who gave you this address?'

'Hey, come on, we're on the same side. Ulstermen.'

He made another attempt at smiling.

'You got your Rottweilers with you?' McLennan asked.

'They're waitin' down there. Discreet, like.'

McLennan produced his Walther and levelled it at Beggs's head. Beggs's attempt at smiling twisted into a dislocating jaw. He lost control of all muscles for a moment. It looked like he might drop.

'Give me a good reason why I shouldn't,' McLennan said. 'Known paramilitary calls at my door in the dead of night. What am I to think? I could at least blow off a kneecap. Which one, Lenny? You choose. I bet you can't. You couldn't give away steam from your piss, Lenny. I told you I didn't want to talk to you. I told you. Now I'm angry. You come here at this time of night, to my mother's home, creepin' around like a hood. But then what else should I have expected? Jesus Christ, Lenny, what is it with you?'

Beggs regained control of himself. He came forward a couple of steps. McLennan lowered the pistol. He stepped back. Beggs looked into his eyes. The threat had passed.

'I know you, Tim McLennan, I know all about you. And you know all about me. That makes us even, doesn't it? And never mind what you think of me, you know better, don't you? Now are you goin' to let me in?'

McLennan thought some more and told himself to tell Beggs to piss off and ring the police. But he stepped aside. He knew why but he did not admit it to himself. And he put the action down to curiosity.

'Keep your voice down,' he said. 'My mother's sleepin'.'

'Sure, Tim.'

Beggs walked past him. McLennan placed the Walther in his pocket and closed the door. He took one more look through the peephole. The sky had an Einsteinian quality and he wondered if maybe time was bending into a distortion.

Loony Lenny, they called Beggs round the Shankill. Good in a scrap, pain in the arse for anything else. A bully. But bullies had their uses. There'd been times, even Robbie Wilson would have had to admit that, there'd been times when having Lenny around was helpful. A fight on a red-brick street between the Falls and the Shankill. Tim could barely remember it, except in snatches. The Taigs coming at them with small stones and marbles. He got hit with a marble. Maybe twelve, maybe older. It was hard to tell, looking at the faces. The minds felt older but they couldn't have been. Taigs. Tims, they called them in Glasgow. That was a bitch. They used to call him Taig at school. He'd hit a couple of them for that. Lenny Beggs used to call him Taig. He couldn't remember hitting Lenny Beggs. You just didn't hit Lenny Beggs at school. Lenny Beggs hit you if he wanted to, or hit for you if you were clever. He had a brain inversely proportionate to his size, Lenny, they used to say. But that was then. The Taigs were yelling at them, taunting them, on a hot summer's day, dirty city feeling, shorts and vests, fists and legs, marbles and stones. Lenny at the front. Charging into the Taigs like a bull. Knocking them every which way. They were scared of Lenny. They were even more scared when he got older.

I called you Tim just so you might know what a simple label can do, his mother had said. He never understood, he never really forgave her.

They all cheered Lenny then. When the Taigs ran off, or their mothers came out and clipped the ears off them. He preferred to think of the Taigs in retreat. And everyone slapped Lenny on the back and told him he was the best, best of the best, King Lenny, victory to King Lenny of the Shankill. Tim could remember slapping Beggs on the back, saying all that stuff, hailing him. He stopped himself then.

'Good stuff, this,' Beggs said.

They were in the conservatory. At the back of the house. Wicker chairs and residual warmth. No lights. Lenny looked like some huge tropical plant. He sipped his glass of Bushmills and then knocked it back. McLennan poured him another. Lenny had a couple of stones wedged in the soles of his shoes. His feet scraped the tiling. He tried to stop doing it but he could not keep his feet still and every time he moved them he scraped the tiling. He made a face halfway between amusement and embarrassment.

Beggs downed his whiskey in one and held out his glass.

'That's good. Jesus, I'm bloody freezin'. I hear you were part of that team that scored over in Tyrone last week, Tim,' he said.

Tim McLennan said nothing. He poured Beggs another glass and sipped some of his own whiskey.

'Good one, that, Tim. Good work. Like to see that. And more. Know what I mean?'

'No.'

'Dead terrorists,' Beggs said.

'You includin' yourself there, Lenny?'

'I'm not a terrorist.'

'No?'

'No. What I do, I do for Ulster. Same as you. And you know it. Don't you?'

McLennan saw Mal Hart's face and heard his words.

He sipped some more whiskey.

'I could have you lifted for bein' here, Lenny,' he said.

'I know.'

Beggs held out his glass again and McLennan filled it. He poured a single and Beggs kept his hand out. McLennan gave him a double.

'You stayin' here now?' Beggs said.

'Who's askin'?'

'Just me. If I can find you then maybe the other side can. Think about it.'

'You threatenin' me, Lenny?'

'Ach, away off with you, Tim, no, I'm not. I want to see you do better. I want you alive. Fuck, SAS, little Tim McLennan. Not fuckin' bad. You were a bit of a snobby snot. Youse and that Robbie Wilson's family. Movin' out here. Youse went up in the world. Afraid to talk to an old pal?'

'About what?'

'What do you think? I never saw what they did to him. But you did. Robbie Wilson. Look what they did to him. Jesus, poor old Robbie. I heard youse went fishin' when you should have been workin'. Mind of your own, Tim. I like that. And doin' some catchin' up with old friends. That's good. Quality time, they call it. I never liked him. Robbie. Stuck-up family, the Wilsons, thought they were above us all. Then the ma gets a bit of money from England and they're off as quick as can be. But look at what happened.'

'Gettin' sentimental in your old age, Lenny?'

'Maybe. Maybe I'm just more aware of who my friends are. Good thing to know in this world, Tim. Don't you agree? You were a Selous Scout, weren't you?'

'You know it all, don't you, Lenny. I was for a bit.'

'Then you know. The Rhodesians ran out of friends. Cut-off and isolated. Gave in too easily.'

'They lost the war. The terrorists were too strong, comin' from too many directions. I was there. Too many fronts. And sanctions.'

'That's as maybe, Tim, but I'm right about the friends. Amn't I?'

'Maybe.'

'Anyway, I want to talk about here, about Northern Ireland. We're gettin' isolated. Or have the Army blinded you to everythin'? We're gettin' isolated and we might just end up gettin' dropped right in it for it. We're bein' parcelled up, Tim, nice and slow like, then we'll be handed over to Dublin. You know it, I know it. Maybe not today, maybe not tomorrow, as Humphrey Bogart would say, but it's comin'. And when it does, there's those of us want to be ready to do somethin' about it. Know what I mean?'

'Your lot, you mean.'

'My lot may well be all that stands between you and a united Ireland one of these fine days, Tim. My lot might be the ones you come screamin' to when the Taigs are knockin' at that door. You want to live in that kind of a country, with Fenians runnin' around lookin' to settle old scores. You want that? For your mother? For your son? Oh, yeah! Face it, Tim, the United Kingdom's becomin' a bad joke for Protestants. Those fuckers over there, those fuckers think we're a bunch of religious bigots. If they could, they'd sell Northern Ireland out first chance they got. They're tryin' to do it now. Look at what's happened. Stormont goes, then they let Dublin in by the back door. Creepin' unity, I'm tellin' you. Well, there's those of us not prepared to let that happen. Ever. There comes a point, Tim, there comes a point when you have to stand up for what you believe in, no matter what. No matter what. Ulster is there. She was there in 1912 and men came together and stopped it. We're there again. But we have friends. We do.'

He nodded and held out his glass. McLennan refilled it. Beggs's tongue was in autopilot.

'I'm fightin' for the union,' McLennan said. 'I'm a British soldier. If you wanted to fight for the right to be British so much, Lenny, why didn't you join up? You never even joined the UDR. Nothin'. Like the drinkin' clubs too much, Lenny. Like the B'mer. I know about you, Lenny. You haven't enough fingers for the pies. I fight for you, Lenny, for all this, so don't lecture me on Northern Ireland and the union. What do you want me to do? Come with you and pick up a Taig or two and start peelin' their skin for kicks?'

'You really look down your nose at me, McLennan. You really do.

Shankill wasn't good enough for youse. Youse had to go to some nice snotty place, where people put garlic in their food and know the temperature red wine should be served at. Youse McLennans got real big when your daddy got shoved up. Twopence lookin' down on a penny halfpenny, I think they call it.'

'Leave my daddy out of this, Lenny, or I'll blow your fuckin' head off right now.'

'Okay, okay, I'm sorry, I'm sorry. The drink's lubricatin' me, Tim. But I know what I done. And I done my time for it. I was a wee boy. They were doin' it to us. You couldn't walk into the centre of Belfast without runnin' into one of their bombs or bullets. We lost good lads to them. So we were out to hit back. They're all the same. I know there's people who say there's only a few of them. If there were only a few of them, we'd have done for them years ago. Every one, every one of them, every fuckin' Taig is a Provo, or a potential Provo, as far as we're concerned. They are an enemy community and as such must prepare to suffer the consequences of their actions.'

He sounded to McLennan like he was recalling a prepared text.

'People like your friend Robbie Wilson will never understand that. Oh, I know all about Robbie Wilson and his reachin'-out stuff, Tim. The kind of good heart that loses wars. You should tell him that. Make him see. Robbie just – Robbie just can't see.'

If Beggs expected McLennan to laugh, he got the opposite and it stopped his own smile mid-tracks.

'I told you, I fight terrorism in this province wherever it comes from,' McLennan said. 'That's my job. I'm a soldier of the United Kingdom. I defend that kingdom from its enemies, wherever they come from.'

'And if they sell us out?'

'You talk like there's a difference. I'm they. I'm part of Britain. Are you sayin' I'd sell out my own people?'

'No, not you, Tim, others. Ever get the feelin' we're like a relative who's overstayed their welcome. Distance, Tim. Look and listen. Jesus, they ring Dublin before they fart now. Sure they're sponsorin' Gaelic lessons in Tigers Bay, for God's sake. They're like a bunch of fuckin' housesitters. The NIO, all the rest. They – youse – youse used to use people like me. I did jobs for youse. Yes, you know I did. Men with upper-crust accents handin' out weapons with the serial numbers filed off. Untraceable. Familiar?

You never knew where they came from, except they had pots of money and information comin' out their ears. Who, where, what, how. They told you you were doin' it for Ulster, to keep Ulster British. We were doin' it for them, to keep them in work, to keep the status quo in London. We'd have been cheap at half the price. Don't worry, we're quiet about it all. We know what happens if lads gò public. It's a dirty game played here. Friends and enemies. Like musical chairs. You know it, Tim. Kill Taigs, don't kill Taigs, bomb here, no bomb there. They fair smashed this wee town of yours, Tim. Your mother okay?'

Tim nodded.

'And they can just keep doin' it,' Beggs said. 'Soon there won't be a town centre left in the whole province. You know? And what if I told you your people know who done it here? What if I was to say they know who done it and they let them do it?'

'I'd say, go on.'

'I'll bet.'

Beggs reached inside his jacket. He pulled out a folded envelope and took a creased ten-by-eight from it and unfolded it and handed it to McLennan.

'That was taken forty minutes before the bomb went off. It's not great. You see this boy, here, he's the bomber. Here, take it, check up if you like. Then go take your mother for a walk down the high street and open your bloody eyes. You're bein' used, son. Just like I was, once.'

'How'd you get this?'

'Friends. Who don't like what they're seein'. Good Ulstermen. Who know. Look, you rubbed out three Provos. Three more will take their place. They're queuin' up to join in the Taig ghettos. And they're outbreedin' us, Tim. Time is with them. And we're expected to stand still while Westminster packages us – because that's what they're doin', this war with the IRA is just a matter of prestige for them now – while they package us nicely and send us down to Dublin. That what you want?'

'It won't happen. They've agreed.'

'Christ! What planet were you born on, man? Look at that photo again. What do they call you over there? Paddy, is it, or Mick? I bet they don't call you old chap, or Timothy. I bet. Ulster's bloody bought them an empire and they'd sell us like a second-hand chair at a car boot sale. Agreed? And when the Taigs pass us out. Not now. But a couple of decades or so. Inside our lifetimes. I have kids. If we don't sort this out, then they'll get it. I don't want that. I don't want my kids stripped of everythin' they are, outsiders, freaks, in a united Republic of Ireland. Not on.'

'We might just end up part of a united Europe,' McLennan said.

'More Taigs. You say my lot. Well my lot has been doin' a lot of reorganisation. Since Andy stood down.'

'Stood down?'

'Was stood down. Good lad, Andy. Too long in the job, though. Needed the rest. Well, we're leaner and meaner, as they say across the ocean, and we've sorted the organisation out, weeded out the chaff.'

McLennan was going to say something about mixing metaphors but decided not to. His whiskey was benefitting.

'We're well armed and we're cultivatin' friends. Networkin', I think the yuppies say. Well, we're networkin'. But in the end we'll have to do most of it on our own. Be prepared to fight. Hit them with everythin' we have.'

'Who?'

'Republicans. No matter which corner they come from. Doomsday. Bible's always goin' on about it. Maybe there's somethin' in it. If it comes to it, we'll have to take power. Here. It'll take doin'. We'll need support from all sides of unionism. It'll be difficult but we'll make a go of it.'

'Independence?'

'Sure. Only solution if we're dumped. Unless you want to go to Dublin and join the Free State Army. I hear it's a cushy number. They definitely don't do much work along the border. Am I right?'

'Not viable. Anyway, I'm British. They can't take that away from me. We went all the way to the Falklands to keep them British because the people wanted it. Lost good men.'

'Times change, Tim. Needs change. Put not your faith in princes. I know my words. The Kesh does that for you. Does other things. Gives you a political education. One thing about the Taigs, they're dedicated, you have to give that to them. They educate, they direct, they aim. I may hate everythin' they stand for but I have to admire the way they go for it. We need that. That kind of direction. Ulster. Our state.'

'And the Catholics.'

'Not with us, against us. That was the mistake we made in the past. Allowin' them to stay and be disloyal. Not next time. Next time it's out. Let them go south to their fuckin' republic. I hear you have to show a marriage licence to buy condoms there. Did you hear that?'

'What do you want from me?' McLennan asked.

Beggs smiled. He held out his glass again. McLennan filled it up.

'Good stuff,' Beggs said. 'I want you to look at that photograph – take a bloody good look at it, ask a few questions, and then maybe we can talk again.'

'No way, Lenny. Your organisation is barely tolerated by law, Lenny. That bit of it you hang around is outlawed. I could arrest you here and now on suspicion of membership. You've spent the last twenty years arsin' your way around this province, murderin' and bombin' and racketeerin', so deep in blood you don't know what you're doin'. What is it you lads say – any Catholic will do? I've seen it on walls. I don't know if anyone used you and I don't care. That was then and now is now. Like I said, if you wanted to defend this province you could have joined the UDR or the RUC or any other army regiment. You boys just don't see. You keep sayin' you're British, loyalists, then you fuckin' do everythin' in your power to subvert the kingdom. You shame Ulster. You shame the men of the Somme. You shame me. I fight and I fight to win, sure. But I'm a soldier and I don't go bumpin' off people on a Saturday night for kicks.'

'Don't you?'

'What's that supposed to mean?'

'What it does.'

McLennan's mouth pressed closed, hard closed. He put his glass down. He put his hand in his pocket. Beggs glanced at the hand in the pocket and moved in his chair and moved his drink in his glass. He licked his lips. McLennan leaned forward.

'I think you better go. I don't know who gave you this address or told you I'd be here, Lenny, but if you call uninvited again or if I hear anyone's been around shouldn't be, I'm comin' callin' on you. I've seen too many men die for this province, good men, to sit and listen to you get off on some kind of coup theory. We'll fight all right, we'll fight the IRA, but we'll do it as what we are, British soldiers and policemen.'

There was a silence and both men finished their drinks for something to do and McLennan felt embarrassed for what he had said. Before he left, Beggs turned to McLennan again.

'Nice speech, Tim. But I don't think you believe it. I'll be in touch again. If you're not interested you'll have peelers at my door tomorrow mornin'.

But I don't think they'll be there. Do you?'

McLennan sat up when Beggs had gone. He sat up and tried to count the stars.

16

JOHN CUSACK STOOD at the door of an outhouse on the small Monaghan farm where Dessie Hart's unit was billeted. The clouds had broken. The sun was out. A sharp winter sun. A corona surrounded him and a thin wall of steam rose from the floor of the outhouse in front of him. He had an oilskin coat on and a kevlar jacket hanging from one shoulder under the coat and he was carrying an Armalite rifle rolled up in a sheet. He walked over to the hay bales where Maggie O'Neill sat.

That end of the outhouse was stacked with hay bales and there were sleeping bags and rucksacks lying on the bales. Automatic rifles stood in an improvised rack next to one bale. And magazines of ammunition beside them. There were farm tools up against a wall. The farm tools were old. The whole place smelled of gun oil and hay and damp. The damp was the strongest smell. It got into everything. And when the temperature dropped at night, the damp froze and the water running from the walls turned to ice and it was so cold you felt like all the heat you had ever had was being drained from you.

Maggie had a stripped-down Romanian FPK sniper rifle on a groundsheet beside her and a Barrett Light Fifty sniper rifle sat on a bipod behind her. She had the bolt of the FPK in her hand. She was rubbing it with a cloth. Cusack watched her before saying anything. She wore a boiler suit and wellingtons and a woollen balaclava rolled up to her forehead. She had a small streak of dirt across her face and her neck had a pink scratch running the length of it.

'Hi,' Cusack said. 'I heard you were here.'

She pressed her lips together and nodded.

Cusack took his oilskin coat off and sat on a heap of fresh logs. They were green and wet and the one he was sitting on left a stain on his combat trousers. He wore a camouflaged cotton vest underneath an open combat jacket. The combat jacket was British Army issue and the boots he wore were French Ranger boots with double strapping at the top. And he wore a .357 Magnum in a shoulder holster.

He put the kevlar jacket down on a hay bale and pulled out the butt of the Armalite and stood it up in the makeshift rifle rack. Then he took a small timber plank from a pile and placed it on two logs and sat on it.

The timber planking was fresh and had the smell of fresh wood. There was other wood in the shed – small sticks and planks and kindling for fires – and in one corner there was bark, a large heap of it, and in bad daylight it looked like manure.

'Wet,' he said, looking at the logs. 'You like that?'

Maggie held her head just below his line of sight, thought, then raised her head and looked him in the eye.

'You like that?' she asked.

She nodded at the kevlar jacket.

'It helps.'

'Not against one of those.'

She looked at the Barrett Light Fifty.

'We're not facing those.'

'Better a round goes right through,' she said. 'That sends things in all directions. Rounds do acrobatics all over you when they hit them. Better clean.'

'I'll remember that. You haven't answered my question.'

'I know.'

'I like the Steyr. The SSG. It's clean. Solid piece.'

'True. But you can't knock it around like this. And this has a customised feel. The round is a good stopper. Put a very hard nose on it and it'll go right through just about anythin' a body can wear.'

'AK-based. Reinforced receiver. You can take the recoil?'

'Don't patronise me, Yank. Just don't. I can take this cannon.'

She reached over and touched the Barrett.

'Awkward bastard, though. Damn monster,' Cusack said.

'Goes through walls. Stopper of all stoppers.'

'So you're ready to go, then. Good. That's good. I -'

'Don't try and get personal, Yank. We're here for a job. I'll do mine. You look after yours. And that's it.'

'Fine. I didn't mean to—'

'To what? Come on to me?' She looked up at him again. Then she laughed. 'Everyone comes on to me. I think it has to do with the sniper thing. This.' She pointed to the stripped-down rifle. 'Phallic. So cut the shite, Yank. I know a come-on. You work with a lot of men, you get to know a come-on. It's the only way most of these lads can deal with me. Not exactly progressive, this army of ours. But I do what I do and I do it better than most so that gets me space. Look, I've been watchin' you. And you've been watchin' me. You know? I've seen you. So don't go all mysterious on me. Anyway, what are you doin' here?'

'Came to clean this. Been giving lessons to the boys.'

He touched the Armalite.

She looked around the outhouse. Then she put down the part of the rifle she was oiling.

'I mean here. The others, well, I know most of them, and they know me, and we all know why everyone's here. But you, here. Your bloody accent screws you up right away. I get the feelin' we're on a film set. I expect someone to say cut, any moment.'

'I was born in Dublin. I lived the first five years of my life in the States. The next twelve in Dublin. I lived the next ten years in the States and other places. I've lived in this country since. Maybe a couple or more Stateside and other places because I was asked to. And now I'm here again. Happy?'

'That you're here?'

'That I've filled you in.'

He sat down on the groundsheet and picked up the Walkman beside her. He opened it and took the tape out. It was opera. He did not recognise the work or the composer so he did not comment. He just knew it was opera. He put the tape back in and picked up the main body of the FPK.

'Nice-looking piece, isn't it?' he said.

He balanced it in his hand. Then he picked up the telescopic sight. The markings were in English.

'Export model.'

He laughed.

'I'm married,' she said.

'I know. I know everything about you.'

He looked into her eyes and the look held her even though she did not want to be held by it. Then she broke free.

'That get you off?' she said.

'No. You have nice kids.'

'Yeah, I do. Do you?'

'Have kids? No, no I don't. Your boy looks a lot like Spike. I knew Spike. He was a good man, Spike.'

'We never called him Spike at home. Pat. We always called him Pat. Mammy called him P. That was because our Jackie couldn't say Pat when he was a wee boy. Did you know our Jackie? Jackie was a great laugh.'

'I never knew Jackie. I've heard about him. I was living in the States then. That was a different time.'

'I remember Jackie dyin' more than Pat, you know. There were four of them in the van. Ridiculous. Kids tryin' to be soldiers. They hadn't a clue what they were doin'. We just got the coffin. Mammy wanted to open it. There was nothin' in it. We knew that. Look, you have me gettin' all nostalgic. You should know better, Yank. You lost anyone?'

'No. My people don't . . .'

'Never in jail, never lost anyone. No one involved. Jesus! You have any connections?'

'None. I'm here because I believe what we're doing is right. They're here by force and the only way to get them out is by force.'

'Wow! You weren't in Sinn Fein, were you?'

'No. I'm here because they're here. Because they've drawn the line. And in my country, I won't be dictated to. Not in my country. Not by them.'

'You have it all worked out.'

'You haven't?'

'I suppose I do. But I don't worry about all that. That's for Staters and people who need it. I don't need it. I know what I'm about.'

She was reassembling the rifle without looking at it. She was looking at a frosted window. The sun and the rainwater threw different colours on the frosted glass.

'You don't wear your wedding ring,' he said.

She examined her finger.

'That's a stupid thing to say, Yank. Who ever heard of a sniper wearin' a weddin' ring.'

'My name's John.'

'I don't want to know. I don't want to know anythin' about you. You were a marine or something, weren't you? Didn't they teach you that? Don't get to know too much. I said this to Dessie Hart years ago. The cells. The longer this goes on, the more difficult it will be to keep any distance. And distance is essential for security. Look at us, Yank, I know everyone here. I know where they come from, who their families are. You know Betty – well, we're related, and my husband is Dessie Hart's second cousin. Brian – he's my husband – he doesn't get involved. But he knows not to ask questions.'

'So what do you tell him?'

'Whatever he wants to hear. He has his own problems. He's out of work. Half the country's out of work. He's good at shuttin' things out, Brian. Comes naturally. Jesus, what am I sayin' this to you for? What's your work, Yank?'

'This.'

'Jesus, you are committed.'

'What's yours?'

'You should know.'

Cusack laughed. He tapped his fingers on the plate in the kevlar jacket. Maggie had re-assembled the FPK. She pointed it at the ceiling and looked through the sight. Then she cocked it, pulled the trigger and put the safety catch on.

'Have to keep this baby in luxury,' she said. 'Treat your rifles like you treat your men, like we used to say in the Cumann – lay them in luxury and squeeze, don't pull.'

She grinned and placed the rifle in the leather holder she had for it. Then she rubbed her hands together and put them to her nose.

'Good smell,' she said.

She placed her hands close to Cusack's face. He hesitated before leaning in to them. The smell was of gun oil. But there was more, somewhere distant, a faint trace, and it was that trace that got Cusack. She touched his nose with her finger.

'You're cute, Yank. I won't call you John. I don't want to. I'll stick to Yank. You want to see my kids?'

She was already reaching into her pocket. She took out a plastic holder and pulled two photographs from it.

'Maeve's like her daddy. She's goin' through that stage, you know?

Hormones all over the place. Ach, it'll pass. Eoin's – he is like Pat, you're right. It's there. You've a good eye.'

'We'll be finished here soon,' Cusack said. 'You can get back to them. You'll—'

'Don't tell me anythin' except what I have to do, Yank. And don't get soft.'

'Okay,' he said. 'I suppose – I have a sister. She just lost a kid.'

'I'm sorry.'

'Me too. Cot death. She's taking it bad. She's—'

Cusack forgot what he wanted to say about his sister and just stared at Maggie's body. Her skin did something to him. The colour was between pale and cream, kind of hanging there, and you could imagine it turning a good brown if it got enough sun, turning brown and then peeling some and then staying a lighter brown. Her hair would look good then. And he could feel something. A sense. It was not something he could define and say, that's it, but it was a part of her, or a part of her and him there in that outhouse, and it had a knowledge attached. Movements complemented each other, unconscious movements, and it was there. He let himself get closer. The lashes turned up and the chin was pointed. A fine craftsman had worked on her, he thought. She curved in the right places. Many women did not curve in the right places. He did not mean catwalk curves, he meant the curves that made women and it did not matter what way they were or how they looked if they had those curves. She looked good and she had the curves. She was not beautiful. But the curves. And the curves and the sense. He felt himself being drawn in.

'—my sister's like that. Her husband's a son of a bitch. I can't stand him.'

'Don't tell me, Yank. I heard you scared the shite out of the lads the other day. Had Danny cursin' you blind. I'd like to have seen that.'

'Just a little training. Test the plaster for cracks.'

'Are there many?'

'Some. But in the end it's all about what's up here.' He touched his head. 'That's something Sheila doesn't understand. She's my sister.'

'You miss her?'

'I guess.'

Sunlight had made its way to the back of the outhouse and into Maggie O'Neill's hair. And her hair was lovely in the sunlight. He looked at her again and held the look and she dipped her eyes and then lifted them again and held the look.

'Good,' she said.

'Why's that?'

'You can get detached here.'

'That's what she says. She thinks the world's all about house prices and whether you live on a road or a park or a close. Says I'm a psycho. Me! She doesn't understand things. The way the world works. Why she has things and other people don't. Says it's because they work hard. Jesus. I tried to tell her. She won't listen. Just spouts the usual terrorism stuff. Called me a murdering bastard. Me! Thinks I'm some kind of Capone.'

'You'd like her to understand?'

'Sure. Doesn't matter, though. None of that lot do. I know them. I grew up with them. They just take what they're given. Have to have someone tell them they're right. Fucking sheep. I think Sheila thinks I'm playing games. Cowboys and Indians. Told me once she wouldn't care if she was Japanese. She doesn't even realise that you gotta be privileged just to think like that. Stupid bitch. You ever get detached?'

'All the time. It has its uses.'

'You miss your kids?'

'All the time.'

'Your husband?'

'None of your bloody business.'

Maggie stood up and rubbed the hay from her boiler suit. Cusack watched her move and the movement of her body against the boiler suit and the warmth and the way she had held the look all made him hard and it was like he had drunk wine, too much wine, and was lying in the sun and the wine was flowing through him, a free flow that made him happy and relaxed and he felt himself released.

'There's nothin' much in it for us,' she said, 'is there? Except maybe a good funeral. We give the best funerals. Don't wear that thing, it'll just make movin' harder.' She looked at her watch. 'I'm hungry,' she said. 'Don't follow me. We've talked enough. Too much. Remember, distance.'

She walked to the door. He watched her walk because he could not stop himself watching her. Even when he told himself she was right he could not take his eyes off her. She walked well and maybe she knew it and walked that way because she knew it. Cusack let breath out and tore a piece of hay in two.

Maggie only got to the door of the outhouse.

'It's off,' the voice outside said.

Cusack lifted his head.

Danny Loughlin had his hands in his pockets. He had his pipe in his mouth. His beard was white in the light and his shape was fluid and it looked like maybe he would vanish. The boiler suit he was wearing didn't fit him properly and his jeans showed under the legs of the boiler suit. He had a white shirt under the top of the boiler suit and a shoulder holster with a Magnum in it. He pulled two Magnum bullets from his pocket and turned them around between his fingers.

'It's off again,' he said. 'Another delay. Like waitin' for a charter flight to land.'

Maggie spun around and headbutted the air.

'Ah, shite,' she said. 'Why?'

'They have someone in Tyrone. It's a bloody woman, would you believe. McCabe's lot are takin' her over to Donegal now. That's all Dessie's sayin'. He's not too pleased himself. He's gone over to find out what's goin' on. Francie Devine'll be there. Council want a say in this one. So it's all freeze until we find out what the score is. It's a bloody pain, isn't it?'

'I thought you'd be happy, Danny,' Cusack said. 'Just what you want.'

'Runnin' half blind, you mean, John. Always runnin' half blind. This is what I mean about an operation like this. All those workin' parts. I've been puttin' messages out all over. And if Dessie comes back with the okay, I'll have to put more messages out. Sometimes I think I should pack it all in and go open a bar on the Costa de Sol.'

'How long do you figure?' Maggie asked.

'Have to ask Dessie, love,' Loughlin said.

'Where is he?'

'Gone off to find out what's happenin'. Wonderful, isn't it? Even Dessie doesn't know what's goin' on. You want to go home? I could get someone to drop you home. I don't like havin' too many volunteers in the one place sittin' on their arses with no end in sight.'

'We need to build a team,' Cusack said.

'Sometimes I think you lot should leave this war to the women, you know,' Maggie said.

'You could have somethin' there, Maggie,' Loughlin said. 'Betty says that, too. You want a lift?'

She went to answer and then looked at Cusack.

'No,' she said. 'I'll wait. I want to see what's happenin'. Anyway, you need someone to protect you from Brit touts, Danny. They're everywhere, aren't they?'

She laughed and then Cusack laughed.

Loughlin tried to hide his embarrassment but his face let him down.

'Sure maybe all this is just a Brit plot to keep us all sittin' on our arses doin' nothin',' Maggie said.

She smiled and left them.

'Tongue like a fuckin' viper but she's a nice bit of stuff, Maggie,' Loughlin said to Cusack. 'Old Spike was a terrible fuckin' eejit, though. Nothin' on his sister. The other fellow was probably the same as Spike. I think the brains in that family came from the mother. The daddy was a fool. I remember him in the fifties. I had a lecture from him on weapons and he couldn't even strip a Lee Enfield. The brains of that family stayed with the women. You better do what you have to do there, John. Soon.'

'I don't know what you mean, Danny.'

Loughlin came in to the outhouse. Cusack picked up the Armalite he had carried in and began to strip it down. They made you sleep with it in the Corps, sleep with it and chant love songs, so it became a mistress and you loved it. He stripped the weapon like he was stripping a lover. Loughlin watched. Cusack stripped it and then re-assembled it and put it back. There was no need. He had done it to show something or relieve some tension that was building. He could not tell which. He felt good with a rifle, whole. It was hard to explain but that was the way it was. An extra voice. There was the power, too. And power was a high and there was no high like power except maybe fear. Not just scared fear, but chase fear, where you were testing yourself and the stakes were ultimate, which was a kind of power thing. There was nothing like it, everything on the line and only you and whoever or whatever was against you. The buzz made you take off.

'Well, anyway, I gave you the message,' Loughlin said. 'It's delayed till further notice. You can pump the lads with more of that Marine shite if you like. I'm goin' for a walk. Don't like the atmosphere much in here.'

'Bad for your health, Danny?' Cusack said.

Loughlin was gone.

There was a tractor parked at one end of the farmyard. It was old and rusted. A trailer lay beside it. The trailer was full of old bits of metal. A couple of car wheels were resting against the whitewashed stone of one of the outhouses.

The television aerial on the farmhouse was swaying in the wind. A collie sat near the tractor, facing out. Ger Kelly in the doorway of a shed. He was reading. He had a long German Army jacket on. The flashes were Bundeswehr. He was smoking and the smoke was scattering in the wind. The wind was blowing Ger Kelly's red hair around. The smoke mixed with the red hair. Loughlin nodded to him and Ger nodded back. He touched his side. Under his German Army jacket he had an AKM hanging from his shoulder. On the other shoulder he wore a holster with a Magnum revolver. His shoes were hillwalking shoes. He'd taken them from a labourer he'd helped shoot two years earlier. They were good shoes, he said. Shame to let good shoes go to waste. Expensive. American. He repeated it every time someone asked him about the shoes. He only wore them on operations. He glanced around the yard himself. There was a football near the dog and a bathtub underneath a window of the farmhouse. The curtains were pulled in the window. The door needed a coat of paint and the wood was rotting at the skirting board.

'Mother Ireland get off my back!'

Loughlin looked around. Cusack was standing in the farmyard. He raised his fist.

'Tiocfaidh ár lá,' Cusack said.

'Chuky!' Loughlin said.

They both laughed.

17

THERE WILL ALWAYS be conflict between the haves and have nots; the haves trying to hold on to what they have, the have nots trying to take it away from them. That's the way it is, that's the way it always will be. It's nature.

Tim McLennan recited Lenny Begg's words over and over again in his mind in some kind of vain hope they would tell him something he did not already know.

He walked right up to Stone and saluted. Stone paused and tried to hide his surprise and any anger that was inside and then returned the salute even though McLennan was dressed in jeans and a jacket. Then Stone smiled a defusing smile because he thought it was needed. He waited for a return gesture. It did not come and Stone stepped back and stood at ease on the balls of his feet.

'Staff,' he said. 'What the bloody hell are you doing here, Tim?'

Across the airfield a resupply flight was preparing for take-off. Two Lynxes and a Wessex. Anxious toms checked their weapons. McLennan glanced over at them.

'I need to talk, boss.'

Stone glanced over at the choppers – their blades were beginning to turn – and then back at McLennan and regained whatever he had lost.

'Yes, right, of course, Tim. What's wrong, Staff?' He looked at his watch. 'You and Vinny Richards should be tooling up south of here right now. Staff?'

'Please, Bob, please, I need to talk.'

'Bloody hell, this had better be worth it, Tim.'

'Oh, it is. It is, sir. I think we could call it special circumstances. I mean, my home town bein' shredded and my mother nearly bein' killed by a Provo bomb youse let go off counts as special circumstances, doesn't it – sir?'

He shoved the blurred photograph of John Cusack into Stone's hand.

Three airmen passed them and Stone stopped what he was going to say until they were out of earshot. Then he looked at the photograph and stared at McLennan.

'Christ, Staff!' he said.

That told McLennan what he wanted to know. He did not need to hear any more but when Stone said they should go somewhere private he went with him anyway.

At first, Stone was going to go to his office, but he stopped at the entrance to the block where it was and turned round and tapped his head.

'Best I mufti up, Tim, I think,' he said.

His tone had changed.

He drew civilian clothes and they took a Q-car and left the base and drove south.

The Q-car was Japanese and McLennan felt some of his anger being rechannelled into self-preservatory road scans. The Q-cars had a reputation. The IRA knew most of the licence plates. Sometimes they sent lists in to Army HQ at Lisburn. A kind of black humour. As between people who have a mutual interest in something. Just as there was talk of talks which no one would admit to. That threw Lenny Beggs and his gems of wisdom back into McLennan's face. Just when he was questioning Stone.

'Jesus Christ, Tim.' Stone said when they were away from the airfield. He said it a couple of times like he was trying to stall. 'Where did you get this?'

'Let's say a birdy gave it to me. I have sources, too, sir. Everyone here has sources. What I want to hear from you is, is it true?'

Stone tried to win back lost ground.

'I don't like your tone, Staff. Remember who and what you are. HMG isn't in the habit of letting terrorists away with bomb outrages. I can tell you that.'

'Then it's true?'

'It's not your business to even ask questions like that, Staff. It has nothing to do with you. Nothing. You have your assignment and you will obey the orders you have been given. And if you don't like it, tell me and I'll have you removed.'

'Ah, fuck it, sir,' McLennan said. 'It's true, then.'

Stone didn't answer. His face was pale.

'Jesus Christ, Bob,' McLennan said. 'Jesus Christ.'

'I would like to know the source of your information, Tim,' Stone said then.

'Fuck the source of my information. I'm out buried in shit day after day, night after night, tryin' to protect me and mine – and yours – and all we believe in and stand for, riskin' my life, and youse calmly let a Provo waltz into my town and let off a van bomb. Am I mad or somethin'?'

'Remember who you're talking to, Staff. You're a soldier and soldiers take orders. Nothing more. I hope you realise that. You have no more rights than Queen's Regulations allow. No matter where you come from.'

McLennan clenched his fist. His eyes were a mixture of fire and water and Stone could not figure out which was winning. He drove on, along the M1, around Belfast, through Lisburn and then down to Ballynahinch and on to the coast. The Mournes stood black against the blue sky, the sea milky green below the black and blue of the mountains and the sky. There were small cliffs, eaten, and sand dunes. There was a couple lying in the dunes. They were still. The sea was angry at the land and a boat moved along the line where it met the sky.

Stone stopped the car and did not speak. He had the look of a computer analysing data now. McLennan expected to see lights flash and a cursor move across his face. McLennan was trying to control himself.

They walked along the promenade of a seaside town that might have been any seaside town. It was one of those places that had never really been touched by the Troubles. The haves, McLennan thought.

And they argued: soldiering, morality, strategy. It was old ground. Then Stone stared out to sea like he was desperately trying to get a glimpse of England.

'I can't discuss this with you, Tim,' Stone said, 'but if I said yes, your information is correct, what would you do?'

McLennan did not know the answer. He did not know what he would do. He had not thought about it. He had not allowed himself to think about it. His mouth was open and his tongue was showing and he felt it made him look stupid.

'Well, all I can say is this,' Stone said, 'and you know it, Tim – there's a real chance to hit them hard. PIRA. And maybe tactical decisions are made for strategic reasons. Battles and wars, Tim. You know the way it works. We let them do things, things we shouldn't if we had all the choices, but we do it for a greater reason. We're not talking rights and wrongs here, Tim. Just tactics and strategy. And sometimes it looks damn dirty. It's a dirty little war we're fighting here, very dirty. And nobody's clean. You understand what I'm saying?'

'And my mother and the others? One lost a hand. Another fellow's still havin' bits of van picked out of him.'

'I am dreadfully sorry about what happened there. The terrorist warning was too short. I can't say more, Tim.'

'I used to patrol that town, when I was in the UDR. I know everyone in it. You should see it now. Have you even taken a look, sir?'

'I have, Staff. You think I get a kick out of this war? I know what you're feeling, Tim. Some of my father's family was in Coventry in 1940. Two of his cousins were killed. Just kids. They knew the Germans were coming.'

He shook his head.

In Belfast, they drank coffee near the Cornmarket. Stone put three sugar lumps in his coffee and stirred it and sipped some coffee and ate the oat cake he had bought with the coffee and put the coffee cup down.

'I feel bad,' he said. 'I'm an honourable man, Tim, like you. I want to stay that way.'

'So are they all, all honourable men,' McLennan said.

'Yes. If your mother – well, we can arrange something there, you know? I know it's difficult, Tim. But try to see the broader picture. The aims here. You're a fine soldier, Tim, a fine soldier.'

McLennan kept turning his head. They were in a corner with a wall behind them and an angle providing more cover but he could not help feeling exposed every time Stone spoke. Any anger he had had wasted itself away on logic and tactical considerations that he could not argue with and he had given up the idea of getting something from Stone that would satisfy him. The wasted anger toyed around with Lenny Beggs's words and their simplicity of analysis and he had a desperate want kicking inside him for Carol, a want that came from nowhere when he least needed it, backed up by isolation and confusion, spinning in his head, tearing up everything he had meant to say, almost swallowing him.

'You're part of it, Tim,' Stone said in the Q-car, driving back to Aldergrove.

The land was flat, stretching to Lough Neagh, and the lake made it colder than it should have been.

'We have a chance to get a dozen or more of them. Think about it. The whole gang between Tyrone, Monaghan and Armagh. Dessie Hart, Francie Devine, the lot of them, in one contact. This has been coming for a long time, Tim. Information coming from all angles. Everyone's involved, whether they know it or not, even the Garda across the border. You see? It's very big – bigger than you and bigger than me – and it's from the very top. Orders, Tim. We don't make policy. That's politics. And HMG isn't keen on its soldiers mixing in politics. Leads to cracks. Look, we're friends, Tim, or at least I like to think we are. You think I liked the idea of letting them bomb and get away. Of seeing your mother being lifted into an ambulance on the evening news. But I'm a soldier and I obey orders. And so do you. So, if you're the soldier I think you are, the soldier I said you were when they were deciding to commission you, you'll understand, Tim.'

In Stone's office, the captain took a photograph from a drawer. Then he turned on his CD player and put the volume up just enough. He leaned across to McLennan.

'That's his face, the chap you want,' he said.

The photograph was a better-quality print than Beggs's.

'Drove straight in,' Stone said, 'dumped the van and drove out in a Dublin hire car. Very smooth. Don't know his name – yet. Never seen him before. Came through on a false American passport. We have a request in with the cousins to see if they have anything but they're being bitchy about it. It's getting now that we have to beg stuff out of them. They're very possessive. Nothing on him in our files till this bomb. Not even a parking ticket. The Garda ditto. We've accessed Dublin but there's nothing there. And we don't want to put in a formal request. Too many suspect characters south of the line for my liking, Tim. Never know who knows whom. It's like walking on a blade. See? We have to play a wide game. Not just the strategy of the last outrage.'

'Can I have this?'

'No can do, Tim. Classified. If Security Service knew, they'd have my balls. They're like jealous lovers with this stuff. I should ask you for yours but I won't. Have a good look at that. Memorise it. Maybe you'll meet him again. You still haven't told me the source of your information.'

'Are you givin' me an order?'

'Not now, Staff. But think about it. Consider your position, so to speak.'

'Sir.'

'I've had words with the C/O, Tim. Training Wing are making noises. And when your commission comes through, they may want you. Don't fuck up your career, Staff. I've three OPs out at the moment, I'm short of men – the whole squadron's short – we have this thing moving and a couple of other things in the pipeline that the big boss wants shifting, so be gentle with me.'

'Do we have one? A Freddy?'

'We have many sources, Tim. You know that. I'll say this: you don't always need to be told what's obvious. Eyes and ears, Tim. Dog-work. All those OPs. Sometimes it pays off.'

'I'll remember that.'

'I understand your anger, Tim. I do, really I do. But I hope I'm not losing you.'

'I don't know what you mean.'

Stone was about to make a joke about McLennan going native. He stopped himself.

'I hope it's all worth it,' McLennan said.

'You're the one who says he wants to neutralise as many of them as possible. Well, we're doing it.'

'And so you let them bomb and shoot their way across the province till you're ready.'

'No one was killed, Staff.'

McLennan thumped the desk. He kept his voice low, though.

'Christ, I hope you're as understandin' as this when they send your local Safeway's into orbit and one of your family gets a piece of the dairy counter lodged in their leg and ends up a walkin' sedative.'

Stone had regained himself.

'I understand your anger, Tim. If you feel you have a decision to make, I suggest you make it now. Clear? Otherwise, get back to what you're paid to do and get those ears in down south. Get them in and get back here where I need you. Well?'

McLennan paused and then looked at his watch.

'Tomorrow,' he said, finally, 'We'll do it tomorrow.'

Stone nodded.

'Fine,' Stone said. 'That's fine. And think about what I said. I know what this means to you, Tim. I understand. When it falls into place, you'll see it was worth it.'

'I hope so.'

That evening, Tim McLennan thought of Lenny Beggs's words about haves and have nots when he wanted to come inside Carol Russell. He was holding himself at the edge, where the pleasure was almost unbearable, concentrating on every muscle in his body, using Lenny Beggs's words to help his control. It seemed ridiculous that he should use Lenny Beggs's words to make love, and he felt phoney, except that what was happening was more important than any words.

Carole's fingers touched his face and she stroked it with the tips of her nails. McLennan brought his mouth down to hers and she lifted her head to meet him. They touched lips, barely, then tongues. Her eyes were almost closed. He pushed again and she threw her head back and pushed at him and he held himself again.

This is nature, Lenny, McLennan thought.

He pulled himself back, right up so that he was almost out of her and Carol thrust her pelvis up at him and he pulled back more and she came to him again, running her hands down his chest.

'Let me see,' she said. 'Let me see, love.'

She bent her head forward and touched him and ran her finger across his balls.

'Swollen!' she said.

Then she put her fingers around his prick and squeezed it with the tips. McLennan used everything he had to hold himself. His breathing was fast now and they were licking, tongues touching. He thrust again. She dug her heels into the bed and threw her legs apart.

'I'm coming,' she said, 'slowly, Tim – oh, darling, wait, very slowly, please, oh, please.'

'You're beautiful,' he said.

'Don't – oh Jesus!'

Her face was red at the cheeks and forehead and beads of sweat gathered above her eyebrows. Her body jerked at the pelvis again. He moved. She ran her hands down to his prick again.

'On your back, soldier,' she whispered. 'On your back. I want you.'

She pulled him out. The foreskin was back and the tip of the prick was dribbling. She put her finger to it and then rubbed it down his chest.

He sank into her and they kissed and rolled over and she sat up and ran her hand through her hair. Her hair was wet and the sandy colour was dark at the roots. She pulled herself up.

'Hold yourself,' he said.

'I am, I am. Come up when I come down.'

He did. She pushed her hands along his chest to his neck and followed them with her tongue. McLennan relaxed his body and closed his eyes. She moved herself on top of him.

He came up to her and held her breasts and put each nipple in his mouth in turn and licked them till they were hard and red and pushed himself with everything he had till they were moving fast, kneeling, interlocked and moving and facing, mouths together and he could feel it coming again. Then they slowed and he pulled himself to the very edge of her and shoved and she cried his name and he said he wanted her and they did this until they could not hold on any longer. It came in quick movements and they fell back on to the bed and Carol dug her heels into his thighs and McLennan said her name over and over again.

They lay apart for maybe a minute. Then he reached out and touched her.

'Did the earth move?' she laughed.

'And the sun and the planets and the stars. The whole bloody galaxy. Maybe even the universe.'

His head was buried in the pillow. He had a hand across her stomach. Carol picked at the hairs on his hand.

'Most bombed hotel in the world,' she said.

'What?'

'This. Great place for an illicit fuck, the Europa. There should be a club. We should have stickers. I committed adultery in the Europa and the earth moved.'

'Cut it out.'

'Why? That's what we've been doing, Tim, or hadn't you noticed?'

'I don't like that word.'

'I do. It's a delicious word: adultery. It makes me feel horny. I prefer being an adulteress to being a wife. Maybe you should stay married, Tim, and just meet me on the side. It'll lose its edge. You'll probably go off screwing other women. That'd be funny. Me at home, barefoot and pregnant, and you off screwing other women. Maybe even Anne. Now that's a thought, having an affair with your ex-wife. Wow! I'd go for it, Tim!'

'Stop talkin'.'

'You needn't get a divorce on my account. I like it this way. My tough SAS body. Meat and two veg.'

'What's that supposed to mean?'

'Nothing, Tim, don't be so sensitive. Police officers have a sense of humour, too. You've got very serious. What's the matter?'

'Everythin'.'

She rolled over on to him and put her chin in between the blades of his shoulders.

'Tell me, lover.'

'Is all this just a war of haves and have nots?' he asked. 'Will there always be wars between haves and have nots? Is it nature?'

'I suppose, yes – and yes. I don't know. It depends on who has what and what right they have to have it. If you follow me. Traffic Branch doesn't deal much with the Provos. Except to give them a speeding ticket. Maybe that's how we should go at them. I don't know, Tim. I'm in the police for a career. I could have gone to Dublin. Good fun in Dublin. Very cosmopolitan. Compared to Belfast, I mean. I used to go out with a medical student from Dublin. Barry.'

'I don't want to hear.'

'Okay. Want to do it again, lover? Oh, I adore you, lover, your body, your balls, your prick. Jesus, I could fuck you till you exploded and then some more.'

She ran her hand down his back and between his legs.

'Soft,' she said. 'Let's see if we can do something about that.'

'No, Carol.'

He rolled away from her. She followed. He pushed her hands away. She lay across him and pinned his arms down. He did not fight back. She kissed him. They held the kiss. It was a warm kiss and they didn't use their tongues till they were well into it and when they did it made it better and the warmth of the kiss was better.

'I love you,' he said.

'Do you? Do you really?'

'I said I do.'

'I've heard that before. If I'd a pound for every time a man told me he loved me I'd be out of the police and living on a tropical island. Men love with their dicks. Women do it with their hearts. And a dick can take a hell of a lot more punishment than a heart. So don't tell me you love me unless you mean it. Really mean it.'

'I do.'

'And Anne?'

'Not any more.'

'Will it be the same for me?'

'No.'

'How do you know.'

'I just do.'

'Rubbish.' She rubbed his hair. 'My God, Tim McLennan. How could I ever go for an ordinary mortal after an SAS man? It's downhill after this. Do they give you special lessons? You know? Maybe for undercover.'

'That's only for paras. They like to give it up the rear. But that's paras for you.'

'Kinky.'

'Come on, Carol.'

She raised her eyebrows.

'Have you ever done it that way?'

'No.'

'How did Anne like it? Was she really horny? Wild? I can't imagine her wild. Not the way you describe her.'

'Stop it, Carol.'

'Checking out the competition.'

'There's no competition.'

'There's always competition.'

She slid down his body and put her head between his legs. He spread them and she stroked the back of his thighs. McLennan bent his head forward and grabbed the pillow when she took him in her mouth. He felt himself harden in her mouth, felt himself go deeper into her, felt her shake and swallow. She moved her hands to cup him. He cried out.

'It's okay,' she said, 'it's okay, enjoy it, let go, it'll be good, I promise.'

He looked back at her. She had a secret face, hidden. He could not say what was hidden or where, but that was how he felt when he looked at her.

She shook her hair back and put her head down again. McLennan felt himself come alive again. He reached back and touched her hair with his fingers.

She moved her mouth from between his legs and licked up his back, massaging the flesh with her hands, to the back of his neck.

'Enjoy,' she whispered, 'enjoy it, soldier. I want to break you.'

Then she moved her hands across the contours of Tim McLennan's body and felt the feel of his flesh. He was tense and the muscles were hard and when she pressed into them, they pushed back. She moved down his body to his legs and down his legs to his feet. She massaged his feet and McLennan felt like a weight was being lifted from him. He could feel his body begin to lift.

'It's good, isn't it?' she said. 'Everything runs through the feet. Controls the feelings. Your head lifting?'

'Yes.'

'Think of nothing. I'll bring you. Oh, I want you. Just relax. Let me do it.'

He turned to her.

'I—'

'Don't be old-fashioned. These aren't performance stakes. Pleasure, love, just pleasure.'

She licked him along each leg and followed her tongue with her hands. She took his prick in her mouth again.

'Please, love,' he said.

'Nothing, say nothing, until you're ready to scream. Lie down. Don't speak until you're coming. Then I want to hear you come.'

McLennan laid his head on the pillow and turned his eyes around as far as they would go. He could see her head and her body moving and the movement of her body made him harder and he thrust himself at her and she moved faster over him, smelling him, the sweat and the seed and the male smell that she could almost taste. She pushed his legs wider and he spread them as wide as he could and she lay on her back so she could get him deeper and she spoke something but he could not make it out because he was inside her and he did not care what she had said anyway. It was like trying to get something from nothing, a fabulous sense of draining emptiness, a desperate movement of lips and tongue and muscle and he could feel himself shaking and he cried out and she sucked and swallowed and he jerked out of control, trying to hold himself up, slamming his pelvis down at her, and he could feel his seed going and Carol swallowed and thought she was going to choke and grabbed his flesh and put her hands between her legs and brought herself when he was coming, wrapping her legs around his leg to feel him next to her when she came.

Later, Carol sat up and ran her hands down her body. It was a small body, maybe a bit of extra weight where there should not be, but it was good when she used it. She felt good. She could come again. She could come all day. She walked across the room to the bathroom.

'Where are you goin'?' McLennan asked.

'Giving you a rest.'

'Come back.'

'I will. I'm going to shower.'

'I want to talk.'

'I want to shower. Come with me if you like. It's good in the shower. Sensuous.'

'I can't.'

'I thought you boys could go on to infinity.'

'That's a totally shit thing to say.'

'Yes, I'm sorry. Come and I'll rub your back.'

He followed her into the shower. She turned the water temperature up as high as they could stand it and they took turns with the shower-head at their groins. Carol said she wanted to make love again but McLennan could not get hard enough and for a moment he felt like walking out because she was smiling but then she changed her face in that hidden way and he put his fingers inside her and made her come. They sank to the floor of the shower when she had come and let the hot water massage them and McLennan spoke.

'I killed a man a while back.'

'I don't want to know, Tim.'

'I thought you understood, I thought—'

'What, Tim? That I'd be a shoulder? I understand what's happening. I know people who've been killed. But I can't change it. I accept it till it's over. I get on with my life. I screw beautiful SAS soldiers, have fabulous orgasms and then put my uniform back on and look to the rest of the world as if butter wouldn't melt in my mouth. If my mother could see me now. Paisleyite, my mother. She'd skin me. I'm ordinary, Tim, I have no great designs. You have a job and you do it. If you can't do it, then go and do something else.'

'Is that all it is?'

'Should it be more? Society has its tax collectors, its doctors, its teachers, its police and its soldiers. And soldiers kill. That's what they do.'

'But there's more to what I do than just killin'. This is a war for our survival. You know? I don't think enough people realise that. You want to go into a united Ireland?'

'It wouldn't bother me, Tim. I told you, I like Dublin.'

'Jesus! Then what did I kill a man for? What will I kill other men for?'

'I suppose because he was going to kill someone and they're going to go on killing people. I don't think too much about that. I can't do anything about it. I do my job and have a good time when I can. Like now. You're so lovely.'

He got out of the shower and threw a towel over him. There was steam all over the room and steam went with him to the bedroom. He fell on the bed.

Carol stood naked at the door. She was running her fingers through her hair.

'What do you want, Tim?'

'You.'

'You have me.'

'No, I don't. I thought – I thought you understood Northern Ireland.'

'I do, I live here. I like it. But it would still be here no matter what flag flies from Stormont, no matter what uniform I wore. It doesn't matter to me. I won't marry you, Tim.'

'Then what am I gettin' divorced for?'

'Because you want to. Because you don't love your wife any more. I told you, I prefer adultery.'

'Jesus.'

'Why do you say that?'

'Don't you have any loyalty?'

She came over to the bed and knelt on it and touched his legs.

'Of course I do.'

Her mouth smiled but her eyes did not. That hidden face again.

'To small things, Tim. My family, friends, Traffic Branch, I suppose – and you. But small scale. I can do that. I support Northern Ireland. Support the Republic, too, sometimes. Even Brazil. I don't know. I don't really want to talk about this now. We don't have that much time. Let's just fuck like crazy and let the politics go and have a quiet drink in The Crown. I haven't finished, have you?'

'No.'

She flopped down beside him and put her fingers between her legs.

'Do this. Just there.'

He touched her and she helped him find the spot. He moved his finger slightly and her pupils dilated. She let out a long controlled sigh and closed her eyes.

'Terribly slowly,' she said.

'I know.'

He did that and when she was starting, McLennan put his head between her legs and used his tongue. Carol held his hair and pulled at it. She wrapped her legs around his body and dug her heels into his back. They stayed like that until Carol lost control. McLennan did not come this time.

When it was done, Tim McLennan left Lenny Beggs and his words and Bob Stone in limbo and watched Carol, panting on the bed, trying to formulate words. He put his finger to her mouth and lay on her and pushed himself inside and it hurt both of them when he did it.

'Tim!'

'More!' he said.

'Tim.'

'Yes!'

He thrust at her. She held him. He moved faster. She pulled him to her. He kept thrusting until he could feel the release coming and when he felt that he thrust harder and faster into her like he was trying to beat the release, like he was trying to control it, win something, and they came like that.

'You'll marry me,' he said.

She was rubbing his back. It was scarred. She wanted to ask him about the scars but she decided not to.

'I won't.'

'I'll divorce Anne and you'll marry me.'

'No.'

He turned and smiled.

'Yes,' he said.

'I mean what I say, Tim. Now enjoy me while you have me.'

McLennan ran his hand across Carol's hair and thought of Lenny Beggs's words again. Haves and have nots. When you had something you had to hold on to it. If you wanted it to mean something you had to fight for it, make it happen, shape it. He closed his eyes and thought about what it was and what it was came and went with her touch and McLennan slipped into a half-sleep.

18

VINNY RICHARDS LAY flat on the soft high ground and felt the prick of pine needles in his flesh through his combats. The smell of the pine needles and resin from the trees and the earthy odour of the soft ground mixed and seeped into him and lifted him and a microscopic mist hanging in lines of droplets from about halfway up the trees redrew the nightscape in a melting form. There was no wind and the sky was clear except for thin strips of orange cloud, and the stars fell away in disjointed lines to the horizon and the moon was low and filtered and the filtered light from the moon gave the strips of cloud their orange colour.

He pulled a pair of nightvision goggles from the small pack on his back and put them on. The grey-green fused with the melting mist and the clear-sky stars and the orange moon and its strips of cloud and Richards saw an animal move. Then it was gone.

Richards checked left and right, took the goggles off because they were heavy to move with and then picked himself and his silenced Sterling up and moved through the trees to a small hollow behind a fallen trunk. Frosted air poured from his mouth and he could feel the sharp edge of the night on his lungs as he breathed. Behind him a twig broke and the snap shot across the forest like a bullet. Richards froze. Then he heard another snap and felt the vibration of running in the ground and heard the frozen breath.

'Okay?' Tim McLennan whispered.

Richards put his thumb up.

They were two miles inside Monaghan, on a drumlin slope, above a twenty-acre farm.

McLennan sat against the fallen trunk and took off one of his canvas shoes and pulled a two-inch-long piece of wood out. He held it up to Richards and Richards pulled a face at McLennan and then they both smiled. McLennan broke the piece of wood and threw the halves away. Then he replaced the shoe and tied the lace and moved off.

The farm buildings were laid out in a broken S formation with the farmhouse in the centre and a gravel path providing the break in the structure. The hay barn was a grey corrugated metal block in front of the farmhouse and a bit to the right and the outhouses at the back were whitewashed and covered in red corrugation and grey slate. One was a shed and it had grey corrugated walls over the remains of a whitewashed wall that had collapsed in the middle. Its roof was red. The farmyard was mud and concrete at opposite ends with slurry covering the join. The slurry looked like it was moving when McLennan looked through his nightvision goggles. And there were no lights.

It was two-thirty in the morning. McLennan moved out of the trees to a dirt path. Richards covered him. McLennan took his nightvision goggles off, put them in his backpack and adjusted his eyes to the night. Then he moved down the path. The stones on the path rolled under his feet, so he stepped off it on to the grass verge when he could. There were blackthorn trees and brambles in a hedge along the path, and nettles, and the nettles stung him through his balaclava when he crouched low in the grass against the hedge.

McLennan listened.

Nothing.

He swung his silenced Sterling over his back and pulled a dart pistol from the pack he was wearing. The dart pistol was for the dog.

The dog was a collie and it slept in a kennel in the yard beside the back door of the farmhouse. McLennan was behind the yard coming down to an outhouse they used for machinery. There was a broken tractor beside the outhouse. It had no wheels and the front bucket was gone. Its seat was on the ground beside the tractor. Richards moved down the other side of the path and felt the cold air burn at the moisture around his lips. He stopped before the outhouse in boggy ground and his canvas shoes sank into the mud. Richards made a face and turned to McLennan. McLennan made a circle with his fingers and indicated his next move with his hands. The pine smell of the forest had given way to slurry and rust and diesel. McLennan moved forward on the balls of his feet.

He slammed himself up against the outhouse wall. It was cold and dripping water and he could hear water on metal inside. Then he slid along the contours of the wall, feeling the brickwork on his body, hands gripping the pistol. He had to get his first shot in. It was a bitch of an angle from the corner of the outhouse. And if the dog woke?

He preferred not to think about that. He'd been mauled by a pit bull outside Strabane one night. Lying in an OP. The local IRA made the OP and sent in Fido. And Fido nearly tore McLennan's arm off before he got his knife into it. He had to cut the dog's jaws off his arm when it was dead.

At the corner of the outhouse, he knelt down and pulled his nightvision goggles from his backpack. He checked his watch. A tingle ran down his spine and he knew he was sweating and the tingle went into his crotch and McLennan felt good. The dog's head was just inside the kennel. Shit! he said to himself. The angle was wrong. He eased along another wall to the edge of the farmyard. There were paint cans in front of him when he stopped. And the broken tractor to his right. He went down on his belly.

Above him, the strips of cloud were bending and changing colour.

McLennan crawled forward two feet closer to his target. He had a shot now. He found himself talking to the dog in his mind. He raised the pistol and then levelled it with both hands and waited till the tension had left his body. Then he fired.

The dog jumped in his kennel and went to bark and get out and McLennan saw a stunned look on the animal's face. It staggered and made another feeble attempt at a bark and whimpered and rolled over. McLennan let out a breath of hidden tension and picked himself up. He closed his eyes and took off the nightvision goggles and looked around the yard. Richards was at the corner of the machinery outhouse, behind him. Tim McLennan felt good again. He raised his thumb to his partner.

McLennan moved to the first outhouse in the yard. He would take the outhouses, Richards would do the hay barn and the farmhouse. The farmhouse devices would all be placed outside. So they wouldn't have to chance a break-in. The equipment was good enough inside or out. McLennan moved past the dog without stopping. The animal was stretched out with its nose touching a pool of slurry. McLennan stopped at the outhouse door. He raised himself on his toes and looked at Richards moving on the other side of the yard. A faint trail of condensation followed Richards down the yard. McLennan pulled his Sterling into his hands for reassurance. Then he slipped the bolt on the outhouse door, holding every muscle rigid while it came out.

He pulled the door open and the orange moonlight dribbled in from the night sky and dappled the walls of the outhouse. McLennan put his head inside.

The first thing Maggie O'Neill felt was John Cusack's hand over her mouth. He was lying beside her, reaching for his .357 Magnum. His other hand pressed against her lips and she felt the touch of his skin on them. His skin was hard and dry and her lips were dry from sleep. He had no expression. He put a finger to his lips. His lips were wet. His tongue came out slightly over the lower lip. Then he flicked it up to the upper lip and across the mouth. He hadn't shaved and his stubble was like a shadow on his face. He pulled the Magnum from its holster, looked around, pointed to the open door with his eyes and then took his hand away from Maggie's mouth.

McLennan had already stepped on Tate Byrne. Tate snored and exhaled and then jumped up from his sleep.

'Jesus Christ!' he yelled.

'Freeze!' Cusack roared.

Tate had knocked McLennan off balance and McLennan was trying to steady himself on a wooden post and get his Sterling into firing position.

'Shite!' he said. 'Fuckin' Christ.'

Cusack didn't wait for any more. He fired. The bullet hit the wooden post beside McLennan and tore a lump from the corner and travelled on through the door. Tate Byrne made a grab for McLennan and his own revolver at the same time. Dessie Hart and Ger Kelly had woken up across from Tate and both of them were going for their guns. And Bruddy Holmes had caught his sleeve in his sleeping-bag zip.

Cusack tried to get an aim on the shadow trying to get to the door. He fired again and the bullet passed an inch from McLennan's head. McLennan felt Tate Byrne grab his leg. He kicked Byrne in the stomach and Tate yelled and McLennan kicked him again in the face and Tate fell back and McLennan made a break for the door. At the door he fired a three-round burst from his Sterling at the figures in the barn. The bullets hit the floor of the outhouse and ricocheted up into the walls. One of them caught Dessie

Hart in the face, tearing the skin below his cheek and carrying on into the wall beside him. Cusack threw Maggie into a wood pile and then hit the floor himself.

McLennan was in the yard now.

'Out, out,' he roared at Richards.

Richards didn't need to be told. He was already moving back. McLennan fired a second burst, longer this time, at the outhouse. Bullets punched through the door and smashed two coffee cups and splintered logs and passed through the back window. Inside, Cusack was up. He had an Armalite and was clipping a thirty-round magazine into it. Maggie O'Neill had her Magnum and was crawling along the floor to where Tate was screaming that he'd been hit. Ger Kelly had made it to the front wall of the outhouse. And Bruddy Holmes had ripped his shirt-sleeve free and was reaching for his gun.

'Dessie, Dessie,' Kelly roared.

Hart was scrambling around in the dark for a rifle.

'Shut up, Ger,' he said. 'Shut up. John?'

'Moving, Dessie.'

'How many?'

'One.'

Maggie had reached Tate.

'You're not fuckin' hit, Tate, you're okay,' she said.

'Shut up,Tate,' Cusack said. He scrambled for the door. He waited, listening. Hart joined him on the other side.

'Get the window, Maggie,' he said. 'Tate, on me. Ger, cover John. Bruddy, where are you?'

'I can't find my gun.'

'Take another. Jesus!'

Cusack was easing around the open door.

McLennan and Richards had retreated to the furthest outhouse. McLennan was trying to figure out what had happened. He kept saying Jesus to himself, like he'd just stood on a nest of rattlesnakes and survived. He was shaking. Scared and excited shaking. He crouched at the corner leading to the farmyard. Richards was pulling back into a covering position. Cusack's Armalite was coming round the outhouse door. McLennan aimed.

'Come on,' Richards whispered to him. 'Let's go.'

McLennan looked at Richards and then at the rifle coming round the outhouse door. It was Hart's gang. Had to be. Maybe half a dozen of them. His mind was racing.

'Come on,' Richards said again.

The whisper was straining.

Jesus, I can take them, McLennan thought. All of them.

He fired.

The burst splintered the side of the door and made Cusack dive for cover. One of the bullets caught the ground and rebounded into the farmhouse. The lights were already on there.

'Shite!' Ger Kelly shouted.

A bullet had hit the stone wall beside him.

Cusack pulled himself up and pushed his rifle around the door with one hand and pulled the trigger. The Armalite sprayed an arc into the yard. Bullets hit the tractor beside McLennan and the ground in front of him and four peppered a window above his head and the glass shattered and fell out on top of him. He threw himself into the wall for cover. Cusack was already out of the outhouse and Dessie Hart was behind him.

'Son of a bitch,' Cusack said.

He was flat on his face in the farmyard, in an inch of hay and slurry. He had jeans and a t-shirt on. The t-shirt was an old Marine affair with the words 'Mess With The Best And Die Like The Rest' on it. Hart threw himself beside a trailer and fired in the general direction of where he thought the last incoming burst had come from.

McLennan fired again. This time he almost emptied his magazine into the yard. Cusack was trying to reload with a spare magazine he had shoved into his jeans. Bullets tore into the concrete and slurry around him, ricocheting around the farmyard. He buried his head in the mess on the ground and Dessie Hart lifted his arms and fired again right where he thought McLennan was.

But McLennan had moved. Richards had grabbed him by the shoulder and pulled him back and McLennan had regained his sense of where he was and what he should do. They had to get out. They couldn't be caught. No matter what he felt or wanted to do. He pulled back through Richards' cover and Richards pulled back through him towards the forest on the hill above them. There was a sense of release in Tim McLennan now, relaxation almost, the release and relaxation of complete concentration. It was just a case of getting back over the border now.

In the farmyard, Cusack and Hart were on their feet and Ger Kelly and Maggie O'Neill were out and armed.

'What the fuck's goin' on?' Ger asked Dessie Hart.

'I don't know. I don't know. John, go wide. Ger, you and Maggie flank that way. Bruddy – Bruddy!'

'Here, Dessie.'

Holmes came out with an AKM and no magazine in it.

'Jesus, Bruddy, cop on. Stay here on guard. Where the fuck's Danny?'

'Fucking bastard's no fucking good, Dessie,' Cusack said. 'I knew it. Fucking bastard's probably grabbing zees. Tate!'

Byrne was at the door of the outhouse, holding an AKM and spare magazines. He gave one to Bruddy Holmes.

'With you, John.'

His nose was pumping blood and his lips had been ripped open. Pieces of skin dangled from his mouth and a flap was loose at his temple.

'The fuckin' cunt's fucked me up,' he said.

They moved out wide of the farmyard in pairs, with Tate acting as a tail-end sweeper. No one spoke. They knew where they should be looking, what should be done. The only communication was by hand.

Two hundred yards ahead of them, McLennan and Richards had stopped at the edge of a field between two tree plantations. They were breathing heavily through their noses to cut down on the condensation from their mouths.

'Jesus, what a fuck-up,' McLennan said, 'a complete arse-up.'

'Come on, Tim.'

Richards grabbed his wrist.

McLennan nodded. He wanted to scream and just shoot anything at that moment. But he held himself.

He reached into his backpack and pulled out his nightvision goggles. He swept the trees and fields around them. Then he took three deep breaths through his mouth, raised his thumb to Richards and led off.

Cusack was cursing himself that he did not have a nightsight on his weapon and trying to calculate their path. It did not matter to him who they were or what they were up to. It was not important then. Importance had narrowed to getting them.

Hart was across the field from him, going uphill at the other hedgerow, low, moving fast, Heckler and Koch G3 extended. Hart had no shoes on.

Cusack pulled himself over a hedge and then slid along on his belly through the grass on the other side and watched Hart do the same. Cusack searched the trees ahead of them for any kind of a sign. He drew a line in his head and then pointed out the direction to Hart and Hart nodded and they moved forward.

They moved faster in the trees, not caring who heard them. If whoever these guys were got deep enough into the forest, then they'd be gone. Cusack ducked low but his head still caught low branches and they snapped in his face and tore skin but he could not feel it and the excitement pounded inside him and lifted his head.

Fifty yards. Cusack could see vague outlines against the brushstrokes of orange moonlight that had penetrated the trees, flickers in the rows of pines. They were coming from his right and he could flank them if he moved faster. Dessie Hart had slipped out of sight now. The excitement almost made Cusack take off. He fired a three-round burst and threw himself flat on the forest floor.

McLennan heard the bullets pass before he heard the shots. He flattened himself and fired. Richards was ahead of him. He fired. McLennan crawled in behind a cover of fallen branches and fired again. Bullets tore the darkness around Cusack, ripping the forest floor and the trees around him. He buried himself in the soft ground and the pine needles and the needles stuck into the wounds on his face.

Then he came up on his knees and opened up on full automatic. The whole magazine in the direction of McLennan and Richards. Richards threw himself back into a hole made by an uprooted tree. He fired and reloaded and searched the grey-green forest and saw something move where he thought it should be moving and fired at it. Cusack was already out of there and moving left. McLennan saw him through his nightvision goggles and fired and broke silence to tell Richards where Cusack was. He did not see Hart.

Hart had flanked right and was coming in behind McLennan and Richards. He could see only what the moonlight teased him with but he was moving to the sound of the firing. Richards was trying to track Cusack and McLennan was moving in behind Richards to cover his retreat. Hart was now twenty yards behind them. He saw McLennan's outline for a second and fired a burst. McLennan swung round and emptied his magazine in Hart's direction before he saw Hart. Hart dived for cover. Cusack opened up on McLennan's firing. Two of his bullets hit McLennan's backpack and sent McLennan around in a spin. The spin saved McLennan's life because Hart had reloaded and was pumping bullets at his silhouette. McLennan hit a tree, regained his balance and then tripped over a root. He hit his head on another tree and then ripped his face on loose branches. Hart fired again and Cusack fired when he heard Hart's weapon. They had a crossfire even if they couldn't see each other.

It was exciting and terrifying at the same time.

Vinny Richards had seen Cusack by this stage. He had knelt down and raised his weapon to fire at Cusack when Dessie Hart's rounds struck home. One caught Richards in the left shoulder and knocked him forward, a second hit him through his backpack. The round passed through the backpack and hit three pieces of equipment and turned down into Richards' back, somersaulting through his body and coming out through his left thigh. He screamed and a third round hit his right hand and passed through his left kneecap. Richards pitched forward.

McLennan had recovered and had targeted Hart. He emptied his Sterling at him and moved towards Richards, reloading and firing. Hart saw McLennan's silhouette and lost it and then saw what he thought was it and fired and the rounds tore up the trees around John Cusack. Cusack cursed and threw himself on the ground and fired where he thought the opposition was. But it was wide.

'Dessie!'

Maggie O'Neill and Ger Kelly were now behind Hart.

'Maggie, they're ahead of you. Move over right. John's on the other side. Ger, pull back and wide of Maggie. Where's Tate? Tate!'

Tate answered from a hundred yards behind Cusack.

Cusack had reloaded his Armalite.

'One of them's down, Dessie,' he roared. 'One's down. They're right of you, Dessie, movin' back.'

Hart was rolling over on the ground. Cusack had begun to crawl.

Ahead of them, about twenty yards away, McLennan had dragged Richards back into the hole left by the uprooted tree. Richards was streaming blood from his leg wounds. McLennan tied the thigh wound with a handkerchief and reloaded Richards' weapon and his own. Inside, he was cursing himself. Nine-mils against assault rifles. Shite, he thought, I should have taken them in the farm when I had them. All he could think of now was the humiliation of being captured or killed. Richards moaned beside him.

'Hang on, Vinny, son,' he whispered, 'hang on, mate. I'll get you back. I'll get you home. Jesus fuckin' Christ, this is a mess.'

McLennan scanned the forest with his nightvision goggles. He could see three of them and then two of them vanished and he fired at Ger Kelly and Kelly dived forward and hit a tree and McLennan swung and fired a burst where he thought Hart should be and then another at Cusack. Both of them stopped. Cusack fired back and rolled in behind a fallen tree. Hart got dirt in his eyes and dropped his rifle to clear it. The dirt mixed with blood from scratches he had picked up in the forest and clogged in his eyes. And he was feeling weak. The round that had creased him in the outhouse was having a delayed effect.

McLennan searched around him for the others. He saw Maggie moving behind him. He fired at Maggie and the rounds sent her diving for cover. She opened up on where she thought the incoming fire had originated. But she missed. And Ger followed. All their rounds passed over McLennan's head. And Cusack was sent diving into a small ditch by another burst from McLennan. He cursed out loud. The ditch was running with water and Cusack felt the cold water on his sweating face and scooped some up and drank it. He put his head over the top of the ditch and searched the darkness.

'For Christ's sake, check your fire, check your fire,' he yelled. 'Or we're going to end up wasting each other. Wait for them to move. Wait and listen.'

The forest had gone quiet and all there was was the smell of cordite with the other smells.

McLennan searched it. This was it. The chance. They could either take it now or Christ knew what would happen. He scanned the forest again.

'Okay, Vinny, you ready to move, boy?'

Richards made a noise. McLennan wiped his mouth.

'Jesus Christ, they're out there, Vinny. Hart. And that bastard bomber. I can take the fuckers. I can.'

Richards had passed out.

McLennan cursed himself and the orders he was obeying and grabbed Richards by the collar. Then he picked him up and threw him over his shoulder and took both Sterlings and stood up and fired in a wide arc around him, screaming while he fired. Rounds sent Cusack and Hart in different directions. Maggie O'Neill fired and missed. Ger Kelly aimed and went to fire but did not. He could see nothing. They were deeper into the forest now and even the slivers of light were gone. And so was Tim McLennan.

Cusack put his head over the top of the ditch he was lying in.

'Dessie!' he roared.

'John! I can't see a fuckin' thing.'

'Me neither, John,' Ger said.

'Maggie!' Cusack yelled.

'Nothin',' she said.

Cusack exhaled and watched the frozen breath disappear into the darkness.

19

'I BET YOU were fucking asleep, man, you fucking son of a bitch.'

Cusack stood right up close to Danny Loughlin, right where he said he could smell Loughlin's fear. Dessie Hart sat against a wall inside the outhouse. There was a bullet-hole in the wall, just above his head. Ger Kelly was dressing Hart's face wound. The bullet had torn a gash below his cheek and the wound was weeping.

'I think you'll need stitches, Dessie,' Kelly said.

Hart winced when Kelly dabbed the wound with disinfectant.

'I was watchin' the roads, like I was supposed to,' Loughlin said. He looked at Hart. 'I was supposed to.'

'And these bastards just walk past you, Danny, and almost waste all of us in our sleep. Fucking shit.'

Cusack slammed his hand against the wooden post beside him. He was still high.

'I was one man, Dessie,' Loughlin said. 'One man.'

'They must have passed you, Danny,' Hart said. 'And you had night gear. Shite, John, we should all have had night gear. Fuck, we could have walked right over them and we wouldn't have seen them.'

'Who the fuck were they?' Bruddy Holmes asked.

He was trying to cover his fear.

'Who knows?' Cusack said. 'Sass, UVF, UFF – UF fucking Os. Christ knows. That lead bastard talked with a Six-County accent. Anyway, right now, that's not the point. The point is that we nearly got creamed and Danny here is nowhere to be seen.'

'So I'm supposed to be Superman, all-seein' Superman, am I, John?

Like you, maybe. I was doin' my duty.'

'And you never once checked around here. You just watched the roads, did you?'

Loughlin looked at Hart again. This time his look had more pleading in it.

'We're gonna have to move now,' Maggie said. 'We can sort this out later. The Staters'll be here soon. I mean, that little firefight isn't gonna go unnoticed. You probably woke everyone for miles. Dessie, are you okay?'

'Head's a bit light, but I'm fine, love. Okay, John, get everythin' cleared. Danny, go arrange what you have to arrange. We'll move overland. I don't want us caught in a Garda checkpoint. Give me that map.'

Loughlin pulled a map from his top pocket and unfolded it. He handed it to Hart.

'Right – we'll meet you here, Danny. What time is it?' Loughlin showed him. 'Okay, in three hours, Danny. So shift yourself, boy.'

'And try and do that without shittin' yourself,' Cusack said.

Loughlin came at him. Tate Byrne went in between them. Loughlin stopped.

'For Christ's sake, John, shut up,' Hart said. 'I want everyone workin'. Clear this place. All equipment. All traces.'

'And Nuala and Benny?' Maggie asked.

Hart shrugged.

'They'll have to come up with an excuse. I don't know. If we leave nothin', then they can't be charged with anythin', so wash the place down properly. They can say someone tried to kill them. Might even get a Garda watch. Doesn't matter. This place is a write-off anyway. Shite, Ger, go easy, will you.'

'Sorry, Dessie. I'm not a fuckin' doctor.'

'Try not to be a butcher either. Tate, how's your gob?'

'Ach, I'm okay, Dessie. Tissues and iodine'll do me. Maggie's cleaned it up, haven't you, love?'

He winked. She did not wink back.

'Well, get up on the hill and keep a watch for the Branch,' Hart said. 'Do nothin' unless they're comin' at us. And if they are, put a round or two into their lead vehicle. Just to scare 'em. But call me first. Jesus, I wish I could tell you to fuckin' do them all, the bastards, I feel like it right now, but Council would go mad. The C/S'd piss himself. Go on.'

Byrne walked over to Maggie's holdall, looked at her, then into the bag, then at her again. She nodded and Tate took the FPK and two magazines. Then he collected a walkie-talkie, nightvision goggles and his own backpack, and went.

Hart pointed at Loughlin and Cusack.

'We can argue this one out later, lads. Clear? I want everyone functionin' now. Clear heads. Now shake hands.'

'Come on,' Cusack said.

'Shake, John.'

Cusack put his hand out. Loughlin hesitated, looked at Hart and Maggie and then put his hand out.

Fifteen minutes later, when Loughlin had left and the volunteers were still clearing out, Tate Byrne came through on Cusack's walkie-talkie. Hart was drilling the old couple who owned the farm on a cover story. They'd been paid for their services, so he wasn't too concerned for their well-being. What he was trying to prevent was a change in loyalty if the Special Branch got hold of a lever. What they knew was minimal, but minimal had a way of becoming important if enough of it was gathered together, so Hart kept staring at them when he talked to them in a way that left them with no illusions about what would happen if even the colour of his socks got into Branch files.

'Branch and soldiers,' Cusack said when he had taken Tate's message. 'Three cars and a Land Rover, Tate says. They're about half a mile away. From the east.'

'Tell him to scare 'em off.'

Cusack did and a minute later they heard five shots, three first and then two.

'They're runnin', the bastards,' Tate Byrne yelled over his walkie-talkie.

They all looked at each other.

'Okay, okay,' Cusack said, 'that's it. They'll be back. Move.'

Maggie O'Neill was down the other end of the outhouse, packing. Cusack watched her for a few minutes. He pulled a piece of hay from her neck and smiled and offered to roll her sleeping bag. She said no. Cusack raised his hands. Maggie smiled and held back another smile when she saw Bruddy Holmes watching.

Bruddy Holmes was at the door end of the outhouse, rifles over his back and a kitbag over one shoulder. He was moving in shakes. Everything he did looked like the result of a shake or more. He had two backpacks and he was trying to get his balaclava over his head. His eyes kept closing, like he was trying to make sure it was all happening.

Maggie pulled combats over her jeans. Cusack threw her a combat jacket and a balaclava and then a bag full of ammunition magazines. He moved through everything and everyone with the same speed and sureness. Like it was an exercise. Maggie found herself watching for a few seconds. Then she laced up her boots, grabbed her Magnum, her holdall and her kit, and moved to the door.

'Hey!' Cusack said.

Maggie stopped.

'This baby.'

He pointed to the Barrett Light Fifty. It was hidden under a tarpaulin.

'You and me,' he said. 'In turns. Dessie, you take the ammunition, right?'

Hart did as he was asked and Maggie came back and helped Cusack with the Barrett.

'I'll go first,' Cusack said.

He laughed and picked up the spare Barrett.

It was barely light outside when they were ready to move. The cold cut like steel. They moved off in silence. Each following whoever was in front of them. They moved along a set route. Outhouses and hedgerows, sunk into ditches where they could, on hands and knees and bellies when they had to.

And Maggie thought about her children and what they would say if they knew their mother was crawling around on a hillside before dawn when other mothers were getting the breakfast. She could hear a sound and thought it was a helicopter, except it was dark, and there was no sign of one. Maybe she was imagining it. Maybe it was across the border, watching them.

Dessie Hart and Bruddy Holmes led the escape up along a bank and a ditch. The ditch was full of water and they crouched in it, holding the equipment over their heads. Then came Ger Kelly, wiping Dessie Hart's blood from his hands in the ditchwater, and Maggie O'Neill; and behind Maggie, John Cusack. Maggie listened again for the chopper.

The treeline was about two hundred yards away, the beginning of a Coilte plantation that stretched over the top of the hill and down and up over three more hills. Then there were gaps and more forests. A couple of the forests had been cleared and they looked like old World War I battlefield photographs – broken and burnt trees, stumps, emptiness and desolation.

'Keep moving.'

Maggie looked behind her. Cusack smiled. He touched her bottom and held his hand there. She did not push it away. Then he gave her a shove and they moved through the ditchwater to the treeline and Tate.

Tate was watching the line of soldiers and gardai moving across the fields. He could see uniformed gardai in overcoats and wellingtons and special gardai in anoraks and jeans, carrying Uzis. The soldiers were regular infantry with a couple of Rangers on each of the flanks. The Rangers had Fiannoglach flashes on their shoulders and carried Heckler and Koch G3s. The regular infantry carried Steyrs.

'Jesus, you should have seen them leg it when I opened up on them,' Tate said. 'They must be shittin' themselves now.'

'And the chopper?' Maggie said.

'There was no chopper.' Tate said.

She exhaled.

Cusack lay flat on the ground. The ground was soft like a sponge. The morning cold made his legs shake. Dessie Hart lay beside him. They could see the line now with their eyes. Cusack was looking for faces. Special men with bloodhound noses. Could smell a weapons dump or a call house or a training camp a mile off. The faces he saw were grim and resigned. Keeping them going. He followed the line to the flanking Rangers. They were out ahead and moving faster.

Cusack looked at Dessie Hart and shook his head. There were dumps nearby. And it was the dumps Cusack was thinking about now. There was a couple of hundred pounds of ammonium nitrate and associated extras in a hole in the ground about two miles north-west of them. And some rifles and ammunition south of them.

'Danny's really screwed up this time,' he said.

'We all did,' Hart said. 'Let's just hope this is it. Maybe we should have left somethin' for them.'

'I could pop a few from here.'

'I don't mean that. I mean somethin' to keep them happy.'

'I could still pop 'em.' He shook his head again and sighed. 'Bastards,' he said.

'Can't argue with you there, John,' Hart said.

Needles clung to Cusack's combats. He could smell the moisture around them and there was a cloud of steam rising from their bodies. Ger Kelly removed the safety catch from a G3.

'No way, Ger,' Dessie Hart said.

Kelly put the safety catch back on and smiled at Hart and then at Cusack.

'We could pot some of the bastards,' Tate said. 'Maggie?'

She let out a breath through her nose and shook her head.

'No, Tate.'

'Be nice, though,' Cusack said. 'Sons o' bitches. We nut touts, they're touts, let's nut a few.'

'For Jesus' sake, John,' Hart said. 'Let's get out of here. Come on, we've transport to meet.'

He pulled a map from inside his jacket and laid it out on the needles. It was wrapped in plastic. Water drops settled on the plastic and distorted the contours and lettering. He moved his finger along the map, through forests, over fields, a wide swinging movement.

'Danny's people'll have another call house waitin'. I hope to Christ there's no general sweep. It could fuck things up really big for us. I've some people billeted five miles from here and we've Tyrone comin' over. Fuck, fuck, fuck.'

He slammed his hand down.

'What do you think?' Cusack asked.

'Who knows!' Hart said. 'I'm open to suggestions, John.'

'Fuck Loughlin out,' he said.

He looked around at the different faces. No one said anything.

'You really don't like him, do you?' Hart said.

'That's the problem, Dessie, I do. But, I don't know.'

'Danny's okay. This – I don't know what this was. Sass?'

Cusack shrugged.

'Well, we can't do anythin' about it now,' Maggie said.

'Yeah,' Hart said, 'come on, let's move, John.'

'Rock and roll,' Cusack said.

He picked up an Armalite and aimed it in the direction of the advancing gardai and troops.

'Pow!' he said.

'You're fuckin' mad, John,' Bruddy Holmes said.

He was trying to ingratiate himself and everyone knew it and said nothing. Except Cusack.

'Fucking mad, Bruddy, fucking mad. One day we'll have to. You do know that? We're not going to stop with those bastards north of the border, Bruddy. We'll have to do a complete clear-out. Fuck Standing Order Number Eight then. Are you ready for that one? We got as far as Blessington last time. We could have taken the place then. They had nothing, the Staters, nothing, and we stopped at Blessington.'

'What are you talkin' about, John?' Tate asked.

'Civil War. Don't any of you know history? That was our chance and we handed the country to them on a plate. And look what they've done to it. Are you ready for the second phase Bruddy?'

Holmes looked at Hart and Ger for help.

'Yeah, sure, I'm ready, John,' he said.

'Fucking right, Bruddy, boy, I think you are. We'll make shit for them, shit for them.'

Hart was crawling away from them. He had a backpack on and a rifle hanging from his neck.

'Come on, cut it out, Yank,' Maggie said. 'Let's go.'

'I'm talking the truth, I am.'

'One war at a time, John.'

Ger touched Cusack's shoulder and then turned and followed Hart. Maggie O'Neill knelt and pulled her equipment on and told Holmes to take the Barrett. Cusack was going to say he'd take it but he did not want to argue and he was feeling embarrassed so he said he'd cover them. Maggie sighed. Her skin was sore like someone had cut it with small blades. She pulled her balaclava over her face.

'Don't go talkin' about new wars, Yank,' she said. 'This one's enough for all of us. So stop actin' like a kid. You have a kid's face, Yank. Your eyes are bright, even now. Bright like you're playin'. We could be out for a walk in the woods. Get a grip. And keep your opinions to yourself.'

'Sorry.'

'You should be.'

She moved off into the trees.

Cusack sat and watched the line advance.

One, two, three, four, he said in his mind, open up the H-Block door. Five, six, seven, eight, open up the Armagh gate. Nine, ten, eleven, twelve, Margaret Thatcher go to hell . . .

It repeated itself without prompting and led him to a demonstration in Dublin and more gardai. A line of them – blue crash helmets, shields, truncheons drawn, like some Roman legion, beating out a battle rhythm, numbers removed, ready for action. And the marchers – men, women, kids, thousands of them, fighters to the front, megaphones to the back, confusion in the middle.

What do we want? Political status! When do we want it? Now!

One of the gardai had a Johnston, Mooney and O'Brien breadboard. A marcher from Omagh threw a golfball at him. Everyone laughed. There were more gardai, they said, you couldn't see them but there were more. Stick together, link arms, watch for snatch squads. If you link arms the snatch squads won't get you. The lad with the megaphone from Finglas demonstrated on some teenager what happened when you walked alone. Someone sang, 'You'll Never Walk Alone'.

He watched the gardai and soldiers advance on the farm.

Fergal Lynch could be down there, Cusack thought. He scanned the line. The soldiers had camouflage on their faces. Impossible to make out who they were. Didn't really matter. The blue boys were the important ones and the blue boys in anoraks were the specially important boys. But Fergal Lynch could have been there. Curragh man, Fergal. Good football player, Fergal, what they liked, fine winger, fast. Good at all games.

Cusack wandered through years, chopping and changing. You could do that with years gone by, re-edit them. Fergal'd be a captain now. He'd met him when he was a lieutenant. In Grafton Street.

Hellos, what you doing nows? handshakes, nervous shuffling, backing off, waiting for the other, interested disinterest.

I'm in the Army.

Pause. Pregnant.

I can't say I'm in the Army, too.

I was in the Marine Corps in the States, Cusack said.

Were you, by God?

Recondos.

Fergal's face nearly dropped. Cusack held himself in his Corps pose.

I'm off to the Leb myself, second tour there, the money's great.

They'll never let him die, a woman had said. Sands. He's an MP now.

Can't let him die. She's caught now – Thatcher – caught and there's nowhere to go. She has to give in. The five demands.

Cusack could not remember what all the demands were: no prison work, no prison uniform, free association, they were the important ones, the others were chancer stuff.

Tony McCabe stuff. Good with words, Tony. An Phoblacht head. But lousy when it came to the real dirty work. Cusack found a scene he had not banked on showing itself. Billy Holmes. He shuddered. Maybe it was the cold.

We'll never forget you, Jimmy Sands.

Who could remember all the hunger strikers?

Even Cusack could not. Frank Hughes, yeah. Everyone knew about Frank Hughes. McGlinchey and Hughes, Villa and Zapata. Waste of a good man, Cusack thought. That whole fucking thing was a big waste of good men. Killing ourselves, saving them the trouble. And the marches: disorganised mobs. Not an ounce of thought. Sit down, he'd said. No one listened. No one was in a listening mood. Sit down, there's a world of television cameras. They won't do anything. But Sands was dying and the boys who liked riots but wouldn't take a weapon and go out on operations were out for a bit of fun.

Bravest man I ever heard of, Cusack thought. Bravest. And these bastards let him die.

He raised his rifle and put his sights on the nearest garda. He was tall and young and he had orange hair under his cap. His chinstrap was down. Head-shot, Cusack thought. Head-shot and adiós. He felt warm, even hot.

The Rangers had made the farm. They were in the yard. Soldiers were coming from two sides. The right flank of the line was closing in on him. Cusack trained his glasses on them. Rangers and infantry, blackened faces. I could take you all, he thought. I could take you all and you wouldn't even know who did it. He put his rifle down and picked up his backpack. There was another bag with detonators and timers and some Semtex and he carried that. He slung his Armalite over his neck with the butt folded. Then he moved back into the pines.

The IRA didn't want him when he first tried to join. It hadn't occurred to him they wouldn't want him. But they made it difficult. Go away and think about it. Marine-trained? What the hell do you want to join us for? Not the regular volunteer. Go away and come back when you've thought about it.

Marines don't make good revolutionaries. Can't think for themselves. We want people who can think. People who can make decisions without having to ask someone. People who can kill because they believe in it, not because someone told them. You kill in here – and the guy pointed to his head – before you ever pull a trigger. Once you've killed in here then the deed is just like closing a door. But the decision comes up here first. Can you do that, Yank?

I'm Irish, Cusack said to himself.

He was running through the trees.

But it was more than that. It was loyalty. You had to prove it. They guarded it like some sacred rite. There were degrees. People outside. If you had no family in Miltown or the Kesh then you were outside. There was no one could vouch for you. Good to have a brother or a cousin or a father who could vouch for you, give you the quality stamp. He laughed to himself.

Fergal Lynch got the cadets third time out. It took two or three goes. Cusack'd gone once and got close and then left for the States. Stay around, go again, you'll get it if you go again, you were this close. Word came back through the vine. They'd had their chance, he said. The Marines took him. The Marines took him and taught him what he wanted to know. How to stay alive, they said. It was a matter of perspective. But it was always shoot to kill. And he forgot about the cadets until he met Fergal Lynch.

The IRA were paying for him to go to college then and look respectable.

Amazing what the right voice and the right degree does for you John, a GHQ man said. Lets you move places people like me couldn't go. It's a weakness. They have us as a type. We've helped that. We're tryin' to change it. Sendin' our boys to college. Gettin' a better class of volunteer, like. Soon you'll have to have more points to get into the IRA than you will to get into medicine.

Cusack laughed to himself: well-spoken volunteers in Armani suits hitting prestige targets and the Brits running around like headless chickens.

I like it, Cusack said.

He came out of the trees on the other side of a hill. He crouched and moved across open country between broken and burnt trees and stumps and black charcoal ground with the smell of fire and the smell of pine mixed together in a sharp scent that made his eyes water. He moved the way he knew how, the way to move so that no one would find you. You had a route and you stuck to it. You went with the land.

He could see Maggie ahead of him, on a ridge. The ridge ran along the edge of a new forest. She was low and Holmes was ahead of her.

Behind Cusack, the flanking Rangers were closing the stable door. Cusack stopped and turned to watch them. He could hear their voices. He sat behind a stump and a downed tree. He had the Armalite ready. They were speaking formula search words. Their voices had a touch of fear. Cusack stayed listening.

When he came down to the road, they were loading a Hiace. Cusack strolled. Danny Loughlin was there waving at him to hurry up.

Cusack grinned and took his time.

Loughlin cursed, showing his curse on his lips.

'You're a fuckin' go-boy, John Cusack,' Danny Loughlin said. 'What the hell do you think you're doin'?'

'Having a walk, Danny. Glad to see you got here. Nerves getting to you, Danny?'

'Ah, fuck off.'

'John!' Maggie said.

'She called me John.'

'For Jesus' sake, John,' Dessie Hart said, 'this is still my unit and I want cooperation from you. Okay? I've enough fuckin' problems without you messin' around.'

Cusack threw his head back.

'They're off chasing themselves,' he said. 'I watched them. The only thing they're going to get from that farm is bigger overtime cheques. So we're clear.'

'We don't know. We don't know if this is a one-off or if they'll launch a general sweep. We have to get clear.'

'Come on, I've got a place arranged,' Loughlin said.

'I'm glad to hear that, Danny. You glad to hear that, Maggie?'

She turned away from him.

20

FOR TWENTY MINUTES, waves of Italian opera broke over the walls of his mind and retreated with a melodic whisper that floated to the edge of darkness. And when it was over, McLennan was calm again. He did not understand it or like it much but it had something, a unity maybe, a strength, and he needed that. He closed his eyes again and sighed and let his body relax. Then he turned off the CD player and got out of the car.

The smell of production-line upholstery gave way to edge-of-town fertility and the drifting taste of urban emission. He stood still and untied his scarf and faced the graveyard. The weather had a sodden quality, hanging, slightly warm, spitting rain enough for the first setting on the windscreen wiper control. It had been cold an hour earlier. He unbuttoned his coat. His scarf swung down over one lapel. He straightened it and picked some hairs from his coat. There was an old woman fixing flowers on a grave by the wall. She had a shrivelled face and her eyes were watering. McLennan figured that was where the moisture from her face had gone. She looked at him. He did not recognise her and he hoped she did not recognise him. That above all things now. He shoved his hands in his pockets and walked to the gate.

The grave was ordinary. Headstone and pebbles, name and date and flowers. No inscription. A tree hung over the wall at that end by a black marble stone for three kids from the same family killed in a road accident. The tree was old and its branches were dipping back towards the ground. Its roots had come under the graveyard wall and broke the ground around the children's grave in snake patterns. The concrete at the rim of that grave was cracked and one corner rose as if it was being pushed up by the earth.

Maybe someone was trying to get out, McLennan thought. Trying to say, Hey, wait a minute, I don't want this, this wasn't supposed to happen to me, I wanted some kind of warning, to get ready. It just isn't fair. McLennan turned his head back to the grave he was standing by and tried to make a sarcastic remark about the flowers.

It said nothing to him and he had nothing to say to it. He looked for changes in it – little things, maybe a root of that tree pushing its way in or up, maybe a crack or a shift in the ground, something changed. Nothing had. Footsteps competed with each other behind him on the gravel paths among the graves.

'I thought it would be appropriate.'

McLennan did not turn. He knew who it was. The voice almost put a hand on his shoulder before it spoke to him.

'I hope you don't mind.'

Stone stood beside him. He wore an overcoat and black gloves and held his hands in a position that made him look like he was praying. He bowed his head and the gentlest breeze took strands of his hair and stood them high on his head.

'You know best, sir,' McLennan said. 'But we'll have to stop meetin' like this or people will talk.'

'Don't push it, Staff,' Stone said. 'I should have given you a right bollocking. Those weapons were for protection, not a bloody gun battle inside Eire. I've let you off lightly, Tim. Again.'

'Quits,' McLennan said. 'That place was supposed to be empty, if you remember, Bob. Next thing I know I've got Dessie Hart and most of his gang gunnin' for me. And that fuckin' bomber was one of them, I'm sure of it. Bastard. I could have stiffed all of them.'

'I'm bloody glad for your sake you didn't.'

'And you're damn lucky Vinny wasn't killed. I'd have had to leave him. How would you have played that one in the press?'

'There're always options. GOC's furious, Tim. It was a mess, but you could have been more thorough. It was down to you, Staff. Anyway, it never happened. That's official. No record.'

'You think the cover will hold?'

'I don't see why it shouldn't. The Irish want to believe it. The Loyalists like the publicity. And PIRA are keeping mum. Everyone's happy. It isn't like the Loyalists haven't done it before. Always screaming they're going to this and that down there. Well, now we've handed them something on a plate and they haven't denied it. Feather in their cap. Makes PIRA and their cronies sit up. Maybe scare them a bit. Show them their Loyalist counterparts aren't the Saturday-night punch-up merchants they used to be. Sammy flexing his muscles. Black have some back-up ready and Security Service are priming the usual hacks. Seems like you've singlehandedly invaded the Republic in the name of God and Ulster, Tim.' Stone laughed to himself. A respectful laugh. 'Which brings me to the real reason why I wanted this stroll in the country, Tim,' he said.

'What do you mean, Bob?'

'You see that farm over there? That one?'

Stone nodded towards a farm. It was tall and Victorian and about half a mile away with a fat hay barn tucked in beside it. It had a treelined driveway and what looked like stables on the opposite side to the barn. There were horses in one of the nearer fields and the car they could see looked new and German.

'What about it?'

'He's having an affair. With a teacher. She's a Catholic. Do you know them?'

'I don't remember. I think one of them used to be in my UDR battalion. It was a long time ago. What's it matter?'

'It doesn't. I was trying to impress you, Tim. My local knowledge. The fact that I know things. Take you, for instance, Tim. Father killed by terrorists. You'd think that'd make you want to rid the world of such people, realise that no matter what their motivation, groups that take it upon themselves to act outside the dictates of lawful authority are no help to anyone, Tim. Not to you, not to me, not to anyone. Don't you think?'

'Except when we need a cover story.'

'Quite. It's a nice spot, this. Do you come here a lot?'

'You should know, sir.'

There was a pause and Stone appeared to be preparing himself.

'Lenny Beggs, Tim,' he said.

'Sir?'

'No more bloody sirs here, Staff. Taking the piss. By the way, I'm having Richards shipped back to Blighty in case you want to have a word before he goes. Now where was I? Oh, yeah. I thought I'd give you a chance to explain yourself, Tim. Show me there's nothing to worry about.'

'I'm not sure what you mean, Bob.'

'Yes, you bloody well are, Staff. You've been talking to this Lenny Beggs, Tim. Don't deny it. I know you have. And if this information got about, people might ask what a regiment staff sergeant in line for a commission was doing sharing his drinks cabinet with a known terrorist. See what I mean?'

'I wasn't aware I had to account for my time off.'

'Your time off on tour is at my discretion, Staff. It's mine. And it doesn't include reminiscing with old kneecappers from your days in the ghetto. So don't piss about, Staff. Of course, it could be in the line of legitimate duty – initiative, so to speak. Potential undercover work. And if anyone pressed, that'd be the answer I'd give them. Unless you have another.'

McLennan swung around to him. Stone's eyes looked colder than the day, unfeeling cold, killer tips in the centres. McLennan was going to step back, more an instinctive reaction to superior rank than anything else, but he felt it would betray something and this was not a time for betrayal.

'I'm sure you know what you're talking about – Bob.'

'I said don't fart around, Tim. You know, some people in the regiment don't like the fact that we have Irish in the ranks. Touch of the Little Englander mentality. I don't mind where a chap comes from, what he looks like, what he talks like, whom he hates, whom he loves, just so long as he gives the regiment one thing. You know what that is, Tim?'

'You're goin' to tell me.'

'Loyalty, Tim. Regiment runs on loyalty. You can't buy it and you can't fake it. It's a very pure thing, loyalty. Know what I mean? Now we have southern Irish, northern Irish, all sorts of Irish in the regiment and they all get on fine and do their work. And you know why? Because they have no other loyalty but the regiment. And the regiment serves the realm. It's very simple. Clean.'

'What do you want from me, sir?'

'Just a chat, Tim, just a chat. Two colleagues out for a walk. You appreciate this is all unofficial. Private matter. You and I. Troop commander to senior staff sergeant. We run a good troop, you and I, Tim. And with you in line for a commission and me in line for a squadron command, we have possibilities. But only if we know where our loyalties lie. And our interests. It's good when interests and loyalties correspond. I know you've been having personal problems, Tim. That's why I've been giving you a certain degree of latitude. So you could sort yourself out. Concentrate on the job. You see, I feel you're worth it, Tim. At least, that's what I think.'

They walked past McLennan's car. The road was narrow and lined with trees. There was no path. The trees had lost most of their leaves and now and then there were piles of leaves on the road, wet and glued and sitting as if they had been stuck there by an artist. The road was tarmacked and the tarmac had potholes and lumps in it and where it was wet the wet flickered in the grey light and slid on the surface and gave it an oily sheen. Their shoes bit into the tarmac and crushed the small stones and broke twigs that had fallen from the trees.

'You're having real problems, Tim, aren't you? And I don't just mean marriage.'

McLennan did not answer. He did not feel he was supposed to. The tone Stone used was hard mono, same kind you used when you were interrogating. Deep interrogation, they called it – white noise, sensory deprivation, sharp-end stuff, but always the sound of reason behind, give them something to hang on to.

'You're asking yourself if HMG is really serious about dealing with the republican terrorist threat. You're wondering why the hell we have to go at PIRA with our hands tied to our penises. You want to have full licence to dish it out to them in the same measure they give it to us. And you feel like dog dirt at having to run from the bastards the other night when you think you could have taken them. You feel let down, Tim. And I understand. You know when you ask me if I feel this is as British as Surrey? Well, I do. Honestly. I know you doubt it. But I do. Oh, I know there're chaps think we're out in wogland, and you people are fuzzies, don't trust anyone with an Irish accent – Provo, Loyalist. And then there's the politicians. I don't think I'm even a democrat. There, you can hold that against me.'

Stone walked over to a wire fence and put his hands on it. The wire was barbed. The barbs had rusting tips. The field he looked into dipped at their end and there was a pool of water ten yards to the right of them before a bank of grass.

'It's a lovely country, Tim.'

'I think so.'

Stone clapped his hands.

'Beggs, Tim. Leonard William Beggs. Out-of-the-blue meeting, was it?'

McLennan did not answer for a minute. 'Somethin' like that,' he said.

He touched a barb-tip with his finger and watched a black dog in a nearby garden jump up and move towards them. It came forward so far, then stopped and barked.

'One of our eye-in-the-sky videos picked it up, Tim. No one else noticed it. But then I have a special interest in faces. This is a war of faces. Very important you know faces when you see them. So I make it my business to remember faces. And who should I spot but our Mr Beggs, out walking the kid. Now you tell me, what are the chances of Lenny Beggs being out walking his kid at the exact time and in the exact place you happen to be taking in the view? I could ask you what you were doing there when you were supposed to be still in England sorting out your marital difficulties. But I won't. So there you are and there he is. Then add that to the sensitive tactical information you came across and alarm bells begin to ring in my head. You slipped up again, Tim. Shows you're below par. My senior NCO.'

'I wasn't tryin' anythin'.'

'Of course not. So, to get to the point, what did Lenny-boy want?'

'Nothin'. Just to talk.'

'Yes. Good talker, Lenny. Man of great erudition. Always one for the *bon mot*, Lenny, everyone's favourite conversationalist. I hear he's developed a bit of a sense of humour, Lenny. Come on, Tim, don't fuck about with me. He was over at your mother's house the other night.'

'You have someone on me!'

'Staff! If I did, a good regiment man like you should have picked the eyes up. Lenny Beggs, Tim. He wants to recruit you, doesn't he? He belongs to an organisation on the way up and they need people like you. Lenny Beggs wants to recruit you. Correct?'

'You could look at it like that, I suppose. It was just talk, though. We argued. And I kind of threw him out.'

'But you expect he will try and recruit you?'

'Maybe. Maybe he just wants to find out where I stand or somethin'. See how the land lies.'

'You stand where you're ordered to stand, Staff, with the regiment and loyal to Her Majesty and her realm. That's it. He can read that in any HMG publication. He can read, can't he?'

'We used to use people like Beggs, Bob,' McLennan said. 'For the unattributable stuff. Like the other night. You know, the direct action. So secret, no one knew what was happenin'. Untraceable weapons, spare barrels, false documents, bags full of cash, targets and trainin'.'

'Different times, Tim. Different aims. Different methods. HMG is good at changing with the times. Anyway, Beggs and his crowd were the original sledgehammer trying to crack nuts. They always left a mess. A habit I'd rather we did not get into. Cowboy tactics invariably lead to heaps of bull excrement lying all over the place. There were officers in our regiment, some no longer with us, some decorated for their efforts, who did not realise the subtleties of trying to fight a low-intensity war in an age of mass communication and the global village. The balance of success and propaganda, the value of prevention: there's a moral there. They were using tactics twenty years out of date. And they were fucking it up for anyone who wanted to apply a bit of logic to the situation. To be quite honest, Tim, some people at HQNI were running around like frightened schoolgirls. And their political masters didn't help. One minute PIRA were terrorists, the next they were being courted like they were a government in exile. Policy changed by the hour. No consistency. Well, we're out of that, and your Mr Beggs and his crew are surplus to requirements at the moment and dangerous except as a plausible excuse when we fuck up an embarrassing job. The ground has shifted, Tim. The battle has moved on.'

'Is this an official reprimand, sir?'

'On the contrary, Tim. You've done nothing wrong, I hope. And this conversation isn't happening. I'm on classified duties right now. Somewhere undisclosed. No, this is by way of establishing common ground. You see, HMG likes to know its allies. You know, for and against people. Team lists. Now, you and I are on the same team, but our Mr Beggs and his crew are not. Maybe once upon a time they used to be – but somewhere along the line they took a free transfer. The thing we want to know is where and what strength their team is at. I hope you don't mind all these football analogies. They're very popular in intelligence circles. You're with me, aren't you, Tim?'

'I think so. Does this carry a Security Service stamp?'

'My links with Security Service are purely professional, Tim. We're on the same side. But naturally they might be interested if we come to an understanding. With me?'

McLennan didn't answer. He had a cold feeling at the back of his neck and a creeping suspicion he could not get rid of.

'Of course you are,' Stone said. 'How could you be otherwise? I'm surprised you didn't put one between Lenny's eyes the minute he showed his face. Nasty bit of work, Lenny Beggs. Rather we didn't have to deal with people like him. No class. Make us look like a South American Junta. It's bad enough having republicans trying to break up the kingdom. We can do without Lenny and his crowd thinking likewise. I think he's paranoid. Too long in the ghetto.'

McLennan was not listening. 'Who?'

'Lenny boy and his gang doing their saviours of Ulster bit.'

The captain had a serious face behind his smile, like he was wearing a mask. Only McLennan could not tell which was the face and which was the mask.

'I don't – I don't know. We should be able to take PIRA out. Go at them with everythin' we have. Destroy them and their allies. Once and for all. And if that means killin' every one of them, that's fine by me. I'll not stop till the job's done. There.'

'Oh, Tim, Tim. You think I wouldn't like to go in top gear? Hit them so hard we'd knock the bastards into the next century? But that's not on, is it, Tim? The world we live in is like an overcrowded lift. If we went in like you say, we wouldn't have a friend left this side of the equator. We'd be pariahs. And PIRA would have a propaganda coup that would keep them going for another hundred years. You see that, don't you? You see what I'm saying. PIRA is an idea, Tim. And ideas are difficult opponents to fight with just bullets. You have to be really smart to beat an idea. You have to fight on fronts that people don't even think about. And the biggest front is the media. They know that. Close them off, hit them when we can, gather information, close them some more. Attrition, Tim. Slow and hard and glamourless. But it can work. It has to work.'

'Does it?'

'We can do it. Possession, Tim. We have possession. And they haven't managed to deprive us of very much despite all their efforts. Meanwhile we erode their bases. Get Catholics on our side. Give them an interest in the state. Get them loyal. That's a hell of a slow process. Generational. But it can happen. Look at all the Catholics moving into Malone in Belfast. Out of the ghettos. You think they're hard core Provos any more? No way. It's slow but it will work. Long war.'

'That's what they say.'

'We can close them down. Their resources are finite. Read Clauswitz.'

'Haven't time. My province is bein' wrecked and my people bein' murdered.'

'That's unkind, Tim.'

'It's the truth.'

'Look, man, look around you. This is our country. Over there, two farms away, man shot dead in his car on the way to work, over there two constables blown to pieces by a landmine, over there UDR man machinegunned in his dayjob van, and I can go on. Come on, Tim, what's got into you?'

McLennan had backed off into the shelter, such as it was, of five evergreens. He switched off and watched the barking dog. The dog had come down to the gate of the house. He had scared eyes and a red tongue and it was dripping saliva.

'So what do you want, sir?' he asked.

'Your cooperation, Staff. We—'

Stone realised his slip and smiled and composed himself.

'I want you to go along with Beggs,' he said. 'Let him know you're interested. We want to know what that organisation is up to and we're short of people inside now. We were so bloody successful penetrating it before we ended up getting the whole damn leadership shot, stood down or behind bars. Now we're back to square one and they've had a clean-out. See what I mean? I don't want you to do anything. Just go along with Beggs and report what happens. So we know. Knowledge, Tim. It's the gold of the late twentieth century. We must have knowledge. Knowledge is power.'

'Is this an order?'

'If you like. But best think of it as your duty.'

'For how long? How far should I go?'

'As far as possible, I think. I think we can arrange things to suit the situation. And we can be accommodating where your family is concerned. You'd like to stay with your mother for a while. That could suit us. You wouldn't mind staying around, would you? I'd hate to lose you from the troop, but if we had a possibility of penetration here, we think we should take it.'

'We again?'

'Of course, if you decide to go along, your controller will be a Five officer. Naturally. It's their area. National assets and all that. It would be a very hands-off affair. You'd have space. And outside that work, you would do normal military activity. Secondment, attachment, something like that. Something very ordinary. Beggs is probably going to ask you to make an application. You just go along with his suggestions. Play it as normal. That's the thing with these fellows, they haven't fully worked out their loyalties. Makes them vulnerable. Gives us a chance to move in.'

'Just like that?'

'Just like that. Take your opportunities, Staff. It'll look well in this commission application. Might even speed it up. Good cover for a new assignment, a commission. Get Beggs and his lads really interested in you. But play it very slow. Argue. I don't have to tell you what happens to people Lenny Beggs takes a dislike to. Fond of the knife, Lenny. Sadistic shit. So, what do you say?'

'Is it an order?'

'It needn't be. You should be volunteering, Tim. I don't know what course your career will take if you turn this one down. Now, I know we don't usually make our local boys go under cover but this is a special case. You were approached. It doesn't happen very often. Think about it.'

'And you're the only one who knows so far?'

Stone smiled. 'Of course.'

'Looks like I don't have much choice.'

'There are always choices, Tim. The thing is to make the right ones. Don't you think? See where your best interests lie. I don't want to order you, Tim.'

McLennan came to attention. 'Sir.'

'Good. Good.'

'And this checkpoint business?' McLennan said. 'What's the situation there?'

Stone pulled a small map from inside his coat.

'Come here,' he said. 'They've moved here. Hart and crowd. See? North of where you found them. They scattered for a couple of days. We lost most of them. But now they're here. Difficult terrain. A lot of bog. Still . . .'

'So?'

'So everything's moving nicely. There'll be a little hyperbole for a few days, then it'll all die down and Dessie Hart and company will get back to their business. They have to. What else can they do? And, of course, we can wait. Works out rather well, really. Considering.'

'So I see.'

'We're still in the game. I've a meeting this afternoon and we'll make a decision there. But as far as I'm concerned this operation is still in business.'

'A suspicious man might say you threw us at them the other night,' McLennan said, 'that you knew they'd be there and you threw us at them to rattle them. Did you? Did we flush them out for you?'

Stone said nothing. McLennan stared at the ground and shook his head.

'Smart. Very smart. I hope it was worth it,' he said.

'Oh, come on, Tim, this paranoia rubbish is getting out of hand. You better get a hold, Staff, or I will have you putting pegs in holes with the shrink. You're not in command around here, Tim. You obey orders, like me. We're soldiers and we obey orders. Remember that. This isn't a private war. You do as you're told. That's it.'

McLennan had stopped listening to him.

21

THE NEW IRA call house was a farm a mile inside Monaghan from the Armagh border, between two drumlins. There was one approach road to the farm, along a track which connected with a small road that crossed the border through a forest. The crossing was blocked by two huge concrete slabs and a hole twenty feet wide which the British Army had blown in the track. Local people complained that they had to do a seven-mile detour to do their business. Farmers with land on both sides of the frontier said they couldn't get their tractors through. They filled the hole in and smashed the concrete with pneumatic drills. The British Army blasted the road again and put up new concrete blocks and a sign saying 'Blame It On The Terrorists'. The locals weren't inclined to. They filled in the hole again and smashed the blocks and brought a French TV crew along to film it. The British Army arrived by helicopter and there were words and a couple of stones and aimed rifles and the French TV crew left happy for an interview with an IRA unit in Derry. The British Army blasted another hole in the road, twice as big, and put up four concrete blocks and a bigger sign saying 'Blame It On The Terrorists'. The locals fell back.

The new call house was squat and grey with some of the cement façade falling away and revealing the brick structure of the building. It had grass growing right up to the door and a bath in the next field for the cows. There was a brick shed with a green corrugated roof behind the house, up against a hedge of tree and bracken. The trees overhung the shed. In another field there were two long semi-cylindrical sheds covered in black polythene where the farmer grew mushrooms. The farmer was a bachelor and he was in Dublin.

Betty Loughlin had just filled a basin with mushrooms when she saw the four-wheel-drive coming along the track. She watched the vehicle crawl its way along the muddy track, dip into a hollow and reappear. She looked up to a hill above them, to a tree plantation that stretched along the hilltop and down the other side to a small lake. Tate Byrne was on look-out up there.

The day was good. Clouds raced across the sky on the wind from the north-west. The cold was a fresh cold and the sunshine made up for the drop in temperature. She could take the cold. All you had to do in cold was wrap up. But the rain and the long periods of dull atmosphere that went with it sometimes left her sapped of energy.

She walked back to the farmhouse with the mushrooms, through a rusting metal gate, past a robin, sitting on a blackthorn branch, red breast brilliant in the sun. And the sun touched her face, even in the cold, and made a promise. She had a scarf on and a duffle coat she had bought years ago in Paris, and wellingtons. Her hands had mushroom compost on them and one of her nails was cracked. Her hands were dry. She wore gloves when she could because the wind would crack them and the wounds would stay open for days and maybe become septic.

A face watched her from one of the farmhouse windows. She smiled. Deano Brady smiled back and looked past her. Brady had arrived the night before. He was a cousin of Dessie Hart's from Crossmaglen. On the run and available. He'd been on the run since a shooting he'd done near Banbridge had been intercepted by the RUC. One of his mates had been killed and they'd had to leave him on the back seat of a car outside a doctor's surgery in Newry. He died. And Deano Brady went to ground and took a job as a delivery-van driver.

This was the last stop before a decision for Dessie Hart's unit. Make or break, Danny Loughlin kept saying, like he was trying to force something. Everyone had been tense in the days immediately after the firefight at the other billet. Then, when nothing happened, the tension turned to frustration. Theories about what had happened got passed around with the cigarettes. And IRA intelligence could come up with nothing more than Loyalist cheering. But Dessie Hart decided to wait. So they waited. And they were still waiting.

Betty rubbed her face and got some mushroom compost on it. Her eyes were on the verge of watering in the cold and it gave them a romantic look. She liked that, too. She looked back at Brady but he was gone from the window. Young men sometimes looked at her. Young volunteers with arrogance in their minds and fear in their hearts, lads with a confusion of directions and emotions, sometimes face to face with real choice for the first time in their lives. They would look at her and say smart stuff if they had a brain and sexy stuff if they didn't. They'd look at her and maybe want her, maybe just because they might be going to die and they just wanted a woman, but she liked it.

She'd seen every kind of face. The names all sounded alike and it was so damn familial she often thought she was seeing double or people returning from the dead. There were psychos, there were fools, she'd seen fellows who were both, there were criminals, there were kids trying to emulate brothers or fathers, there were friends, there were fellows out for revenge, out for kicks, out because it beat standing on a corner doing nothing. Then there were the idealists, fanatics maybe, hard men, who the more you beat them, the more they suffered, the more they came back for more and the more convinced they were of their right. There were a million different reasons, from social club to homicidal licence, there were kids chasing dreams and old men running from them; born guerillas and gangsters; superior intelligences and lads you wouldn't put in charge of a match. But they kept coming. There was a time when she thought it would stop and they would stop coming but they never did. And every time they lost a volunteer another turned up, ready and willing. She could not explain it. And because she did not believe in any of it herself any more, she could not really understand anyone who did.

Then John Cusack came out of the shed and walked across to her. He had an oilskin coat on, knee-length, and a tweed cap. She made a face at him. He pulled a detonator out of his pocket and a parking-meter timer and held them up.

'Present,' he said.

'Romantic,' she said.

He put his hand into her basin and pulled out a mushroom. Then he peeled a small piece off the skin.

'Nice. What's the rations?'

'Chauvinist. When's the Army going to get a progressive policy on women?'

'We do. They're volunteers. Didn't we get rid of the Cumann.'

'And I suppose Command and Council are packed with women.'

'There aren't enough.'

'I don't know why I do this, John. But then you lads are going out soon, aren't you?'

'Can't answer that. But the war goes on. Speaking of women, you seen Maggie?'

She laughed and took the mushroom off him and put it back in the basin.

'She's up there with that bloody cannon of hers. She has Bruddy up there with her. In the trees. Ger's on watch for them. Eddie's watchin' for Ger. Jesus, everybody's watchin'. Why?'

'I just wanted to talk about something.'

'I bet. Maybe she and Bruddy . . .'

Cusack went red and looked away. Betty laughed again. She touched him on the shoulder.

'Be good, John,' she said. 'And make peace with Danny, please!'

Then she went into the farmhouse.

Cusack watched the four-wheel-drive come up the last few yards of the track. He put the detonator and timer in his pocket and walked over to the vehicle. It was blue, with chrome and stickers everywhere. The man at the wheel nodded to him. He was ordinary with a kind of hangdog face and a moustache that made the face more pronounced. His eyes were sad and resigned, more resigned than sad. Behind him were two twins, both with curly red hair and one with a beard. The beard didn't make him any less like his brother. They had smart smiles and they held themselves like they were always expecting a fight. Cusack put out his hand.

'Francie, man,' he said.

Francie Devine's hangdog face attempted a smile and he put his hand into Cusack's. Cusack's was the tighter grip. Devine put his other hand over Cusack's to show they were good friends. Cusack did the same and then patted him on the back.

'Here we go again, lads,' Francie Devine said.

He looked around at the twins for support. They gave it. The Beattie twins walked like they were drilling on a parade ground. Cusack shook their hands. They both nodded and didn't say anything. They were both good snooker players, and they had the concentration of snooker players. They were wiry and had a pallid snooker-hall colour in their skin. Cusack looked round at the horizon and gestured towards the shed. They followed him.

'Dessie's checking the cracks for cracks,' Cusack said. 'You eaten?'

'Yeah, we had fish and chips,' Devine said. 'Army marches on it stomach. Who said that?'

'Napoleon,' one of the twins said.

'We've been doing some marching, Francie,' Cusack said.

Devine nodded and looked past Cusack. Then he touched Cusack's hand and put his finger to his lips. For a moment Cusack was reaching for the Magnum in the small of his back. Then Devine nodded towards the edge of the yard. The rabbit had a brown coat and a white tail. They stopped and watched him. He was scarred, bleeding above the eye and from his back leg. The blood had coagulated in the brown hair on the leg. The blood above his eye was coming down his nose, a line and a drop at the end of the line at the tip of his nose. There was coagulated blood on the side of his head. Cusack looked at the three faces around him. He took a step towards the rabbit. It did not move. He took another step. The rabbit looked at him. It rose on its legs. Cusack held back. It sank. The bearded Beattie went to speak and Cusack cut him off with a look. Cusack moved. 'Battle casualty,' he said.

He had the rabbit in his hands. It made no attempt to escape. He stroked its fur. The rabbit tucked its head into Cusack's chest.

'We could eat him,' the clean-shaven Beattie said. 'Army rations.'

'No fucking way,' Cusack said.

Devine laughed. And his face seemed to break up.

'We're going to fix him up, aren't we, boy?' Cusack said.

'City boy,' Devine said. 'He's a meal or a pest where I come from. Good stew if you're hungry, John.'

Cusack moved away from them. They looked at each other and made gestures.

'He trusts me,' Cusack said.

'He'd trust anyone now. Kill it and eat it or let him go and let nature take its course, John.'

Cusack shook his head, slowly.

'No. We'll fix him up. Let him go free then. Fair chance.'

'Is he a Taig or a Prod rabbit?' Devine said. He laughed more. Like he was looking for an excuse to laugh. 'Better interrogate him, John. Maybe he's a Sass tout. They'd try anythin', you know. Are you, son? Robert Nairac?'

They all laughed.

Cusack lifted the rabbit and looked it in the eyes. They were brown and they were scared and the rabbit moved its mouth so that it looked a bit like a child.

'You Sass, son?' Cusack said. 'Answer. Francie here wants to nut you. You better tell us now. We might consider an amnesty. Let me see. Sing – sing us a verse of the – of the "Broad Black Brimmer".'

'That's no proof,' the bearded Beattie said. 'The Brits learn that in basic trainin'. Ask him to sing "Jerusalem". No Brit knows how to sing "Jerusalem". Sing "Jerusalem", son.'

The rabbit leaned his head into Cusack's arm.

'Staying quiet?' Cusack said. 'Must be one of ours. Knows how to keep his mouth shut. Okay, you're clear. If you want to join us all we can promise you is mud and shit and prison and . . .'

Cusack stopped himself and stared at each of them in turn and then went back to the rabbit.

'. . . and death,' Devine said.

They stayed silent for a moment.

'But we give good funerals,' Cusack said.

They laughed again.

Francie Devine went over to Cusack.

'Welcome to the movement, Volunteer,' he said to the rabbit. 'Do your best. That's all we ask.'

In the shed, which was stocked with tyres and cans of beer and gallons of petrol, Dessie Hart sat on a drum, reading a tabloid paper and looking at a map. He wore a shoulder holster with a .357 Magnum in it and was eating a sandwich. The crusts lay beside the map on a pack of Dutch beer. He had a can open beside him on another drum of petrol. Behind him, Danny Loughlin sat on crates of bottled Danish beer, loading ammunition magazines and making notes in a small red notebook. Danny was smoking his pipe. There was a third man, sitting beside Danny Loughlin, rolling a cigarette. He wore an anorak and he had a face that had recently been clean shaven of beard. He had a paperback book and was swigging from one of the Dutch lager cans. His shoes were desert boots and they were streaked with mud. A shadow was draped over his face. There were no windows in the shed. Two battery lamps hung from wooden rafters. The light was yellow and the yellow was a sad yellow, a kind of afterglow or dying-flame colour.

'How's the men?' Francie Devine said.

Hart looked up from his paper. He was reading the sports page. He looked up and his eyes opened wide so the whites were nearly swallowed by the pupils. He grinned and showed his teeth and then stood up and threw his arms around Francie Devine. They slapped each other on the back.

'Youse got here okay?' Hart said. 'Jesus, at least youse got here okay. We had a hell of a time.'

'So I heard. Lot of scarred faces, I see. That was some firefight, lads. Orangies are jumpin' around, sayin' how they're gonna wipe us off the map. You better keep your political profile down, Tony.'

Tony McCabe closed his paperback book and put his hand out to Francie Devine.

'I don't know. Maybe it's best to have a high profile. Good protection. Look at these fellows. Not expectin' nothin'. Sass or otherwise.'

'Sure keeps us on our toes,' Cusack said. 'Know what I mean, Francie?'

'I do, John. By the way, I got word from Council, Tony. We can go ahead with our problem any time. I'd give it to Donegal. Let them look after it. Okay?'

'That's settled then,' Hart said.

'They were gonna let her go. Insufficient evidence. C/S and Council say nuttin' housewives is not on unless we have a sure case. Too much bad publicity. Tony brought in Boxer Murphy. Old Boxer showed what he could do. Scared the shite out of her. And more. She said she rang the Confidential. Tony doesn't believe that.'

'I think she was molin' there. Long time. Twenty-quidder. Regular stuff. It's just a feelin'. Anyway, we got a confession. And that's that.'

'If we had the time you and me'd go and deal with her, Dessie, not leave it to Donegal. I have no problem there. I know she fuckin' touted. I know. I know the family and they're all scum. Fuckin' sell each other for a Lotto ticket. How are you, Danny?'

Loughlin was caught off guard.

'Good, Francie, good,' he said.

'I'm glad to hear it.'

Loughlin shook Devine's hand in a kind of confirmation.

'Had to take a long route here,' Devine said. 'Much cloak and dagger. But we managed to avoid wanderin' eyes.'

Sean and Dermot Beattie shifted around him like wings.

'You movin' to Sinn Fein, Dermot?' Dessie Hart asked. 'Fancy yourself as a councillor? Takin' up where Tony here left off. Like I was sayin', be careful of bein' noticed. Cousin Terry got too much exposure for his own good, remember that. Stick to the Army. At least when the Prods come for you, you'll have a weapon. Like the other night.'

Dermot Beattie looked unsure of himself. He looked at Devine and then back to Hart.

'That bloody beard, son,' Hart said. 'I'd get rid of it. Like Tony done.'

Hart shook his hand and then his brother's. Danny Loughlin followed. If the cell structure had been working the way it was intended, they wouldn't have known one another. But they did. And the Beatties had done time with Dessie Hart years earlier.

'Sorry about Terry, Dermot,' Hart said. 'But you see what I'm gettin' at? He was . . .'

Then Danny Loughlin saw John Cusack with the rabbit under his coat.

'What the hell is that, John?'

'It's a rabbit, Danny. Haven't you ever seen a rabbit?'

'What's he doin' with you?'

'He's a casualty, isn't he? A fellow warrior. We're going to treat him – with respect.'

'John thinks he was wounded in a scrap with the Sass. He's not sayin' much.'

'The quiet type,' Hart said.

'Knows to keep his mouth shut,' Cusack said. 'Bugs is his name. Bugs, meet Dessie and Danny. Dessie, Danny, say hello to Bugs. New volunteer.'

They all laughed. Then Hart touched the rabbit. Loughlin went to grab it. Cusack pulled back.

'Stick it in the pot, John,' Loughlin said. 'Give it to Betty.'

'No way. He gets the treatment. He's a hero. Look at those scratches. Purple heart, at least.'

'We're not in the Marines, John. Kill him or just dump him and let's get down to work.'

'No fucking way. He lives. I say he lives.'

Loughlin went red and forgot where he was. 'Oh, right, he lives. He lives and we go chargin' into this.' He pointed at the map and then looked around and held what he was going to say.

'You're not going charging anywhere, Danny,' Cusack said.

'You're still on for this?' Loughlin said to Devine.

'I am, surely, Danny,' Devine said. 'Is there a problem here? Dessie?'

Hart ran his tongue around the inside of his mouth. Cusack could see it make indentations in his skin.

'No. If we decide now, it's on. Danny's just bein' Danny. Aren't you, Danny? He has some reservations. That's fine.'

'Yeah, sorry, I'm tired,' Loughlin said. 'Gettin' old. We had that fuckin' mess. Caught us on the hop. My fault.'

Loughlin looked around, proud he'd taken full responsibility, like it meant he was stronger.

'So I believe, Danny,' Devine said.

He looked at Loughlin as if he knew everything Loughlin had ever thought or was ever going to think. Loughlin turned to Cusack.

'Put that fuckin' animal away, John, will you? This is your play, so let's get serious with it.'

'I am serious, Danny. Very serious.'

'So what's the view on your wee incident, Dessie?' Devine asked.

'Two men. Silenced nine-mils. They ran off. The rest you know. Tony?'

McCabe shrugged. 'Sass,' he said. 'Or somethin' like that.'

'Yeah, but why? If it was a stiff they were after, then why only two and why run?'

'They got surprised. Didn't expect all of us there,' Cusack said.

'So what did they expect?'

Hart moved his face and looked at Cusack.

'Maybe it was a routine black-bag run. They've done that. Could have been a wet job. More likely the silencers were just protection.'

'Look, we don't know,' Hart said. 'Maybe it was Prods. That's all Intelligence are gettin'. Maybe they came for Benny. To stiff him. It's happened before. If it was a Sass job, what was it about. Two of them and they run off. I think we scared the shite out of them. That right, John?'

'I guess. I think we got one. Didn't hang around to find out. Whatever it was, it's over. And we're still here.'

'Yeah, I'd like it to stay like that,' Devine said.

He thought for a moment and sighed. 'Who knows everythin' about what's happenin' here, Dessie?'

'Just people directly involved,' Hart said. 'Can't keep people in the dark with a target like this. Back-up units don't know more than they have to. But nine at the minute know all of it. And I'll have a couple more probably. What you thinkin'?'

'Tout?'

'No, Francie. If it was a tout set-up and they wanted to hit us, they wouldn't hit us here,' Cusack said. 'Not the Sass. Not all of us. And not here. Be hell to pay. Why not wait for us to cross the border and get us proper?'

McCabe was going to speak. Hart beat him to it.

'The people who know my end are cast iron,' Hart said. 'And you're lookin' after things your end, Francie?'

Devine nodded. 'Yeah,' he said, like he was walking on broken glass. 'Tony?'

McCabe's political sense made him hold back.

Danny Loughlin took his chance.

'I think we should hang on,' he said. 'Till we know what's what. See what Intelligence come up with, I mean, we shoulda been safe where we were – that was a good billet – but we got surprised. And they had silencers. What does that tell you? They were out to stiff. Maybe they're on to us.'

'You're right about one thing,' Cusack said. 'We should have been safe, Danny.'

'Okay, John,' Hart said. 'Whoever they were, all they done was nearly get stiffed themselves. Sass wouldn't do that kind of job. Maybe for one man, maybe, but not a unit. And not here. John's right on that. Kick up murder in Dublin. If it was a stiff job on us, it wasn't Sass. That means the Prods are gettin' more aggressive.'

'If it was the Prods,' McCabe said, 'then they know at least one of our billets here. Where are they gettin' that kind of information?'

'That's Intellingence's and your job,' Devine said. 'I was just thinkin', how many people knew we used Benny's place, Danny?'

Loughlin looked embarrassed.

'Over the years,' Hart said, 'maybe over a hundred. More maybe. Jesus, probably everyone that's ever been active here.'

'Jesus, Danny,' Devine said. 'The fuckin' dogs on the street must have known about Benny's place. And what about this place?'

Loughlin was sweating under his clothes.

'This one's new,' Hart said. 'Brand spankin', Francie. Never used before. And no one knew about it till now except me and Danny.'

'Is this place swept, Danny?' Devine asked.

'Sure, Francie.'

'When?'

'Day we moved in. Standard procedure.'

The sweeping had been done the day before they'd moved in, but Loughlin figured a few hours didn't matter and he did not want to be in Devine's bad books again so he stuck to his lie.

'I'm glad to hear it. Better see there's more of your people around this place so no one falls over youse here. Bad habit to get into, Danny. So, what do you think, John?'

'I'm for getting on with the job. Whoever they were, they're gone and they didn't get what they came for. We nearly stiffed one of them. First blood to us. I think Tony's probably right. We should be ready to expect more attacks this side of the frontier. Loyalist or otherwise. That means everyone from Sinn Fein people to volunteers will have to be extra vigilant. This isn't a rest zone any more. The Sass could be up to their old tricks. Arming Prods and sending them south. Gives them access and deniability. Standard practice in any counter-insurgency. I've seen it done. Hell, I did it. And with the Prods more militant, maybe they feel they can do it and get away with it. It doesn't mean I don't want to continue operations. No matter what Danny says. I don't see any reason to hold back. But I think we need to get a move on this checkpoint soon. We can't hang around like this. We're vulnerable. The other night proves that if nothing else. Anyway, that's my say.'

'From a pro,' Hart said.

'Who can argue with that?' Devine said.

Loughlin lit his pipe and looked away.

They sat around the map.

22

THE FIRST STAR had been there about fifteen minutes before she saw the next one. When the others came they lay in lines between the tunnelling clouds. Maggie O'Neill scanned the night with her nightvision goggles. The grey-green umbral world gave away nothing. She sat back on the groundsheet and changed the tape in her Walkman. She had to take her gloves off to do it and the wind swung around from the north-east and licked the warmth from her hands and carried it off. She rubbed them and put the black gloves back on. Then she went back to watching. There were signs of life, far away – headlights, cars moving, the odd human being walking home from the pub late, or from wherever. But around her, there was nothing. Not even the sound of an animal. She hunched her shoulders. She had thermals and a combat kit on, and a German Army winter coat, but it was still freezing. At least there was no rain, she thought. Then she glanced at the tunnelling clouds and the menacing smile of the crescent moon.

She was up there to get away. When you were used to working alone, working with a unit again was claustrophobic. Positions, orders, straining to gel, building-workers playing soldiers, and Cusack trying to inject his Marine Corps knowhow with all the finesse of a charging rhino. Bullshit, she thought. But she did not know if she was thinking it because it annoyed her or he annoyed her. The fact that she knew she wanted him doubled her anger.

She was trying to stay loyal to Brian in her mind and finding pity was the only emotion she had left when she thought about him. She could have gone home for a few days. Hart had said so. She rang instead. The investor had fallen through. She put the phone down.

You make vows to someone, she thought, and you mean them and then time passes and the vows don't mean as much and things change and whoever you made the vows to has changed and you hate yourself for not sticking to your vows. Sometimes she wanted to scream.

Then Cusack was strolling towards her with an Armalite over his shoulder.

He had a balaclava rolled up on his head. Maggie watched him through the nightvision glasses. His face was paler and he looked like he was talking to himself. But she liked it. She liked him. And she felt bad, watching him and liking him and feeling want for him. She told herself not to feel it, that she could stop this, that men came on to her all the time, that she did not need him, that she preferred to be alone, worked better alone, all that, but it did not work and she felt her heat increase and her skin come to life and part of her life left wherever it had been and became something she wanted again now. She stopped watching him with the nightvision goggles and waited for him to come along the track enough so she could see him with her eyes.

'Hi,' he said.

He always sounded like he was on a fun run. That annoyed her, too.

Cusack crouched beside her and looked around them. He had come up to seduce her. He told himself different, made up excuses in case it didn't work, argued with himself about her being married and having kids and a home and all that. But he had come up to seduce her and he did not completely like himself for it.

Maggie nodded to him. 'Hello, Yank.'

'My name is John.'

'I know, Yank.'

He sighed. He could have taken the message she was giving out but the message did not correspond with the feelings he was getting and he had made up his mind anyway.

'Anything?'

'No. We have radios, Yank, there's no need to come and check on me. I know what I'm doin'. I've done it before. And I amn't Danny. You want anythin'?'

'Couldn't sleep.'

'I'll bet.'

'It's true.'

'Well, I can. I've another hour of this and then I'm out cold.'

Cusack sat down on the ground beside her. He reached into his pocket and pulled out a bar of chocolate and an apple.

'Not much, I know, but I thought you might be hungry. You know?'

'Yes. Thanks.'

She took them and put them in her pocket. Then she put the nightvision goggles on again. She left them on for five minutes. Cusack watched her and tried not to look like he was watching her. He was trying to stop the noise of his heart coming through his mouth. His mouth was dry and he kept licking it. He had not been able to sleep. In part it had been the cold.

'You cold?' he asked.

'No,' she said.

Lying in his sleeping bag, he had been able to smell her. It was the strangest feeling, knowing she was not there and smelling her. And he carried the smell of her everywhere. He examined her face, all the contours, in as much detail as the stars and the nightvision goggles would allow. And he wanted to reach out and touch her, just the barest touch. But he did not.

'Mind if I look?' he said.

'At what?'

'Whatever.'

She sighed. Long and deliberate and meant to mean something. She let her eyes wander over him. It was a good feeling and she did it again.

'I'm still married,' she said.

'So you say.'

She turned to him and moved her mouth and he lifted his hand and reached out and let his finger touch her face.

'There's nothin' happenin',' she said.

Cusack's heart raced faster. He had to concentrate to keep himself together. He took his hand away. She took off the nightvision goggles and handed them to Cusack. Cusack moved in to her place. He could smell her more. He did not bother looking when he put the nightvision goggles on.

'You were burnt out,' he said, 'in Belfast.'

'So were others.'

'Was that why you joined up?'

'Does it matter? You shouldn't be askin' me all this. It's a breach of security. You should know that. You'll have Tony McCabe all over you. Doesn't like fraternisation, Tony. Especially men and women.'

She told herself she was being a bitch.

'I've worked with Tony before,' Cusack said.

'Closely?'

He turned to her and smiled and then went back to watching.

'Theory and information man, Tony. No good for this kind of work. See him this afternoon? Couldn't wait to get out of here. Scared the Sass will come. Or the Prods. I think he's more scared of the Prods.'

'Zealous, though. The Felix Dzerzhinsky of the RA.'

'Who?'

'Lenin's pet. Head of the Cheka. Very zealous. You see, I'm not a brainless housewife gettin' off on playin' soldiers. I'm a clever woman. I could have got a degree if things had been different. Queens.'

'I have.'

'From Queens?'

'No, UCD.'

'Brains and brawn. You gonna be another movement intellectual? Like Tony? Full of polemics? I'm a fighter myself. I mean, speeches are fine, and policy statements look good, but you can't beat a stiff Brit for gettin' the message across. They understand that. Gives them somethin' to explain. Keeps us goin'.'

'Ruthless, too,' Cusack said.

'Don't patronise me. I think you're right though.'

'What do you mean?'

'I think we should go for more of these things. Up the stakes. We have to.'

He looked at her.

'Checkpoints, yeah. Stuff like that. Don't pay heed to Danny. He's against it because he's scared. A blind man could see that. Danny's losin' it. Maybe he lost it years ago. I like Danny but I think we should drop him from this. Only good for logistics and enforcement jobs now. He drinks. Do you know that? Everythin' has booze in it. He's scared shitless. Worse than McCabe.'

'And you?'

'No. I've lost two brothers, I've lost friends, I've seen our house burnt to the ground, I've seen my father beaten. Fear doesn't come into it any more. I don't want my kids to have to do this.'

'They won't.'

'You sure?'

Cusack moved his head around in a scan.

'Do they know?' he asked.

'About this? Don't be stupid, Yank. Jesus, you can be stupid, you know.'

'You let your old man slap you about, though.'

'Fuck off, Yank. Who the fuck do you think you are?'

She raised her hand and he caught it and held it. He pulled the nightvision goggles off.

'Hey, hey, it isn't me. I'm not the one,' he said.

She pulled her hand away and put it down.

'No, you're not,' she said. 'Sorry. Jesus, you've a way of gettin' close.'

'Only when I want to.'

'Tell me another. You've a sweet tongue, you know, Yank?'

'It's the truth. I tell the truth.'

'I bet.'

'Why don't you do something about it?'

'About what?'

'Your man.'

'I don't want to talk about it. It's private.'

'Nothing's private so long as you're in this army, Maggie. Nothing.'

'Except that. Funny, isn't it? Look, Brian – he's my husband, the father of my children – he's been out of work for a while now. He never used to be like that.'

'So you let him hit you?'

'What do you want me to do? Stiff him? It'll pass.'

Cusack put the nightvision goggles on the ground.

Maggie picked them up.

'That'd be your solution, wouldn't it, Yank? Good at nuttin' touts, I hear. Keen'

'Always had a case.'

'I knew a couple. That's the problem with you lot. Southerners, others. Youse have no links to the pain. You're there on a kind of academic level. No one ever came to your door and broke it down and carried off your father. No one ever called you Taig. No one ever threw petrol bombs at your front window. So it's a nice textbook revolution to you. Well, there's others of us. And we feel everythin'. I knew Billy Holmes, you know.

Remember Billy? Bruddy wouldn't know this. Far too bloody young. But me and Billy were first feelers.'

'What do you mean?'

'I mean that one Saturday night after a dance, somewhere in Andytown, Billy put his hand up my skirt and I put my hand down his pants. Does that answer your question or do you want a full statement? Maybe I should be nutted for cavortin' with a tout when I was a teenager. He was a good feel. Gentle, like. Other fellows'd nearly rip you in half.'

'Stop.'

'Hurtin' you, is it? We know how to hurt. Maybe you should have me tarred and feathered. We used to do that. To girls that went with Brits. I went with a Prod once. Years ago. On a school trip. By a river. He was a nice lad, I think. Billy was a fool. I know he did wrong and I can hate him for it but I can't help feelin' sorry for him. I know his wife. Good with the women, he was. Popular around Andytown, then.'

'Are you trying to get at me?'

'Why should I? There's nothin' to get at. Nothin' between us. We barely know each other. And we're not supposed to. Security. Remember?'

'He set up Roddy Jordan and Barry Lennon.'

'Billy?'

'Yeah, lover boy.'

There was a silence. She wanted to take back what she had said. She wanted to reach out and touch him and maybe hold him and feel him close and just sit there and be with him.

'I knew Barry Lennon's brother, too,' she said. 'Fergus. We all called him John. You know, after the Beatles. Fergus and me used to go out together. I did my first job with Fergus. I was a kid. We were told to go to this house and shoot the man in it. It was vague. Fergus had the gun. It was a Brownin'. But I didn't know what a Brownin' was then. I was there because that was the way it was then. Everybody was doin' stuff. And because of Fergus. I was mad about Fergus. He had Donny Osmond looks. Do you remember him? Anyway, we went to the house and I kept watch. Fergus knocked on the door. An old man opened it. Fergus shot him. The bullet went through his throat. It didn't kill him. He turned out to be the wrong man. We got pissed that night. It was really romantic. I think it was better he didn't die, that old man. Made us feel good. We had it off in the back of Fergus's dad's van..There was a bomb nearby. Have you ever done it when a bomb went off? Fergus was killed a couple of months later. Brit patrol shot him.'

'I better go back,' Cusack said.

'Have I hurt your feelins?'

'I think you're right about knowing too much.'

'Maybe I just want you to know what you're tryin' to buy.'

Cusack leant his head back against a tree behind them. He felt the bark on the back of his head. His heart had slowed its beat. He cursed himself for being obvious. They taught you that in the Corps, too, not to be obvious. Special training in how not to be special. He could see hills and lights, static lights and lights moving across hills. There were shadows on the hills and sometimes the moving lights lit up the shadows. The shadows were treelines. Sometimes they looked like giants, in formation. You could put faces on them. He began to imagine.

'They could be watching you, you know,' he said. He looked up. 'Satellites.'

'It's a risk we take. You never know, do you? A few hundred of us and thousands of them. But we still manage it. I've never been arrested either, you know. I think I'm considered too quiet. I play at it when I'm home. Maybe that's why I let Brian hit me. Maybe that's an excuse.'

'Do you love him?'

She smiled. 'I must. I married him because I loved him. He was different. And there was no chance he'd get himself shot or blow himself up with his own bomb. Brian's not political.'

'I know.'

'Are your hands not cold?'

She took off a glove and touched his hand. 'Jesus, you're freezin'.

'No, I'm not. It's my natural temperature. I've ice for blood. My sister says it.'

'I'm sorry.'

'She doesn't tell,' he said, as if it was a redeeming factor.

'You'd have to nut her.'

Cusack felt his heart race and he fought to control it.

'She'd be okay if she wasn't such a stuck-up bitch.'

'You still love her?'

'I guess.'

'Billy Holmes. Was it money or fear?'

'I don't know.'

'Okay. What was it like, in the Marines?'

'Hard.'

'Harder than this?'

'You ask a lot of questions.'

'Look who's talkin'. I just wonder.'

'I'm not some half-assed son of a bitch high on grandad tales, if that's what you think. I know what I'm doing and I know why I'm doing it. I came a different road. But we're at the same place.'

'You get off on it?'

'On what?'

'All this. There's boys who get off on it. Ger and Tate. They're big men round here. I know them. Everyone does. Real hard men. Go to all the dances. Girls jump at them for a ride. Status to have one of the boys screwin' you. They did a part-timer in the UDR a couple of years ago, when Dessie was shut up, over in Fermanagh. He delivered milk. They shot him when he was puttin' the empties away. They came back cheerin' like they'd scored a goal in a Cup Final. I was around. I saw it. I don't cheer when I work.'

'Do you get off on it?'

'If it ended tomorrow then I'd find somethin' else. I'd miss it maybe, yeah, but I'd find somethin' else. I don't think Ger and Tate would. They need it now. They're good lads but they're hooked. There's only one way they're goin'. Are you like that?'

'Sands,' he said. 'I joined after Sands. It just happened. I never thought I'd see anything like that. The sacrifice. The sheer – strength of will. There we were, living like the world was rosy, cocooned, only looking forward to the next Spanish holiday. *A la carte* supermarket world. Then this guy says he's going to fast to death for a principle. And he does it. Then nine more of the lads do it. We handled that all wrong, though. I suppose with all the emotion you couldn't have done any better.'

'My cousin went out with him. Bobby Sands. Years ago. They were burnt out, too. The Sands. I knew him. Look at you, you're starin' at me as if I'd just said I knew Jesus. I knew Bobby Sands. He was all right. Dessie knew Frank Hughes. Dessie and Dominic McGlinchey and Frank Hughes hung around together. Then McGlinchey went over to the INLA. Bunch of wild boys, the INLA. Old Sticks. Old sticks are only good for the fire. It's a joke.'

'I know Oliver North,' Cusack said.

'Who's he?'

'North. You know, Iran-Contra.'

'Oh, him. That's old news. Tell me you know Michael Jackson. I'd be impressed with that.'

'You're beautiful,' he said.

He turned to her. She did not respond. She put the nightvision goggles back on and moved her head in an arc.

'I said you're beautiful.'

'I heard.'

'Don't you have anything to say?'

'What should I say? You want me to strip and jump on you? Do women always do that? You click your fingers and they spread their legs. If you think I'm some cheap little Andytown ride, forget it. Go somewhere else. I know what I look like. And I don't look terrific right now. I feel like my face is about to break up.'

'Maggie Oakley,' he said.

'Don't say that. I hate that. Makes me sound like a fairground attraction. I'm a soldier, just like you. Give me the respect I deserve. You can be right bastards, you know, you boys.'

'I'm sorry, I don't seem to be able to do anything right here.'

'That's because you came expectin' a conquest. And you didn't care what I thought. You had a drink of that beer down there, you got any courage you were lackin' and you came up here expectin' me to fall over. Funny that, you needin' courage to approach me. And yet you could walk up to someone and kill them without a thought. Do you get scared? I mean scared like you are with me?'

Cusack went to stand up. Maggie reached out and caught his hand. She held it for a moment and then pulled him down. He did not resist.

'I'm always scared some,' he said. 'But not like this. This is different.'

'Never ceases to amaze me that men can be confident and direct in everythin' they do except how they deal with women. I remember I had to force Brian to kiss me. Then he was all over me. But I had to force him first time. So you think I'm beautiful. It's nice to hear. It's a chat-up line but it's nice to hear anyway. You're nice, too. You have good lips. And I like your smile.'

She leaned across and kissed him. They held the kiss for maybe a minute, just lips. Then she stroked his face and his hand.

'There,' she said, 'was that what you expected?'

He shook his head. Then he licked his lips. Then he laughed. It was a soft laugh.

'Danish, by the way,' she said.

He made like he did not understand.

'The beer. You're probably in breach of regulations. If Peter Best ever found out, we'd be on our arses. Drinkin' on active service. Might even get kneecapped. You know what Peter's like for discipline. Useless for anythin' else, Peter. Kind of C/S Council likes these days. Dessie thinks he's a prick. Francie hit him once. Don't worry, I won't tell on youse. Might have some myself.'

'Are you playing me along?'

'What do you think?'

'I don't know what to think.'

She picked up the nightvision goggles again. Cusack touched his lips and put a finger in his mouth.

'Movement!' Maggie said.

Cusack jumped up and moved in beside her. He picked his rifle up and took the safety catch off and cocked it. The sight was a nightsight. He followed her directions.

'Car,' she said. 'See it? Toyota Corolla. Southern reg. Dark colour. One – no, two.'

'I'm with you.'

'I'll call in.'

'No, wait. Watch. They're a long way off. They can't see anything from there. Look around them. They could be a decoy. You check left, I'll check right.'

The car had stopped at a junction about a quarter of a mile north-west of where they were. The headlights were still on. It backed up and the passenger window came down. Cusack could see a figure. It was a man. He could not make out much of the man's features, except that his hair was short and tight to the scalp. His face was round. He rolled the window up. The car moved forward. It stopped again behind a blackthorn. Then the lights were dimmed.

'He's getting out,' Cusack said.

The man was out. He walked to the front of the car and then went down the unapproved road that led to the border blockage. He walked along it. Cusack followed it. The man stopped and waved. The car turned into the unapproved road.

'Not ours,' Maggie said.

'Not here, not now.'

The car stopped beside the man about a hundred yards up the unapproved road just after a bend that hid it from the main road. The man got in again. The lights went off. Cusack watched the car. The driver turned to the man in the passenger seat. It might have been a woman. Cusack was not sure.

'You able to hit from here with that?' Cusack asked.

He nodded at the AKM beside Maggie.

'What do you think?'

'Well, get ready. Use my fire if you need it.'

Maggie focussed her nightvision goggles on the car.

'I don't think we're gonna have to, Yank,' she said.

The driver's door opened. Then the passenger door. Cusack had the man's head in his sights. He heard Maggie laughing to herself.

'Take a good look,' she said. 'At least someone's gettin' lucky.'

The driver was a woman. She got out and followed the man over to the bank of grass at the side of the road. The he rolled something out on the grass. She lay down. The man lay on top of her. He had a long coat on. Cusack could see his trouser belt just below his coat. He could see the woman's legs. He focused on the woman's face.

'Leave them, Yank.'

'No, could be a set-up. Keep tracking around them. Keep going. Everywhere. I'll keep on them.'

'You get all the fun.'

'This isn't fun.'

'Are they bein' safe?'

'I don't care.'

The man came in under a minute. The woman showed no expression on her face. Afterwards they sat in the car, smoking. Then they backed out of the unapproved road and headed back the way they had come. Cusack watched the road and the area around it for another half an hour.

'Seedy,' Maggie said.

She looked at her watch. The rain was very close now. She could see it falling a few miles away. It looked strange in the night, like prison bars, and the clouds looked like the jaws of a mouth. The stars were fewer on that side now. The wood around them was disappearing. All there was was the sound of the animals.

'Is that what you have planned for me?' she asked.

'No. Don't talk like that. It could have been trouble.'

'I can smell trouble. That was a quickie. A desperate quickie. I bet he lives at home. I bet she thinks sex is borin'. Maybe they're related. Happens around here. I know a couple of twins who've had twins. You should see them. They don't look like each other. I know fathers who are their own sons' grandfathers. And other combinations. You still want to have this wonderful republic, this united Ireland? Because sometimes that's the only unity I see. You don't like this side of it, do you?'

'We'll sort it all out, drag this place out of the stones.'

'Confident.'

'I know what I want.'

'I know.'

A branch cracked and they swung around with their rifles levelled.

Bruddy Holmes came out of the trees, carrying an AKM over his shoulder and a small rucksack on his back. He wore combats and a balaclava over his head. It came down to his eyebrows. He walked with an uneven step, like he'd been disabled earlier and had never recovered. His eyes raced around the trees and there was confused fear in them. Cusack could see the fear best. There were other things but the fear dominated. He wore a green anorak over his combats. His boots were British.

'Relief,' Holmes said.

Cusack frowned. He had to hold his temper. It was hard to hold it. Bruddy had no idea what he was doing and held himself like a kid who had no idea what he was doing. You're going to get someone into a heap of shit some day, boy, Cusack thought. Probably yourself. Then he stopped himself doing that, finding fault with Bruddy Holmes. Anyone who volunteered deserved the benefit of the doubt, deserved a chance. You had to learn somewhere. Most people learned on the job. It was a good master. Clean and efficient at weeding out the no-hopers. They got themselves killed or arrested pretty soon. Sometimes they turned tout. He found himself studying Holmes more and feeling his anger subside.

Holmes's arrival made Cusack abort what he had planned, he told himself. It was not true. Not all of it. There was more. When they had left Bruddy Holmes at the watch and walked down the track together, sometimes touching hands when they walked, Cusack and Maggie stood beside the house. The rain came when they were beside the house but they did not move. They stood and looked at each other and the rain got heavier. Cusack smiled and Maggie smiled and rain ran down his balaclava and on to his nose and down into his mouth and she watched it and felt the rain hit her eyes and drops fall from her nose and water run down the back of her neck but she did not do anything. Sometimes she let her eyes drift to the rain tap-dancing on the slates of the house. The taps were random and even if she tried she could not predict where each of them would go.

23

TIM McLENNAN HAD not slept again. He had not even tried. He had sat at the window in the dark, gun in hand, watching the road. Now and then he slipped the ammunition clip out of the pistol and then snapped it back in. Now and then he lifted the weapon and aimed it at the window and the road. He could not say he wanted someone to come because he did not know if it was true, but there was something in him in the dark after the central heating had gone off and the warmth was slowly slipping out of the room, something that felt right. He thought a lot but his thoughts were in snapshots, interruptions almost, of a synchronicity that he knew he was part of but could not fully explain. And the only voice he heard was Lenny Beggs's and the only face he saw was John Cusack's.

In the morning, he had that elation that going a night without sleep brings, like you're so fragile you're close to tearing. And it helped slow his thoughts more and widen the delays between snapshots. He carried the Walther in his trouser pocket and when he needed to he put his hand in the pocket and touched it and put his finger to the trigger.

The doorbell rang after his mother had insisted on making him breakfast, and he could not rally the will to argue with her when she was limping around the house, talking about his father and Marty. He watched the two faces through the peephole, wide and friendly and maybe drifting in his mind, bits he could not remember, surprises he did not know about. And Eric Johnson's patched-together mutilation grin dragged a kind of deathwish with it.

'Timmy!' Johnson roared. He grinned his patched-together mutilation grin. 'How's the man?'

He put his hand up from where it lay in his lap.

McLennan threw his hand into Johnson's. 'Eric!'

Robbie Wilson smiled and kept his hands on Johnson's wheelchair.

'I found him wanderin' the streets,' he said. 'Tryin' to score with women again.'

'Don't we make a team or what? My eyes, his legs. My eyes are better than his legs. Are you goin' to ask us in, Timmy? It's bloody cold out here!'

McLennan felt he'd been shoved out of somewhere safe.

'Yeah, sure, come in. Jesus, I can't believe it. Mum'll be glad to see youse.'

'We rang your base yesterday on that number you gave me,' Robbie Wilson said.

'I was out.'

'Hush-hush.'

'I thought you were in Edinburgh, Eric.'

'Can't a lad come home for a holiday? See his old friends. Catch up on what's been happenin' in Northern Ireland. Christ, you can't beat it. Is that a bloody Ulster fry I can smell? Mrs McLennan, you always did the best Ulster fry I ever tasted. My God, you've joined the walking wounded, too. I heard.'

Mae McLennan came down the hall from the kitchen on a walking stick with her arm out and smiling like Tim McLennan had not seen her smile since he had been staying with her. Her bad leg looked as if it might give way under her and her hands shook. She shook all over now when she heard a bang. Even a door slamming. And despite her efforts to pull herself together, she had a stale look. Past some sell-by date. Good only for nostalgia. To remind.

He watched her embrace Johnson and Robbie Wilson and say things and make gestures and comments that made him feel like he was watching an action replay. He wanted to press a button that would stop it but he could not find one and, anyway, the feelings it produced were a release from the tension of the tearing and the release was slow and pleasant.

'Will youse come in?' Mae McLennan said. 'Come in and I'll make youse both the biggest fry you ever had. Tim's not had his breakfast yet. Youse'll eat fries, lads. A big Ulster fry?' Then she turned back to Johnson and Wilson and pretended to lower her voice so her son could not hear her. 'Of course, bein' a soldier, he's not used to good cookin'.'

'You can't beat your mother, can you, Tim?'

'Too bloody right.'

She smiled again. She had been sad half an hour earlier. The divorce, Marty, her husband, other things. There did not seem to be a need for a reason any more.

I'll not see my grandson again, she had said, Anne'll keep him away.

No, Mum, I'll have visitin' rights. There'll be times.

Is that all you have now with your son, visitin' rights? He's my grandchild. My only grandchild. For God's sake, Tim, I'm not gettin' any younger. I've no husband, my son spends his time far away, doin' God knows what, and now all this. Jesus, I don't think I can stand it.

He had watched her face fall into despair. Desperately fighting to hold on to any dignity it had left, on the verge of begging, holding herself back. The broken lines on her face spreading, the skin dropping at the jaws, the lines around the lips, the down and the darker hairs, the fatigue in her eyes, the thinning of the hair on her head. She had never been a beautiful woman and Tim McLennan was grateful for that. He thought it must be difficult for a beautiful woman to grow old. A kind of nasty trick nature played on them.

They sat around a veneered kitchen table and Mae McLennan fried everything she had in her pan. Sausages lined up like corpses, black and white pudding melting into the oil, rashers turning up at the edges with the heat, oozing hard salty fat into the rest of the meal, tomatoes bubbling. Then she put the fried bread on and the pan spat a frenzy of excitement and the three men stared over like they were small boys again and waited.

'We were thinkin' of goin' for a drive, Timmy,' Robbie Wilson said. 'Now Eric has a car, but since you have a better one we thought we'd get you if you had spare time. Maybe to the beach. Maybe we'll just go and have a drink. I told him about our fishin' trip. He doesn't believe we caught anythin'. Tell him we did, will you. You don't have anythin' to do, do you?'

'No, he doesn't,' Mrs McLennan said. 'He's a couple of days off. He'd be just sittin' round the house, wouldn't you, Tim?'

It was like she was pre-empting him. He did not fight it.

'Go on, Tim, it'll do you good,' she said. 'The three of you eat this and then head off there and enjoy yourselves. Do youse remember when I used to bring you one of these when you slept over after one of Timmy's parties?'

'I remember the one when Timmy tried to eat grass to show off to the girls,' Eric Johnson said. 'Then made us all try it as a dare. We all had bellyache. I remember your fries, Mrs Mack. I remember Robbie's ghost stories. Good for gettin' the girls close. Scared the hell out of me, too. I work in a library now and guess what? I read nothin' but ghost stories, horror, all that. Now what do you think of that?'

'Are you married, Eric?' Mae McLennan said.

She still had a hard side to her, Tim thought. Fought hard. He did not know what to think about it. Johnson half came to his rescue.

'I am, Mrs Mack,' he said. 'Second time lucky. Great girl. Two wee ones.' He winked. 'There's still things a man with no legs can do.'

They all laughed.

Mae McLennan composed herself before turning around from the pan again.

'Isn't that great,' she said. 'Nice family. Good for a man.'

Johnson realised the nature of the interplay he was involved in. He changed the subject.

'So, will you come, Timmy?' he said.

'How long are you here for?'

'Few more days. But I've my granny to see and I've to go visit Tommy Boyle in jail.'

'Tommy Boyle!'

'He's in Crumlin Road, Timmy. Didn't you know? They say he was passin' information to the UDA or somethin'. I think it's rubbish. But there you are. This is Northern Ireland. Maybe you could find out about it.'

'I'll try. I will.'

'Lenny Beggs says it isn't true.'

Tim nearly went through Robbie Wilson with his head.

'You seen Lenny Beggs, Robbie?'

'Inasmuch as I can, Timmy. Yeah. I bumped into him. The other day. Just like that. Out walkin' and who taps me on the shoulder only Lenny. Got a fright, I did. Well, you would with Lenny. Hasn't changed much. Nearly ended up invitin' me to tea. No thanks.'

'Is this the Lenny Beggs?' Eric Johnson said.

'Yeah. We grew up together.'

Robbie Wilson looked in the general direction of Mrs McLennan.

'That right, Mrs Mack? Our old Shankill days. Before youse and my mam and dad saw sense. He was askin' me about you, Timmy. Tryin' to be subtle. Do I see you? You know? I told him I never see you any more. I laughed. He didn't. Lenny never had much of a sense of humour except for his own jokes. I didn't say anythin', Tim. What do you think of that? Keep clear of him, though. He's dangerous. Lenny Beggs will always be Lenny Beggs.'

'Yeah.'

Tim nodded and looked at Eric Johnson. Johnson winked at him. McLennan turned to his mother.

'How's that fry, Mam?'

In the afternoon, they were in the mountains north-east of Ballymena, on the edge of a glen. The day was good and the wind had died. Fat white clouds punctuated the cold blue sky. Leaves covered the ground, yellow and brown and wet. The castle was overgrown and crumbling. It was sixteenth-century on an earlier structure. Some archaeologists had been digging there and there was a dig site marked out on the west side of the castle. Creeper clung to the walls like a beard.

The path up to the castle was soft and grassy, made by feet more than anything else. On either side of it, the grass was high, and brown at the top, and the ground it grew in was uneven. Tim wheeled Eric and Robbie Wilson linked arms with Tim. The wheelchair sank some in the path and left tracks in the grass and mud and the grass on the tracks came back up in blades here and there and gave it the look of a bad haircut.

'Ulster will fight and Ulster will be right,' Eric Johnson said.

He laughed and looked back at Tim and Robbie.

'Ach, Ulster's done too much fightin', Eric,' Robbie said. 'Good place for a day out, though.'

'He's still into this cross-community do-gooder stuff, Timmy, what do you think of that? Sleepin' with the enemy.'

'It's more fun than killin' each other.'

'You ever had a Taig, Robbie?'

'I'm a married man.'

'You, Timmy?'

Lower down the castle, where it was older, the stonework was uneven and worn away in places, making it unstable. There was a notice saying the walls were unsafe but someone had defaced it with marker and hit it with a stone. They entered the keep, or what was left of the keep, through an arch that dripped water. There were sweet-wrappers and drink cans in holes and moss grew where it was very damp. The smell was stone and damp.

'When we lived in Belfast. Must be twenty years ago,' McLennan said. 'There was a convent girl. Remember that, Robbie? We used to say that if you could get a convent girl you were made. They had this mystery about them. Like findin' buried treasure. A kind of El Dorado in knickers. What the hell was her name? I think she was from Andytown. We were at school, weren't we? It was one of those get-to-know-the-other-side trips, before the real fightin' began. Christ, I think it was near Bangor they sent us. Few days. It all ended in a huge fight. The Taigs got pissed off when we got pissed on cider and sang "The Sash". I remember this organiser guy, all pimpled like, long hair in a ponytail, all full of social-worker ideas, tryin' to stop us, tellin' us it was non-sectarian. What the hell did he want us to do? Get rid of everythin' we were just because the Taigs didn't like it? That's the problem, Robbie, that's the problem with what you do, we have to give up too much. There'd be nothin' left to enjoy.'

'Life, Timmy.'

'Bloody do-gooder,' Eric said.

Robbie Wilson reached down and found Johnson's ear and clipped it with his fingers.

'Talk and dialogue,' he said, 'isn't it fun? It's what we're doin' now. Would you prefer it if we were killin' one another?'

McLennan rubbed his chin. He had a vision he could not completely capture. There had been a girl. There was no face he could put on her. A body but no face. A teenage body with teenage breasts and a teenage hunger. A day with her. They had walked through fields together, instead of being where they were supposed to be. She was pretty. But that was a guess. She was his first. Not Helen Wright. That came to him in flash. His first had been a convent girl. Except he could not remember what had happened. He juggled the years. Must have been my first, he thought. You'd think I could remember my first.

'If walls could talk,' he said.

'Was she good, Timmy?' Eric asked.

'I don't know. I suppose so. But you know what it's like when you're a kid, you're goin' from one girl to another, whoever's willin', as fast as you can.'

'Jesus, I wasn't,' Robbie said.

'Timmy must have been a ladies' man, Robbie. Dark horse, Timmy. You know the type. Always kept it to himself.'

'In Belfast. Jesus, you couldn't keep the colour of your underpants to yourself in Belfast. You've no idea, Eric. You had a nice middle-class upbringin'. We're Shankill men, aren't we, Timmy? Lads of the Royal blue. We—'

'Gettin' sectarian there, Robbie.'

'It's my eyes. I can't always see into my mind. You had it good, Eric.'

'Till some bastard did this.'

They stayed silent for a minute. It felt like an hour. Tim went to wheel Eric through another arch to a broken-down stairway. Eric pushed his hand away. He wheeled himself forward. Tim took Robbie Wilson's arm.

'Hang on to me, Robbie,' he said.

She had a soft body. The convent girl. They all had soft bodies and he could not tell if her soft body was the one he was thinking about. But it was soft. And it was young and they swam in the river. She dared him.

Hey, Prod. She called him Prod. Hey, Prod, take your clothes off and jump in the river. My brother told me Prods can't swim. Prods can't swim 'cause they're heavy with sin. They sink when they go into water. He heard that. I bet you sink.

He took his clothes off to his underpants. She laughed. He hardened and she laughed more.

He could see the mouth now and hear the laughter.

He jumped in because she was laughing. It was the only way to escape her laughter. She sat on the bank of the river. She had good legs. Her hair was shoulder-length, straight. He showed off.

Look, I don't sink. I don't sink. Prods know how to swim. Born to it, he said. Come in.

She shook her head.

Come in. Take your clothes off and come in. Or is it true what they say about convent girls?

What's that?

They've nothin' underneath. Just nothin'.

Oh, I've somethin'. I'm tellin' you. You wouldn't laugh if—

If what?

If I let you do it to me.

Do you want me to?

Do you want to?

Take them off.

We'll get into trouble.

We're already in trouble.

She had her shirt off.

It happened on the bank in the sun. They lay close. It was difficult to get into her. She tried to relax and he forced and had to try again and use his fingers. He brought her close with his fingers and then pushed himself into her and when he was in he had to move quickly because she was coming and he could not hold himself. She said she loved him. He remembered that. And he said it, too. Only knew each other a day and they were saying they loved each other. Rocking there in the sun, white bodies on the grass, feeling the sun caress them. They laughed afterwards and did it again.

'Never saw her again,' Tim said.

'Who?' Robbie asked.

'Convent girlie. Can't remember her name, would you believe.'

Eric had stopped at a stone wall. He was staring ahead of him, into the mountains. They were green like gemstones and you felt you could pick them and wear them.

Tim helped Robbie sit on the stone wall. The stones were cold and Robbie tucked his coat under his bottom. Eric pulled out a whiskey flask and took a drink. He offered it to Tim. McLennan took it and drank and wiped the head and gave it to Robbie Wilson.

'Wow!' Robbie said. 'Great on a day like today. Let's go find a pub and get pissed. Great thing about bein' blind, you know. You can go and get pissed. You never have to worry about havin' to drive. Anythin' great about bein' legless, Eric?'

'Not much, Robbie.'

McLennan put his hand on Eric's shoulders. They were developed and hard as the stone wall. Eric was playing basketball again, from a chair. He was going to run the London Marathon next year. He said it kept him going. It and the kids. He went on about his kids and Tim had wanted to tell him to shut up in the car, but you don't tell people with no legs to shut up. Maybe Eric didn't realise what he was doing. Maybe he couldn't see the connection. Sometimes connections aren't visible unless you're involved.

McLennan sat on the wall beside Robbie. They had another shot of whiskey each.

'I bet it's a gorgeous day,' Robbie said. 'I bet there's different blues in the sky and a kind of autumnal fire, especially with the fire. Am I right?'

'Right, Robbie,' Eric said.

'I remember goin' to Canada from New York years ago. And Jesus, it was on fire. It needs to be dry and sunny for you to see autumn. The shades. The feelin' it gives you. Like the whole world is on fire with expectation. Like it's tryin' to remind you of what'll happen after winter. Gettin' ready for sleep. Sayin', don't worry, it'll all be back in the spring. Keep this in your mind. It gets better. It does. I could be worse off. I know people who've never seen, never, some who've never heard either. Imagine that.'

There was another pause, and then Eric Johnson.

'I just want my legs back,' he said.

'I feel left out,' McLennan said.

'You just keep drawin' blood for us, Timmy.'

'You know what they say about an eye for an eye? Leaves everyone blind.'

'Yeah, but it makes you feel good. Doesn't it, Timmy?'

'No politics. Let's enjoy the day.'

Four women passed by and disappeared into some trees, very tall trees, losing their leaves. They saluted and Eric nudged Robbie.

'Fine bit of skirt, Robbie. Want me to describe them?'

'I can still remember.'

McLennan looked at the castle. He could feel the Walther in the small of his back. It did not irritate him now. It felt comfortable, part of him, and he could not imagine it ever not being there. He let his eyes drift back over the stones in the walls, dark stones, and the ones that had fallen and lay alone, and he tried to remember the convent girl. All he could remember was Carol. Leaving him with a kiss on the cheek. An I'll ring you on the end of a dash through Donegal Place. Her scent, a kind of cloak of reassurance, then a bus or a lorry passed and it was gone and she had vanished around a corner. He watched an RUC patrol question a man at the security checkpoint across the road, beside a grey Landrover, one man levelling his Ruger at the suspect's body, the other going through a bag. There was a camera, and maybe a book. It looked like a book. A child ate a bar of chocolate. It was drizzling.

McLennan brought his eyes back to his friends. The tearing sensation was back. He felt confused. It was difficult, adapting. They said it was difficult and you said yes but you could cope and on the surface you thought you could cope, but below that the confusion was sowing itself, very slowly, and you could not see it until all there was beneath was confusion and any confidence you had collapsed in confusion. He wished he was back in an OP. Up to his head in mud and rain and waiting. Finish it, he said to himself. Finish it and get back before there is nothing to get back to.

'Let's go to the South.'

McLennan turned to Robbie Wilson and then realised his gesture would have no meaning.

'You're jokin'?' he said.

'I am not. I want to go to the Free State.'

Eric looked at Tim McLennan.

'Why not?' he said.

'No.'

'When was the last time you were there, Tim?' Robbie asked.

McLennan turned his head away from Wilson and realised that gesture too meant nothing. He jumped from the wall and walked down a grassy slope. There were weed-ends growing in the grass. He picked some then threw them away. He realised he had to speak; nothing else meant anything to Robbie Wilson.

'I've never been,' he said.

He was going to say officially, but he held it back.

'What!'

'What's the matter with that? Sure they're tryin' to take us over, why the hell would I want to go and visit a place like that?'

'I've never been either,' Eric said.

'Ah, come on.'

'No. Honest to God. Same reason. Fuckers want to see Northern Ireland wiped off the map. They've been out to get us since the twenties. Where d'you think the Provos get their support? I heard there's Provos with brothers in the Free State Army. They're one and the same. They use the Provos to get what they want. Sure who helped arm the Provos? The Free State Government. But I'd like to go now. To see it. Like a raid. The three of us. We could go and take somethin'. Jesus, I'd love to. Maybe a road sign.'

'You're bloody mad. You're worse than him.'

'What the hell else could they do to me? They've taken my legs. I think a road sign is a small return.'

'I want to see the place.'

'You're bloody blind, man.'

'What's the matter, Tim? You'd swear we'd asked you to go to hell.'

'Worse.'

'Ah, come on, Tim, everyone goes to the South now. Even Ian Paisley. We don't have to like them.'

'It'd be a betrayal. Of all of them. All the lads that's died. You know? Do you boys not see?'

'No, I can't.' Robbie laughed.

'Anyway, there's some good folk in the South.'

'Who?'

'If we took a road sign. That'd be a victory. We could burn somethin' down, I suppose.'

'None of that,' Robbie said.

'Okay, take a road sign, though. The three musketeers ride again. Do you remember, Timmy? All for one and – come on, Timmy. All for one.'

'And one for all.'

'That's settled, then.'

'I've a problem,' Tim said. 'I'm armed. And I'm not takin' it off. Rules. If I'm caught armed, we could be in serious trouble. I'd get a bollockin'. Might even be RTU'd.'

'For Ulster!' Robbie said.

'It's serious.'

'Maybe we should hold off, then,' Robbie said. 'You know. Tim's right. It could be dangerous.'

'No fuckin' way. I'm on my holidays. I want to go to the South. I want to take somethin' from them. Like they did to me. Fuck the problems. I'll be our ticket. When they see me and Robbie they won't ask any questions. Super spies. Fancy doin' a bit of spyin' in the South, Robbie? For God and Ulster.'

He wheeled himself towards McLennan. The wheels dug into the ground and he had to shove hard to make the chair move. He stopped in front of McLennan.

'Well, there, young Tim McLennan, you gonna come South with us, your best friends that you see once in a blue moon now? Nice havin' the Army with us. You could look out for bad lads. You're not afraid, are you?'

'I wish I was. You always were a mad bastard, Eric. Why the fuck d'you ever get in that car without checkin' it?'

Johnson let his head sink. He shook it. He scratched the back of his head and looked at McLennan. Tears welled in his eyes. He began shaking his head. His face grew redder and his cheeks expanded and the water poured out over his eyelids and down his swollen cheeks. The tears ran all over his cheeks in all directions, into his mouth, down his nose, down the side of his face, even back towards his ears. McLennan moved towards him and then stopped.

'I don't know, Tim, I don't know. I just never – well, you don't do you? And then it's too late. Too fuckin' late, Robbie, you know?'

Wilson was moving slowly towards him, along the sound of his voice. He measured out each step and McLennan thought it would take an infinity for him to reach Eric Johnson. McLennan felt out of it. All he could do was watch them. Robbie Wilson put his arms around Eric Johnson and Johnson cried like a child into Wilson's embrace. McLennan bowed his head.

24

JOHN CUSACK BENT over the stream and cupped some water in his hands and splashed it on to his face. The water was cold and it tightened the skin on his face and put his brain in sensory overload for a moment. Then he was awake. There were other ways to keep awake when you had to – dexies, nettles, fear. Fear got worn down too easily, dexies brought you down like a stone from a clifftop, nettles gave you lumps. In the end, it was what went on up top that kept you going.

He splashed his face again and watched a fish on the other side dart between the rocks. Now you see it, now you don't. The water bubbled around the big rocks and pieces of weed and twig caught in the current and moved with the rhythm of the water. And the sun moved and the water went from morning silver to brown because the bottom was brown and the trees behind him threw their reflections into the water and Cusack stopped splashing himself. He sat back and felt the cold morning air on the water on his body. Drops criss-crossed his chest and ran down to his pants. His skin goosed and each of the lumps had a hair standing up from it in a kind of frozen attention. He resisted the cold. The wind was stronger now and from the north-east again and warmth left his body with the speed of life from a dying man. He lay back in the grass and began to shiver.

Over him, a bird sat on the edge of a branch and sang. He watched it. He did not know what it was. He did not care. That it was there was enough. He touched his arm. His arm had been torn by gorse thorns. He'd had the unit out overnight, in the forest, chasing each other. Danny Loughlin complaining that it was a bloody kid's game and he wasn't playing. They nearly drew fists except that Dessie Hart got in the middle. Danny went and got drunk on the Dutch lager in the shed.

One scratch was deep and the blood had dried in streaks either side of the wound and given it a stitched look. He could see inside the skin, the way it changed to pink and became weepy. Cold river water had settled on the scabbing. He threw himself around on to his stomach and began to do press-ups. Any amount. A Marine drill instructor in his mind's eye. We're not going to do ten press-ups, maggots, we're not going to do fifty press-ups, maggots. We're not even going to do a hundred press-ups. We're going to do press-ups forever and ever. And you did them till he said drop, and then some more. Cusack kept repeating that to himself while he did his press-ups. It wasn't those who could inflict the most, it was those who could endure the most.

He carried his press-ups beyond fifty. Warmth was returning to his body. Faces came to him now. Dead friends. Army friends. He didn't have any other friends now. Not possible. You took a step when you joined. Maybe a bigger one when you came from where he came from. A kind of exile. And there was no going back.

He thought of the faces again. Policemen, touts, soldiers, civilians. He never counted. You kept yourself free of that. They were enemy and collateral. Depersonalised. You had to. If you thought about each one, about his wife and his kids and his friends, you'd put your gun down and never pick it up again. Never individualise. Some lads did. They were gung-ho till they pulled the trigger. Then when they saw the man's brains all over their clothes they ran like hell to get away. A face came to him.

An RUC officer watering the grass.

They came at him from behind a van. His kid was looking out of the window. Three shots to the torso. He got caught in the rose bushes, kind of jerked, tried to free himself. They shot him again. His face. The kid's face.

And Deco Hynes.

That was a firefight between Dundalk and Forkhill. An hour and a half. And Deco lying there with his stomach beginning to spill. They were stuffing things into him. Back to Dundalk. Friendly doctor. Frantic. Deco digging into his arms. Drew blood. John, Jesus, John, hold on to me, Christ. I'm spillin' out, John, fuck, mother, fuck, white going whiter, butcher shop stink, curses from the doctor, curses from Deco, curses, spitting blood and blood bubbling like a prestrike well. He died, Deco, he died in a convulsion.

Screaming for his mother. Mother Ireland get off my back, Cusack said to himself.

One hundred press ups. Go for one fifty. Push yourself. Nothing you can't take.

And Charlie Brennan. Hunger striker.

Didn't die. Might as well have. Not mentioned in the list of the saints. Cusack allowed himself a moment of resentment for Charlie Brennan. Good footballer, Charlie Brennan. Might have won All-Ireland. Brain damaged, half blind, walked like an out of control special effects creature from a B-movie. Kids laughed at him, called him names. Charlie threw himself in front of a car.

At one hundred and fifty, Cusack stopped. He was warm again. The sun had gone. The clouds had grouped around it and forced it out. His body was hard like reinforced steel, and just as cold, but he felt warm. He pulled the woollen jumper lying beside him over his body and stood up.

'Doin' the Rambo thing, John?'

Cusack swung around to Danny Loughlin.

'I could have popped you, John,' Loughlin said.

Cusack pulled his Magnum from the small of his back.

'I could have had you dead back there when you were getting over the wall, Danny. Difficult shot with one of these but I could have had you, boy.'

Loughlin's smile vanished. Cusack had levelled the revolver at his head. 'Go ahead, punk, make my day!'

He laughed. Loughlin did not.

'Smart, aren't you, John?'

Cusack put the barrel of the gun to his head and tapped it against his skull. Then he shoved it into his pants at the small of his back.

'Up early, Danny? I thought you'd be nursing a hangover. Jesus, you went through a fair amount of that beer last night. Still have it in you, Danny. Still put it away.'

'Youse playin' games didn't appeal to me. You think all this is a game, don't you?'

'Games have their uses, Danny.'

'That what she says?'

Cusack's features froze. He tensed and Loughlin stepped back. He watched Cusack's fists clench and the veins in his hands pulsate and the skin stretch to breaking point. Water and sweat had mixed on his forehead and the drops were balanced at his eyebrows. His eyes were narrowing, nothing getting in he did not want to let in. Loughlin felt himself shaking. He tried a smile. It did not work. He folded his arms because it was the best way he could keep himself from showing his feelings.

'You better watch your mouth, Danny. I'll take so much from you. Go count bullets for the QMG. I hear he's looking for an assistant. You'd be better off a step removed from the war zone, Danny. You're not up to it any more.'

'And you'll fuck up operations here by throwin' everythin' we have at that checkpoint.'

'We're at war, Danny. That's the way wars are fought. We hit the enemy where we can and how we can. You're getting too cosy with company duty. Maybe coming along with us, getting your hands dirty again, maybe that will get you back in line. You haven't done anything for a while, Danny. Too much time playing politics, too much time on the Army Council. You're too damn old anyway, Danny. Jesus, man, you're a relic. Should be touring the States making speeches, stuff like that, enjoying your retirement. Not this kind of work. Not good for your heart, Danny. You're the only one that's against it, Danny.'

'And that makes me wrong?'

'Maybe.'

'I was at this when youse were still suckin' on your mammy's tits, son. And I've seen everythin'. There's nothin' I haven't done for this army. Nothin'. And I can smell a bad one a mile off. I was on the Brookeborough raid, you know that? A skinny kid. That was another mess. I don't like bravado. And this little scheme is all bravado.'

'Well, Danny, you just go tell Dessie you want to stand dow. You're not even up to support fire any more, are you? Go to the pub and we'll sort it out ourselves. Go on. I don't know what's happening to you, Danny.'

He walked past Loughlin. The ground was soft from rain and his boots made prints in the grass. Loughlin reached out and touched his shoulder. Cusack stopped. Loughlin took his hand away and put it back. Cusack turned and looked at him. He knew Loughlin was scared. He could feel it. They taught you to feel for fear, the Corps. Feel for weakness. Loughlin's mouth was dry. His beard moved slightly with the breeze. There were more grey hairs.

Cusack placed his hand on Loughlin's. He smiled. He could feel Loughlin's hand trembling.

'We're going ahead, Danny,' Cusack said. 'It's done. You can come or go.'

'You always get what you want?'

'Don't press it, Danny. I'll knock you into tomorrow.'

'You think there's others don't want a legover there? Maybe you'll have to join a queue. Or maybe you could get the whole unit. Good operation, that. You—'

Cusack grabbed his hand and his forearm and pushed them back. Loughlin tried to get out of it but he could not move. Cusack pushed harder against the joints and Loughlin's mouth sealed itself and he went to grab Cusack with his other arm but Cusack stepped sideways and allowed Loughlin's weight to unbalance him. The older man went down on his knees and Cusack caught him and the shoulder and pushed the arm to near dislocation. Loughlin cried out.

'I told you, Danny, lay off. I could break your arm, or dislocate it, whatever you want. I could do it without thinking. I'm trained like that. There's a part they find. It can objectify. It happens automatically now. When I need it. I could kill you, too. I don't want to. But if you keep pressing this, pressing me, fucking things up, I'll come at you, Danny. I don't care what Dessie says. I don't understand what it is with you. You were always a good volunteer. Me and Dessie, we looked up to you, you know. And here I am about to do you harm. That's not what I want.'

He released Loughlin and Loughlin fell forward on to the grass, clutching his arm and moaning. Cusack walked away.

Danny Loughlin came at him. Cusack knew he would, he had it timed and Loughlin obeyed the timing. Cusack stepped to one side again and left his leg out and Loughlin tripped on the leg and ploughed into the soft ground. When he pulled himself up, he had grass stains on his hands and at his elbows and knees, and there was muck and grass on his face, around his nose.

'Come on, Danny, stop it,' Cusack said. 'That's an order.'

'Fuck orders. I'm gonna teach you a fuckin' lesson. You better do me, son, if you want to avoid it, because I'm gonna keep comin' at you, again and again.'

He came at Cusack and swung his right fist at him. Cusack moved the minimum distance to avoid the blow and caught Loughlin with a kick to the ribs. The older man roared and bent double and Cusack spun and caught him with the other leg across the side of the head. Loughlin fell again. He stayed on the ground and then pulled himself up on to his knees. There was blood coming from the side of his head. His nose was running. His face was red. The red was changing shades and it made his beard brighter. His lower lip was bleeding, too.

Cusack backed away.

'I told you, Danny.'

'And I told you.'

Loughlin wiped his nose on his sleeve and sucked on the blood from his lip. The blood from the side of his head had run into the hairs of his grey beard and was spreading out among the bristles. He threw himself at Cusack. Cusack moved again and brought his hand down on the side of Loughlin's neck. Loughlin groaned and fell flat on his face. He lay there, body flat to the grass, arms out, the only movement from him his breathing.

'You just won't listen, Danny.'

Cusack pulled a stem of coarse grass from the ground and wrapped it round his finger. He stepped closer to Loughlin. Loughlin made no move. Cusack took another step.

'Come on, Danny, you're too old for this. It's ridiculous.'

Cusack moved to Loughlin's legs. He stood beside him and watched the older man. Loughlin just lay there, breathing deeply. Cusack crouched down.

Loughlin swung the back of his head into Cusack's face. Cusack fell back. The Magnum in the small of his back dug into the base of his spine. He cried out and jerked on the ground. Loughlin was up and coming at him. Cusack's nose and eye were pumping blood and the pain in his back had near paralysed him. Loughlin kicked him in the balls. Cusack almost bounced along the ground. He rolled away from Loughlin and tried to get himself up. Loughlin followed him and kicked him in the ribs and Cusack folded and Loughlin kicked him in the face and Cusack nearly backflipped.

'I told you I'd keep comin', I told you, son. I told you I'd get you, one way or another. It's a fuckin' great drivin' force, revenge, you should try it. Sweet, they say.'

He kicked Cusack in the stomach. Cusack felt like all he had ever breathed or was ever likely to breathe had been taken from him, like his insides had been squeezed out of him. And the pain from the balls and the base of the spine was worse. He rolled on the ground and coughed till he was spitting.

'Fancy, you are, John, I'll grant you that, fancy, but you forget the first rule of survival, always cheat. Always do what they least expect. It's what kept me going these years. Jesus, I feel fuckin' good now. Come on, get up. Get—'

He did not get the next 'up' out. Cusack's legs had caught him at the knees like a felling axe and Danny Loughlin went over like a felled tree. He was getting himself back up when Cusack came into him with the second kick. It caught him in the side and it felt like a high-velocity bullet. Loughlin had once been shot with a high-velocity round, in a firefight in Belfast in 1972, when he worked there, when such things were an everyday occurrence, when they ambushed at will, when they had barely enough time for a sandwich before they were battling it out. Then the thing closed in and the British got more sophisticated and casualties on their side became unsustainable.

Cusack picked him up and threw him. He somersaulted across the field and tried to stop himself by clutching the grass. Cusack followed him and kicked him in the face and Loughlin tried to pull himself up and Cusack hit him with his fists, one after the other, into the face, and Loughlin's face seemed to explode into a bloody mess and Cusack still came at him in a dance-like routine, blow after blow, kick, fist, hand, head. Loughlin looked like he was on the end of a string. He folded and collapsed. Cusack stood over him, fists extended.

'Enough,' he said. 'I told you I could kill you, Danny, and maybe I should. Maybe you should have put one into me. Then you'd have solved your problem. Not now. Get up and get back to work.'

Loughlin could not move. His body was broken, his spirit was in worse condition. He had drifted. To a roadside in Armagh years earlier. A winter night when everything was frozen. There was frost on the road and they were driving slowly. Coming home from work. It did not matter what work. They knew the van. Snow began to fall. He could remember thinking how beautiful the snow looked when it was falling, in the headlights of the van, clinging to the road, settling on the wall they sat behind. One of them stepped out on the road. He wore military dress. He flagged the van down.

The driver smiled when he slowed down. He didn't smile when the rest of them came from behind the wall.

Danny Loughlin had never seen a face change like that. From smile to terror.

Out of the van, all of youse.

Ah, come on, lads, don't shoot us, please, please don't shoot us . . . I have a wife, please . . . come on, lads.

Up against the wall. Which of youse are Taigs?

Looking, one to the other, trying to figure it out, twelve of them, guns levelled at them.

Which of youse are Taigs? Fuckin' answer, fuckin' answer or we'll stiff the lot of you.

Fear, all round, fear so thick you could reach out and touch it.

Jesus, lads, no, come on, please . . . please, let us go . . . we saw nothin'.

Taigs, the fuckin' Taigs.

The power, the feeling of power, it was like a hundred orgasms coming together, watching them, smelling their fear, a trigger away from oblivion and a finger away from the trigger.

The Taigs!

Rifle to one lad's throat. He shook and pissed himself and you could see the piss running down his leg into the virgin snow, melting it. And the three Catholics stepped out like they knew they were done for. Guns followed them. They stepped out and walked to the side and stood together and Danny Loughlin found himself hardening and he wanted to do them, just for the hell of it, do everything, just for the hell of it, hard to control, turn to face the others. More begging, more pathetic pleading, contempt and power fought for control.

Please, Jesus, no, please, oh, Jesus, Christ, fuck . . .

He could see their faces, even in the dark beside the wall, trying to stop the bullets with their hands, and the bullets smashed into them from three feet, broke spines, ruptured spleens and kidneys, burst lungs and hearts, tore brains, gouged eyes and ripped flesh, a hundred, two hundred rounds, magazine after magazine, bodies dancing in a grotesque parody of ecstasy, stone and blood, blood and stone, the smell of death, the feeling of kill, the pleasure.

They were high for three days after. Then the down and the down never ended.

Details came. A coat with a tear. One man's eyes were crossed. Loughlin had followed the rogue eye. It led to another man. Fat with two teeth out and a yellow colour on his lips. His nose was broken. The fifth man had huge hands, like spades, with a wart on one and a blister on the other. There was a scarf and blue overalls and a smell of tobacco and mint and there were gloves and the gloves disintegrated with the fellow's hands when he tried to stop the bullets. Boots stank of lime and the van had cement on it.

They turned their weapons on the van after. Till it blew up. The Catholics watched. They said nothing. Two of them pissed themselves. They stood together and watched and didn't move and said nothing. Loughlin thought they should have said something. Then he remembered he didn't say anything either.

One of the dead men held himself proud, never begged or pleaded, didn't look down the way some people do when they're going to be done. Some of them give up, like little animals. One or two hold dignity. Loughlin wanted to rip the dignity out of him. Make him crawl. Lie down and crawl, you fucker. All the anger he could summon, years of it, pulled the trigger. He kept saying it inside his head. Lie down, cunt, lie down.

Cusack placed his Magnum to Loughlin's head. Then he pulled the hammer back.

'You hear this, Danny? You mess with me again and I'll put one in you. You'll obey orders and do your job or you'll go. And I don't think you want to go, Danny. You need us. Don't you?' He shoved the gun into Loughlin's head. 'I said, don't you?'

'Yes, yes.'

Cusack saw the two women out of the corner of his eye. They were coming from the treeline above them. He took the gun away from Loughlin's head and released the hammer and shoved it into the small of his back. It touched the bruising and he winced. He grabbed Loughlin by the collar and pulled him up to his knees. Then he stood back. Loughlin tried to raise himself. His head was spinning. He could smell cordite and there was blood in the snow and they were heading south-west and the van was burning.

'I fell,' he said to his wife.

She looked at Cusack. He shrugged.

'Me too. We both fell.'

He pulled his handkerchief out and went over to the stream and wet it and cleaned his nose.

Maggie O'Neill went up to Loughlin and touched his face. It was split below the right eye and at the lips and the left temple. And there was bruising at the cheekbones and the bridge of the nose. She touched a couple of the wounds. Snot ran from Loughlin's nose. He wiped it with his sleeve. His eyes were watering and it looked like he might cry.

'I fell,' he repeated.

He wiped his nose again and sniffed and pushed Maggie's hand away. She stepped back. He walked past her and past his wife and said nothing. They watched him climb over the stone wall and move up the hill to the treeline and disappear into the trees. He limped when he got over the wall.

Betty Loughlin looked at Cusack. He was touching his eye-cut with the wet handkerchief he had dipped in the stream. His nose was clear of blood but there was bruising at the bridge.

'Differences,' he said.

She shook her head. She took her hands out of her anorak and rubbed them.

'He's gettin' dangerous, John. He's my husband and I don't like sayin' it but he's getting' dangerous. Stand him down.'

She took a tissue from the anorak and walked over to the river and dipped it in the water and came back. Then she rubbed Cusack's cuts. There was one above his eye and one at the side of his mouth. His lip was swelling there. He stood still while she rubbed his cuts. He watched Maggie O'Neill and she looked at him. They did not say anything. Maggie's eyes squinted slightly in the breeze. It was colder now.

'Stand him down, John,' Betty said. 'He needs it. A court martial if you have to. But get him out. He's way past his sell-by date. Danny's livin' on time he hasn't even borrowed. It's stolen, John, and unless you do somethin', I'm gonna have no husband. You see? This is selfish for me. I want my husband. He's a good man. Circumstances, John, circumstances have made him what he is now. He's a good husband. Let him be a good husband.'

'After this, Betty,' Cusack said.

He had not taken his eyes from Maggie. And she had not stopped staring at him. He could feel the cold now and he was not sure if it was the wind or her stare or what he was feeling or what he wanted to do.

'Why?'

'Because it has to be done. Danny knows that. He'll do it. He'll do it because he knows it has to be done. He's an Army man, Betty, more than you'll ever know. He needs us as much as we need him. It's a two-way thing. What we share. You should know that.'

'You're a hard man, John Cusack.'

Maggie had stepped closer and Cusack was trying to make out what was in her eyes. There were layers and the layers were multicoloured in the minutest flecks and the flecks only appeared with the sun from behind the clouds. And her hair glistened, strand by strand, like they were queuing up to reflect the rays of the cold light. Cusack thought he was shaking and he thought he would shake more.

'Danny knows, Betty,' Maggie said. 'He knows.'

She turned and began to walk back. Cusack followed her but he did not catch her up. Betty Loughlin watched the two of them and went to shout. She did not shout. She watched and felt out of it, distant, and trying to catch up with something that was gone. Around her the grass moved and whispered and the river kept moving and Betty closed her eyes.

'I want my husband,' she said.

She did not want to open her eyes again.

25

THAT NIGHT A black taxi pulled into a street in loyalist west Belfast. The street was red-brick Victorian to Edwardian working class. The street lights were white bursts and the white-burst light burnt through the thin mist of night. The footpath was freckled with left-over drizzle patches and the kerbs were painted blue, white and red. Tim McLennan put his foot to the right of a dog turd getting out of the taxi. His eyes drifted along the sharp light, through the mist, to a corner house. King Billy stared back.

McLennan dipped his eyes to the footpath to make sure he had avoided any more dog droppings. There was a squashed Coke tin and a crisp packet in the gutter. The crisp packet had a small pool of water resting in its folds. The Coke tin had been crushed by a heel. He knew from the way the indentation was formed. He leaned into the front passenger side of the taxi and put his hand into his pocket.

'I can get you back?' he said.

The driver nodded. He looked shrunken. There had been no ID in the taxi, no picture, no name, no address. He told McLennan his first name.

'Ask for me by that name. Give this address, I'll come,' he said.

'Fine.'

McLennan handed him a tip. The driver's hands were sweaty. McLennan stepped back. He glanced down at the dog turd. The taxi did a U-turn. McLennan swallowed some of the exhaust. He could taste it on his tongue when he was ringing the bell of the house.

The house was exactly the same as every other house in the street. Except maybe the paintwork was better and there was trestling running around the door and creeper on the trestling. The garden was tissue-sized and the plants in it would have had a better deal in a window-box but they were laid out with precision and well-kept. The whole house had a well-kept feel to it. Nothing more. McLennan watched his breath mix with the mist and his breath made patterns in the light when it burnt the mist.

'Staff Sergeant McLennan.'

McLennan tried not to be seduced by the respect for rank but he had spent so long trying to get where he was now, he could not stop himself feeling a surge of pride at the flattery, even though he knew it was flattery. A weakness, he said to himself. He nodded.

Lenny Beggs looked bigger in his doorway. Maybe he had constructed the doorway to make himself look bigger McLennan thought. The door had a metal plate screwed to its reverse side. McLennan saw it only when he was inside. Beggs kept him standing for a few seconds longer than he should, watching the street. It was his street on his turf and he had people watching everything that needed to be watched but he always watched himself anyway.

Practice, he said. You never knew when the Fenians might slip in and take a pot-shot or stick a mercury tilt package under your car. His car was driven by someone else. A precaution. When he wanted a car, he made a call and a car appeared. The call was coded to prevent the IRA or one of the more fanatical left-wing republican splinters in the Lower Falls and Divis appearing in a similar vehicle with a surprise. Caution and watchfulness, Beggs said. McLennan wondered if Lenny could spell watchfulness.

Beggs led McLennan upstairs. Another precaution, he said, better for defending. There was a door in one of the bedrooms through to the next house and the next house was occupied by one of his bodyguards. All the upstairs doors had reinforced steel panels screwed to them on the inside. All the windows were bullet-proofed. You wouldn't notice it, Beggs said, unless you were looking for it. That was the way it was designed.

'But they're safe if that's what you're worried about.'

'I trust your instincts, Lenny.'

'Sure don't we have the peace line over there and youse lads to protect us from the Taigs,' Beggs said.

He pointed out of the window to where the corrugated wall that cut the Belfast cake into religious and political slices ran the length of three streets. There was wire caging stretching out from the wall on both sides as far as the nearest buildings to prevent people lobbing dangerous objects at one another. Peace had never been much in evidence along the peace line. Lenny Beggs said she'd packed her bags and gone to Beirut. He laughed at that, too. He laughed at all his own jokes. McLennan smiled now and again.

McLennan sat down in the bare chair provided for him in the back bedroom. There was a single light hanging from the centre of the ceiling and a veneered table separating Beggs from himself. Beggs sat on the opposite side of the table. There were two flags at angles to the horizontal on the wall behind him. The Union Jack and the Ulster provincial flag. The Ulster flag had a legend under it: For God and Ulster. To Beggs's left was a bare wall with the door in it. This was the door that led to the next house. The get-out clause, Beggs said, laughing again. At the window end of the room was a television set with a VCR and a camcorder. There were tapes in a box and beside the box was a fax machine. And that was the room. McLennan didn't like the idea of having his back to the window but then again he wasn't sure he much liked the idea of being there at all.

He did not know why he was there, yet. He had not made up his mind. And at that moment, in front of Beggs, he did not want to make up his mind and he did not want to know why he was there. But these things would come.

The first ten minutes, Lenny Beggs talked about when they were kids and pointed out families they had known and gave potted histories and judgments. And McLennan sat and nodded and listened. Sometimes he smiled for effect. The odd time he smiled because Beggs had brought up a name he had forgotten, or an incident. And when Beggs had done his anecdotal introduction he sat back in his seat and folded his arms.

'So what can I do for you, Timmy?' he said.

'Well, you can fuck off with the takin' the piss bit for a start. Keep the respect, Lenny. You can stick to Staff Sergeant. And the thing we're here for is what I can do for you.'

'Yes, of course. Okay, shoot. Here, that's funny, isn't it?'

McLennan showed no emotion. 'You first, Lenny,' he said.

'This house is secure. You can say what you like. We sweep and scramble and we're ninety-nine per cent sure.'

'It's the one per cent that kills you.'

'You want to go somewhere else?'

'Maybe.'

'Okay. I – we – are in the business of the possible disengagement of

Great Britain from Northern Ireland. And we're interested in people of a similar mindset. But you know that, Staff Sergeant, or you wouldn't be here.'

'Who exactly are we?'

'The organisation I represent – others, many people, in fact, many more than you'd think. People who've been watchin' the way things are goin', people who've been watchin' the Taigs grow in strength while we weaken. Good Protestants who don't want to see their province destroyed by Fenians. And the very fact that you're here means that you're thinkin' that way too.'

'What if it does happen? What then?'

Beggs leaned over the table and broke a pencil he had been moving in and out of his fingers. McLennan smelled sausages and kidneys from his breath. His pores had blackheads and there was a small incision in the lobe of his ear.

'Take a look at this,' he said.

He handed McLennan a sketch map of Northern Ireland.

'That's the kind of blueprint we'd be aimin' at. We'd have to leave some of the border areas to the Taigs. But that's tactical. You'd know that. I'd be interested if you had any comments, Tim.'

Beggs's eyes were brown and had a bovine quality to them that made McLennan want to stand up and walk out. This was Lenny Beggs he was talking to. He knew at least three killings Beggs had been the trigger for. None of the victims anything more than an easy Catholic. McLennan didn't like Catholics much, there was no way of getting round it, it was just the way it was with him, based on experience and observation: they were dangerous, conspiratorial, subversive people. He had no Catholic friends, and not counting that girl he had had all those years ago, he had never had a Catholic friend. They were superstitious, repressive, childish almost, he thought. These were thought-out views, not just the kind of prejudice he was raised around, though he could not say where the thoughts came from. Given the chance, he would rather live in a Protestant state than a Catholic state, it was as simple as that, and he made no apologies for his views. Protestantism meant liberty to him. The other lot legislated for what you thought. He liked the freedom to pursue his own mind. But walking up to men, drinking or putting a bet on a horse and blowing them away just because they had the luck to be born Catholic, no way, he thought. I'm a soldier, not a terrorist.

'I'm serious, Tim,' Beggs said after a while. 'The doomsday scenario. And we're lookin' out for real talent. Yeah, I know what you think of us. There's others think the same. But when the time comes and the bottom falls out, who are they goin' to turn to? They're goin' to turn to us, Tim. And you will, too. Because you're too good a Protestant to let this province slide to Dublin without a fight. Jesus, just look at it economically, Tim. Westminster puts billions into us. You think Dublin could do that? We'd end up down at their level. A third-rate banana republic, waitin' for the next EC handout. Unemployment would go through the roof. And who do you think would get the fuckin' jobs? Not Protestants, I'll tell you. Fuckin' Taigs would. Everythin' that was goin'. We'd end up havin' to take the boat to England. Boat people, that's what we'd become, Tim. Just think about it. Of course, we want to stay in the kingdom, but . . .'

'And you're still gonna walk into pubs and bookie shops and spray them?'

Beggs leaned back.

'I know what you're thinkin', Tim. I know, and there's no way I can give you a good answer, except to say this is war. And in war, civilians get killed. And this is a war with terrorism and you can only fight terror with terror. Do you not think we'd like to take them on in a clean fight? But they don't fight clean. They've been killin' Protestants along the border at will. Sons of farmers, so the farm will die in a generation, key people. They say they kill members of the security forces only. That's fuckin' rubbish, a nice cover. They hit the key Protestants. And we're goin' to do the same. Terrorise the terrorists. Hit Sinn Fein and anyone else that wraps the green flag round them. We have better info now, we're better organised, we know what we're doin'. I can't say more but you'll see. The right people will fall and they'll know that if they cause us pain we'll cause them a lot more. And Dublin isn't goin' to get away lightly. That's the real string-puller. They shelter behind that fuckin' agreement and they say they have no ambitions and yet they do nothin' to stop terrorists trainin' and launchin' attacks from the south. They're scum. They will know they'll have to pay a heavy price for their united Ireland. We'll bleed them fuckin' dry before they get their hands on our province and if they ever do there'll be nothin' left for them in the place by the time we've finished with it. That's the way it has to be, Tim. War footin'. This is to the death. There is no compromise with republicanism, with Catholicism. We've fought for hundreds of years to keep away from Rome. You think we're gonna go peacefully now?'

'What kind of support do you have?'

Beggs took a sheet of paper from his pocket and placed it blank side up on the table.

'Right, this is a risk I'm takin',' he said. 'You could be a spy. I'd never know. So take this as a sign of trust.'

He turned the paper over and shoved it at McLennan. McLennan looked at the names. There was no one on it that surprised him. He did not say that to Beggs. He went down the list a couple of times without betraying any emotion. Beggs had another pencil between his fingers. He dug it into the table. McLennan let his eyes run to Beggs' fingers. The nails were bitten and there were scars on the hands. Beggs had had a run-in with a rival years earlier and the rival and his mates had come for Lenny one night with steel bars and cut-throat razors. Lenny beat them off but they got a few implements in. Lenny kneecapped the whole lot three weeks later, complete works. He killed the rival.

'You're sure?' McLennan said.

'Of course. They know what side their butter's on. They won't come out and say it but they're with us.'

'And the police people? The Army?'

'We have our contacts. But you know that. You're here. The more we can get, the better. Some of them politicians are dodgy. They think we're a bunch of guttersnipes, only good for their marches, their speeches. They wouldn't have a drink with us. They used us before. Made fools of us. Well, we're callin' the shots now, and we're shoppin' about for talent.'

'Me?'

'If you like.'

'What would I have to do?'

Beggs smiled. He leaned forward again.

'Now? Nothin'. Except what you're doin'. Maybe we could meet, discuss the situation, now and again. Incognito. Mutual interests. Maybe explore links you might have in South Africa. You still have friends down that way, Tim? We got a shipment in from there a while back. We'd be lookin' for another. And maybe somebody who could give us some advice on what we need and other places we might acquire it. Then there's trainin'. We want to train ourselves. We have people in the UDR, in the Territorials. Good for them. Youngsters need trainin'. We need everyone. Like Israel. Like the good Afrikaaners. War footin'. It's a slow thing. Our timescale is open. But we must be ready. This Ulster, this province, it's either gonna be fought over, and won, or it's gonna be lost. That's the choice. Now, I know what you think of me, Tim. I know how you lot think about us. Ghetto Prods. Only one step up from the Taigs. A kind of buffer. Well, there's a focussin' goin' on here and you lads are gonna have to take sides. Simple as that. You used to be one of us, Tim. Used to be. Then you moved out. Got deghettoised. Then they put you up for a commission. Tryin' to grab you good and proper.'

McLennan shoved the paper back.

'Except you lot killed my father,' he said.

Beggs sat back and his face reddened.

'I was waitin' for that, Tim. I thought you'd hit me with it immediately. I remember that, Tim. And all I can say is I'm sorry. I had nothin' to do with it. I want you to know that. That was a different time. This movement, well, we were wilder, stupid, but you have to see it in the context of the times. Stormont fallin' apart, the whole Protestant state we had constructed over fifty years being systematically destroyed by the Taigs and their terrorists. I will not try to excuse what happened. The lads that done it, they're dead, if you want to know. But they didn't know there would be Protestants in that bar. That was a Taig bar. Jesus, why did they drink in a Taig bar?'

'There wasn't any reason not to. It didn't mean anythin' there, not the way it does here in Belfast. No one gonna beat the shite out of you if you did. He threw himself on her, you know. On my mother. Right across her. He was brave, my dad. Good man. They came in and sprayed and he threw himself across my mother and she lived and he died.'

Beggs raised his hands.

'I won't excuse it. But there were circumstances. And now is now. And the time has come for takin' sides.'

McLennan could still remember the phone call. It rang longer than it should have, on and on, like it wasn't going till it told what it had to tell. Bad news ringing. And he came down from his bedroom and picked it up and there was a pause and he knew. So stupid. In a Catholic bar, shot by Protestant gunmen. Fucking Monty Python couldn't have thought up a better piece of comedy. And at the funeral they sent a wreath, Beggs's pals, saying how sorry they were, from this or that battalion, this or that brigade.

'And what'll it lead to? You want me goin' around with your gangs, pottin' Taigs because they're Taigs, just murderin'. I'm not like that. There's a government here and there's security forces and I'm a member of those security forces and we fight the terrorists within the law. Sure we'd like a wider brief but that doesn't include old men and taxi drivers and barmen. There's laws and they take care of the terrorists we don't get. The law, Lenny. Once we give that up we're sunk. We become as bad as they are.'

'Are you a religious man, Tim? I don't suppose you are really. I am. Ach, I used to be a wild boy when I was younger, but I found order in religion. It's good. Disciplines you. The Taigs have that. They get discipline from their Church. Sure the southern government has to ask Rome before it takes a piss. Now that's the way we've got to be. We've got to have discipline. Demonstrate we can hit them where it hurts when we like. And that's where you come in, Tim. You're the kind of fellow can hit a target.'

He picked up a briefcase he had at his feet and laid it on the table. Then he took a manila folder out. He shoved the folder at McLennan.

'Chinese Type 67. Good job, Tim. And the right boy, too. I'm impressed. I've no doubt you could do me right now if you wanted. You still carrying a P5? The Provos give their border people Magnums. But this job was good. Really good, Tim. Professional. Maybe if we'd been runnin' things, you'd have got a medal. Now you'd do life.'

The folder contained a photograph of the dead IRA man in Donegal and a typed report detailing McLennan's moves.

'We were on to him. Our boys were doin' a dry run. They were watchin' the place. That's you in the photograph.'

'It's outside a pub.'

'True. Five minutes from where the lad was killed.'

'What's that supposed to mean?'

'Okay, okay, listen. I think it's bloody terrific. I think we should let you loose on the whole fuckin' lot of them. But don't play the moral judge when you speak to me, Staff Sergeant McLennan.'

McLennan put the pictures and the report back in the folder and shoved it back at Beggs.

'I could kill you now, Lenny. I could put one between your eyes. I feel like it. I feel like gettin' some of what's inside me out and you'd be a good target. For my father if nothin' else. He never did anyone any harm. He was a good man. He worked hard, liked a drink on a Saturday night. One fuckin' night a week.'

McLennan thought about reaching for his pistol. He could feel it against his ankle but he was not sure why he wanted to kill Beggs. For himself, for the humiliation of having his father killed in a Catholic pub by people like Lenny Beggs, for having to sit down with Beggs and discuss an inescapable logic which any way you looked at it kept coming up with the same answer? I want to break your fucking neck, Beggs, he thought. I want to break your fucking neck and put the magazine into your thick skull because you show me what I am, what a dumb fucker I am, and where all this shit is leading to. There was no way out. He slapped the table and stood up.

'I'm glad we've been able to talk, Tim. Maybe we can meet again. Maybe a neutral venue. You know, where we can relax. This ghetto shite gets me down. My kids can't go anywhere on their own and I've to bring a bloody escort any time I want to take the family out, even to a Linfield game. Isn't that fuckin' ridiculous? The wife doesn't like it. It's makin' her old. She's on Valium. The whole fuckin' city's on Valium.'

McLennan thought about Beggs's wife. The woman was only slightly smaller than Beggs. She had a tight soldier's haircut and skin that looked like a mixer had worked on it. He told himself he was a snob, that these were his people, not the men he worked with, the ones with the Tyneside and scouse and cockney accents, these were his people, and he did not have a choice about where he should go. He shook his head.

'I have to go,' he said. 'I want to call a taxi.'

'It's already been called, Tim.'

McLennan shook his head and laughed and told himself this wasn't happening to him.

26

MAGGIE O'NEILL TOLD herself it would not happen with Cusack right up to the edge of the forest; she told herself it would not happen when they were staring at each other; she told herself it would not happen when they kissed. And when he came inside her the first time, she arched back and pulled from the pleasure until she could not hold herself any more and then she came close to him and dug her nails into his skin and felt the chill of the soft wind around them and their heat and she cried out to him that she wanted it to happen.

He had followed her to the forest, knowing what would happen. Part of him argued that it was wrong, that he had no right, but he wanted her and she was there for him and he was going to have her and to hell with everything else. So he followed her, brought sleeping bags and bread and a few bottles of Danish lager and followed her thirty yards behind when she was going on watch, and watched her move in the blue darkness, the clear cold-sky darkness of the in-between time before full-winter, on a long walk up the track over uneven ground, silent, pulse racing, pulse pushing, a kind of panting expectation present, and he told himself it was what he wanted and it was his will and his will was right and what he wanted he should have because that was the line, what was there and his will to take it.

She came on top of him with his mouth over her breast and her hands between his legs, holding him when he pushed, her head back, frosted breath on clouds over her mouth.

Cusack rolled over. Her breast hung to the side and the nipple was hard and he put his mouth to it again. She touched his head. There was sweat in the hairs and sweat gathered at the hairline and she ran her hand along the hairline and closed her eyes. The wind had chilled the sweat and she pulled the sleeping bag over her shoulders. Her body was shaking. She could feel individual muscles shaking, put her fingers on them and feel them shaking.

'I hope I'm pregnant,' she said. 'I want to be pregnant. Make me pregnant. Love me again, John, and make me pregnant.'

'I can't. I'm wasted.'

'I can wait. I think I'm in love with you. I want you. I've wanted you since I saw you with Dessie. I wanted to strip you immediately. God, if you knew what I was thinkin'. I was cold, wasn't I? But I wanted you. Are you ready?'

'No.'

'Does it matter to you?'

'That you're in love with me?'

'No, me bein' pregnant?'

'No. Might be nice, I guess. I've never been a father. We can get somewhere, I suppose. Okay?'

'Yes. This is all stupid and doesn't mean anythin'. I know, but it doesn't matter. I like it.'

'It's not stupid. And it means something.'

'I want to tell Brian. I want to scream it at him. Jesus, it feels so easy. Maybe I should have done this years ago.'

'With whom?'

'I don't know. I'm thinkin' out loud. My kids – I'll be able to get my kids, won't I? They have to come with me. I'll do anythin' else but I won't leave them. Oh, God, I want to be pregnant. Make me pregnant, John.'

'Lie on me.'

Cusack could feel the lumps in the forest ground beneath the sleeping bag they lay on. The wind moved in the branches of the trees around them and whispered. The trees were packed tight in plantation formation and some of the branches came down to their heads and one had scratched Cusack's back when he was coming the first time and when he was on his back and she was lying on him he reached out and touched it. There were some stars out. The stars played hide and seek with his eyes behind the trees and the small dark clouds coming in from the south. Cusack shoved his body closer to hers and ran his tongue across her. He could smell the needles around them and the oil from their rifles on the night air and

Maggie's scent and the needles mixed with the oil and with her scent and it was a good smell.

He had expected the seduction to be harder and maybe he was disappointed it had not been harder but there were other things to be disappointed with and he was glad it had happened the way it had.

Maggie kissed him and ran her hands around him and down between his legs and touched him there with the tips of her fingers and felt him move and drew her finger along the length of him.

'Beautiful,' she said.

'I love you,' he said.

She laughed.

'It's good to hear. Say it all the time, will you? Say it and make me pregnant. I always want to be pregnant when I'm goin' to do a job. That make sense?'

'Yeah.'

She reached up and pulled some bark from the tree behind him. She touched his face with the piece of bark. It had another smell but the smell could not break free of what wrapped them.

'I was aching for you,' he said. 'And you played me along. You played me along to keep me aching.'

'I like it that way. To watch your face, feel the energy buildin', holdin' you right off. We were always goin' to do it but I was goin' to say when. That's the problem with men, they don't know when to wait, to allow it to build and make it better, right until you can't hold on. Drives you crazy, doesn't it?'

'Who taught you all that?'

'Experience.'

'Much?'

'Enough. You must know how to play a man. And he must know how to play you. You play well.'

'Be a fine mess if the Sass caught us like this,' Cusack said.

Maggie laughed.

'If Dessie caught us. Could be court-martialled.'

'Let them,' he said.

He closed his eyes and travelled on her voice and her feel and her smell.

He was running. Through another jungle. He could see the figure ahead of him, in and out of the growth. He fired, one round, two rounds, three, then the magazine, reload, cut across, heart beating, eyes turning in their sockets, feel it, smell it, obey your gut, moving faster, branches in the face, thorns, eyes down for booby traps, eyes up, eyes across, snakes, poisoned sticks, spring-loaded spikes, man-traps and tripwires, move faster, got to catch up. Witness.

They made love twice more and when they had finished and each of them wanted no more Cusack took the watch and Maggie slept and when she had slept she took over the watch and Cusack slept.

It was dawn when Cusack woke. Maggie was sitting away from him by a small fire she had made in a clearing in the trees. The smoke tongued its way to the sky and the flames cloaked the wood in a kind of warm velvet. Cusack sat down beside her. She had a long stick in her hand and a hunk of bread on the end of the stick. The bread was in the fire and butter from the browning surface of the bread was bubbling into the fire. The butter made tears in the velvet of the flames. Cusack placed one of the sleeping bags over Maggie's shoulders. He threw the other around himself. They did not speak. Around them, forms changed with the minutes from ill-defined lumps to detailed structures and a haze settled across the drumlins.

It was an Indian woman. In the jungle. He dropped her with a single shot between the second and third ribs, left side. Exit was down at the hip. The exit wound would have taken his fist. She was a woman with dark hair and dull, dedicated eyes. She had facial hair above her lip and a scar across her neck. She was maybe forty, she looked older. Her hands were rough and they looked like they belonged to someone else and that she had only borrowed them. She was still alive when he found her.

Dios, she said.

She had seen him. She could identify him. His face. *Norteamericano* when there weren't supposed to be any *norteamericanos* around. The target had gone down and Cusack was away and she was strolling through the jungle, whistling, carrying fruit. Never expected to die. Expected to eat fruit. Look looked at look and dull eyes met killer's. Killer's moved and dull ran and then she was dying on the jungle carpet. Her blood stayed with her. She bled into herself. There was some bone on a leaf near her. She shook like she was cold. He held her hand until she died.

'You'll have to put it out,' he said to Maggie. 'The fire.'

'A few more minutes. I like it. It makes me feel warm.'

'Dios,' he said.

'Why?' she said.

'A prayer,' he said.

'Do you believe?'

'I don't know. I suppose.'

Cusack picked another piece of bread from the plastic bag at her feet and put it on the stick.

Maggie allowed a smile on to her face. She turned and shared it with Cusack.

'Betty told me to screw you,' she said.

'Why?'

'*Carpe diem*. Means seize the day. You know? Latin.'

'I know.'

'I think I was doin' it for her, too.' She touched Cusack's head. 'You mean well, John,' she said. 'Know that?'

'I mean what I say,' Cusack said. 'And I want to be with you.'

'I know. It's good. Eat.'

They ate and there might have been something in the fact that they each gave the other their pieces of toast to eat or it might have been the time of the day.

Maggie could feel a headache coming on. Sometimes it happened. After she had enjoyed herself. She never told anyone. Difficult to say she got a headache after sex. People would laugh. Her headache was at the top of her neck and she could feel her head beginning to expand.

'Where is it?' Cusack asked.

She'd told him about it. An act of trust. A test. He did not laugh. He touched her neck and she told him where it was and he rubbed with his fingers, thumbs first, under the skull, then tips on top and through her hair.

'Will you remember it?' she asked.

'Of course. I mean what I say. I'm a man who says what he means and does what he says.'

'I believe it.'

'You don't—'

She turned and stopped him.

'If you're goin' to say I don't have to come with you, I don't want to hear, and if you're goin' to say I don't have to go on this operation, I'll be insulted and get angry. I don't want to get angry. If I told you you didn't have to go, you'd be insulted, you'd be angry.'

He did not say what was on his mind.

'Are you one of these heads who need to feel the women are safe? Is that it, Yank?'

'You called me Yank again. I thought you said you wouldn't.'

'I can't help it – John. There.'

'Is that a victory?'

'In a way. You're close now. I could love you without lettin' you close. But now you're close. Maybe you have made me pregnant. I felt warm when you came, it's a warm feelin' when it comes, you can feel it, it touches inside. They're probably fightin' their way towards an egg now. Kiss my neck.'

The light was up and there were noises in the forest now and Cusack put his foot in the fire and stamped it out. He threw muck on it to cloak the smoke and more muck to bury the embers. The muck and the smoke mixed for a while and floated up in a sheet and then fell away. The embers crackled and cherry smiles stayed on the black sticks and in the ashes and sap dripped from the edge of some of the sticks that had only started burning when they put the fire out.

'I feel like a kid,' Cusack said. 'We used to camp out a lot when I was a kid. Summers in the States. Catskills.'

'Where's that?'

'New York.'

'New York's a city.'

'It's a beautiful state, too. You know, wild. Bears and cats and skunks and stuff. There were a lot of things you could see. You have to hang your food away from your camp in case the bears come for it. Bear'll take everything it gets its claws around. Racoons, too. But when you hang it they can't take it. Only the bears. And you should see it in the fall. It's like someone's put a match to it or thrown paint on it. Reds and yellows and browns and greens, and the fall light's like an oil and it all mixes and seeps right into you.'

'Jesus, you're a romantic, aren't you?'

'Not really. I can appreciate beauty.'

'Don't you dare tell me I'm beautiful.'

'You're a fantastic fuck, Maggie O'Neill.'

She grabbed him by the face and kissed him on the lips.

'That's the most marvellous thing anyone's ever said to me,' she said. 'Thank you, John.'

She made a confession – the woman in the jungle – before she died. He listened and gave her a blessing because she asked for one, and when she was dead he said a prayer over her body and dug a hole in the jungle floor with his knife and buried her. He said a prayer over her grave. Then he covered the grave so that there was no trace of it and wondered if she had anyone, anyone who would never know what had happened to her, kids maybe, a man, folks, people who cared, people who saw her go out or maybe asked how long she'd be, or were waiting. And they'd never know. He knew.

Maggie walked down on her own. There was a bird near her. She had twigs and pieces of bark and needle in her hair and she had his smell on her jacket. She carried her sleeping bag in her arms like she was hugging it, and she could smell him in that, too.

Betty Loughlin stood at the back door of the farmhouse. She had one wellington on. Maggie smiled at Betty Loughlin and Betty tried to smile back but the night had all of her energy. At the corner of the farmhouse, going towards the hill she had come from, loaded up for his watch, Maggie could see Bruddy Holmes. He still walked as if he did not understand what he was supposed to be doing. He had a boy's walk and he carried an AKM as if he was an untrained militia fighter in a Third World civil war, with no respect, by the grip, pointing directly down at the ground. Maggie watched him walk up by a line of larches and blackthorn and she wanted to yell at him: Did he not know what the fuck he was doing? Did he think he was playing some kind of game? He was just like his fucking brother, and look what happened to him! But Betty was in front of her and she had lines on her face that spoke of more important things than Bruddy Holmes.

'You had a nice night?' Betty said.

'I did.'

'I'm glad. It was right.'

'I know.'

'Husbands.'

'Love.'

'Love, indeed.'

'Need help with the breakfast? Troops need feedin', I suppose. So much for feminism, Betty.'

'Don't you ever get tired, Maggie?'

'Sure. All the time?'

'I don't think Danny'll last. I don't. Maybe none of youse will.'

She came right up to Maggie and stood so that her body touched the sleeping bag and her hands touched Maggie's hands. Her wrists were cold and the skin was loose and there were hairs running from the wrists to the backs of the hands and down to the thumbs. Her wedding-ring finger was red and the red became purple further up. The nails were long and brittle and there were cracks in three of them. Maggie grabbed the sleeping bag with her elbows and took Betty Loughlin's hands and rubbed them.

'I was thinkin' of going back to school,' Betty said. 'Get myself a good qualification. Maybe study the law. I like the law, you know. Maybe I could defend you lot if you come before the courts, plead mitigatin' circumstances. I'd have to move. Danny could come with me.'

'I always wanted to give a great speech from the dock.'

Maggie swung her head. John Cusack sat on the stone wall behind her. He had his Armalite across his lap with the butt folded. He smiled and picked a piece of weed and folded it.

'You would,' she said. 'I could see you refusin' the court. All brave and Robert Emmett.'

'It had class,' he said.

'Not a lot of room for nobility any more,' Betty said.

'Yeah,' Maggie said. 'We gotta use their system against them. Otherwise we'd all be hoisted on principle and it's a hell of a sharp instrument, principle. Be practical. Their biggest strengths are their biggest weaknesses. Remember that.'

'They may kill the revolutionary but never the revolution,' Cusack said.

'Bravo, Che Guevara,' she said. 'Any more enlightenment?'

'What have the Brits ever done for us?

They looked at one another and smiled.

'Roads are good,' Betty said. 'The ones they haven't blown up.'

'The ones we haven't blown up,' Cusack added.

They laughed.

'Social welfare. If you're a Taig, you need it. It's all you're likely to have.'

'Housing. Six-County ghettoesque. Nice views of Land Rovers and camouflage and corrugated iron. Very tasteful.'

'Education. Remember, man, thou art a Brit and a Brit thou shalt stay.'

'Safe to walk the streets at night.'

They all laughed again.

'Soldiers who say have a nice day,' Maggie said.

'Long Kesh.'

'Castlereagh.'

'Sensory deprivation.'

'Inhuman treatment.'

'When is torture not torture? When it's inhuman treatment.'

'Supergrasses: it was him, your lordship, I swear by the grand you're goin' to give me. Maybe it was him and them two, and he was probably there, too. Do I get my money now, your lordship?'

'Okay, okay, but besides the roads, social welfare, housing, education, public safety, soldiers with manners, prisons, prisons, more prisons, interrogation centres, torture, show trials and paid informers, what have the Brits ever done for us?'

They all buckled laughing and Cusack raised his rifle and gave a clenched-fist salute.

'Chuky,' he said.

Bruddy Holmes had stopped about a hundred yards up the track and looked at them and looked like he wanted to join them. He raised his hand in a fist and then his rifle and was going to yell but held himself. And Cusack saw Billy Holmes and could not help feeling angry at Bruddy and blaming him. Bruddy lowered his rifle and stopped smiling and went to shout something again and did not. He waited for one of them to shout to him, to show him something special they had between them, to share it with him. He was scared all the time now. Scared so much he drank when he thought they weren't looking and used chewing gum to cover the smell. Scared so much he thought he'd shit himself every time he woke from the lousy sleep he was getting. There was a part of him wanted to be caught, wanted the gardai or whoever to come along and lift the whole lot of them and stop it all.

None of them yelled at him. Cusack waved him on.

He backed off without saying anything and felt his stomach turn.

'I like Radio Four,' Maggie said.

She put her hand on Betty Loughlin's hand and stroked it.

John Cusack picked up the sleeping bag he had laid on the wall and threw it at her.

27

THE CLIPPED CONFIDENCE of a Security Service briefing officer oil-on-watered the memory of Anne McLennan's appearance at Carol Russell's flat the day before.

Tim and Carol had been naked. They were sliding down the door when the bell rang. Anne was standing in the video screen. Black and white and stooped. Carol pressed the buzzer to let her in before McLennan could stop her.

'Don't. I don't want to,' he said.

'I have to. I want to have it out, anyway.'

Anne stood at the door, watching them button up. Carol had opened the door before McLennan was ready. He was still buttoning his shirt. Anne stood there in her coat, looking. There were no emotions on her face. He expected to see something. He was embarrassed. He wanted to yell at Carol but he needed her. She stepped forward to the door. She did not go over the threshold. She smiled at Anne and straightened her clothes. McLennan moved over to the side, out of the view of his wife.

'I'm Carol.'

Carol put her hand over the threshold and Anne took it.

'Won't you come in?'

Anne had been inside for two or three minutes before she said anything. McLennan thought the room was going to explode with tension. Anne looked older. Older and wiser, he was going to say, but older sufficed. She carried a small holdall. She wore make-up that stood out too much on her face and lipstick that was lumpy on the top of her lips. Put on in a hurry. Everything about her looked hurried. How the hell did she find the place?

Off off-the-Malone Road. In the middle of middle-class respectability. Outsiders didn't even know Belfast had middle-class respectability. It was a well-kept secret. The bombs and the bullets didn't stray too far from their natural habitat. He resented Carol for being middle-class. Never felt the heat of the ghetto, where the Taigs were so close they had to be kept out with a wall; that close and getting closer. Never felt that.

Anne studied them, still without saying anything.

'Tea?' Carol said.

She looked at Tim McLennan and smiled. It was a joke to her. She had the luxury of allowing it to be a joke, like she had the luxury of not being too pushed about Northern Ireland, like she had the luxury of going where she wanted. She was a bitch at that moment, he thought.

Anne shook her head and directed her looks at her husband. She walked towards him and stood in front of him and let him finish getting his clothes in order and then slapped him across the face. He remembered thinking how English she was then. An Irish girl would have taken a knife to him. The term Irish caught in his mind and he replaced it with Ulster and then thought that it did not matter. But that was dangerous thought.

Then she exploded.

'Bastard, bastard, bastard, fucking bastard.'

Anne McLennan kept hitting her husband across the face. Her wedding and engagement rings tore into his face and ripped skin from his cheek and his nose and blood ran from the nose wound. McLennan did not try to stop her. Anne McLennan turned away from him and put her hands over her face.

'Maybe I should leave you two to sort this one out,' Carol said. 'I mean, I'm just the mistress really, and I'm not keen on scenes. There's tea and coffee. Tim knows where it is. Tim knows where everything is. Don't you, love?'

'Don't you call my husband love, you fucking bitch,' Anne said. 'Don't you fucking dare.'

'I'm sorry. Slip of the tongue. Listen, I want nothing to do with this. I find all these hystrionics a bore, frankly.'

'Nothing to do with it, nothing to do with it. You're taking my husband from me and his son. You're here screwing him and you want nothing to do with it. Fucking whore.'

'I'm not taking anyone's husband, love. And what Tim and I do in private is our business. Just like what you and Tim do is your business. I'm willing to respect that. Now I think I'll go. And I'd keep my mouth shut with language like that, deary, when you're in my flat. I always wondered what you were like. I'm not disappointed.'

Anne took her hands away from her face and reached into her pocket for a tissue. She wiped her face and saliva and mucus and make-up came off and streaked the tissue. McLennan came over to her and held out his hand. He just held it there, doing nothing with it, and Anne kept looking at it and sniffing. The blood from McLennan's nose had stopped at his lip and welled up and run round his mouth to the corner and was dripping into his mouth from there. She could see the blood making its way round the contours of his face and the small shaved hairs and a small scar he had above his lip. She brushed his hand away.

Then she launched herself at Carol. It happened when Tim had turned his back on her and was walking towards the door. She caught the policewoman by the hair and knocked her against the wall and smashed her head against it and then fell over still holding her. Carol pushed her off and then tried to fix herself while Anne McLennan was struggling to get herself up. Tim was coming across the floor.

'Stupid bitch,' Carol said. 'Torn my shirt. I'll have her run in for attacking a policewoman. Bitch.'

But Anne McLennan came at her again and hit her with her palm and knocked her over. McLennan caught his wife and pulled her back and she kicked him on the shin with her heels and he cried out and fell back against a chair. Carol got to her feet and backed off, holding the tear in her shirt and trying to get control of herself. Anne McLennan came at her and caught her with a punch and Carol fell back across the couch and hit her head on a lampstand. Anne stood over her. Holding the fist she had hit her with.

'Bitch, bitch, bitch.'

'Jesus, what are you doin'?' Tim said to his wife.

Carol was trying to get herself to her knees. Her eyebrow was bleeding.

'I hope it hurts.' Anne McLennan said. 'Like you've hurt me. I hope it fucking hurts.'

Tim caught her and dragged her away and she did not resist this time.

'I think I've broken my hand,' she said.

Dangerous, Tim McLennan thought, maybe more dangerous than the Falls at one in the morning.

He had left Anne on her own in Carol's flat to go and meet Lenny Beggs. And when he was finished, the taxi driver wouldn't take him to the Falls. So he had to walk. It was a test or something like that. He had a few pints in him so it was probably more of the latter. More than a few pints. A sensory buffer. Between Lenny Beggs and himself and himself and everything else.

Yes, Lenny, no, Lenny, is that right, Lenny?

It was easier to get pissed than decide anything.

He stopped at Miltown Cemetery and stared through the gates. He had a plan. He could not put it all together. It had something to do with the cemetery. And death. The common thread, the shared experience.

There was a foot patrol and a couple of Land Rovers across the road at the bus depot and a helicopter hovering overhead, right above the security wedge that sliced into the fork at Andersonstown and Glen Roads. It was his first time on the Falls. He had been near the Falls, around the Falls, next to it, fought gangs from it, maybe fancied girls on it, but this was the first time he had ever stood there. The soldiers came up to him and he showed his card. Undercover, he said. They smelled his breath and told him he'd picked the perfect spot, why didn't he just go and dig a hole and throw himself in. The NCO in charge told him to get the fuck out, he was putting them all in shit, did he not know what happened to soldiers who strayed into the Falls?

He had visions of himself being taken by an angry mob and beaten and shot, his body a swollen cadaver slightly arched with torn underwear down below the pubic hairline, maybe a trickle of blood coming from his mouth, maybe a Catholic priest giving last rites. That would be ironic, he thought. The soldiers asked if he was armed. He said yes.

'Best move on, Staff.'

The NCO in charge of the patrol spoke with a Birmingham accent. He radioed in for advice. McLennan smiled and shoved his hands in his pockets. The advice was short and sweet.

McLennan had forgotten the sounds of west Belfast at night, the distance wheelspins, the shouts, the monotony of patrol movements. There was a closet feeling. Claustrophobia. It was sweaty even on a cold evening, and there was a feeling of danger.

'It's dangerous, Staff, come with us, Staff, we're heading towards town centre, Staff.'

They sniffed his breath again and indulged in the kind of piss-take only British toms were capable of – unfailing respect, courteous to a fault with their words, but everything was dipped in contempt. He'd seen it once, when he'd been in the UDR. They'd pulled in a couple of drinkers, there'd been a fight, a weapon had gone off, there were accusations and a couple of bleeding heads, nothing serious. Then the senior officer came down. Scots Guards. English. Smoking a cheroot. The Scots Guards stood to attention and explained what had happened. The UDR stood by and watched the pantomime. The prisoners kept telling everyone to fuck off, that their wives, mothers, girlfriends were being fucked by black men with dicks the size of telephone poles. As if a black lover was something that really hurt. The major came down dressed in a silk dressing gown and slippers. He wore his combat trousers and carried a novel by Nadine Gordimer. He looked a bit like Oswald Mosley. He looked at each prisoner in turn, as if there was a screen between them. They told him about his mother's sex life and his sister's predilection for group sex and his wife's cucumber fetish and he just walked around them. Behind him, his men made facial expressions and gave a two-fingered salute and answered sir when he asked a question.

A round soldier, who looked too young to be allowed out after midnight let alone into the Army, offered McLennan a cigarette in the Land Rover on the Falls. He had little-boy cheeks and his kevlar helmet looked as if it would have come right down over his eyes if he hadn't secured it so tight it stopped the blood leaving his head. Maybe that accounted for the cheeks, McLennan thought.

They crept through the Lower Falls at walking pace. Shadows moved in doorways, cars moved faster than they should, taxis moved faster than ordinary cars, buses didn't move at all. The place talked to you if you cared to listen. It had the ulcerous feeling of rupture and no amount of repair was going to do it any good. McLennan did not talk to the soldiers and they did not talk to him. They had resignation on their faces. There was a certain automaton nature to their movements, as if someone else controlled them. He could smell the gun oil and the boot polish and all the other lotions and polishes soldiers rub things with, and there was fear.

He wasn't afraid. The pints gave him any back-up he needed. But he wasn't afraid anyway. He could handle himself. He went through the death recipe book: maybe an RPG, maybe a nail bomb, maybe a bullet, maybe a petrol bomb, maybe all or none of the above. He'd seen them all. An RPG could make a hell of a mess in a Land Rover. Like watching meat being minced. He could smell the smell of a petrol-bombed tom, screaming, beating at the flames with his hands. He could see the back entrance of a high-velocity bullet in a tom's skull, skull contents spread all over the road. He could see more if he allowed himself to.

They passed a wall mural: Oglaigh Na hEireann. Balaclavaed terminators with Armalites and machine-guns, very aspirational. Good for the fundraisers in the States. Good for morale. The occasional village along the border secured for an hour or two. They made the best of what they had. It brought him back to Lenny Beggs's arguments and he could find no real fault in the man's logic. He cursed Beggs and then himself.

He had a hangover during the briefing later that day.

'Our sources say we can expect between twelve and fifteen PIRA terrorists,' the Security Service officer said.

The Security Service officer was local and pretty and she kept looking over at the TCG liaison officer every time she spoke. McLennan figured they were either hot for each other or TCG South and Int and Sy Group were pissed off at the Security Service for elbowing in on their territory and she was trying to calm things. His head was too fuzzy to go too deep. Anyway, he knew it was pointless. Maybe no one knew everything, he thought.

'A big one, I think you'll admit, gentlemen,' the Security Service officer said. 'Basically, everyone that's anyone in Armagh and Tyrone at the minute. E4A have tails on a couple of them and we've been getting a certain amount of cooperation from the people across the border. Although they are unaware of our intentions. Francie Devine has been seen in Monaghan and Donegal. And I think we can take it he's not there for the weather. Mr Devine rates about the highest marks on our wanted lists, as you all know, and – need I say it – he is to be approached with the caution you would reserve for a first encounter with your mother-in-law or a rattlesnake. Whichever you consider the most dangerous. Handle with care, as they say.'

It had to be a Security Service asset they were playing, McLennan thought. He pressed.

'Are our sources absolutely reliable?' he asked.

The Security Service officer looked at him like he'd just asked if the Pope was a Catholic. She squinted and lost some of her calm.

'The best, Staff. This is highly valuable material. Very valuable. I can say no more than that.'

She looked at the TCG liaison officer who betrayed an inner-circle arrogance and indicated she should continue. She continued.

'Dessie Hart tried this very successfully a few years back. In Fermanagh. You all have a briefing on how that one went. Francie Devine's been using similar tactics on police stations these past few months. However, they are about to learn you can be a victim of your own success. There hasn't been a lot of variation in their tactics and that's their weakness. Basically, this'll be based on the police station attacks Francie's been at and Dessie's checkpoint job in Fermanagh. But don't let that make you complacent – that's a big word for lazy, lads. I don't have to remind you, these boys play for keeps: flamethrowers, body armour, assault rifles, grenades, rocket launchers. The works. So, as they say on television, let's be careful out there. Captain Stone.'

Stone stood up, nodded to the TCG liaison officer, in a way that made McLennan want to curse, and went to the front.

'This troop will be the assault group,' Stone said. 'With reinforcements from Hereford. Staff Sergeant McLennan has ground command. Okay, Tim?'

McLennan nodded. 'There'll be a fuller briefin' on positions, layout, liaison with the police, later on. This is a rollin' operation, lads,' he said.

He looked at Stone.

'Maximum firepower, gentlemen,' Stone said. 'Apply the usual codes with the usual latitude. And this comes from the very top. You have all the licence you need to do what's necessary to neutralise this threat. Just try not to inflict civilian casualties. It's very bad for our press relations.'

'Difficult when the shooting starts, sir,' a trooper said.

'Direct your fire. Make your rounds count. That's what you're paid for. Short of evacuating the entire village there isn't much else we can do. This crossroads here gives a killing ground with minimum risk to civilians and other collateral. And if we set our assault groups up right, we should be able to use maximum effort with minimum collateral effect.'

'What about this bomb, sir?' McLennan said.

'What about it?' Stone said.

'It's to be allowed to explode, I take it?'

'Unless you want to run over and blow the fuse out, Staff,' the Security Service woman said.

There was laughter. McLennan smiled. Some of his head cleared.

'I mean it's goin' to cause a lot of damage.'

'I don't see we can prevent that without major risk to our personnel, Staff,' Stone said. 'It's their bomb. They must bear responsibility for what happens when it explodes. We will be evacuating these houses here, immediately around the checkpoint. I'd like to have people in this one across the road and maybe a couple here. But I think it's best we let them carry out their attack and then catch them where we minimise risk to ourselves and maximise it to them. I needn't remind you that many of the local citizens aren't going to be welcoming you with open arms, Tim. Clear?'

'The local paras will remain in their positions until the very last moment,' the Security Service woman said. 'The PIRA dickers must see that it's business as usual.'

'We'll have two of our own men inside the checkpoint when they hit,' Stone said. 'I'll be asking for volunteers there. Don't everybody jump at once. It'll be just to create the illusion of occupation. Just show yourselves and then leg it out the back gate. Make our friends feel good. Otherwise, we'll have dummies in the control box and in the tower. Remember, it'll be dark and they'll be excited.'

'There are risks here, Staff,' the Security Service woman said. 'But may I remind you, risks are what you are paid to take. This is an active-service situation and you are soldiers, volunteers. You may withdraw at any time.'

McLennan did not smile this time. He wanted to tell her to fuck herself and her Queens University accent.

'I think we can have assault positions set up on these hills, Tim,' Stone said. 'Our major problem is once we go in, staying concealed until they come. Any delay on their part would fuck up our schedule. This end of the village is distinctly unfriendly. We'll cut phone lines and pull in anyone who leaves but it's up to you lot to make sure you remain unseen for however long it takes. After that, it's just a matter of operational tactics. That I leave to you gentlemen. And for God's sake, remember to say halt and that kind of thing before you open up. Maximum effort, though, chaps.

This has Downing Street approval.' He looked over at the Security Service woman. 'Anything to add?'

'Not at the minute.'

'Dick?' Stone said.

The TCG liaison officer shook his head.

The Security Service woman sat down and scratched her head and pulled out a packet of cigarettes. McLennan watched her light up. It was a covert action and if he had not watched it directly he might have missed it. The woman seemed to blend in. She had a class of innocuity McLennan thought was reserved for members of the Anglo-Irish Secretariat. He could see a kind of oily film on her skin. It gave her flesh a reddish sheen. And her eyes were vacant. Like she was closed down. They were always the same, her kind, no matter where they came from – icebergs. DI this and MI that and various other combinations of letters and numbers. They competed with each other so you never knew what the hell they were at. And some of the plans they came up with defied belief. There was a ridiculous conceit they all carried with them and they played every side there was. He looked at her head again. It rose to a point and all the hair came from the point and ran straight across the head in tight lines. Her jacket was a different colour to her skirt and her scarf was silk. She might have been a librarian.

McLennan moved his eyes away from the Security Service woman and watched his commanding officer pull down an aerial photograph of the checkpoint.

'This was taken by a Vulcan yesterday,' Stone said. 'You can see the kind of terrain we're dealing with. And there's the border. The checkpoint's about a mile back from it.'

He circled fire and concealment positions with a felt pen and pointed out likely directions and calculated times. He was still speaking when McLennan spoke.

'Why?'

Stone jerked his head back. McLennan had raised his eyebrows.

'Why what, Staff?'

'Why's it there, boss? There's a dozen hills with nice sniper lines, there's roads coming from three directions, and there's nothin' but fuckin' trees everywhere. It's a second-rate road. Why the hell haven't we blown the damn thing up? It's just sittin' there.'

'That would be giving in to terrorism, Tim. There's been a police station there since the last century. You of all people don't expect us to just retreat because PIRA can take a shot at us. This is the British Army, Tim, not a bunch of untrained wogs. We don't give in to terrorism and abandoning that checkpoint would be a defeat. Anyway, they were going to come for it sooner or later.'

McLennan saw that the TCG liaison officer was about to speak. The Security Service woman beat him to it.

'It's HMG and HQNI policy to engage PIRA terrorists in the greatest numbers possible and inflict the most serious casualties possible,' she said.

She stood up and walked over to the photograph and touched it with the back of one of the fingers holding her cigarette.

'Bait, you mean,' McLennan said.

'Staff!' she said.

She shook her head.

When the officers had left, the troop sat around McLennan and he went over what was likely to be the killing ground. It would be a standard ambush. Type A. They all knew the routine. But this was their time, and before he left Stone had a look on his face that said he envied Tim McLennan. McLennan did not want to believe it. The troopers wore sweatshirts and combat pants and runners and scarves and shorts and open boots and two or three of them carried half-stripped weapons. The smell of gun oil was everywhere. And the musk of mouldy canvas. They had hard faces, harder than the kids in the Land Rover on the Falls. They had a knowledge that those kids did not have. One of the NCOs had a knife and he ran his finger up and down the blade while the briefing went on. His finger was fat and the skin was dry and the blade indented the dry skin but it did not cut it.

'There's a good site for a GPMG, Staff . . .'

'Cut-off squads here and here. Nothin' gets by . . .'

'Ben and Harry, you're on this side. Maximum prejudice, lads . . .'

'Who nuts the nutters, eh . . .?'

When he had finished, McLennan walked down a bland corridor to Stone's office. All the corridors had a nondescriptness about them, as if they were trying to hide from themselves, and McLennan had the feeling that the whole place could be stripped and carried away in a couple of hours and no one would ever know it had been there.

In Stone's office, McLennan sat down. Stone stayed standing. He lit another cigarette and offered one to McLennan. McLennan refused it.

Stone paused before he spoke and tried a smile. McLennan did not reply.

'You're okay, Tim?' Stone said.

'Yes, sure. Why shouldn't I be?'

Stone pointed to the scratches on McLennan's face. 'You tell me, Tim.'

McLennan leaned over the desk and looked at the maps and photographs laid out on it. Stone smoked another cigarette and offered one to McLennan again. McLennan refused.

'You look like shit warmed up, Tim. Good night last night?'

'My wife's in town.'

'Oh! Are things settled yet?'

There was more to that question than there seemed.

'Almost, I suppose.'

'Good. Best get these things sorted quickly. By the way, I'm told you were found wandering down the Falls early this morning, Tim. GOC asked me if there was something going down. I was left with a lot of egg on my face. What the hell were you doing there?'

'Walkin', boss. I've never been down the Falls. I was born in Belfast and I've never been down the Falls. I used to live off the Shankill. Then we moved. I met Lenny Beggs in a bar, as per orders, and I was walkin' around the old neighbourhood. Hasn't changed that much. Neither has my wife. A few toms gave me a lift.'

'Jesus Christ, Tim, were you armed? GOC'll go fucking crazy if he gets to hear you were alone. All they think about at HQNI is the corporals' murders. Never again, Tim, clear?'

'Sir.'

Stone turned from him and then swung back.

'So you met Beggs again, Tim. Any progress to report? The wheels are in motion this end.'

'We're goin' to meet again. I'll talk to you after the contact, Bob, okay?'

'Fine. Good. One job at a time. By the way, I have a name for that chap you ran into in Monaghan. The bomber.'

McLennan's eyes opened wide. He had had Cusack on his mind, not in any substantial way, because without a name and a personality he had not seemed real. But now Stone was reading out a bio and Cusack came alive and McLennan had somewhere to direct his feelings.

'It's not much,' Stone said. 'The cousins say he was a fine Marine, this

Cusack. They were a bit shocked, actually. Used expletives.'

'He'll be there, with Hart?'

'I think you can expect to meet him, Tim. And that's unofficial.'

'Bloody bastard. I'll personally put one through his head.'

'I didn't hear that, Staff. I heard you say you'll do your very best to apprehend any terrorists you might encounter on your next assignment. Using, of course, minimum force. Think of me when you're doing it.'

McLennan shook his head and smiled. 'Sir!' he said.

'God, I wish I could come on this one, you know,' Stone said. 'I might just get myself reduced. Just to get out there.'

McLènnan wanted to tell him he was bullshitting, to tear into him, tell him all the buddy-buddy shit was transparent. He didn't need it. Don't fuckin' insult me, Bob, he said to himself. Just don't. You think you have me right where you want me, don't you? Yessir, nosir, threebagsfullsir. Well, it isn't like that, sir, it just isn't, is it?

28

THE RADIO SAID a GAA club in Fermanagh had been burnt down by the UFF and a thousand-pound bomb had been defused in Belfast. A night watchman was belted over the head with a crowbar at the GAA club. A policeman was injured evacuating people from the street where the bomb was. He ran into a reversing RUC Land Rover. Cusack laughed at the RUC officer's accident. He cursed at the burning-down of the GAA club and the night watchman's injuries. He dipped his disposable razor into the water in the bowl in front of him. The bowl was enamel, the water was lukewarm. Shaving foam bobbed in the water in disintegrating balls. The foam on his face cooled his skin and the razor blade massaged his face. The bowl was balanced on a plank of wood between two barrels. The barrels were full of rainwater. There was a bathroom in the farmhouse but they'd given that to the women. It was sexist and Betty Loughlin said it was sexist and Maggie O'Neill backed her, but they took the bathroom anyway.

The day was bright like polished chrome. There were clouds massing in the west but they were far off and the wind was coming from the north. The wind was colder. Cusack stretched his focus to the furthest drumlin and the tall treeline that ran across its back. There was nothing there, nothing except the shapes of the trees and the shapes were people shapes, thin people with frozen feelings, caught somewhere, maybe waiting, giant, fixed in some natural memory, unable to break free. And there was the light.

The light was sharp like the blade of the razor, maybe sharper, and it cut into the landscape and the buildings and opened them. The blades of grass turned shades when they twitched, the hills split with hedgerows looked like a child's puzzle with no conclusion, the dirt road appeared and disappeared and reappeared and Cusack felt that maybe there was a whole other place existing alongside them, just out of their reach and all they could do was imagine it. The stones of the walls were bleached white where the rain had dried off and soaked black where it never stopped. And on the house behind him, the stones looked like the scales of a fish and sometimes he expected the house to move and wriggle and slide to the small river below.

The river was a brown stain in the green, and the green never stopped except when someone had ploughed a field, and then it looked like a skin disorder on the face of the land and you wanted to rub something on it. The light was different now from the light in spring. The spring light was warm and it had life in it and when it touched things it made them smile. This light was hard and it carried death and the land bled something when it touched it.

Cusack rubbed his hand around the edge of the enamel basin. Some of his stubble became attached to his fingers. He wiped the cream and the stubble on the plank of wood. The wood was wet and rotting and he could extract splinters with his fingernails. He had seen a man's fingernails taken out with splinters. It was hard to do. You had to get a good splinter and then you had to get people to hold the hand down and then you had to get the splinter in under the nail and kind of wedge it off. The man would scream and try to get free and even if he was tied and people were holding him he always managed to get some way free. Sometimes the splinter would stick in him and he would just die from poisoning.

He ran his hand around his face and felt the even feeling and the cool spice of the skin. He had a small mirror hanging from a nail in the corrugation in front of him. The rust from the corrugation was gathering in a pool beside one of the barrels and the grass and mud there was red and a bit yellow. Cusack licked his lips and tasted the freshness.

Dessie Hart took the cap off the bottle of Danish beer by catching it against the corner of the shed wall and cracking it with the side of his hand. Froth oozed over the edges of the bottle neck and down the green glass and Dessie dipped his finger in the beer froth and licked his finger. He swigged from the bottle and walked over to John Cusack. Cusack focussed on the bottle. Hart looked at Cusack and then at the bottle and then drank.

'Bit early,' Cusack said.

'It's good for me. Liquid breakfast. I think I need it.'

Cusack picked up the hand towel which lay on the splintered plank and rubbed his face. Hart had a look. Cusack had seen it before and knew what it was. He said nothing. He wanted to say something but he could not say anything that would do any good. There was nothing you could do for a man with that look. It would go away by itself and everything would be fine again or it would stay and get worse and that would be that. Hart downed the rest of the bottle and threw it into a hedge. 'Vandal,' he said.

Cusack did not reply. Hart put his hand on Cusack's shoulder. He looked around him.

'Butterflies, John. I gave the word. Francie's on his way. The boys have their positions. Tonight's a good night to die, as they say in all the best films.'

He tried to smile. Cusack smiled for him. He knew Dessie Hart wanted to smile. That was enough. Hart's body had softened. It was not a physical thing, though there were traces of it in the way he stood and looked and held himself. His eyes were losing life.

'You don't need any courage, do you, John?'

'All the time, Dessie.'

'Good. That's good. You know, right up to now, right up to this point, I've felt confident about this. But—' He shook his head. '—last night – I didn't sleep much, I kept thinkin'. You know; everythin' that can go wrong. All these lads followin' me. All the messin', all the delays. Bad omens. You believe much in omens? Maybe Danny's right. Where is he?' He looked around and then showed Cusack another bottle. 'Anyway, I need some help now. What do you think, John? You think I could become a liability? Maybe I should go company. You know, let fresh blood through.'

'Nerves, Dessie. We all get 'em. They're good. Keep you sharp.'

'I must sound like a real old woman to you, John. You know?'

'It's okay, Dessie, I understand.'

'Ah, it's probably just jitters. And maybe Mal. I can't help seein' him. In the coffin. They shot him on the ground. He was still alive. I want to do this for him. For Mal.'

'That's it, Dessie, concentrate on the job. For Mal. For the others. Then after this one, maybe, if you want, I'll take the load here. Give you some time to yourself.'

'Don't say anythin' about this, John. They need me here. You know the feelin'. There's too much's happened, will happen. But I wish – I wish – all this waitin' around, it doesn't do a man any good.'

'You didn't sleep at all?'

'No.'

'Well, I didn't much either. I'm scared, too, Dessie, if it's any help. I'm always scared some. But that's good. And I want to do this. We can take it. And remember, our day will come.'

Hart found his smile and it showed a false silver tooth he had among his canines. He slapped Cusack's shoulder. His body tried to regain some of its shape. Dessie Hart, the this and that of the border, on the run for years, hiding punctuated by jail terms, life stamped with a public health warning. It was a hard thing to carry, a hard thing to walk into a house and hope that someone hadn't informed, a hard thing to sleep and hope they wouldn't come at night, a hard thing to run a war with a handful of half-trained people surrounded by disinterested normality, organise and lead operations, knowing the other side wanted you dead, not caught and jailed, but dead. And Dessie Hart tried to forget it then.

'Thanks, John. I thought maybe we'd try that landmine we planted a while back over Aughnacloy way. The one Danny keeps goin' on about. Ger thinks there's a chance of manoeuverin' a patrol into it. Be worth a try after this one. They'd be kickin' up shit over this one and we hit them again. Kind of a delayed Warrenpoint.'

'Whatever we can, Dessie. Hit them where and when. I'm in for the duration.'

'Or until they tag us and bag us. Jesus, I'm really soundin' like Danny. I think I'll have to give Danny some time off. I've been talkin' to Francie about him. Francie says not to risk him any more. I'm with him on that. Danny's fine but I don't like what's been happenin' to him lately. I heard he had a go at you.'

'Nothing much. Fancy an arm wrestle? Get the blood going?'

Hart grinned. He rolled up his sleeve.

'On the ground?'

Cusack was down ahead of him. They lay flat on the grass and joined hands and took the strain.

'Jesus, would you look at that?' Hart said. 'You keep in shape, John. And Danny went for you? Can't be all gone, Danny.'

'That's over, Dessie. Ready when you are. Danny's back in line.'

Dessie made a facial gesture that showed he was not convinced. Neither of them spoke. Cusack wanted to say something reassuring but he could not think of anything. Then another voice spoke and there was nothing he could say.

'I don't think so.'

They both loosened their grip and turned their heads to the voice. Betty Loughlin stood leaning against the house. She wore a polo-neck and a tweed skirt and the tweed skirt was creased and the polo-neck hung forward from her neck and showed her skin and her skin had small moles on it. She tapped her feet in a pool of stagnant water. The water spat at the grass around it.

She folded her arms and began to cry. The two men did not do anything. They had not expected her to cry and when she did they did not know what to do about it so they did nothing. They let her cry and she went from a tightened face with tears rolling down it to losing control of her face and then the rest of her body and she bawled her eyes out.

Danny Loughlin came out of the farmhouse and moved behind his wife and placed his hand on her shoulder. He was pale and he hunched his shoulders and Cusack could see a shake in his hand and a shadow in his face around the eyes. He stood behind his wife and tried to straighten himself but he could not manage it. His eyes had a look of torment under the shadow and inside the torment there was more agony.

'We're goin',' he said.

Hart stood up.

'Goin'?' he said. 'What do you mean, goin'? Goin' where, Danny? It's on tonight, Danny. I gave the word. I need you.'

'I can't come. I'm goin' home for a bit, Dessie. I need some time off. So I'm goin'. Betty's comin' with me. Aren't you, love?'

She nodded. She was still fighting the tears. But under the tears and the pain on her face, Cusack could see something hard, resentful maybe, and then it was gone, as if it had realised someone had seen it. She cried and Danny Loughlin raised his free hand and pointed the gun in it at Dessie Hart and John Cusack.

Cusack stood up beside Hart. Hart looked at Cusack. He wiped his mouth. He could see the top of a bottle of spirits in Danny Loughlin's jacket pocket.

'Youse just had to make me do it, didn't youse?' Loughlin said. 'Had to force it. Well, I can't. I just can't, Dessie. Now, youse know and youse can laugh at me. So I'm goin' and I'm takin' my wife.'

'What is this, Danny?' Cusack said. 'Took a look in the mirror and saw the yellow streak running from your ass?'

'John!' Hart barked.

'Shut your fuckin' mouth, John Cusack, or I'll fuckin' blow your brains out. You really wanted this, didn't you. Wanted to come in here, into my patch and put all that Marine horseshite around and do me. He did, Dessie, he did, from the minute he came here. GHQ. Fuck GHQ. I've been at this longer than most of them lads have been alive.'

He waved the gun.

'Put the gun away, Danny,' Hart said. 'Put it away. Come on.'

'Can't do that, Dessie. Can't. I suppose this means I get stood down and court-martialled. Just what you wanted, John, eh?'

'Not true, Danny,' Cusack said.

'It won't happen, Danny,' Hart said. 'You're tired. You need a rest. Okay, take a rest after tonight but for Christ's sake put the gun away. Come on, son. Jesus, if a chopper goes over and spots it, we're all in for it. And it'll fuck up the operation. Put it away and we'll talk. I promise, nothin'll happen.'

'Oh, yeah, sure. I've seen too many broken limbs, Dessie. Quick court, quick decision, quick punishment. I don't want to stand down. Do you hear? I don't want to stand down. I want to go on doin' what I was doin' well. Company stuff. Lookin' after youse lads. Jesus, Dessie, I was good at it. Had everythin'. Why'd you have to order me on a job? You wouldn't let me make beds now. Not after this. Would you? I told you, I can't go out. I just can't.'

Hart moved forward and watched the grass bend under each step. After three steps, Loughlin ordered him to stop and Hart stopped and looked up. Twenty yards behind Loughlin, to his right, tucked in against a hedge, Maggie O'Neill had an AKM aimed. She signalled to Hart for a sign. Hart shook his head. Loughlin saw it and swung around, pulling his wife as a shield.

'You gonna kill Betty, Danny?' Dessie Hart asked.

Cusack was reaching for a Magnum in a folded newspaper beside him. Very slowly, Loughlin swung back to Hart.

'Leave it, John,' he said.

Hart turned to Cusack.

'Leave it, John. Do as he says. Hold your fire, Maggie. No one's goin' to get killed here. We're all on the same side. Jesus Christ.'

'I have a shot,' Maggie said.

'No, Maggie,' Betty Loughlin said.

'I'm sorry, Betty.'

'No, Maggie,' Hart said.

'I have a shot.'

'Please, Maggie,' Betty said. 'Please. For Jesus' sake.'

'Do as Dessie says, Danny,' Maggie said.

'And get my kneecaps taken off? No.'

'I said, it won't happen, Danny,' Hart said.

'Sure.'

'You okay, Betty?' Hart said.

'I'm okay, love, okay. Don't hurt him, please.'

'I still have a shot, Dessie.'

'No, Maggie. No.'

She looked at Cusack and he shook his head. Cusack leaned back against the wall of the shed and felt the cold of it on his back. His hands were sweating.

'This is ridiculous, Danny,' Hart said. 'For Christ's sake, put the gun down and talk. You're not goin' anywhere. The rest of the boys are on their way. We're goin' tonight. I can't let you go. You know that. Now put the gun down and let's talk before this gets out of hand.'

'It's out of hand already,' Cusack said.

'John, shut up,' Hart said. 'This is my command.'

'He's right,' Loughlin said.

He loosened his grip on his wife and she moved forward. She could have moved away but she did not. Maggie was down on one knee. If she hit him it might go right through and kill Betty, too. She was close enough. She thought about it. If Dessie Hart gave the order, could she do it? Risk killing Betty? She tried to shift her angle. Wind tickled her nose and she shoved herself in closer to the hedge that grew out of the stone wall to her right. Some kind of protection, she thought. There was still sleep in her eyes and she had that dry feeling you get when you're woken before your time. She wet her lips and kept the rifle aimed.

'What the fuck's goin' on?'

Tate Byrne came out of the shed in his y-fronts and a t-shirt, scratching his head and picking his nose. The first thing he saw was Loughlin's Magnum.

'On the ground, Tate,' Loughlin said.

'What – what's – what's the matter?'

Byrne looked round, at Cusack, at Hart, at Betty Loughlin, at Danny Loughlin. His pneumatic flesh undulated as if it was being filled with air and his face went red. Then deep red. Then purple.

'Flat on the ground, Tate,' Loughlin said. 'Shut that door and face down. You too, John, you should know the routine. On your fuckin' faces.'

Hart turned to Cusack and Byrne and indicated that they should do it. Cusack obeyed first. Byrne was thinking about something and his thinking betrayed itself and Hart shouted at him to get down.

The scene settled – two minutes, maybe more, quiet. Then Hart spoke.

'What do you think you're gonna do, Danny? Where do you think you're gonna go?'

'I'll go home. For now. Then I'll talk to the C/S. He'll listen. And Francie. Francie's a fair man.'

'And me, am I not fair?'

'You're fair, Dessie, but you're here and now and you listen to him – to the Yank and his shite. I just need to think. I do. I just need to go and to think. Let me do that, Dessie, and—'

'And what?'

'I can't, Dessie, I just can't do it. Harry McCusker'll take care of what needs takin' care of my end. Someone else can do the fifty. Just let us go, me and Betty. Just let us go.'

'And if I don't?'

'Ah, Dessie, please. Don't make me. Please.'

'You'll be dead before me, Danny. And even if I let you go, what do you think'd happen then? Where would you go? This is my unit, my rules apply. The C/S'll keep out. Francie'll chew you up, Danny. You're fuckin' up an operation we've spent months plannin', Danny, puttin' volunteers' lives in danger, puttin' this army in danger. Now put the gun down and I promise we'll talk. And you're out of the operation, okay? I'll get someone else to replace you if I can. But you're jeopardisin' the operation, Danny. And the more you go on with this shite, the more you're diggin' a hole for yourself. Put the gun down. You can stand down. You can stand down and I promise you nothin' will happen to you. The worst you can expect is a minder or two till we get things shifted about. That's fair, isn't it?'

'Ah, you're just talkin' now, Dessie. I don't want to stand down, Dessie. I want to keep doin' what I do best. This is my life, Dessie, the Army, the work. It's just – it's just, sometimes a man gets – you know – it happens, and he's not up to the rough stuff any more, he's better at other stuff.'

'Fucking chicken, you mean.'

'Shut up, John!'

Loughlin fired. The bullet hit the gutter of the shed. The echo of the shot danced on the wind and rebounded around the drumlins. Bruddy Holmes came out of the shed with a rifle, trying to get the magazine in. He had the safety catch still on when he was raising the rifle. Hart came back at him and knocked the rifle down and pulled it from Holmes's hands. Holmes stood with his hands down at his crotch and a confused milkiness in his eyes. He blinked and scratched and lay down with Byrne and Cusack when he was told.

'What's goin' on, lads?' he asked.

'Shut up, Bruddy,' Loughlin said.

'Touch of yellow, Bruddy,' Cusack said.

'John, shut up,' Hart said.

'Fuckin' fucker, Cusack,' Loughlin said. 'All full of it, aren't you? Were you like that with his brother, were you?'

'Danny!' Hart said.

'Oh, yeah, he can say what he likes but no one's allowed to say anythin' about him. That's the lad that nutted Billy, know that, Bruddy?'

Bruddy Holmes lifted his head from the grass and looked at John Cusack.

'It was orders, Bruddy,' Cusack said.

'Someone had to do it, Bruddy. It was a fair execution. Billy said so himself. You saw the letter. John pulled the trigger but this army executed him. So if you've anythin' to say, say it to me. I'm in command here. That right, Danny?'

Loughlin was already regretting what he had said. It showed on his face.

'Yes, Dessie,' Holmes said. 'I'm – I understand, John. I do.'

'It's okay, Bruddy.'

'He wasn't such a bad lad – Billy. I mean, he could have – I don't know. I don't't—'

Everyone told Bruddy Holmes to shut up and do what he was told. He did. He nodded at Cusack and put his face into the grass.

Cusack watched Loughlin from where he lay, face down in the grass, blades of grass touching his nose. Signs of fear gave themselves away on Loughlin's face like contours on a landscape. It was an uneven landscape, fear, fighting itself, hiding so many things it could barely keep itself together. And Cusack felt sorry for Loughlin. It was a distant sorrow and it did not come hand in hand with mercy because it had no empathy, it was a sorrow of disappointment and maybe some disgust.

Hart was still talking to him – polite, diplomatic talk. Upper-hand talk. Loughlin wasn't going anywhere. Even he knew that now. And in a way he did not want to go. He was waiting for Dessie Hart to walk over and put his arms around him and sit him down and ask him to talk about it. A quiet chat in a quiet room, maybe, cups of tea or a snort of whiskey, talk about the old days and the struggle and the continuity and keeping faith, just taking the strain. He needed someone to take the strain, someone to set him free for a while, until he was ready to come back.

Hart took two steps closer and Loughlin threatened him and Hart took another step and Loughlin's threats rang as hollow as the shot he had fired at the shed gutter. He lifted his hand from his wife's shoulder and held the palm up to Hart. Hart stopped and raised his own hands. He was feeling some of what Cusack was feeling. They were all feeling it. It reflected on them all, and they could feel sadness and anger in the same moment, hate and affection. But feeling had to be put aside and cold decisions made, decisions that calculated.

Maggie O'Neill was calculating. Points of entry and angles of exit and velocities.

'You could have let me go, Dessie,' Loughlin said. 'You could have said it was okay, I didn't have to come. I don't like it, I don't. I think it's too risky. I told you that. You should have listened to me. I've been around long enough to be listened to. I've seen things. I deserved that, I deserved to be listened to.'

'Give me the gun, Danny. Give it to me and we'll talk, okay? You should have come to me, you know, Danny, should have come to me, told me what was wrong. I'm here for that. I need you, you know. Not just for this job. You're valuable, Danny. So put the gun down and talk to me, son. Or do you want to do what the Brits have never done? If you do, put it in my heart, Danny. Right in. Take slow aim and hit me here. You're tired, Danny. Tired and probably pissed off. I know. I get that way, too. It takes its toll, doesn't it?'

Loughlin managed a smile of sorts. He almost had to. The strain was tearing him apart.

'I don't want to, Dessie. I just – I don't know. I just couldn't hold myself. I'm sorry. What d'you think'll happen? Nut job?'

'No, Danny. But I think it's time for you to retire. I'll forget this if you will, Danny, and the lads here, too. So give me the gun and it'll go no further. I promise. You have my word.'

When he made the promise, Hart did not know or care whether he could keep it. It was a necessary promise and if it worked then it would have been worth it and it would have ended there. Hart was more concerned with the operation. Francie Devine and his men were on their way. The Hino had been fitted out, the bomb was ready, back-up units were getting into position, everything was ready. If they had to cancel again – Dessie Hart did not want to think about that.

'I'll be fine in a few days, Dessie. I'll be back. You'll see.'

'I know, Danny. Then we'll talk about it. We will. I promise. Now, come on, give me the gun.'

He came up to Betty Loughlin and stood before her. Her face was impassive like she was somewhere else, waiting to be called.

'Don't, Danny,' she said. 'You're dead if you do.'

'Betty!' Hart said.

'Jesus, Betty,' Maggie said.

Hart had the gun by its barrel. He pushed it down.

'No!' Betty Loughlin screamed.

'Betty!' Hart roared.

She pushed him back and shoved her husband with her elbow and Danny Loughlin jerked the gun up. The bullet went through her spine.

Dessie Hart held Betty Loughlin in his arms. Blood dribbled from her mouth. Her legs gave way and she looked at Hart and then one eye closed and her head dipped into his chest and she said his name and Danny's name and coughed and tears came from her open eye and ran down Hart's t-shirt and mixed with the blood from the exit wound in her chest.

'Jesus Christ!' Hart said. 'Betty!'

'Oh, no, oh Christ, no,' Loughlin said.

He dropped the gun on the grass and backed away and sank down against the wall of the farmhouse.

Maggie O'Neill and John Cusack rushed to Betty Loughlin. They held her with Hart. The three of them laid her on the grass. Cusack tried to stop her bleeding with his t-shirt. It had no effect. He put his ear to her chest but there was nothing there.

'Betty, Betty,' Hart said.

He pushed his hand against her bloody chest like he was trying to get her heart going. But there was no heart left to get going. Maggie felt for a pulse at Betty's neck. There was none. She took her hand away and sat down on the grass and dipped her head.

'She's gone, Dessie,' she said. 'She's gone.'

She leaned her head on Cusack's shoulder. Tate Byrne and Bruddy Holmes backed off to the door of the shed. Tate had a weapon cocked and raised as if he was waiting for something more to happen and Bruddy Holmes had a stunned expression on his face. He had never seen anyone die before.

By the wall of the house, Danny Loughlin was talking to his wife.

29

THEY PUT BETTY Loughlin in two polythene bags and laid her out on a bed in the farmhouse. The polythene bags did not stop blood running into the mattress and the mattress was stained deep red in the middle under the body and the stain spread out and seeped through the mattress and blood dripped on the carpet underneath the bed. The body and the bags and the blood and the mattress had their own smell and the smell was heavy and dead. And Danny Loughlin sat beside the body.

Dessie Hart and John Cusack stood behind him with Tony McCabe. One of McCabe's men sat outside the door with a gun in his lap, reading a Sunday magazine.

'I couldn't go, Dessie,' Loughlin said. 'I just couldn't. I loved her, John, ah, Jesus, I loved her. What'll I do, Dessie?'

'It was an accident, Danny,' Hart said.

He went to touch Loughlin's head with his hand but held off. Loughlin scratched his grey stubble and put his head in his hands.

'You sure you want to stay here, Danny?' Cusack asked.

Loughlin turned slowly. He nodded.

'Yeah, John. Yeah. Sure where else would I go?'

'I'm sorry, Danny,' Cusack said. 'I really am. She was a fine woman. I . . .'

He was going to make a kind of speech he had been putting together in his mind but there did not seem any point.

'She was a fine woman, Danny,' he said again.

McCabe gestured to Cusack with his head and Hart went to the door.

In the kitchen, Harry McCusker and Maggie O'Neill drank coffee from broken cups and chewed on stale biscuits.

'What's to be done there?' McCabe asked Hart.

'I'll leave him here with you for now, Tony. Harry, you're runnin' Danny's end of things here, okay?'

McCusker nodded and drank his coffee.

'Who's up above?' Hart asked.

'Eddie,' Cusack said. 'Says he's freezing his balls off.'

He laughed.

'Get someone to bring him soup or somethin', Harry. And anythin' happenin' with those shots, I want to know. You think they heard on the other side?'

Cusack shrugged.

'So what? They can guess. Things are still with us.'

'Yeah, yeah, I know. But I wanna know anyway.'

'And keep Danny here, Tony,' Cusack said. 'Till we get back. Okay?'

Hart went over to the sink and poured himself a glass of water and drank it. Then he rubbed his head and turned to Cusack.

'Can I have a word, John?' Hart said. 'Private, like?'

'Sure, Dessie.'

'I've business to take care of, Dessie,' McCabe said. 'I'll be back when I'm finished. Okay? And I'm sorry about all this. I really am. There's no one didn't like her. I don't know what the fuck we're gonna do.'

'Why don't you just dump her in a boghole, Tony,' Maggie said. 'Go on, just dump her. She's an inconvenience now, isn't she?'

'Hey, Maggie, come on!' Cusack said.

'Well, youse are actin' like she's a fuckin' dog. That's Betty in there. Christ. She deserves better, Dessie. She deserves better than bein' an inconvenience.'

'Yeah, I know. We'll keep Betty here, too, Harry. Okay?'

'Sure, Dessie.'

He looked at McCusker and then at McCabe. 'I mean it.'

'Yes. Okay, yes,' McCabe said. 'Council are gonna want a word on this, Dessie, anyway. This is serious stuff. And your man in there.'

'But not without me. Okay?'

'Okay.'

'John,' Hart said.

Cusack and Hart went outside. Hart stood where Betty Loughlin had been shot. Her blood was still on the ground. Drops of blood had coagulated on the grass. Hart looked at them and then at the landscape. It was a lonely landscape, he thought, and in early-coming winter it had a chill to it, but it was his and he shook his head like he was agreeing with himself and then looked at John Cusack.

'I'm gonna call it off, John,' he said. 'I don't know – I just – I don't know, John. Christ, did you see her face? They were like family to me, those two. Visited me in Portlaoise, sent me stuff. I've known Danny since I was a kid. Him and my old man did time in the Curragh. I mean, Danny Loughlin, John, Danny, he's a fuckin' legend. I don't know. Jesus Christ.'

'What does Francie say?'

Hart shook his head. He shoved his hands into his pockets and pulled out a packet of sweets. He pulled the wrapper off one and placed the sweet on his tongue and offered one to Cusack. Cusack took it and repeated Hart's movements exactly. They both folded their wrappers till they could not fold them any more. Hart used his to clean his fingernails. Cusack put his in his pocket.

'I haven't said anythin'. Can't. They're still on their way. It's down to me anyway, John. I'm in charge here. Francie may outrank me in Command but I have the say here. And you. That's why I'm askin' you. Jesus, I'm hurt, John, I'm bloody hurt. I can't tell you how much. Mal. Now this. How's everybody else takin' it?'

'They'll get over it. Bruddy's like this.' He moved his hand from side to side. 'Needs handling. Look, there's a greater issue here, Dessie. There's no one liked her more than me but there's a greater issue here. Even Betty would have seen that. She saw things, Betty. She saw Danny was cracking. He'd have fucked up if he'd come. At least she saved us from that. Hell, I like the old bastard, but it's gotta be said. No one's that special, Dessie, no one. Not even Betty. You gotta be hard here, Dessie, no matter what. We've put a lot of time and effort into this. You gotta put aside personal feelings and think of the war. The war's what counts. You know that. Mal knew that. Think about it. What would Mal say? Give it all up because we've had a tragedy. It's a tragedy, Dessie. Christ, my heart's tearing apart too right now, but we have to go on. And I'm for going on. Don't cancel.'

'He would have been fine. I had my fingers on the gun. Why did she do it?'

'She loved him. It's a damn fine thing, love.'

'I love him too, John. And her. Both of them. They're like family.'

'There's nothing you can do about it now, Dessie. Nothing. What counts is this operation, Dessie. We've had cancellations, delays, a whole bunch of shit with this one. If we don't do this thing now, then call it off for good and send everyone home and send out a dump-arms notice around here. Because, I'm telling you, if you do that, it'll be damn difficult to get people back here again. Especially after this. You understand? We need it, Dessie. You don't have a choice now. What's done is done and that's the way it is. The war, Dessie, the war.'

'Ah, John. First Mal, now this. Jesus, I'm worn out, John. I didn't realise it till last night. I just couldn't sleep. I knew how Danny felt and I didn't help him. He was my friend and I pushed him when I knew he couldn't do it. I could have dropped him. Left him in company. I think I was pushin' him to push myself. Because if I let him drop out then I'd drop out myself. It was like Danny was my own defence. You know, when they were lettin' me out of Portlaoise last time, I nearly didn't want to go. I don't even know if I didn't get myself caught on purpose. You see, I don't know. It's not that I'm not committed. I'm as committed as I ever was, more maybe. But I'm tired, John. And bein' tired sometimes just gets to you. I sometimes wish I'd had a family. Know that? Maybe a kid. Maybe a county football champion. I used to be a footballer, you know. I can't even turn up to a game now without risk. Ah, Jesus, Danny shot Betty. She's dead.'

Cusack put his hands on Hart's chest.

'Dessie, come on, man, come on. Don't let them see you like this. Come on. You're down, you're down and you're out of steam. I know, it happens. But for God's sake don't fuck up the unit and the operation. Come on, Dessie, dig deep, dig real deep, man. Pull it out. Remember what we're here for. Remember. Keep the faith.'

He slapped Hart's face. It was a soft slap. Hart faked a smile and dipped his head again.

'Smile or I'll sing "Kevin Barry",' Cusack said.

'No, please, anythin' but that, John. Please, I'll do anythin' you want, but not "Kevin Barry".'

'Good lad.'

'So you want to go ahead?'

'We have to. Because it's there. Because we said we would. Because we planned it. Because we're ready. You can't just stop the war because we take a casualty, Dessie. You know that. Betty'd even tell you that. It's down to will, Dessie. Think about it, about will, Dessie. That's where this war will be won and lost.'

He pointed to his head.

'Battle of wills. That's the war, Dessie. Keep going. It has to be done, Dessie, and it has to be done now. Understand? Or do you just want to give up? And maybe next time you'll come up with a reason to cancel again and again. And next thing you're talking ceasefires and stuff. You want all the fighting to be written off as just some kind of extended vandalism rampage? Remember what we used to say during the hunger strikes: that Britain might brand Ireland's fight eight hundred years of crime. Well, fuck it, Dessie, if we call a halt on this one, if we don't go out and hit them, that's what it'll mean. They'll have won. Because that's all there is between us. Our will to fight.'

Hart rubbed his face and smiled. He threw his head up to the sky and watched a bird and thought of a girl he had once known and a day out when a bird had flown overhead. That path was gone now. His options had narrowed. That was what life was, he thought: narrowing options. Until there were no more options. He felt an emptiness in his stomach when he thought about that. But Cusack had ignited something deep inside him and it was glowing and there was a warmth rising.

'You should be workin' for An Phoblacht, Cusack, you know that? I bet you've got your speech from the dock ready for when they get you. Real way with words, John. I think I'd follow you anywhere after that.'

'They're not going to get me. I'm going to get them. Hit and hit and hit again, Dessie. We're in now, there's no going back. You know that. Not if you believe.'

'You're a fuckin' evangelist, John Cusack. A fuckin' evangelist.'

'Sure what else would we do? Can you imagine yourself sitting at a desk, shifting papers? Come on, Dessie. You're hooked. You believe and you're hooked, and you know we're right. Not a lot of people can have that in their lives. That's something special, son. What was it Cromwell said: let me have men who know what they fight for and love what they know. That bastard knew what he was about. We could take a leaf from the son of a bitch's book. He knew how to win wars.'

Cusack slapped Hart's arms and Hart began to shake his head and laugh and then Cusack laughed and they arm-wrestled and tried to bring each other down and support each other at the same time. The support won and when they were warm and sweating they stood back.

'Okay, okay,' Hart said. He paused. 'If Harry's boys clear everythin', we'll do it then,' he said.

It was a moment of unadulterated corn and both men knew it was and somewhere inside they laughed at themselves for it but it was all they had then and when Dessie Hart pulled open the shed door he had recovered whatever he had lost when Danny Loughlin had killed his wife.

'Hey, John, what'd you do with that rabbit?' Hart asked Cusack when they had split up and Cusack was going into the house and Hart was at the shed door. 'The one you were lookin' after.'

'Why?' Cusack said.

'Nothin'. I just saw Danny fixin' its wounds yesterday. I thought maybe we could give it to him. Keep him occupied.'

'We ate it last night, Dessie.'

'Oh!'

Hart turned away.

In the shed, Tate Byrne was cleaning a rifle. He had the parts laid out on a groundsheet in a symmetrical order. Bruddy Holmes sat beside the groundsheet against a pile of wood and a crate of beer. He sat on the floor and the floor was concrete and mud and hay. Holmes was holding a rifle and doing nothing. He had strips of hay in his hair. Behind him, Ger Kelly and Deano Brady, who had arrived with the bomb and a Toyota pick-up for the 50-calibre machine-gun, were loading magazines and checking weapons.

Hart stood at the door.

'I just want to say a couple of things,' he said.

And he did.

When John Cusack brought Maggie O'Neill in twenty minutes later, Hart was at the other end of the shed with a map and sketches and photographs of the checkpoint, talking. 'What kept you?' he said.

He smiled and Cusack smiled and Maggie managed a movement that might have been a smile except she didn't like the grins on the men in the shed.

They had made love in one of the bedrooms against a wall and then on the floor, nothing said, just the sheer desperation to make love after seeing a death and knowing what was going to happen. And when they had finished they got dressed without saying anything or even looking at each other.

'We were just goin' over a few details,' Hart said. 'You okay, love?'

'Yeah,' Maggie said. 'It's still on, then?'

Cusack touched her and then became self-conscious fearing that some of the others would see. Then they moved down to where Hart had the map stretched out. He had bricks at the corners and pieces of hay drifted across the topography and Hart pointed his finger to the checkpoint.

'Sure,' Hart said. 'Just waitin' for the rest of the boys to come. John, I'm goin' to need someone to replace Danny on the fifty. And you're the best qualified.'

Cusack looked at Hart with his mouth open. 'Ah, Dessie!' he said.

'You're the best qualified. Tate and Ger know how to use it but you've had the most experience, John. And you said yourself, the operation's the most important thing here.'

'Yeah, but you need me up front. In the assault group. I'm needed there. My experience, my firepower.'

'Yeah, we do. But it's a matter of resources now, John. I need you on the fifty more than I need you in the Hino. Anyway, one assault rifle more or less isn't goin' to be as critical as a heavy machine-gun. You know that. I need someone to pour fire into that tower, John. And keep pourin' fire into the area when we're makin' our withdrawal. Someone who knows a fifty back to front, someone who can correct a fault. You're it, John. You're critical, son. Critical. And Bruddy here'll be your driver. That right, Bruddy?'

Holmes nodded and raised his fist to Cusack. 'Yeah, sure. Glad to, John. You know?' he said.

Cusack stood with his hands on his hips, looking at the map on the ground.

'Jesus, yeah, Dessie, but I know this job, I've been over and back and across it. No one knows it better than me.'

'Then no one knows better than you, John, that we need the fifty workin' and we need concentrated, directed back-up. Now, I have Maggie as final line back-up and you're heavy support fire. We'll have nine volunteers in the assault group and two drivers. Deano can add to our firepower once the bomb's been placed. Help cover the withdrawal. It'll work. I wanted more but that's not gonna happen, is it? We just don't have the people to spare at this point. Unless you want me to ask Danny. I'm only thinkin' of the operation, John. If it's to go ahead, it has to go ahead with fifty-cal back-up. You must see that. Bruddy does.'

'We'll do all right, John,' Holmes said. 'You'll see.'

Cusack sighed.

Holmes looked at everyone in turn.

'I'll make up for what Billy done. I will, lads. Me and John. All right, John? And John, I don't – don't think I – well, what Danny said back there – I know you were doin' your duty. I know that.'

He reached up and Cusack took his hand and they shook and nodded to each other and Cusack opened his mouth and felt himself choke and then go dry.

Maggie touched Cusack's wrist. 'Dessie's right, Yank,' she said.

Cusack looked at her. He wanted to argue with her but he could not. He looked at the others and then at Dessie Hart again.

'But I'm the most experienced man here, Dessie. That's why I'm here, to give you my experience.'

'And I want to use you where I think you'll be best, John. So do as you're told, okay. This is not some kind of trip, John. You follow orders like everyone else. It's not like I'm droppin' you. Just movin' you to our best advantage. I need you on the fifty. I need consistent firepower from there. I put someone else on that and they get a jam or somethin' goes wrong, then we're left out in the open with no cover. No, John, I've made my mind up, you're on the fifty and Bruddy backs you up.'

Cusack's brain was trying to work out what he was feeling. Everything Hart said made sense. It was sound military sense. But he was being dropped. And it was a kick in the teeth.

He searched Hart's face for an explanation. But Hart had moved on, pointing out pieces of the target where special attention had to be paid, assessing the effect of the firepower they had decided to bring with them.

Just after dark, Francie Devine and Martin Burke arrived with Sean and Dermot Beattie. Sean Beattie drove a Hino truck. The Hino was sandbagged in the back. Beattie had two late inclusions with him in the Hino, men Dessie Hart had managed to round up almost at the last moment: a new volunteer named Anto Doyle, who was related to Hart by marriage, and an older one, Hughie Donnelly, who'd done time in the Maze with Devine and

Hart a decade or more earlier but had been out of things for years.

It was a Thursday evening and the wind had died.

30

TWO HOURS BEFORE dawn, Dessie Hart snapped a magazine into his Heckler and Koch G3, cocked the weapon and put the safety catch on and stood up. Then he took six more magazines and put them in the pockets of his combat jacket. He slung the rifle over his shoulder and took a balaclava out of his top pocket and pulled it down over his face. He made a motion with his finger. Tate Byrne made a zero with his thumb and forefinger in response and fitted his Magnum into its shoulder holster and checked the GPMG at his feet. He straightened the armour-plated vest he was wearing under his German Army anorak. The vest was pulling on his chest, making it difficult to breathe. He shifted his body until the weight of the vest was evenly spread. Then he knelt down and laced up his Nike boots. He had a knife strapped to his left thigh. His pants were khaki jeans. It was time.

John Cusack picked up an Armalite and spare magazines and put the magazines in his pockets and slung the Armalite over his shoulder. Beside him, Bruddy Holmes carried a spare ammunition box for the 50-calibre machine-gun and an AKM slung over his shoulder. Both their personal weapons had nightsights. Cusack nodded to Dessie Hart and Dessie Hart nodded back. Tate Byrne and Ger Kelly hugged one another and the two Beattie brothers shook hands. And Francie Devine finished off a cigarette. He smoked it right down to the filter and then stamped on it with his running shoe and slapped Martin Burke on the shoulder. Burke pulled a flamethrower pack on to his back and Deano Brady stopped buttoning his blue boiler suit and helped him with it.

Brady had a Belgian FNC slung over his shoulder and he wore Reeboks with his boiler suit. He picked up two grenades and hung them from the back of his belt and stuffed four spare magazines into his pockets, two either side. Hart reached over and picked up the keys to the Hiace outside and threw them to Brady and put his thumb up to his cousin. Brady nodded at Hart and took a deep breath and then went back to Martin Burke. He slapped him on the back when the flamethrower was ready and Burke raised his fist. His fist had a latex glove on it.

Behind Burke's fist, almost hidden in the shadows of the shed, Eddie Barnes checked the AKMs of the two volunteers who'd been brought in that evening for extra firepower. Anto Doyle had never fired a weapon in anger before. Barnes saw his hands shake when his rifle was handed back to him. Doyle had been hanging around the fringes of the IRA for three or four years and had only just been sworn in. He was a pale shade of ash, standing there in a boiler suit and runners. Barnes bent down and gave him a grenade but Doyle refused it because he did not know how to use it. Barnes looked over at Cusack and Maggie O'Neill who were watching him and each other. They both shook their heads and Barnes sniffed and went to the second man.

Hughie Donnelly was overweight and his breath stank of cigarette smoke. The front of his combat jacket was stained with beer and a tomato someone had thrown at him earlier on. He had a double chin and stubble that came at you in lines and on his right cheek he had a spot that had come to a head. Donnelly had been active with Hart before and had then gone away to Australia to work and got on the wrong side of the law – a bank job someone said – and was now back. He hadn't been jumping to get back into the IRA but Hart had come asking and since he was sitting around on the dole in Clones and Dessie Hart wasn't someone you refused if he was intent on getting you, Donnelly had signed up again. There was talk of a lump of cash and an American visa if he came good and it sounded fine for Donnelly who'd married a woman he did not want to live with any more. He never asked where the visa would come from.

Donnelly gave Doyle a few hints on cover and reloading and then picked up a kevlar jacket and put it on. Doyle asked Barnes if he could have one. Barnes shook his head.

'Not enough, kid,' he said. 'But if I die, you can have mine.' He smiled and Doyle laughed.

John Cusack stood beside Maggie O'Neill, saying nothing. She nodded her head and he touched her hand and then they saw that the rest of the shed was watching and Cusack felt embarrassed and backed off a couple of steps.

'Go on, John, kiss her,' Hart said.

Everyone laughed.

'Kiss him, Maggie. Hurry now. It's time for you to go, love.'

Barnes and Tate Byrne began humming 'Some Enchanted Evening' and the others joined in and Cusack gave them two fingers. Maggie stepped forward and kissed him.

'See you, Yank,' she said.

Cusack could not think of anything to say and he was sorry when she had gone that he had not said anything. He pulled out a grenade and checked it and then hung it from his belt and when he saw that Bruddy Holmes had stuffed a grenade in his front pocket he walked up to him and pulled the grenade out.

'A round hits you here, Bruddy, and you and anyone beside you go straight to forever land. Wear them behind if you have to. Or carry them separate. Take one, anyway, you won't need more.'

'Right,' Devine said.

He looked at Hart and Hart looked at Cusack. Cusack nodded. 'Right,' he said.

'Okay, let's go,' Hart said.

Dermot Beattie pulled his balaclava down over his face and then pulled it off and scratched his beard. Cusack could see sweat beads on the hairs. Hart looked at Beattie and touched his chin and shook his head. Beattie pulled the balaclava down. Cusack checked the floor of the shed. A sweeper team would be through the place after them but he wanted to make sure there was nothing there that could incriminate. He wandered around the place, looking at rolled-up sleeping bags and dog-eared novels and magazines lying in a cardboard box. A polythene bag was crammed with beer bottles and cans and breadcrumbs were mixed in with the loose hay and the dust and mud.

Outside, the Hino was a solid outline in the darkness and Sean Beattie climbed into the driver's seat and pulled his G3 in beside him and threw a donkey jacket over it. The back of the truck was covered with a tarpaulin. One by one, the volunteers got in and took their positions. There was no talking now. A soft drizzle had begun to fall with the sound of a gathering wind and the drizzle was the back beat to the sound of men taking position.

Cusack and Holmes shook hands with everyone and went to the Toyota pick-up behind the Hino. The pick-up had a tarpaulin draped over the 50-calibre machine-gun and Cusack pulled it back and checked the gun.

'You ready, Bruddy?' he asked.

'I'm with you, John. Victory.'

He held up his gloved fingers in a V sign that Cusack could just about make out. It had a pathetic quality that Cusack had seen in the Philippines or somewhere like that when he'd trained a group of militia and they were going out on their first anti-guerrilla raid. But he did not think about it. He did not think about anything now except what he was going to do and there was a release inside him and a feeling of elation that made it all worthwhile even if he had been relegated to support fire only.

'John,' Hart called through the dark. 'Keep the faith.'

Hart raised his fist and climbed on board the Hino. Deano Brady had already started up the Hiace with the bomb on board. He waited for the Hino to start up.

The Hino moved off first. The volunteers in the back lay flat under the tarpaulin, holding their weapons. Dessie Hart had a walkie-talkie. No one spoke.

Sean Beattie pulled the truck out of the farmyard and down the dirt track to the small blocked road leading across the border. Then he drove back down that for a mile and turned left towards the concession road. About half a mile behind him, Deano Brady followed with the bomb. He was in radio contact with Hart and Sean Beattie and they kept their speeds constant.

When the Hino got to the stone bridge, it slowed and almost came to a stop. The angle of the turn on to the checkpoint road was tight so it had to slow anyway. In the back of the Hino, Dessie Hart got the final okay from two dickers on a hill. They'd sent a team through five minutes earlier and it was all clear. Hart smiled to himself and told everyone in the Hino.

The Hiace had caught up to within fifty yards of the Hino at this point. Sean Beattie brought the truck over the stone bridge and accelerated and the Hiace slowed and fell back as the Hino increased its speed.

Bruddy Holmes and John Cusack had taken a separate road and were coming directly at the checkpoint from the main road leading to Monaghan Town. Without headlights. Cusack was in the back of the Toyota under the tarpaulin with the 50-calibre. There was an opening in the tarpaulin and he had nightvision goggles and could see through the driver's cab. They did not reach the stone bridge until the Hino was approaching thc checkpoint.

In the Hino cab, Sean Beattie saw the checkpoint corrugation at the very edge of his headlights and slowed for a moment before pushing on the accelerator. Once they were inside the sheets of protective corrugation beyond the trees, they would be committed. He could see a small light on in the Victorian house under the checkpoint fort. He reached into a bag under the donkey jacket on the passenger seat of the truck and pulled out a pair of nightvision goggles and placed them in his lap. They were not necessary. The light around the checkpoint was good and there were lights in the village, too. He touched the nightvision goggles and then the G3 under the donkey jacket and came to the first barrier. The barrier was down. He pressed on the brake and the truck slowed.

The Hino stopped.

The Hiace, coming along about fifty yards behind now, also slowed.

Beattie rolled down his window. A voice from a megaphone asked him to wait till they checked his licence plate. Beattie obeyed. The Hiace pulled in behind him.

Back down the road towards Monaghan, at the money-changer's, Bruddy Holmes and John Cusack had slipped into their covered firing position and Cusack was pulling the tarpaulin off his 50-calibre machine-gun. He cocked the gun and looked at his watch. He could see the tail of the Hiace. He could not see the Hino any more. Bruddy Holmes climbed into the back of the pick-up and cocked his rifle and took the safety catch off. He pulled down his balaclava and took aim. Cusack turned the 50-calibre on the checkpoint observation tower.

The first barrier rose and Sean Beattie stepped on the accelerator and the Hino passed an unoccupied pill-box and approached the control box sticking out of the wall of the checkpoint fort. Beattie could see a figure inside but he could not make out who it was. He could feel his veins bursting out through his skin. The night had clouded over and he could see the empty village street now and two lights in one house and a single light in three more houses. The red-brick house to his right was dark. He was slowing down. He passed the control box, and still could not make out what was behind the bullet-proof glass. He reached the gates of the checkpoint fort and saw that the pill-box on his right, before the second crash barrier, was empty. He looked into his rear-view and saw the Hiace moving through the first barrier. Beattie slammed on the brakes and blew his horn.

The first up was Dessie Hart. He threw off the tarpaulin covering him and opened fire at the checkpoint control box with an RPG. The rocket exploded at the top of the control box and blew a hole in the wall of the checkpoint fort. He was followed by Francie Devine and Martin Burke. Devine fired at the pill-box ahead of them with an RPG. The rocket went right into the pill-box and exploded, blowing it apart. Burke, backed by Hughie Donnelly with an AKM and Tate Byrne with a GPMG, turned his flamethrower on what was left of the control box in the wall of the checkpoint fort. All three of them roared as they fired as if they were releasing an infinity of tension and emotion. And they could see Cusack's 50-calibre armour-piercing and explosive rounds strike the observation tower above their heads. In the middle of the Hino, backed by Doyle and Barnes, Ger Kelly also directed his GPMG at the tower.

Dermot Beattie was already out of the Hino and at the gate of the checkpoint fort. He threw a grenade over the gate and then signalled to his brother in the Hino.

Sean Beattie was now in position with the Hino to reverse into the gates of the checkpoint fort. He screamed at Hart through his walkie-talkie and Hart ordered a ceasefire and everyone got down in the back of the truck. Then Beattie revved up the Hino engine till it sounded like it was going to explode, slammed the gears into reverse and let off the brake. The Hino jolted, knocking over two of the volunteers who weren't fully down behind the protection of the sandbags. Martin Burke nearly ignited his flamethrower in the back of the truck and Anto Doyle fell over and had to drop his rifle to stop himself falling out.

'Down!' Francie Devine shouted.

The Hino smashed into the gates of the checkpoint fort, braked for a second, jolted and then went through.

Inside, Francie Devine and Dessie Hart stood up again. Devine saw two figures in berets at the corner of the station house. One of them fired a round and then retreated behind the house and Devine threw a grenade at the other who disappeared before it exploded. Hart cursed in a kind of cheer and fired a rocket into the main door of the station house and Francie Devine fired an RPG into the accommodation block. Then Martin Burke turned his flamethrower on both buildings.

Burke, Devine, Hughie Donnelly and Dessie Hart jumped down off the Hino and began spraying bullets and throwing grenades. Devine called for anyone inside the buildings to come out and no one did so they threw grenades at the buildings and Devine and Hart put two more rockets into them and Burke set fire to the station house with the flamethrower.

Ger Kelly fired at the observation tower again with his GPMG. Tate Byrne was now firing at anything he considered a target. Pieces of slate and stonework flew off in all directions. Doyle and Eddie Barnes jumped from the truck and took up positions on the road outside and Dermot Beattie covered his brother in the Hino.

Sean Beattie revved up again with the brake on, put the Hino into first and tore away from the buckled gates that wedged him from both sides. Then Deano Brady brought the bomb through in the Hiace.

The Hino had smashed through the second checkpoint crash barrier and moved slowly through the village to the crossroads, covered by Doyle and Barnes. Barnes was sniffing under his balaclava. Francie Devine and Martin Burke were already out of the checkpoint fort and running behind the Hino, covered by Tate Byrne and Ger Kelly. Hughie Donnelly had joined Barnes and Doyle, and Doyle was pulling back through Barnes's cover. Inside the checkpoint fort, the bomb was set.

Deano Brady and Dermot Beattie moved through Hughie Donnelly and Eddie Barnes's cover and Dessie Hart pulled back, last, through them. The idea was that of a collapsing box.

There were under two minutes now till the bomb went off. Sean Beattie had stopped the Hino at the crossroads on the school side, picked up the rifle beside him, stuck it out of the window and fired at a signpost in an act of pure bravado.

Dessie Hart had reached the Hino, flanked by Ger Kelly and Tate Byrne with their GPMGs. Anto Doyle, Deano Brady and Dermot Beattie were in the middle of the village, firing into the air and at the checkpoint. And Martin Burke was trying to get his flamethrower pack off as he ran.

'Brostaigh!' Devine shouted.

Hart turned to help Devine back into the Hino.

Sean Beattie had opened the passenger door of the Hino and was spraying the school. Hart roared at him and Beattie stopped and Hart gave Devine's foot a shove and Devine threw his rifle into the Hino. Dessie Hart had time to look back down the main street of the village and see his volunteers moving back to the Hino, covering one another. He had time to see the moon appear and disappear and watch John Cusack's rounds ripping into the observation tower. And he had time to feel good that everything had gone the way he'd planned it. He also had time to wonder. About the rest of the garrison. If it had all gone too easily. If they hadn't walked right into an ambush. If a sense of doom touched him at that moment, it didn't matter.

Deano Brady and Dermot Beattie vanished on the furthest tongues of the explosion. Brady's head was severed by a sheet of checkpoint wall. The blast pulped his body and tore his right leg off below the knee. His body was found beneath the rubble of part of the accommodation block from inside the checkpoint fort. His head was found in a hole in the ground. Dermot Beattie was thrown through the collapsed front wall of the first terraced house on the east side of the village. He bled to death.

The explosion had blown the checkpoint walls out and across the road. And on the east side of the street, the walls of the first three houses had holes in them and pieces of checkpoint corrugation embedded in them like teeth. All their roofs were gone. And the first house front had completely collapsed, its contents spilling out on to the street.

Tate Byrne and Anto Doyle were blown through a front door. Hughie Donnelly was blown into a derelict house which then collapsed on him. He was not dead.

Ger Kelly and Martin Burke were flat on their backs in the middle of the street. Kelly's left arm was broken. He reached around for his GPMG, cursing and wiping the dust from his eyes. Ahead of him, he could see the observation tower in what was left of the checkpoint, keeling over like the tower of Pisa. It felt like he had been watching it for ever before it finally collapsed. It could only have been seconds.

'Jesus!' he kept saying. 'Jesus!'

Dessie Hart and Francie Devine were beneath the Hino. Hart had his G3 levelled, ready to fire. Devine was sitting up looking at a spike of metal lodged in his stomach. It had come through his flak jacket and his back.

'Dessie!' he said.

Hart swung around. Sean Beattie was out of the Hino. A rear tyre on the left side was hissing and the fuel tank was streaming petrol on to the road.

'Early!' Hart screamed. 'Fuckin' early!'

The first round caught Sean Beattie through the upper back. Beattie turned as if he'd been bitten by an insect. The exit wound was the size of his hand. Two more rounds from the school caught him in the shoulder and the hip. He tried to turn and fire but more rounds spun him against the Hino and he cracked his head on the truck and dropped his rifle to the road. Then he sank to his knees and fell over on to the road. His hand made another attempt to reach his rifle. Dessie Hart was already firing back in the direction of the SAS team in the school.

Tim McLennan's general command to open fire had reached all the SAS teams by now and rounds hit the IRA unit from almost every conceivable angle. The two main killer groups were on hills north-west and south-east of the village. There was a group in the lane opposite Ger Kelly and another in a derelict house on the north side of the road east of the crossroads. And five SAS soldiers in the school.

Tate Byrne crawled out of the doorway he had been blown into and raised his GPMG to where he thought the hostile firing was coming from. He was concussed and one lung had collapsed and was bleeding inside, but Byrne threw his ammunition belt over his shoulder and stepped out into the street, firing as he moved along the walls of the terraced houses towards the Hino. Two bullets caught him in the legs and Tate went down and dropped his weapon and then picked it up and dragged himself up along the wall. He roared at Anto Doyle to cover him.

But Anto Doyle had panicked. He had dropped his weapon and was out in the middle of the street in front of Byrne. He was caught by at least four different firing positions, including the one down the lane on his side of the street, no more than ten yards away. Some of the rounds that hit Anto Doyle also hit Tate Byrne as he tried to get up again. He fired and called for cover and fell back through the broken window of a terraced house. Byrne's body armour had little or no effect on the rounds hitting him. Fire hit his head, taking away the left side of his face and one of his eyes. Anto Doyle danced when he was already dead and rounds smashed his spine and tore his chest apart and took the back of his head off and sent three of his fingers across the street.

Martin Burke was caught before he could get the flamethrower off his back. Ger Kelly was trying to give cover fire in four different directions, yelling for Tate Byrne and Dessie Hart and Francie Devine to cover him. He didn't know Byrne was dead.

Devine hadn't moved from where he sat under the Hino, his guts emptying through his combat jacket below the level of his body armour, blood spilling from a bullet wound to the thigh which had split an artery. Hart was moving towards the cab of the Hino, firing. He had been hit at least twice already but he was still firing, and throwing the grenades he had left. They landed short and some of his own shrapnel caught him and threw him back against the Hino.

Back down the street, Martin Burke's flamethrower burst into flames and Burke, already hit by eleven 7.62 rounds, was engulfed in his own flames. He screamed and moved and then stood still and then turned and more rounds hit home and there was a scream and a yell of defiance and then more screaming.

'Oh, fuck, Jesus, shoot me, fuckin' shoot me, fuckin' . . .'

Burke collapsed on to his knees and the screaming started up again and then stopped and Burke fell forward.

John Cusack knew what had happened the second he heard the first shot after the explosion. For a few seconds he could not move. He just froze and listened. Then rounds punctured the ground around the Toyota from a hill to his right and three hit the wall of the house behind him and Cusack swung the 50-calibre and fired back. Bruddy Holmes tried to level his rifle in the direction of the incoming fire but the sound of the bullets striking the Toyota made him drop his weapon. He jumped from the pick-up and lay flat on the ground.

'Get up, you fucker,' Cusack yelled. 'Get up and drive, Bruddy, drive. Go, go.'

Holmes half picked himself up and Cusack pulled his Magnum and pointed it at him.

'Move!' he said.

Holmes hesitated.

'I said move, or you'll join your fucking brother,' Cusack said.

Holmes's eyes were terrified. A round passed close to his head. Another hit the Toyota by the driver's door.

Cusack grabbed the 50-calibre and emptied another twenty rounds at the SAS hill position and then fired his Magnum past Holmes's head.

'Fucking drive, Holmes.'

He bent down and threw Holmes's rifle at him and three rounds hit the ground and ricocheted into the Toyota. One of them tore flesh on Cusack's left shoulder and he spun with the 50-calibre and fired in the direction of the checkpoint again.

Bruddy Holmes fired his rifle without looking and then turned and jumped into the driver's seat and drove.

He drove towards the checkpoint.

More SAS rounds hit the pick-up. From other directions now. And Holmes wasn't even looking where he was going any more. He had his head below the dashboard. Cusack fired the 50-calibre in an arc in the direction of the heaviest incoming fire. Three SAS rounds struck the body of the pick-up, five more hit the tyres and the tyres blew and Holmes lost control right at the moment his windscreen was shattered. Cusack kept firing. A round caught him between the neck and the shoulder and knocked him off his feet. He picked himself up and poured a sustained burst into the SAS position above him and forced them into cover. More rounds hit the driver's cab and two hit Bruddy Holmes in the abdomen and the leg. The pick-up was out of control.

Holmes slammed on the brakes and fell flat on the seat. Cusack fell over in the back of the pick-up and on to the road. He smashed his head on the tarmac and another round hit his foot and he crawled to the grass bank at the side of the road. The grass was long and wet and Cusack sucked some of the moisture and pulled his Magnum out of its holster again. SAS rounds ripped into the Toyota.

When Cusack got to his feet again, Holmes was already running towards the village, firing from the hip, screaming at the top of his voice.

'Bruddy!' Cusack yelled.

If Holmes heard, it made no difference. The next SAS round went through his neck, the second severed his arm, three and four hit him in the chest and came out through his backside, and after that Bruddy Holmes was dead no matter what hit his body. He spun across the road into a piece of torn corrugated metal and bounced off it and spun back over pieces of rubble and fell forward on to two sandbags and rolled over.

Cusack fired off his whole Magnum chamber without being able to see whom he was firing at any more.

He could see Dessie Hart, though, at the far end of the village, kneeling down beside the Hino. And he could see Francie Devine beside him, jerking. And he wanted to call out to them. Dessie looked his way but Cusack did not know if he saw him. He climbed back on to the Toyota and grabbed the 50-calibre. He might have yelled Dessie Hart's name.

A bullet hit his hip and Cusack swung the 50-calibre around and loosed off a burst in the direction he thought the shot had come from. His rounds hit a tree and took pieces from the red-brick house beside the checkpoint and hit the petrol tank of a Mercedes in the driveway. The Mercedes exploded and the car leapt up and spun and landed on its side.

'Jesus!' Cusack screamed.

There was a triumph in his scream.

Another two rounds hit him. One into the shoulder and across the top of the lungs and out behind his body armour. Two rounds went through the side of his kevlar jacket and exited in the lower part of his back. Another knocked him out of the pick-up on to the road again. He crawled to the wall and reloaded his Magnum and stood up and fired three shots and felt another bullet hit him below the neck and two more go into his right leg. Cusack went down against the wall and stood up and was hit again in the chest by a round that did not go through his body armour. He fell back over the stone wall behind him and down a steep bank into nettles and a small trickling stream that had begun there with the rain.

At the far end of the village, Dessie Hart was dying by the passenger door of the Hino. He was screaming for John Cusack. A bullet from above and behind caught him in the back of the head and sent him forward. His G3 fell from his hand and Hart fell flat on his face on the road and tried to get his rifle. But he could not reach it.

McLennan gave the order to cease fire and the village was quiet. From the time the Hino had stopped at the first crash barrier five minutes had elapsed.

31

MAGGIE O'NEILL SAT up and took her earphones out and turned her Walkman off. All she could think about was the silence. She let her eyes adjust from the nightsight on the Barrett Light Fifty to the dark of the attic she was lying in. Then the door of the attic was pushed aside and light came in from the house below.

A fat man came up the ladder into the attic. He had an orange beard and two chins and his ears stuck out so that you thought he'd catch himself in the opening to the attic.

'Jesus, love, they've all been stiffed,' he said. 'The whole bloody lot of them. Come on, love. Move.'

'No. No. What's goin' – what's happenin'?'

'I don't fuckin' know. Now, come on, love. It's orders,' he said.

He pulled his body into the attic. His stomach was pouring out over his trouser belt and his tweed jacket was torn at the shoulder where he was bursting through it. And the leather patch at his elbow was ripped and hanging loose. He slid along on his belly.

'They'll be all over here, the place will be crawlin' with Branchmen and State soldiers, love. Let's fuckin' get outta here. We can't do anythin'. They're dead. Do you hear me, love? They're dead. They're all fuckin' dead. Jesus.'

He reached over to her. She shoved his hand away. Her mind was racing. Images jumped around. She tried to control herself. She pulled her latex gloves off and opened her boiler suit and allowed herself to breathe. The dicker had a pleading look. He was on his knees now. Fidgeting with his big chip fingers. He had the look of a man who wanted to scratch his nose or pick wax from his ear.

'You go,' she said. 'You go.'

'They'll be all over us, love, for Jesus' sake. Come on!'

He grabbed her again. She moved and then pulled back and he lost his balance and nearly fell through the hole. He recovered and raised his hands.

'Right, then, you fuckin' do what you want, love. I'm goin'. There's nothin' in orders says I have to sit here and get slammed up with you. They're just down that road. The whole barracks'll be out. You think those lads over there haven't called in support from down here?'

'One round,' she said. 'One round and I'll follow. Go and get the car ready. Wait for me. Go on, go on, I'll follow. One round. Just one. I still have a shot.'

'Then we'll be sittin' ducks.'

'Well then fuck off if you haven't the stomach. I'll get myself out.'

She pulled out her .357 Magnum and aimed at his head. He raised his hands and tipped his head and smiled.

'See you, love. I don't get enough for hero stuff.'

Maggie put the gun away and pulled her gloves back on and the dicker shook his head and turned. He had to push himself through the hole.

Maggie replaced her tape and stuck the earphones into her ears. Beethoven beat through her head. She took the Barrett, checked the lasersight and aimed at the checkpoint.

In the village, Tim McLennan walked up to the body of Francie Devine and crouched beside him. Fuel from the Hino had leaked on to the road and Devine was sitting in a pool of it, head bent forward like he was asleep. His .357 Magnum revolver was lying beside him, unused, soaked in fuel. His intestine had come through the front of his flak jacket with the metal spike. It came out through a small rip in his combat jacket and one of his latex gloves was lying on a piece of his intestine. Both were shredded. More of his insides were slipping out below the flak jacket.

McLennan pulled back what remained of Devine's balaclava. Part of it had stuck to congealing blood on his head. The wool made a tearing sound when McLennan pulled it up. He touched Devine's face with his hand. It was cold. Blood ran from his face to McLennan's hand. McLennan looked at the blood and turned to his corporal.

'Dead,' he said.

'All dead here, Staff,' Chris Evans said. 'Power to the regiment.'

They could hear the Quick Reaction Force choppers coming in from the north and see the searchlights ride the treetops. It was a set routine. Cut off sweeps along the border to catch anything that had escaped, troops in to seal off the village from the press. The SAS would be all gone in fifteen minutes. Like they were never there. And the conflict would return to the headlines.

McLennan drew breath in through his nose. Cordite cloaked everything. Soldiers and policemen were still running up and down the street, high on the contact, shouting at each other, charged, the kind of bloodlust you couldn't explain to a civilian. The kind of high anyone who'd never killed and won could ever understand.

He crouched down over Dessie Hart. Hart's eye was gone, and part of his left ear; his right arm was severed and the sinews were hanging loose and blowing in the breeze.

The rain had begun, spitting, large cold drops, one at a time, travelling fast on the wind. Hart had an exit hole right through his forehead, almost dead centre. It looked like he had been killed instantly. McLennan knew he hadn't. The head-shots had come last. Maybe even after he was dead. It was clean enough. Troopers had kept firing even after all the players were down. To make sure. You had to make sure. Those down stayed down. A couple of troopers almost shot each other in their excitement.

You go mad, McLennan had once said to Anne, trying to explain himself. When you're in battle. You just go mad. Shoot anythin' that moves. It hadn't worked on her.

He pulled Hart's balaclava back over his face and touched the body with his boot. Maybe he expected to feel a heartbeat.

Villagers came out of their houses and started screaming curses. One was a fat man in pyjamas and a holed sweater. He came out of the shop with the redundant petrol pump and went over to Ger Kelly.

'Fuckers!' he yelled, looking around.

Two SAS troopers felled him with their rifles and dragged him back into his shop. They forced a couple back into their home. For their own safety, they said. Then there was another exchange of heavy cursing and one of the villagers threw a punch and missed and an SAS trooper felled him with his rifle. The two remaining villagers withdrew to their terraced house. Its windows were gone and its walls were peppered with holes and slates fell from the roof at intervals. There was screaming from another house.

A couple of rounds went off. Then there was silence. Then more rounds went off from the south end of the village.

Tim McLennan stood up.

'Cease fire, cease fire,' he roared. 'Do not fire unless you identify a target. I repeat, do not fire unless you identify a target.'

The firing stopped. It was replaced by radio noise. Cut-off team and QRF paras at the border.

McLennan did not listen. He was looking for John Cusack.

He walked from body to body on the street. Each time, he pulled the balaclava back and looked at their faces. And he noticed something about them. No matter what their wounds, and they had all suffered multiple wounds, they all had a surprised look on their faces, even those not killed immediately. And he felt sorry for them. He thought that was strange. But he did not say so to Evans. He was about to turn to his corporal and say the place looked like a bomb had hit it when he realised how stupid it would sound. So he said nothing. It was a personal time.

McLennan moved on towards the wreckage of the checkpoint.

SAS troopers were still emerging from their hides. A couple sat against the walls of a terraced house being dressed for minor wounds: glass, masonry, pieces of shrapnel. One trooper had a piece of Hiace engine in his shoulder, just sticking there, like some obtuse sculpture. McLennan looked at it and then into the eyes of the trooper. The trooper was morphined and his eyes were dilated and he had a giddy look on his face. Two of his colleagues held him still. McLennan nodded to him and walked on.

'What's the state of play on our side?' he asked a medic.

'Few minors, Staff. And this.' He touched the man with the Hiace in him. 'Nothing too special. Their bomb went off early, yeah?'

McLennan nodded. 'Caught a few of the lads off guard, I think.'

'These bastards, too. But it doesn't matter to them any more, does it?'

The checkpoint was ripped apart. The whole top floor of the station house was gone and the corrugated walls were in twisted pieces at post-modernist angles, sprinkled here and there with slates from the roof of the station house and sandbag remains. One of the gates was twisted and hanging over the back wall and surrounded by blank sheets of computer paper. There was a toilet roll and a chair and a coffee mug. And the observation tower lay diagonally across the station house and the remains of the accommodation block in three pieces. One of the mannequins they'd put in the tower lay naked on the ground with both its arms gone. Its torso was peppered with holes. McLennan picked his way over the debris, through the remains of the station house, to what had been the south wall. One jagged piece was left standing. The rest of it had sliced into the Victorian house next door and collapsed a tree through its roof. The nearest wall of the house looked as if it would collapse at the slightest touch.

A helicopter swung in low with a searchlight. It stationed itself over the checkpoint and its searchlight gave the place the look of a stage set. Someone had told him once they used to jump into the searchlight beams in Belfast when they were a kid and do dance routines. He could not remember who. Maybe he was making it up.

He made his way out of the checkpoint and down to the Toyota pick-up. The 50-calibre was dipped like it had died. The Toyota was a series of holes held together by thin strips of metal. Two RUC officers were examining Bruddy Holmes. One of them touched Holmes's face with the barrel of his rifle, as if he was still not convinced Holmes was dead. The other turned to McLennan.

'Not bad, Tim,' he said.

They knew each other from school and the UDR. The fellow had been a policeman with Eric Johnson. He was not a friend of Tim McLennan's but there was something they shared that made it easy for him to speak. They'd had a talk before the operation. At the final briefing. You did that kind of thing. There was a sudden bonding. But they were both alive now. They could smile and Tim could revert to the distance they were supposed to maintain in their respective units. Lenny Beggs had mentioned this fellow's name. In passing. McLennan had Beggs on his mind now, Beggs and Cusack. They were linked, he felt, and he could not think of one without the other coming to mind.

Sure there's no need to rush it, Tim, Beggs had said. There's time. Decisions take time. Take your time. But have a look, that's all I ask. Have a look and ask the right questions and make up your mind where you want to see Northern Ireland goin'. Just do that.

'He's not here,' McLennan said to Evans.

'Who?' Evans asked.

They were standing beside the Toyota pick-up. One of the RUC officers had left Bruddy Holmes and was examining the 50-calibre in the back of the Toyota. The other RUC officer, the one McLennan knew, had stepped back from Holmes like he was going to take a photograph.

Bruddy Holmes lay stretched out on the road in a crucified pose. His head was propped up on a sandbag. Blood ran from his body in a diluted stream. The rain was heavier and the rain had mixed in with Holmes's blood and was worming its way through the bullet-holes in the road surface.

McLennan followed Bruddy Holmes's blood trails as if they could lead somewhere. Fifteen or twenty yards ahead, around the corner, almost out on the open road south, the remains of the control box from the checkpoint lay in a hole in the road with half a mannequin still inside, charred like a half-used briquette, and still smoking.

Part of the surrounding wall had embedded itself in the red-brick house across the road from the checkpoint. Right under a bedroom window. And slates still fell from the roof along a broken drainpipe.

McLennan went over and touched the barrel of the 50-calibre and then bent over Holmes.

The RUC officer McLennan knew had crouched in a ditch ahead of him. The grey corrugation that had protected people operating the checkpoint on the road had been ripped open and bent back. What was left of it was about to collapse.

'Who is he?' McLennan asked the RUC officer about Holmes.

'Not sure,' the officer said.

'He's young.'

'Was.'

They smiled.

The police officer told McLennan to get out of the centre of the road; there was still a chance there were terrorists in the area. McLennan touched his kevlar jacket and grinned.

'Body armour didn't do him much good, Tim,' the RUC officer said.

He moved back and slung his Ruger into his arms and crouched on the road facing south.

McLennan was staring back at Holmes's remaining eye. It was open and glassy and the pupil looked like it wanted to swallow something. Maybe he can still see me, McLennan thought. Maybe he was physically dead but his brain was still receiving signals from the eye.

'There was a second lad here,' McLennan said. 'I know there was, I saw him.'

The RUC officer shrugged.

An SAS trooper came running along the road from the village.

'Choppers in five minutes, Staff,' he said.

'Get on to the paras,' McLennan said. 'Tell them they're chasin' at least one, maybe more, PIRA players, out there. Definitely wounded. Chris—' He turned to Evans. 'Get me five blokes. That bastard's out there.'

'C/O says we're out of here, Staff,' the SAS messenger said.

'Like fuck we are,' McLennan said.

He started walking along the road south.

Down that road and to the left, maybe two or three hundred yards, still a quarter of a mile on the wrong side of the border, John Cusack regained consciousness against a dry-stone wall. He was cold. Raindrops touched his face and he felt wet in his body. Eddie Barnes was trying to get his kevlar jacket off. Cusack moaned.

'Shut up, John,' Barnes whispered. 'For Jesus' sake. Shut up.'

'Oh, Christ, give me some morphine, man, give me morphine,' Cusack said.

'I don't have any. Now shut up, we're not home yet. Can you move?'

Cusack tried to move. His wounds prevented him. A face wound bled into his mouth and he kept spitting the blood out.

'Will you stop fuckin' spittin', John. Now hang on, let's get this fuckin' thing off.'

Cusack winced when Barnes pulled the jacket free and Barnes had to put his hand over Cusack's mouth.

'Jesus, it's crawlin' with them.'

Barnes looked over to the direction of the voice.

Hughie Donnelly crawled in beside them, carrying an AKM rifle. Barnes passed him the kevlar jacket.

'Get rid of it,' he said.

He examined Cusack's wounds.

Donnelly took the jacket, wiped it in the grass and pushed it under a hedge. He had found Cusack unconscious when he was making his own escape along the stream where Cusack had fallen. The two of them had fallen over Barnes further on. Donnelly would have shot him only he dropped his rifle and Cusack fell on top of it. Barnes had crawled, flat on his belly, right through two SAS positions above the red-brick house across the road from the checkpoint. No more than five feet from one trooper who was too busy firing into the main street to check the area immediately around him.

'They can do tests on the blood,' Cusack said when Donnelly threw away his vest. 'Take the goddamn thing.'

'Shut up, John,' Barnes said. 'If they want to do tests, there's enough of you back there to do all the tests they need. I can't carry you with that thing. It's too heavy. Christ, you're a fuckin' mess. I'm goin' to put you on my shoulder. Is that okay? We're near the river. You'll have to hang on till I can get you across. It's not far. So hang on. And keep quiet. I'll help you. But you have to be quiet, John, do you understand? There's Brits everywhere, son.'

Cusack was in danger of passing out again. He moved to hurt himself. He slapped his face and spat more blood. The pain did the trick.

'We were ambushed,' he said.

'Terrific, John, the bleedin' obvious.'

'Fucking shit. Where's Bruddy? Where's Bruddy?'

'Will you shut up, John.'

He passed out.

Donnelly crawled to the river's edge. A Lynx that had been circling the area had flown back towards the village. Another chopper swung west of it and flew low along the border in that direction, covered by a third chopper higher up. There were more choppers coming in to land in the village.

About twenty yards behind the IRA trio, and to their right, they could hear voices, English and Scots voices, directions being given, orders barked. Donnelly could hear footsteps in the grass. He thought it was funny that he could actually hear footsteps in the grass, at night, over the sound of helicopters and troops and yells and commands.

Cusack came back to consciousness when they were trying to get him under a barbed-wire fence. The wire tore through his combat trousers and into his thigh and caught his hand and ripped the length of one of his fingers. He was aware and unaware at the same time. There were flashes of what could have been reality mixed with other times, other places.

A patrol in the Philippines. A hide in Central America.

It was night then, too. They'd gone out to discover what was going on in a rebel village, tooled up: night glasses, day glasses, food, silencers on the weapons. All the good stuff, Cusack had said to someone when he was telling the story once. And they walked in a spread for mines, three of them.

He could hear his own instructions: a mine will kill everything within ten yards, injures up to one hundred yards. He saw the tripwire and the man to the left of him touching it. But there was not enough time to get down. It was a grenade, not a mine. And Cusack took the full force of the blast. Arms and legs. He sat shivering in a hole, in steaming jungle, sat shivering in a hole with his pistol to his head. They weren't going to get him. No way. If they came, he would kill himself. He told his companions to kill him if he passed out.

'Shoot me,' he said to Eddie Barnes.

He was half there, half somewhere else.

Barnes looked at him like he had two heads.

'What the fuck are you goin' on about? Will you fuckin' shut up. You'll get us all stiffed.'

Barnes pushed him face down in the dirt and Cusack smelled the wet grass and the mud and felt movement. The faintest trace of movement. They were by the river now. It was a small river really. With a run-up you could maybe jump it if you were good. But with Cusack the way he was and the voices around them, Barnes did not think they would make it across. He thought about dumping Cusack but decided against it. He did not dwell on the reasons. He desperately wanted to sniff but he checked himself. He dragged Cusack into long grass and crawled down to the river. Donnelly covered them from a gorse bush. He could see shadows and chopper searchlights sometimes showed a figure, but there was never enough time to study what the chopper lights showed. Anyway, maybe it was better not to know how many were out there.

Eight hours, Cusack thought, eight hours with his gun to his head. I won't let them get me. Don't let them get me. We won't let them get you. His leg was split from the hip to the knee and his left arm was peppered with shrapnel. He kept looking at his balls, to see if they were still there. Putting his hands down his trousers, touching them, sighing when he touched them. They had a habit of leaving ball-crunchers, booby traps specially constructed to take your balls off. It was a good morale-killer. Bad enough watching a friend maimed, screaming with his leg in two pieces; worse when his balls were chewed into mince.

A hundred yards behind Cusack, a para fire team fanned out along a hedgerow. Every ten yards they stopped and listened. Cusack heard an English voice and the words boss and fuck and heard a tear and thought he heard breathing but it might have been his own.

Eddie Barnes dragged John Cusack to the edge of the river and slid him in. Then he slipped in himself and lay back into the water and pulled Cusack with him. His head touched the opposite bank with his third kick.

'Shoot me, shoot me,' Cusack muttered.

Barnes threw his hand over Cusack's mouth and put his mouth to Cusack's ear.

'Jesus, John, if you don't fuckin' shut up I will fuckin' shoot you.'

He shoved Cusack's head under the water. Cusack passed out. He drifted into the hole in the jungle again.

They got him out after eight hours. Can you walk? I can't fucking move. Trying not to scream. They rammed a morphine capsule into him and the flow was gentle and the pain drifted and he swam on something he could not understand.

Donnelly moved into the water with his rifle pointed over his head. He could walk but he ducked low and let the water come over his shoulders. He still had body armour on and the body armour brought him lower in the water. He swung his rifle around while he made his way across. A chopper flew to the left of him in a sweep back towards the checkpoint and the searchlight touched the fields behind him and he saw the outline of a soldier. He looked through the nightsight on the rifle and took aim. But he did not fire.

The para flanked right of him.

Barnes and Cusack were across the river now and Donnelly was by the bank. The border was ahead of them, unmarked across the concession road and the patchwork of fields towards the woods that stood tall against the night skyline. Donnelly could see another para moving along the southern bank of the river to his right. He threw himself flat and looked at Barnes ahead of him. They spread themselves and Cusack on the grass. There were more voices now.

English voices: West Country, London, Newcastle; a Welsh voice; and then a couple of Scots. One of the Scots was out in front, directing. Barnes shoved his hand over Cusack's mouth and whispered into his ear.

'Brits, John. Quiet. We're dead if you breathe.'

Cusack was still in a jungle hole with his pistol to his head. Kill me. They were out looking for them. Popular Front teenagers. They came out to the explosion. Came out in sections. Babbling Spanish. They were scared.

He could tell from their accents. He could see a couple below them, slipping in and out of the trees, shoulder-length hair and olive faces. You could see some of the face colour and the movements of heads and the way they twitched when there was a sound in the trees.

The paras moved past them. Slowly. Swinging round with their weapon nightsights.

Cusack came round but not enough. He could feel himself floating. He could see the campesinos in the jungle below him. Smoking. They smoked and you could see the cherry light of their smokes when they moved through the trees.

A radio started up and a London accent gave a position and a check. No contact. Barnes saw a boot step close to him. It caught a moonray and he could see detail in it, undulations, laces dripping mud, a piece of dog turd sticking out from under the sole. The paratrooper twisted quickly and pointed his rifle at the far bank. He had a blackened face and his nose was thin and pointed and he was taking deep, sudden breaths, as if he'd run a couple of miles. He had high cheekbones. And metallic eyes. The moon showed the eyes an instant and then took them away.

Then there was a noise. A shout. A para had caught himself in the hedge. He dropped his rifle and a round went off. Everyone went down. Another shot was fired, then two more, then a three-round burst and then uncontrolled fire. A sergeant ran around, yelling at his men to hold their fire until they had identified a target. But they did not obey.

It was a moment of comedy in the tension, paras moving, turning, crouching, pointing, almost shooting one another, an officer shouting now, NCOs chasing the officer, shouting, walkie-talkies gone mad. Then it was over and the officer was in control and the paras had moved on.

Barnes dragged Cusack across the grass to the concession road. Donnelly covered them from the river bank. He followed another para with his rifle till the para disappeared through a wall of trees. The trees blew in the breeze and the breeze sighed. Donnelly bent low and ran. Barnes grabbed Cusack by the collar, picked him up, threw him across his back and carried him across the border.

'Is he alive?' Donnelly asked on the southern side.

'Just.'

Cusack was conscious again. Cold and conscious and feeling his wounds. Like someone had used a spoon on him and scooped out pieces of his body.

He was wet all over and he could not tell which wet was blood and which wet was just water and rain and the rain kept coming. Barnes and Donnelly took his arms and legs and moved up a hill. The hill was a hard climb and the ground was slippery and muddy and the moonlight shone on the long wet grass and the trees sang a chorus.

Tim McLennan stood in the centre of the road south from the checkpoint.

'The bastard's out there,' he said.

He moved out further down the road. Evans followed.

'We're out of here, Tim,' he said. 'Come on.'

McLennan turned.

'Let's go get the bastards, Chris. Get a few of the boys. We'll have them in an hour.'

'No can do, Staff. QRF job, Tim. There'll be another time.'

'Tim, get in,' the RUC officer tucked into the grass bank at the side of the road said.

'Come on, Tim, leave it,' Evans said. 'Nosh and a brew.'

'You just don't understand, Chris,' he said.

McLennan walked further. He looked at the dark hills ahead of him. They had a sombre feeling to them. Then he twisted on his heel. He was thinking of a kiss when the 50-calibre shot hit.

Maggie O'Neill watched McLennan fall. Her laser was already off. It had been clean. The one who came further elected himself. It was that simple. First rule of sniping. Let your target elect himself. She had tightened her grip and the trigger moved and he fell right where he stood.

The shot went through his back. Through his kevlar jacket and out through his chest. Evans made a move towards him. Another trooper pulled Evans to the side. The RUC officer shouted for cover and edged his way along the grass bank. Blood had already reached the grass.

I've been hit. Jesus, Jesus, McLennan thought, he wanted to scream, but he could not speak. The bullet had smashed his spinal cord and his lungs were filling up with blood. Evans and the RUC officer knelt over him and cursed. There was nothing they could do. Evans said McLennan's name and screamed something back at the faces watching him from cover.

No, this isn't supposed to happen, McLennan thought. No, no, not to me, not now. He fought to think and thought fought thought and Evans and the RUC officer begged him to hang on and tried to stop his body shaking.

Maggie O'Neill had a numbness in her when she reached the treeline on the hill above the house. She could see two Garda cars moving along the road from Monaghan Town with a Japanese overlander behind them. She did not think about the man she had killed. She thought about a river years ago and a Protestant boy and love.

WHEN THEY HAD skimmed the ammonium nitrate from the fertiliser, they let it dry and crystallise. Then they mixed it with castor sugar. And when it was mixed they put it in beer barrels and mixed it with diesel oil. The detonation mechanism was a parking-metre timer and a slab of Semtex and some explosive cord.

John Cusack helped manoeuvre the last of the beer barrels into place in the back of the truck. There were three men with him. He knew their names. They did not know each other except by first names. Two of them spoke with lower-middle-class Dublin accents. The other came from Kerry. The two Dubliners worked as commercial travellers in Reading and Basildon. The Kerryman worked as a night watchman in Acton. Cusack was in command. The Kerryman was an explosives expert. He had finished his job now. Cusack and one of the Dubliners would ferry the bomb and the other Dubliner would drive ahead as a dicker. There was a fifth volunteer ready to make a telephone call but only Cusack knew her.

The lock-up was in Wimbledon, near the railway track. The truck was a Volvo with false number plates. They'd bought it for cash the week before through *Exchange and Mart*, resprayed it and wiped it down. Each man wore latex surgical gloves and a boiler suit and when they had loaded the explosives, the suits and the gloves were dumped in a holdall and taken away by the Kerryman to be burned. The lock-up was plain and empty except for a workbench and the stench of diesel. The walls ran with damp. Water dribbled along the cement lines, twisting and turning its way down.

They had a tarpaulin spread on the floor of the lock-up under the truck so there would be no chance of tyreprints or anything else being left behind, any hint that they had ever been there.

At eight o'clock in the evening they shook hands and wished each other luck. The explosives expert left first and took all the left-over gear with him in a Transit van to a new lock-up on the other side of the city. The Basildon man walked three streets and picked up a car that had been left there for him. Cusack and the other Dubliner, who was maybe thirty, got into the cab of the truck and started it up. The Dubliner drove. They wore casual clothes and both of them wore an anorak and a plain scarf. There were security cameras everywhere. You could be picked up from the end of a dozen streets and not even notice it. The hoods on the anoraks were big and they could cover your face if you used them with a scarf. It was a wet night and the wind blew the rain horizontal so no one would ask questions if they saw men with anoraks and scarves.

The bomb under the tarpaulin contained around fifteen hundred pounds of explosive.

They drove towards Tower Bridge and then round the back of the City of London, through Wapping, coming into Bishopsgate from the east side. There were two international banks on a small street off Bishopsgate. The street would help channel the explosion and maximise the effect of the blast. One of the banks was a worldwide head office, the other a European head office. One was an Anglo-American concern, the second Japanese. The Anglo-American building was about thirty storeys high.

They parked the truck under the Anglo-American bank. Cusack checked his watch. They were ten minutes late. They had fifteen minutes to the warning, and half an hour to the explosion. The timer was running. They checked the street and jumped out of the truck and walked to the end of it and then kept going. They had their hoods up and their scarves around the lower halves of their faces.

A security guard saw their truck and made a phone call to his own head office in Wembley. Then he went out into the street. There were four cars on the street with the truck. The darkness and the rain made it difficult for him to make the vehicle out. The tarpaulin made the truck look as if it had sand or something like that in the back of it. He walked towards it and then halted. Then he turned and walked back towards his own building, but he did not go back in. There was no one inside anyway. He knocked on the glass of two other buildings on the street and yelled.

Bomb!

Cusack and his partner had separated. Cusack headed into the West End. He bought a *Standard* and sat at the end of the tube carriage and flicked through it. A small paragraph on an inside page named Danny Loughlin as the man found naked and shot on the Armagh border the night before. Cusack read the television page. He looked at his watch twice. Maggie O'Neill was waiting for him when he got to Oxford Circus. Her hair was dyed. They took the Bakerloo line to Paddington to catch a train to

Slough. The call house was a semi-detached estate house on the road to Eaton.

In Paddington Station, they held hands and made like they were lovers. Cusack looked at his watch. Two minutes. Maggie kissed his ear and whispered something he did not hear. Cusack watched people grab taxis and buy fast food and stand like zombies watching the arrival and departure times above them. It was so ordered, he thought, like there was a point to it all. One minute.

Thirty yards up the street where the bomb was, a father and daughter had pulled up in their car and the father had gone round the corner to collect some files from his office. His fourteen-year-old daughter sat in the car and waited. They were going to a film in the West End. At the other end of the street the police were already warning people off.

It was the eight hundred and twenty-second year of the war.

GLENN MEADE

BRANDENBURG

Berlin. A political activist is assassinated.

Asunción. A smuggler is killed in a hit-and-run incident. An elderly businessman blows his brains out. A journalist who suspects a link between the deaths is himself brutally murdered.

Strasbourg. Joseph Volkmann, an agent with the EC's newly-formed security unit, is getting a feeling of déjà vu. What he is about to uncover is an audacious plan that will turn the clock of European history back half a century.

Set against the backdrop of a reunified Germany where nationalist feelings are resurfacing for the first time in fifty years, BRANDENBURG is a gripping mixture of spellbinding invention and tantalising fact that heralds the arrival of a major new talent for the nineties.

'A rare treat – sheer, nail-biting suspense'

Sunday Telegraph

'Terrific entertainment, a page-turner in the best tradition of thrillers – unsettlingly plausible'

Campbell Armstrong

'It has all the signs of a bestseller. First-class plot, credible characters and dialogue, and exotic settings. Definitely a winner'

Ted Allbeury

HODDER AND STOUGHTON PAPERBACKS

BOB REISS

THE LAST SPY

1991. The world watches with bated breath as the Soviet Union disintegrates.

Prize-winning Washington journalist James Ash is particularly concerned. For he is not the high-flying yuppie he seems. He grew up in Siberia, in an exact replica of an American town. Where children learnt to assume an alien personality in preparation for the KGB's most spectacular act of espionage.

But where are his orders coming from now? Why is the nature of his assignments changing so radically? And who can he trust, apart from himself?

'Sparkling and fast-paced . . . a thoroughly engaging thriller'

The Washington Post

'Combines an ingenious plot with an utterly engaging central character . . . one of the best recent espionage thrillers I have read'

Gavin Esler

'Reiss makes it believable and tense, and he captures powerful emotions: the constant fear of agents leading a double-life and the schizophrenic terror of betrayal as they turn on each other to save themselves'

The Daily Telegraph

'A compelling story of treachery and deception'

Newsday

'A stylish, up-to-date espionage novel . . . clever, literate and even believable'

Sunday Telegraph

JOHN CALVIN BATCHELOR

FATHER'S DAY

Seven days before Father's Day, US President Teddy Jay makes an unprecedented address to the nation.

Five months ago, he collapsed with depression and voluntarily turned over the White House to Vice-President Thomas Garland, who has since transformed the administration's fortunes with vigour and confidence.

But now Teddy Jay announces that he is fit to resume office. Within twenty-four hours America will be embroiled in a monumental constitutional crisis. What looms is not only Garland's challenging of Jay's competence to govern, but also something far more momentous.

Waiting eagerly in the wings is the ruthless Chairman of the Joint Chiefs of Staff, Lt. General Lucius S. Sensenbrenner. And if the crisis of presidential succession cannot be settled, he'll head a military coup on Father's Day.

HODDER AND STOUGHTON PAPERBACKS